ANGEL 24

BOB FOX

THE FOUNDING OF THE 1607 JAMESTOWN COLONY

AS IT HAS NEVER BEEN TOLD

Angel 24 is the story of Scion, a powerful angel who is emotionally damaged from the Great Rebellion in heaven. Now, he has been assigned to protect the Jamestown Colony from the wicked schemes of his former best friend!

In this unique story, you will discover:

The **unlikely partnership** between a 14-inch female angel named **Angie**, a defective demon called **Morph** and a jealous, Dark Angel named **Voudoc**—all colluding to defeat **Okeus,** the god of the Powhatan Native Americans at Jamestown.

Paquiquino, a real-life Powhatan warrior who changed the history of America!

The simmering conflict between rebel, **dark angels, and the demons** they spawned to serve them.

The **love story of Pocahontas and Captain John Smith** told from a fresh Christian perspective.

Dozens of little-known historical facts based on a Christian historical analysis of the Jamestown Colony: *Healing America's Soul*—also by Bob Fox. **Asterisks (*)** in the text denote historical facts.

The Past Is Prologue

Although based on history and fiction, **Angel 24 is about America today**.

Angel 24 illustrates the power of sin to destroy and the power of repentance to give life as II Chronicles 7:14 declares.

If my people, who are called by my name, will humble themselves and pray and seek my face and turn from their wicked ways, then I will hear from heaven, and I will forgive their sin and will heal their land.

Sin almost destroyed Jamestown. **Sin is again destroying much in America**—but there is a way to heal the land according to God's word.

This book can give genuine hope to Christians that **God will heal the brokenness of America** when His people humble themselves in prayer, seek His face and repent for their sins and for the sins of America.

Angel 24 is a book for such a time as this.

WHAT OTHERS ARE SAYING...

We all know the importance of Jamestown. This book draws us into the spiritual realm of that time in a way you have never imagined. Angel 24 has it all: a clear, biblical worldview, rich historical details, and a cast of wildly creative characters, both human and non-human, who will captivate readers of all ages who enjoy an epic thriller. If you liked *This Present Darkness* by Frank Peretti, Angel 24 will become an instant favorite!

Randy Clark, Phd

President of Global Awakening Theological Seminary

Overseer of the Apostolic Network of Global Awakening

In his book, Angel 24, Bob Fox uniquely and creatively brings light to the realities of the wars that rage in the unseen realms, and to that which are increasingly manifesting in the natural realm. Although the book is written as fiction, it is rooted in many historical and spiritual illustrations and facts that reveal the prophetic drama of our day. There is a clash of cultures not just in the spheres of society, or as some call the seven mountains, and it is becoming clearer there is a battle for the soul of the nation that has global implications.

Bob, in gifted fashion, has given us an excellent illustration of the importance and urgency of the hour. I believe that this type of historical and spiritual drama could help awaken us to the power that comes from the posture of prayer and repentance.

Duncan Campbell, during the 1948 Hebrides Revival, said, "It takes the Supernatural to break the bonds of the natural." Angel 24 will take the reader into a journey that recognizes the need for the supernatural of God, through His people, to break the bonds that surround us today.

Doug Stringer

Founder/President: Somebody Cares America

Somebody Cares International

Houston, Texas

PREFACE & DEDICATION

In 2005, I was serving hurricane Katrina victims in Houston, Texas with two amazing humanitarian ministries: *Operation Blessing and Somebody Cares*. While there, I met an old friend, Eddie Smith and his grandson, Zachary, at a Macdonald's restaurant. Eddie and his wife, Alice, led the US Prayer Center for many years.

As I began to leave, I suddenly sensed the Lord communicating with me. He seemed to say that He wanted me to write a novel based on a history book I wrote in 2003 about the Jamestown Colony called *Healing America's Soul.*

For a moment, I just stood there—stunned. I had no idea how to write a novel. Then, the Lord seemed to say that He wanted the story written from the *viewpoint of angels and demons*. That was such an unusual thought. I knew it had to be from the Lord.

I pleaded with the Lord, "Please get Peretti to do it." Frank Peretti's 1986 novel, *This Present Darkness*, actually started the novel genre that *Angel 24* attempts to follow. It sold millions of copies!

But the Lord quickly respond, "No, I want you to do it." *Sixteen years* later, many online writing courses later and forty thousand edit corrections later, I have finally finished what has become *Angel 24.* God did it—through me—to my great surprise. Obedience draws His grace to do the impossible. Writing this book has proven that to me.

Please note the asterisks (*) throughout the book. I put them next to statements that are historically true so you can see how much actual history runs through this novel.

Blessings to all of you! I hope to see you in heaven, if not sooner.

Bob Fox

~

Dedication of Book

I dedicate this book to my incredible wife, Beth. *Angel 24* would never have been written without her patient and wise support. Thank you, honey, for loving me so well, for so long! You are a great gift to me and to our family! God knew I needed you to be the person I am today.

~

I also want to dedicate this book to **Frank Peretti,** author of *This Present Darkness*. I read it non-stop in one day. I could not put it down. His 25 books have sold over 14 million copies! Frank actually started the Christian fiction genre that this book tries to represent. Now, if I could only write as well as he does :)

Thank you, Frank, for making the vast, mysterious, spiritual realities of angels, demons and prayer much more believable and important to all of us in your wonderful books!

Cover design by Wayne of YWAM and Orlen Stauffer
Fantasy portraits by Amelia Kaiser
Editors: Allison-the Great, Kelly Bixler, Beth Fox, Steve Schoenhoff

His Heros Press (https://hisherospress.com)

ISBN: 978-1-7366916-2-5

For a **free digital gift** from the author, email to: bob@angel24book.com

More info at https://angel24book.com

Facebook: https://www.facebook.com/angel24book

Facebook Messenger: https://m.me/angel24book.

PROLOGUE

Angels were everywhere.

Thousands of six-foot choir angels swirled above the fiery Throne of God in an ever-expanding cone of concentric circles, moving in opposing, alternating directions as high as the eye could see. Faces of brown, black, yellow, and white spun together in a blur of light and motion. Their childlike shouts of joy and ringing peals of laughter formed a contagious counterpoint to the massive choruses of praise echoing everywhere across the vast expanse of heaven.

Just below that whirlwind of worship, a rippling, iridescent rainbow arched regally over the Throne. Lightning and thunderous staccato bass voices shot up into the angelic cone from the throats of eight-foot, golden-headed Cherubim and Seraphim as they soared up and down its center, adding a complex vocal drumbeat to the rhythm of the rotating choir.

All around them, watchful and majestic, a hundred thousand fierce, ten-foot Warrior Angels with faces like burning bronze lined the walls of heaven—wings furled, arms akimbo, massive swords at the ready.

Multitudes of six-foot angels sped past them, racing out of Heaven's Gates, headed for Earth with assignments to serve the saints.

It had not always been that way.

Once, there were no huge Warrior Angels or swords in heaven—just one hundred eighty thousand, unarmed, six-foot angels to serve the Court of Heaven. They all lived in great contentment, enjoying one another and the incredible pleasures of heaven. Although they were male angels, their love for one another was stronger, deeper, and purer than any human couple could ever know.

But, just as God decided to make Adam and Eve, eighty thousand beautiful angels disappeared in a way no angel could have ever foreseen.

The Great Rebellion

When Lucifer rebelled against God, the Lord had no choice but to cast Lucifer and sixty thousand of his rebel angels out of heaven. Lucifer called it "The Great Emancipation." Heaven remembers it as the "Great Rebellion." Twenty thousand loyal angels died in the fierce battle to protect heaven. The sixty thousand rebels became Lucifer's *Dark Angels*. God's loyal one hundred thousand angels lost their best friends, closest companions and comrades-in-arms . . . forever!

The"Great Grief" immediately followed the Great Rebellion. God himself grieved for centuries for the loss of eighty thousand beloved sons.

For hundreds of years, this Great Grief muffled the joy of heaven. Angel poets later wrote that God and the angels flooded Earth with their tears of sadness during the Great Flood in Noah's time.

Shortly after the Great Rebellion, the Lord restructured heaven for war. God transformed most of his six-foot angels into ten-foot-tall giants with formidable physiques and long, sharp swords. These became the Warrior Angels in the Host of Heaven, the ones who now protect heaven under Archangel Michael's leadership. God also established a War Room where Michael and his angelic staff would coordinate heaven's plans against Lucifer's Dark Angels. At roughly the same time, Lucifer somehow spawned billions of evil spirits to resist God's work among humans. These satanic creatures would later be called demons.

But after thousands of years of vicious combat between the Host of Heaven and Lucifer's evil empire for control of humanity, God revealed his ultimate solution to rescue mankind: God would send his Son, Jesus, to destroy Satan's wicked works on Earth!

The angels were ecstatic! But God knew there were not enough of them to do what needed to be done.

So, God created billions of new angels to serve the vast throngs of people who would soon become disciples of Jesus. Their angelic assignments varied according to the needs of each believer. Sometimes, these ministering angels passed messages to a Christian from the Holy Spirit in a vision or dream. Even the human parents of Jesus experienced that. At other times, the angels guided believers away from danger in ways that were usually unnoticeable. Most of the time, however, these angels just brought the presence of heaven to followers of Jesus when they needed God's comfort and encouragement. Believers who risked their lives for the Gospel usually had a steady stream of these angelic messengers serving their needs.

These new angels were called Alpha Angels. They are all six-foot-tall, handsome males with glowing skin in stunning shades of black, brown, beige, yellow and red. Their eyes sparkled in hues of brown, green, blue and grey framed by shoulder-length platinum hair and wings whose feathers perfectly matched their skin color. Even though they carry no swords, these muscular Alphas look formidable in flight with massive, twelve-foot wingspans and glistening white full-length robes cinched at the waist with a wide, golden belt.

At the same time, the Lord created six million Beta Scout Angels to monitor the movements of Satan's forces. Betas are small and hard to detect by the enemy. They range in size from fourteen to eighteen inches. However, God equipped them with the most powerful visual and auditory sensors any angel has ever had.

To the surprise of every angel in heaven, God made all Betas *female*—the first ever in heaven. Most Alphas were somewhat shocked when they heard it. They were even more stunned when God allowed the new Betas to change the color and arrangement of their hair, clothes and wings as often as they desired. An older Alpha openly complained to Jesus, "But, Lord, we have never had angels like *that*. It's just a little embarrassing to have them called angels. They are so different from us." Jesus just laughed as He put his arm around the frowning angel and quipped, "*Just wait*. You will thank Me later." The angle left—but his frown didn't.

To train all those new angels for service in the Earth war zone, God created Angel Academy. After six months of intense training, each angel would be released to serve the saints on Earth. Every angel could hardly wait for the day when they would serve and protect God's people from demonic temptations and attacks.

After God created all his new angels, He did one more thing to help the saints defeat the wicked schemes of Lucifer—He saved one continent for Christians for thousands of years. From that continent, the Lord planned to launch His final assault on Lucifer, whom He now called *Satan*.

So, in the 1500s of earth time, God led Great Britain to start a colony of Christians on that previously hidden continent. God intended to use this new settlement to birth a nation *unlike any other*—a nation that would help vast numbers of people from all over the globe make it to heaven.

To protect this special colony, God picked a special angel—but one that the other angels would never have chosen.

Angel 24.

CHAPTER 1

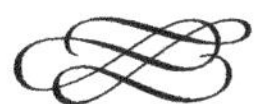

12,000 BC

Deep in the frigid, inky fringes of the universe, a dazzling, golden angel sped past a pale, red planet as he furiously wrote in a notebook. He was measuring the rate of expansion of the universe at its outer limits. His mind tried to focus on the final complex mathematical measurements he was making, but a checklist of personal needs kept nagging him for attention.

This angel was one of twenty-four prototype angels being trained to become heaven's first archangels to serve Earth. Although this flight was just a class exercise, the platinum-haired scout knew he had to do his very best. After all, Lucifer, the Headmaster of Archangel Academy, had personally chosen him for this challenging task. He also wanted to look his very best when reporting his findings to Lucifer, so he was wearing a new pair of shoes he had just borrowed from Kai, his best friend at the Academy.

Now, after a week of hard work far from heaven, he was eager to finish the last few measurements and return to heaven. Just before he left on this mission, Kai, had nervously confided to him that Lucifer was planning a big surprise for heaven. Kai was not allowed to say what it was—just that heaven would never forget it. Now, even in the four-hundred-and-fifty-four-degrees-below-zero vacuum of space, the lone angel felt warm all over just imagining the excitement and fun that surprise would be. Lucifer was famous for being bold and creative. *No angel had ever planned to surprise all of heaven. This is going to be spectacular!*

But there was something about how Kai acted that still puzzled Scion. He has never seen Kai so passionate. When he told him about Lucifer's surprise plans, Scion noticed that Kai's hands trembled a little, and his eyes filled with tears. Stranger still, just before Kai left him, he hugged Scion so tightly and for so long that Scion almost felt embarrassed. Then Kai suddenly flew off, looking back with that smile of love Scion always treasured. All Scion could think now was, *Wow! That was different. Kai was so emotional! Whatever it is, I can't miss it. I must get this done and get back to heaven,* the golden scout vowed to himself just as he completed the last steps of a mission no other student had wanted.

Who could blame them? The assignment required that an angel go to the very edge of the universe for an entire week *alone* and be out of contact with other angels the entire time. Like every other student at Archangel Academy, Scion didn't want to be alone in deep space that long. But when Lucifer personally asked him to do it, his love for the Headmaster made him say yes. But now he was finished.

"I can finally go home to that fantastic surprise Lucifer is planning," he sighed into the darkness. He glanced at Kai's gleaming white shoes one more time and then at the pulsating edge of creation just yards away. A wide smile filled his face.

Just as he turned around to head back to heaven, he saw three Sentinel angels speeding toward him. Sentinels were usually the quiet, introverted types who silently stood guard over remote sectors of the universe. But as the trio drew closer, Scion saw that something was terribly wrong. Terror covered the faces of each angel.

"*Treason! Treason*!" the three shouted to Scion. "Lucifer has gone mad. He is leading a rebellion against the Lord, and many angels are following him. Come at once. General Michael has ordered everyone to return to heaven and fight off the rebels."

As the terrified Sentinels sped off to alert others across the cosmos, Scion froze with a fear that no angel had ever felt. He had recently shared a Throne Room secret with Lucifer that had visibly upset Lucifer— but Scion thought Lucifer would get over it. But now *this!*

Scion suddenly felt dizzy. His shaking hands dropped the notebook. His heart raced. His body felt almost limp. With a cry of *Nooooooo!* the huge angel dove toward the surface of the dark planet faster than he had ever flown. But a few thousand feet into his descent, he suddenly passed out. His body tumbled head over heels into the planet's surface, slicing through the hot, volcanic crust with such force that his body did not stop until it finally splashed into the fiery, molten core, ten thousand miles underground.

LIGHT YEARS AWAY, "ALL HELL" WAS BREAKING OUT IN HEAVEN. THE once glorious choirmaster of heaven was enraged with wounded pride. He was screaming curses and savagely slicing through dozens of angels with one swipe of his eight-foot sword. His once brilliant blue eyes were now fiery black with hate. Thousands of rebel angels swarmed around him, fighting for him with a fury never seen before in heaven. Angels were being butchered by old friends. Angel wings, arms, and heads flew everywhere as twenty thousand unarmed, loyal angels were beheaded and dismembered by their fellow angels. The hideous, rhythmic sounds of death exploded all across heaven : a cry for mercy—then *thwack*—a scream of terror—*thwack*—a surprised shout of the attacker's name—*thwack...thwack...thwack*. The swords of death hacked down the unarmed angelic ranks with monstrous precision.

When the attack began, the emotions and bodies of the loyal angels were frozen with shock for a moment. Then their eyes exploded with terror while their bodies trembled and shook— faster and harder until they could not stand as waves of hideously howling, cursing angels raced toward them. None of the innocent angels had weapons —or the desire to fight their friends. Then, as if on some invisible cue, a cloudburst of tears erupted from the horrified eyes of the helpless victims. Like lambs led to the slaughter, they died with no resistance.

But all was not lost. The Four Living Creatures who guarded God's Throne Room shot into heaven's blue canopy, high above the battle. Each Creature had six wings and enormous bodies completely covered with eyes. They moved like lightning above the battlefield, seeing everything and giving rapid-fire orders to General Michael and his army of Cherubim and Seraphim warrior angels. None of them had swords. *They had something better.*

As Lucifer and his sixty thousand rebels pushed forward toward the Throne of God, the Four Living Creatures guided Michael to array the remaining hundred thousand angels in sixty-four concentric rows encircling the Throne of God. Six-winged Seraphim took their positions at the front while Cherubim stationed themselves in the rear ranks. Then all were in place, Michael's voice rang out like a deafening trumpet call to battle, "Worship!"

Instantly, the surviving angels fought back their tears of shock, grief and anger and began to worship, "Holy, holy, holy is the Lord God, the Almighty, Who was and Who is and Who is to come. Worthy are You, our Lord and our God, to receive glory and honor and power; for You created all things, and because of Your will, they existed and were created." The piercing staccato blasts of many golden trumpets released a powerful anointing that appeared like a glistening, golden blanket floating down on the weeping worshippers.

Then, the air suddenly became electrified with the unseen Presence of Almighty God. Lucifer and his rebels halted for a second as they felt the atmosphere shift. An instant later, Lucifer roared defiantly and charged the Throne even more ferociously.

As the rebels came within three hundred feet of God's Throne, they raised their swords for the final, vicious assault on the worshipping angels surrounding the Throne. The Seraphim on the front ranks were now so close to the rebels that they could recognize former friends, former teammates in games, and former choir members—their faces now contorted with evil, their voices screaming curses.

It was over in an instant. Michael shouted, "Fire!" and six thousand Seraphim angels—whose name means "burning ones"—shot a wall of white-hot flames one thousand feet high out of their eyes and mouths. Lucifer and his rebels slammed into each other as they fell to the golden streets of heaven just before hitting the deadly ring of fire. Now Lucifer knew He would never reach the Throne. With a hideous, animalistic roar of rage, Lucifer commanded his army to retreat to Earth. Michael's army pursued them until they reached the upper atmosphere of the new, blue planet.

The Great Rebellion had begun.

CHAPTER 2

It was just an ordinary day in heaven.

Thousands of gold filigree crosses glistened on the horizon of the shimmering teal sky. Yesterday, the sky had been a pale yellow with shades of peacock blue and raspberry red edges. Multicolored words in ever-changing languages slowly glided across the sky. Each word twirled and bounced to the different rhythms of the songs that were being sung by different groups of saints as the words passed over them. "Jesus Is Lord," "God Is Our Savior," "Glory to God in the Highest." The words moved with easy dignity as they hovered right over a group of Scandinavians, singing with great gusto. But, as usual, the sky-words spun into a blur as they drifted over the passionate dancing of African worshippers. Heaven was constantly and gloriously alive with worship.

The very atmosphere of heaven was saturated with a sense of love, joy, and peace, far beyond anything possible on Earth. The Presence of God radiated from The Great White Throne in waves of glory that made redeemed humanity giddy with delight *every* day. No one was immune. King David himself loved to greet the astonished new arrivals from Earth, shouting and leaping in dance, "See, I told you so!

'In his Presence is the fullness of joy!'" The cheers of welcoming saints were always deafening.

On this particular day, a river of purple, pink, and red dahlias bobbed their heads in the breeze along the golden sidewalk as throngs of families walked and laughed in a lush green park frequented by Jewish believers.

Near a towering sycamore tree, a Jewish family of three stopped and gathered around a ten-foot statue. Wide circles of hot-pink stargazer lilies, purple hydrangeas, brilliant yellow daffodils, and red begonias carpeted the ground around the magnificent sculpture. The fragrance of white camellias and red roses also filled the air. Children nearby giggled as bluebirds swished through the magnolia trees near the pond, dodging stingerless bees filled with nectar, headed home to honey-filled hives. Yes—a very ordinary day for a family walk in a city park.

But this city is anything but ordinary.

Deep in the endless darkness of the cosmos, the walls of this city sparkle like crystal-clear jasper—a perfectly square jewel radiating brilliant rainbows of God's glory in every direction. Each side of the city is fifteen hundred miles long, with massive walls fifteen hundred miles high and two hundred feet wide at the base. Twelve gates, each made of one gigantic pearl, are the only entrances. Each gate is five hundred miles apart from the others. The name of one of the twelve tribes of Israel is engraved above each gate. Precious, multicolored gems form the foundation of the walls. They glisten with a brilliance that pierces the cosmic darkness for millions of miles.

Within the fifteen-hundred-mile-high walls are fifteen hundred levels, one level every mile above the bottom level. Each level contains an entire heavenscape covering the length and breadth of heaven, like the floors of a king's castle. God's Throne is in the center of the top-level, where he meets each believer as they arrive in heaven through the middle East Gate. This is also where the new arrivals see their family members for the first the time in heaven. No one ever forgets that glorious and highly emotional scene.

From there, an angel escorts each saint to their eternal home on one of the lower heavenscapes. Only angels, the Twenty-four Elders, and a few select saints live on the top floor of heaven. Everyone else may choose whichever other heavenscape they desire. Most prefer to live where it is always 72 degrees with low humidity. Others choose heavenscapes with towering, snowy mountains or lush tropical beaches. Because there are so many beautiful places in heaven, many citizens change locations every fifteen hundred years just for a change of scenery and weather. Angels have noticed that those who moved around a lot on Earth tend to change heavenscapes more often. Some American military families even move *every three years*—just like on Earth! Variety and freedom are two of heaven's most popular features.

There is never a housing shortage. Billions of exquisite homes for the faithful followers of Jesus cover every heavenscape below the top level. A hundred and forty-four billion miles of pure gold roads connect each home to all other parts of heaven. Since fatigue is unknown in heaven and it never gets dark, the saints usually visit their neighbors just by walking on those golden roads. Long-distances can be travelled simply by thinking about the destination. In an instant, the residents can go to any place in heaven. It is common to see visitors from even one thousand heavenscapes away suddenly appear for a short visit to a friend or relative. In fact, deep, satisfying fellowship with generations of family members and saints from Old and New Testament times consumes most of the time in heaven. As any angel will be quick to tell you, everything in heaven is about relationships.

Unlike Earth, heaven has neither sun nor night. The light of God illuminates all of heaven with a brightness and clarity never seen on Earth. Plants, animals, angels, and humans all radiate a soft, golden light. Heaven also has no clouds, no rain, and no sea. But a large river of pure water runs steadily from God's Throne through all fifteen hundred heavenscapes. The river replenishes the lakes, ponds, and streams in heaven's magnificent parks.—which are everywhere in heaven.

Each park is different and unbelievably gorgeous—vast areas of the greenest grass, the most fragrant flowers, and trees with delicious fruit always in season. The small ponds in the parks are filled with colorful, glowing fish of every shape imaginable. Animals from every continent on Earth also freely roam these green meadows, but remarkably, they do not need to eat anything. Usually, all the animals live in the parks, but every child who comes to heaven without their parents is allowed to have two animals as personal pets in their homes. Koala bears and lions are always the first to be picked!

In a word, heaven is—well—*heavenly.*

~

"LOOK, PAPA! LOOK, MAMA," THE RAVEN-HAIRED SEVEN-YEAR-OLD BOY exclaimed. "It's Moses!"

Like all the statuary in heaven, the tall statue of Moses was solid gold and yet translucent, shining from within with a soft yellow light that grew brighter when people prayed or worshipped nearby.

This statue of Moses shows him standing with his hands lifted in prayer. The engraving at the bottom read: "And the Lord repented of the evil which he thought to do unto his people." (Exodus 32:14)

The father smiled at his curious son. "Yes, Ari. Moses is the founder of our people, and he led God's people to the Promised Land, so that Jesus could be born there one day."

Ari furrowed his brow in confusion. "But Papa, why did God want to bring evil on his people? I thought God loves the Jews."

"He did, Ari. God graciously rescued them from four hundred years of slavery in Egypt with many great miracles. That was a promise God made to Abraham long before Moses. God even parted the Red Sea for them to cross over to escape the Egyptian army. But then, when Moses was on the mountain getting the Ten Commandments from God, many Jews decided to abandon God and instead, worship the statue of a calf! This was the greatest sin they could commit against their God who had just rescued them from Egypt with many miracles. Because of their extreme and stubborn rebellion, God was going to punish them severely— even though he loved them dearly. But God changed his mind!" the father said with a big smile.

Ari's eyes grew wide. "Papa, why would God change his mind? God knows everything. He cannot make mistakes."

"Because Moses pleaded with God not to judge Israel. Moses did something the Bible calls 'standing in the gap.' Moses stood in the gap before God and pleaded with God to forgive the great sin of our people. And God listened to Moses! By standing in the gap, Moses saved Israel. I know it is hard to believe, but people can actually change God's mind sometimes. He loves us *that much!*"

"Wow, Papa, I want to go to the Great Library tomorrow and read about that."

Suddenly, three angels swooped out of the sky, laughing and shouting, "Look out below!" as they dove toward the startled Jewish family. Ari tried to run away, but he tripped and fell, skinning his knee. His parents ducked to avoid a collision with the reckless trio.

"What in heaven's name—?" the father fumed. "They almost hit us!"

But the raucous laughter and swoosh of wings disappeared as fast as they had burst upon them. The three tricksters had accelerated into a high-speed climb. They were *very late* for class at Angel Academy.

CHAPTER 3

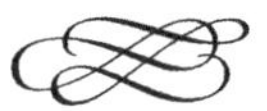

Angel Academy stood tall and serene on a low hill on the top floor of heaven. The flat plateau was in the middle of a long, oblong island surrounded by the river that flows from God's Throne just north of there. It was known as Angel Island. Majestic, tall trees lined the banks of the island. They are the Trees of Life. Each month, the angels harvest a new crop of succulent, reddish-yellow fruit to share with the saints. There was always enough. Jesus would come each month to multiply whatever the angels gathered so that billions of saints and angels could each have a taste. Once a year, when heaven celebrated the Resurrection of the Lamb, the archangels guarding Earth's continents would gather leaves from the Trees of Life to help heal the nations they protected.

For almost sixteen hundred Earth years, the new angels created by God have come to Angel Academy for six months of training to serve God's people on earth. If the angels failed to graduate, they could retake the class. If they failed the second time, they could never qualify for a coveted Earth assignment. Instead, they would be limited to strictly administrative duties, mainly archiving and indexing billions of life records for each human in the Great Library—a job every angel dreaded. Angels knew they were made for adventure!

Angel Academy is beautiful. Its pink granite spires jut into the deep blue sky. The massive, golden front door faces due north to bask in the direct light of God's Throne. Dazzling stained-glass windows wrap the entire circumference of its gem-studded walls.

From above, the academy looks like a giant cross. The vast, rectangular part of the building contains twenty-four spacious classrooms splayed out on all three floors, eight classrooms on each floor. A central hall that runs the length of the academy from north to south, connecting each classroom. Full-color, detailed maps of every major city on Earth are embedded in the sky blue floors of the massive complex. To further orient the students to their future worksite, three-dimensional, high-definition images of Earth's geography floated next to the ceiling of each classroom.

Near the front of the building and perpendicular to the classroom halls, two enormous wings of offices bracket the academy. These wings house the offices for the six archangels of Earth's six continents. Heaven counts the continents as Europe, Asia, Africa, South America, North America, and AFO (Australia/Frozen South Lands/Ocean Islands).

Archangels serve under General Michael to oversee all the Alpha and Beta angels assigned to that continent. They also teach three weeks of classes in each six-month cycle. The head of the academy and guest speakers teach the remaining weeks. Only angels are allowed as guest speakers.

But one archangel office is empty. General Michael has not yet chosen the Archangel of North America. But that is about to change.

Today, the hallways of the academy buzzed with chatter. Rumors were out that the Archangel of North America was about to be announced! To many students, their Headmaster seemed like the perfect choice—and for obvious reasons.

Scion had been Headmaster of Angel Academy since it opened shortly after the Great Rebellion. He was one of the few remaining prototype angels—some of the largest and most powerful angels in heaven. No one ever forgot about meeting him.

He stood twelve feet tall with a burly barrel chest and arms as thick as the thighs of most angels. But despite his size, he also very fast. His pearly-white, twenty-four-foot wings propelled him faster than all but the fastest warrior angels.

Besides his formidable physique, Scion was unusually handsome. Beneath his shoulder-length platinum hair, piercing ice-blue eyes and long, straight nose, a firm jaw jutted out slightly. His good looks were legendary among the female student angels. One Beta requested a transfer to Scion's class from her current class. The administrator asked why. Without a moment's hesitation, the little Beta responded enthusiastically, "*Have you seen him?*"

Despite all that, Scion never tried to draw attention to himself. He could have worn a chest-full of angelic badges for his long service to the Lord, but he wore none. His only piece of jewelry was a small silver pendant on a chain around his neck. Oddly enough, he was always *barefoot*. No one quite knew why—or dared to ask why.

But what made him unique more than anything else was his *skin*. In heaven, all angels and humans glow softly. But when Scion worshipped, his light golden skin shone so brightly that other angels had to shield their eyes. It was a quirk of his makeup that Scion often regretted because it embarrassed him in worship services.

Scion did have one obvious weakness. Although he knew he was greatly respected, he didn't feel comfortable in close relationships. He was always "all business". Taking time to just relax with other angels was never on his checklists—and he had lots of checklists, most of them full of rules.

Student angels were *acutely* aware that Headmaster Scion was a stickler for rules. Few ever dared to test him on that—especially when his emotions were less than joyful. Some days, he appeared sad. On rare occasions, he had panic attacks which frightened his students. Most angels suspected that Scion had suffered a painful trauma—but no one knew what—and no one took the risk to ask him.

Today was a down day for Scion. His legs felt heavy as he walked with his head down, lost in thought. "*Aaaaaah,* another day— here we go," he muttered as he approached the large, ornate door of the academy. It had only been two months since a new class of angels started at the academy, and this bunch was proving to be quite rowdy. *Nothing I can't handle,* he thought, *but I hate conflict. Why can't we all just get along?*

As Scion pushed the door open, he heard a noise. He looked over his shoulder just in time to see three of his most unmotivated students flying too low and frightening a family in the nearby park—a family he knew. His right hand tightened into a fist as he gritted his teeth.

"Stop that and get to class!" Scion yelled as the students flew closer. *More conflict, just great,* he fumed to himself.

Nacham, the ringleader, grabbed his two friends, Stanis and Thomas, and the three quickly touched down in front of Scion at the front door. They knew they were in trouble.

"Well, boys, nice to see that you had time to come to class today." But the look on Scion's face was anything but welcoming. "You know what this means. This is your third time being late for class," Scion scolded.

They all hung their heads. "Yes, Master Scion," they responded in unison.

"You are not even halfway through, but now you will all have to repeat the entire course. If you fail to graduate one more time, you will be disqualified from ever receiving an assignment to Earth." A pained look darkened their faces.

"But we were just having fun, Master Scion!" Nacham shouted. "Don't you know what fun is? Give us a break!"

Scion shook his head. "I'm sorry, boys. You've made your choices, and I am compelled by the rules to dismiss you from the academy. If you cannot keep the rules here in a school, what will you do when human lives depend on your obedience on Earth? Clean out your desks and report back to your base to await further instructions. And before you leave the area, apologize to that Jewish family. I know them. They have already suffered enough on Earth at the hands of Roman soldiers. And now you scare them with your childish pranks!"

As the three downcast angels trudged inside to retrieve their personal items, Nacham suddenly turned, ran back and dropped on his knees before Scion. He looked up at the scowling headmaster with tears in his eyes. "I know I don't deserve it, Master Scion, but please forgive me. Please forgive my friends, too. I will never be late for class again. I will come early and stay late. I was wrong for scaring that family. Please allow me to finish with this class. I want to serve the saints on Earth as soon as possible! In fact, I've always wanted to serve the Jewish saints in Israel and protect them in every way!" Nacham pleaded sheepishly.

Scion looked at the young angel for a long moment, and his face softened. "*Israel. Jews.* Hmm. Nice try, Nacham. If that's true, you picked the wrong family to frighten today.

"I'm sorry, Nacham. Rules are rules. Believe me, I know what happens when you break the rules. Rules protect you. They protect others. Without rules, all kinds of things would happen that should not happen. When you get more experienced, you will understand the need to do things by the book—as I have."

Just then, little Ari ran up to Scion and Nacham. "Sir Angel, my dad wants me to tell you something."

Scion smiled and got down on one knee. "Sure, son. What did your father say?"

"My dad says he forgives the angels, and he wants you to forgive them if they say they are sorry."

Turning sideways, Scion looked over at Ari's father, who was waving at him. Scion grimaced and shook his head to tell the father he could not do that.

Turning back to the boy, Scion put his hulking hand on the boy's head and said, "I know it is hard to understand, but rules must be obeyed."

Just as he was to stand up, the boy's father came walking up to them. "Greetings, most honored angel. I am Ari's father. Could I have a word with you?"

"Of course, my brother. I am honored to meet one such as you. I remember you telling me that you actually saw the Lord on Earth."

For a moment, Ari's dad gazed at the kneeling student, then looked back to Scion and said, "Yes, I was about Ari's age when I saw Jesus. I will never forget the compassion he showed for others. I once saw him give a woman a great gift—a gift even he was reluctant to give."

"What woman? What gift, dear brother?"

"You remember—the Syrophoenician mother whose daughter had a demon. At that time in his ministry, Jesus said he was allowed to help only his people, the Jews. But, when this non-Jewish woman humbly begged Jesus to help her daughter, Jesus broke his *own rule* and gave her what she asked for. You should have seen the look on the mother's face when Jesus did that."

Looking a little confused, Scion mumbled, "Yes—brother, that is a beautiful story."

"Yes, it is, Great Angel. And that statue of Moses over there reminds me of how God changed his mind about killing all the Jews when they worshipped the golden calf. Moses asked God to give them a second chance—and *he did*." Again, the father looked at the heart-broken angel kneeling near Scion.

Scion was speechless. As the father smiled and began to walk away, Scion pulled little Ari close and whispered to him, "I have a secret mission for you, little man. Later on, when you get home, tell your dad that he changed the life of one angel who scared your family. I will give him another chance even though he broke the rules."

"Wow! I've got a secret to tell my dad!" Ari yelled as he ran over to his smiling father and grabbed his leg.

As Ari and his father walked away, Scion turned to the Nacham and lifted him upright. "I assume you heard all that. I want you to know that you will be the first angel I have ever allowed to break academy rules and avoid the penalty. But anyone who can repent like you just did can become a great angel. I want to help you be that angel. Welcome back to class, Nacham!"

"Oh, thank you, sir! Thank you, sir," Nacham shouted as he hugged the wide waist of Scion's twelve-foot torso.

"That will do, Nacham," Scion said half-jokingly. "Now you are scaring me. Please go to class. You are late, so you will have to sit in the back near that little Beta who perches on the windowsill. I'm teaching on something very significant today."

"Yes, sir. I think you mean that Beta named Angel 442. She's so much fun," Nacham grinned.

"And Nacham. About Stanis and Thomas—your two friends—I'll do whatever I can to make sure they complete the next class and get an earth assignment—if they apologize to that family. Tell them that."

Nacham disappeared into the building, just ahead of Scion, hollering with joy. Scion smiled. Today was going to be a good day after all.

CHAPTER 4

Earth Date: September 10, 1561

As Scion entered the academy, the massive building hummed with the energy of fifty thousand angels waiting for their instructors to arrive. In every enormous classroom, plush, blue-padded, stadium-type seating sloped down from the high ceiling in the back of the room toward a small podium centered in front of a large screen where three-dimensional images would appear to illustrate the main points of each lecture.

Scion entered the classroom and moved toward the podium. Instantly, silence filled the room. "Good morning, class. As you know, I am your instructor today. I am sorry to be late, but some of your classmates needed . . . uh . . . help."

A few subdued snickers embedded in fake coughs broke the stillness. Many students had seen the near-collision in the park through the tall wall-to-wall windows. Most, however, looked soberly on the two empty seats formerly assigned to Stanis and Thomas. They knew what that meant. Meanwhile, Nacham eagerly moved to sit near the window. A tiny but beautiful angel next to him eyed him skeptically. She had witnessed his earlier antics.

Scion cleared his throat and said, "As Headmaster of Angel Academy, it is my privilege to oversee the instruction of all newly created angels here at Angel Academy. I hope you are enjoying your new life here in heaven and learning much from the other classes you have been taking over the past months. Your regular instructors tell me that you are a bright and promising class. So, let's get right to work so that you can graduate on time. I know you are all eager for that first Earth assignment!

"Class, you all have probably heard that many of the saints in Europe have been falling into terrible sins due to the violence against each other since 1520.* Most of the sins have been committed by our Catholic saints who have been harshly persecuting the new Protestant saints.* I know it's hard to believe but Catholics have actually killed tens of thousands of Protestants since the Protestant Reformation began in 1517*. Catholics have even burned some Protestants alive simply for not agreeing with Catholic teachings.*

Fortunately, there are signs of hope in France. The Edict of Orleans has stopped the persecution of Protestant French Huguenots as of last January 28.* Then, on April 19, the King of France issued the Edict of Fontainebleau, calling for peace between the two groups.* Despite that, however, many French Catholic leaders continue to punish anyone who leaves the Catholic Church.

"Of course, God always knew these terrible times would come to his children due to their sins. Because of the great suffering of his Protestant sons and daughters in Europe, the Lord has decreed that he will soon open a new land for them where they may find peace and safety. That's why he set aside an entire continent thousands of years ago as a place of refuge for them. The Lord plans to establish a spiritual fortress in that new continent for the spread of his Kingdom through Protestants. And, as you have heard, the last archangel—the

Archangel of North America—will soon be assigned to help serve the saints there."

Cheers erupted for several long moments and then, dead silence. Seven thousand pairs of ears strained to hear who that new archangel would be. The air seemed to go out of the room as Scion silently stood there with a knowing smile. Finally, he said, "As of now, no one knows who will be chosen by General Michael." An audible sigh of disappointment filled the room.

"But enough of all that. Today, we will discuss how to help the Lord's followers in Europe rebuild the peace, unity, and blessing of the Lord in their war-torn lands. Please see page five hundred thirty-three of your syllabus."

As the clacking of books and rustling of pages saturated the room, Scion paced in front of the class, looking more and more serious. Finally, the students looked up quietly. Scion gazed at them intently and slowly began to speak.

"As you know, class, sin is the deadliest enemy of humanity. Sin deceives, sin corrupts, and, if not corrected, sin will kill forever. One of your primary tasks on Earth will be to help your assigned believers obey the promptings of the Holy Spirit to repent for their sins *as quickly as possible*. Repentance can change the course of a person's life —or even a nation's life. God *always* honors repentance. Repentance opens floodgates of blessings on a follower of Jesus or on a nation— blessings that can come no other way."

An angel in the middle of the room stood up and asked, "Master Scion, what exactly is repentance?"

"Good question, Angel Jonah," Scion replied. "In a word, repentance is changing your mind so that you agree with God's mind and act accordingly. It means that you confess and renounce your sins to God and and commit yourself to righteous behavior."

Scion took a deep breath and looked around the room. He knew where this might lead— and he dreaded that. Most of the angels nodded in agreement, but some seemed confused. He continued in a compassionate voice. "People who love God usually want to repent, but sometimes they wait too long, and sin captures their hearts, and many blessings are lost. Sometimes, their sins are so great it even affects the very land they live on. The land becomes defiled with sin. God's blessings are withdrawn from that land and Satan's forces have greater access to corrupt and deceive the people who live there. For instance, this often happens in lands where false gods are worshipped."

"Question, Master Scion!" A muscular angel near the back stood up and looked around the room to make sure everyone was listening. "I know that's true about humans, but what about angels? If angels disobey God, can they repent and be forgiven?"

"Great question, Angel Tomas," Scion responded with a slight tremor in his voice. "Actually, angels don't really sin. They may make innocent mistakes, but they do not deliberately disobey God because—"

"Um, uh, Master Scion, with all due respect," Angel Tomas interrupted, "What about the *Great Rebellion*? I heard about it from Samos, an older angel I met last week. He said no one likes to talk about it, but long ago a third of the angels chose to rebel against God and followed an archangel named Lucifer—the one we now call Satan."

The room grew *very* silent. This was the first time these new angels had heard of the Great Rebellion. Tomas looked around at the stunned faces; he was enjoying the rapt attention of the class. "So, Master Scion," Tomas asked with a repressed snicker, "what happened when 'all hell broke loose' in heaven like Samos said?" Most of the class laughed nervously, but some of the more tender-hearted ones felt fear rise in their hearts. "Those angels sinned big time but they did not repent. Why"

The powerful twelve-foot headmaster froze. The question hit him like a sucker punch to the gut. He always dreaded answering questions related to the Great Rebellion. But every class of new angels brought this topic up at one point or another. Every time they did, gory images flooded Scion's mind—pieces of angel wings scattered near the twelve gates; distraught, weeping angels everywhere. Worst of all, Scion suspected that the secret he illegally shared with Lucifer may have triggered all that carnage.

Scion slowly looked around the room at the eager faces waiting for his response. He took a deep breath. "Well, Tomas, you are right. Lucifer did lead what we call the Great Rebellion, and sixty thousand angels followed him. Those sixty thousand, who once spent their days with us, are now Dark Angels—the principalities, thrones, dominions, and authorities that rule for Satan over all the lands of Earth. The reason those angels did not repent is because they have no permission from God to repent. They are banished from heaven forever in eternal exile."

"No repentance? *Eternal exile*?" Tomas sniggered out loud. "I thought you said God always wants and honors repentance."

Suddenly, the atmosphere in the room shifted. A stifling gloom drifted down over the students. Scion felt it, too. Some angels looked like they were about to cry. If anything made an angel nervous, it was the thought of eternal banishment from heaven. Scion knew he had to get past this topic quickly—*but how*? He had hoped to broach this sensitive topic later in the curriculum when the student were better prepared for what he was about to say.

"Tomas, you are right; God is quick to forgive when angels make innocent mistakes— *if* the angel repents. But the Great Rebellion was a premeditated, full-scale rejection of God's authority by angels who knew God *intimately*. No angel who has seen the very face of God for centuries can rebel like that and stay in heaven. Humans can rebel and repent because they have not seen God and are, therefore, *less accountable.* And as you know, Jesus paid for the sins of humans, *not* angels.

"Listen, Tomas, like you, I grieve for the sixty thousand who were once part of family. But the Lord has banned them and Lucifer from heaven *forever.* Sadly, one day they will enter a place of eternal torment that Jesus has prepared for them. That is God's righteous and final decree."

A shockwave of fear and grief washed over the room. The entire class just sat there like shiny statues—unable to even blink. Scion knew this was one of the difficult things angels have to learn—the goodness *and* the severity of God.

Tomas broke the graveyard silence with fresh energy in his voice. He knew every member of the class hung onto his every word. "Master Scion, how could Lucifer deceive that many angels? He must have had help. Who helped him?"

Another sucker punch, only harder. Scion's heart started to thump in his chest, his palms felt clammy and an old facial twitch returned. *Can I tell the truth without telling all the truth? What if they find out who I am?* he nervously mused.

CHAPTER 5

Scion looked directly at his smirking inquisitor, trying to appear calm. "Brilliant observation, Tomas." Scion forced a grin to hide a stab of stomach pain. Mola, the class assistant, saw the twitching on Scion's face and knew he was struggling.

"That is a very insightful question," Mola interrupted with a broad smile and loud voice, "but we really need to let Master Scion complete his lecture. There's a lot more material to cover today. We need to move on."

"It's okay, Mola," Scion said with a wave of his hand in front of his furrowed brow. "I think I need to answer the question.

"Well, Tomas, you are right—*again*. Lucifer did have help. They were called the 24. Just before God created the universe, he made twenty-four special angels to be trained as archangels by heaven's three original archangels—Michael, Gabriel, and Lucifer. Lucifer was put in charge of most of their training. The names of the 24 are Anak, Og, Nephil, Goliath, Baal, Chemosh, Dagon, Osiris, Marduk, Milcom, Amon, Ashtoreth, Poseidon, Bel, Molech, Zeus, Artemis, Buddha, Hermes, Ra, Ganesh, Kali, and Kai." Scion held his breath and nervously scanned the faces of the class. He only named *23* of the 24. He hoped no one would notice.

"But those are the names of false gods and murderous giants," one student called out.

"Yes, they have made themselves infamous that way," Scion conceded with a pained look. "But, long ago, they were famous and highly admired in heaven. The 24 were the most powerful angels God ever made, except for Michael, Lucifer, and Gabriel. Almost every angel was in awe of them. Many angels secretly wished they could join the 24 and have Lucifer as their leader. Tens of thousands of angels would flock to Archangel Academy just to hear Lucifer and the 24 speak during the annual Open House Day.

"Then, when the fullness of pride corrupted Lucifer's heart, he convinced 23 of the 24 to secretly side with him against God so they could rule humans in their own kingdom on earth. Using their special powers, the 23 made thousands of swords on a planet not far from heaven to equip other angels they hoped would join them. They snuck the swords into heaven just as all the angels were distracted by the news that God was about to make a new species of life called humans.

"Then, these highly esteemed 23 angels helped Lucifer deceive a third of the heavenly host into leaving heaven to reign on earth under Lucifer. Sixty-thousand angels concluded that if Lucifer and the 23 were willing to leave heaven for earth, they would, too. When Michael learned of Lucifer's rebellion, a brutal war broke out in heaven. Finally, General Michael's loyal angels drove Lucifer and his rebel angels out of heaven and banished them to earth. And the rest, as they say, is *very* sad history."

As that reality of all that sank into the minds of these young angels, the traumatic tension in the class broke like a dam. They heard more than they could bear. Soft weeping and stifled cries became loud moans and raucous cries of grief. Little Angel 442 wailed like a small child lost in a dark forest. Nacham reached out his big hand to comfort the tiny Beta. She looked up in gratitude, her eyes awash in tears.

Finally, the thunderstorm of grief subsided. Class members got back in their seats, wiped their faces with their long, silky sleeves and tried to look normal again. But just when everyone thought the exhausting stress was over, Tomas raised his hand *again*. The class groaned. But Tomas grinned. His eyes had not shed a tear—he was too excited to ask his next question.

"Is it true that the 24 can be killed only by one of the 24 or by Michael himself? Is it true that other angels can only wound the 24 temporarily—and that the 24 can heal themselves within a few hours?"

"Yes, Tomas—what your friend told you is all true," Scion answered nervously.

"And the twenty-fourth . . . where was he while the Great Rebellion was happening?" Tomas asked with obvious enjoyment.

"The . . . uh, well . . . the twenty-fourth . . ." Scion felt his throat closing tightly. His thoughts whirled with fear. *Just tell them the truth—at least part of it,* he thought. "The twenty-fourth was on a practice recon assignment in a remote quadrant of the cosmos where there was very minimal communication with heaven. When 'all hell broke out in heaven,' as you so aptly put it, Tomas, everyone was in a panic, and no one in heaven thought to contact angel twenty-four until after the Rebellion was over."

Tomas looked around the class with a knowing look and then proclaimed in an overly loud voice, "Well, *that* was very convenient. But why would Lucifer send him on that remote assignment during his planned rebellion? And why was he left behind by his best friends? For such a tightly bonded group, that seems odd—*very odd,* if you ask me," Tomas laughed scornfully. At that remark, many in the class suddenly looked at Tomas with disgust.

"Tomas, how dare you imply something devious about another angel without proof," Mola scolded harshly.

Realizing his mouth had gotten him into trouble again, Tomas's cheeks turned bright red. "Of course, Master Mola," he sheepishly conceded. "You are right. I was wrong to insinuate evil motives like that to a fellow angel." But still wanting to justify himself, he added, "But *who* exactly is that lone survivor of Archangel Academy? Are we sure he can be trusted? Remember, this is an angel who has the power to destroy any of us with impunity. That sounds like a serious security risk for sure."

Just as Mola was about to force Tomas to sit down and be quiet, loud noises in the hallway caught his attention. Scion shot Mola a questioning look. Mola quickly nodded and made for the door. As he entered the hallway, Mola's eyes widened as he greeted a gigantic visitor. It was General Michael himself—and he looked irritated. The sixteen-foot hallway ceiling was too low for him and he had bumped his head. Leaning down further, General Michael whispered in Mola's ear. Mola gulped and turned to go back to alert Scion.

Back in the classroom, Scion refocused his attention on Tomas and took another deep breath, only deeper now. Nodding his head slightly, Scion said, "Tomas, you are are certainly blessed with a strong, analytical mind to ask such questions. I can only tell you that the twenty-fourth angel has been serving the Lord in heaven faithfully and that he is in a position of great trust— but he wishes to remain anonymous."

Tomas reluctantly sat down.

"And with that, I think we will conclude today's class," Scion said, trying to hide his immense relief. "Come back tomorrow for the rest of my lecture on repentance. I plan to—"

"Master Scion," Mola whispered loudly from the half-opened doorway. "General Michael is in the hallway. He is asking for you."

A sudden tightness rose in Scion's chest. *O God, what would the Commander of the Armies of Heaven want with me?* "Uh . . . yes . . . um, tell him I will be right there, Mola."

Scion swallowed a lump in his throat. His face twitched again from his nervousness.

As the first angel God created, Michael had no equal. No angel had a closer relationship to God. It is no wonder that everyone in heaven considered an encounter with Michael as a visit from the Lord himself. Everything about him shouted authority, strength, courage, wisdom, and yet also compassion. Beneath his brilliant shoulder-length white hair, Michael's golden face gleamed like the sun, while his beautiful blue-green eyes seemed to dance with joy and high intelligence. Every angel in heaven loved and respected this gentle giant who spoke with a strange accent. It wasn't until about AD 800 when other angels discovered people in a place called Caledonia who spoke just like Michael. Old rumors say that Michael once asked the Lord to make a warrior race of humans who would one day defend the Gospel on Earth like he defended God's Throne in heaven. And so, God made Caledonians—who are now called *Scots*.

So, for all these reasons and more, Almost every angel felt intimidated standing near Michael's eighteen-foot frame. They often just stared at his bejeweled golden belt buckle with CHH engraved on it: *Captain of the Host of Heaven*. Even at twelve feet tall, Scion was feeling very nervous. He had not talked to Michael since just after the Great Rebellion.

"Okay, class dismissed!" Scion announced.

Scion's face paled a little as he moved toward the door. He was so distracted he stumbled on the leg of a student's chair. "Mola, something's wrong," Scion whispered. "General Michael never comes here! Have I done something wrong, Mola? Is there something you are not telling me? I trust you more than any other angel. You have always stood by me when others would not. *Please* tell me if I have made a mistake. Is he here to correct me? I cannot afford any more mistakes, you know that," Scion pleaded. His bright blue eyes suddenly became tight and watery.

"Peace, Master, peace! Everyone knows you are the most competent and loyal Headmaster we have ever known," Mola assured Scion with obvious respect. Looking up into Scion's strained face, Mola grabbed Scion's left arm affectionately. "Relax, Master, it's just a special recon request. Michael told me that he needs one of your Beta students to spy out part of that new continent where the Lord is going to send some of His English saints. He just wants a recommendation on which of your students to send. He said it is a sensitive mission that requires your best Beta scout."

Scion nodded, looking greatly relieved. "Oh, thank God! I think I know just the Beta to do this job—Angel 442. Go get her right after this meeting with the General. Remember, Mola, it's important to give General Michael immediate support at all times. I need to make a good impression. I cannot afford to offend anyone, especially *him.*"

And with that, Scion stepped into the hallway to meet his distinguished visitor. As he did, Scion also stepped into an adventure he never saw coming—and one he *feared* more than anything.

CHAPTER 6

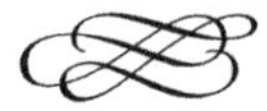

As Scion walked through the doorway, Michael's massive body filled his view. Even though Scion had met Michael before, the sight of the most powerful angel in heaven still startled him. Mola followed right behind Scion, but Scion noticed that Mola seemed strangely calm. That made Scion even more nervous. *What does Mola know that I don't?* Scion drew in a tight breath and smiled. "General Michael, what an unusual surprise to see you here. How can I serve you?"

"Can we talk privately, Master Scion? I 'ave good news for ya, but it be confidential," the massive angel whispered in his thick Scottish brogue.

Scion glanced at Mola and smiled. "Please allow my class assistant and personal confidante, Mola, to hear this good news. We work as a close team here."

Michael eyed the little assistant angel. "Hmm, 'ave we met before, Mola? You look a wee bit familiar."

At that remark, Mola swallowed hard. "Not to my knowledge, General. I would be honored if it were so," he replied with a slight bow to the great warrior.

Michael nodded and then pulled his enormous sword out of its golden scabbard with a clang, and held it horizontally just above Scion's head.

"Very well! Scion, here 'tis the good news: Ya've served the Lord here at Angel Academy fer a long time. Yer reputation as a trainer of angels is unsurpassed. Now, the Lord desires to honor ya in a special way."

Michael paused for effect. Scion and Mola exchanged excited but nervous glances. *Wow—I can hardly believe it. I never thought this would happen after what I have done,* Scion thought with his heart racing. *A rush of joy flooded his heart*—just like when he was a new angel about to fly solo beyond heaven for the first time. His grinning face was glued upward toward the shining giant.

"Angel Scion, after consulting with the archangels of the other five continents, the Lord and I have selected ya to start yer training ta become da archangel of da sixth continent, now called Da New World of da North. Yer new title will be 'Angel of Virginia,' for that is what yer region will first be called fer many a year. When ya accomplish yer first mission, da Lord will promote ya to full Archangel of Virginia. Ya will begin yer duties immediately, and ya will report directly to me."

Scion's body suddenly went limp and his left cheek began to twitch violently. Mola became stiff as a soldier, his face darkened.

Finally pulling himself together, Scion looked up and asked, "But why me, General? The Lord has better . . . um . . . more capable angels for such a task. I am just the Headmaster of this Academy. I've never had a real Earth assignment. All I have ever done on Earth was lead those fourteen wise men to Jesus. Surely, you need someone better qualified than me."

Michael stepped back and squinted at the two angels. "Really, Scion, I thought I had good news. It's an Earth assignment, and a good one, at that. We're all made for this, right? Aren't ya tired of just running a school? I know I would be!"

Michael got down on one knee to see their downcast faces better. "Look, laddie, maybe ya don't get my drift. This be a bonny opportunity for ya! Once ya do this, ya will never be stuck here in a school again. You'll get to do what ya have been training these young angels to do! And, you'll get promoted to an archangel! How aboot that? Just imagine what yer success will bring. All of heaven will rejoice in this victory for the Lamb, and all of hell will surely tremble at the name of Scion, Archangel of Virginia!"

Scion was silent, but his heart raced as a tidal wave of panic swept over his mind, already foggy with fear.

"The truth is, Scion, that yer our best hope to protect that colony. As ya know, ya have . . . shall we say 'special' qualifications for this assignment. Yer one of the few angels in heaven who has personal knowledge of Dark Angels. Ya know more about angel tactics than almost any angel in heaven. After all, ya trained most of them," Michael concluded with a wink and quick tilt of his head.

Scion moaned weakly, staring at the floor and then looking up again. "General Michael, you know that all I have ever done since the Lord closed Archangel Academy was work here at Angel Academy." Then Scion motioned for the general to come closer as he whispered, "Sir, you know what the Rebellion did to me. I've never been the same. That's why you put me here. You said I would be safe here until I could clear my name someday. This assignment you are proposing sounds anything but safe. You know my closest friends are down there on Earth. I can't risk meeting them. It would crush me.

"If I may say so, General Michael, you need someone who has been on Earth dealing with demons for a long time, someone who is strong and wise in battle. I only know the theory. I've never done it."

Scion looked quickly around with tear-filled eyes and then whispered even lower, "Sir, If I go down there and make a mess of it, it will only make me look worse to all those angels who already don't trust me. I've already made at least one *very* serious mistake. Heaven cannot afford another failure like that. *Neither can I*. And what if I run into my old friends from Archangel Academy? Or worse, what if I have to fight against them? I could *never* do that!" Scion almost whimpered.

"With all due respect, sir, it makes no sense for me to accept this assignment. It is, indeed, a great honor to be asked. But I cannot do what you are asking me to do now. Please find someone else. My students need me."

"Hmm. This is harder than I thought it would be," Michael muttered. He leaned even closer to Scion. "Listen closely now, Master Scion. Let me tell ya once more. I kin see 'tis a shock to ya. Ya've spent thousands of years since the Great Rebellion training angels to serve and protect the saints on Earth so they kin finish what Lord Jesus started, right?"

"Yes, I have, General. That's why I must stay here to prepare angels to protect the saints," Scion weakly countered. He was feeling faint. The room started to spin. The walls seemed to be closing in on him.

"Precisely my point, Scion. There are many saints the Lord is about to send to a new land to establish a nation that will fill the Earth with the Gospel. The Lord God himself is planting this colony as he planned long ago. The new nation that will arise from this colony will be great in the eyes of the Lord. And the enemies of the Lord know this, so the battle for that colony will be fierce. Scion, listen. For other reasons I cannae say now, I know ya are the most qualified for this assignment. Do ya hear me, sir?"

With great difficulty and obvious emotional pain, Scion managed to respond, but very slowly. "General, I am truly grateful for this wonderful offer to serve the saints on Earth, but as much as I would love to do that, I cannot! I need to respectfully decline this gracious invitation. I beg you, General, please find someone else."

Michael shook his head in disbelief. Putting his massive hand on Scion's trembling shoulder, the General replied, "Dear brother Scion, I am so sorry. I can see now how difficult this is for ya. I was hoping it would not be so." Michael frowned in frustration. "I know what happened back then. I know who ya are. Few do, but I do. Truly, laddie, me heart goes out to ya. Yes—yer dearest friends are oot there somewhere, as we all know. I truly wish I could tell ya that ya won't have to deal with them traitors, but I cannae. They were once part of us and now they are no. They and their demons must needs be opposed, and if ya meet one of those Archangel Academy deserters, no angel in heaven is better equipped to oppose them than ya are."

A wave of intense pain suddenly crashed across Scion's face. His eyes squinted completely shut as an eruption of volcanic emotions burst from his gut toward his mouth. With lightening speed, his hand muffled the cry, "But *Kai*, my best friend, is out there somewhere! I cannot face him," Scion gasped into his huge hand.

"Master, you said you would never say his name again!" Mola exclaimed softly.

Scion reached out and grabbed Mola's hand. A long moment of silence blanketed the three of them as Scion quietly wept.

Finally, with unusual tenderness Michael spoke, "Dear brother Scion, how I wish I could respect yer request, but I cannae do it."

Michael stood up again, towering over the two angels. His eyes glowed now with heavenly blue-green fire. "My dear brother, ya teach yer students that the Lord of Heaven never makes suggestions or requests—only promises or commands. This assignment is not a request."

In a voice brimming with authority and love, Michael declared, "Master Scion, yer commanded by the Lord 'imself to serve the saints of a new colony in Virginia. You may choose a wee Beta angel ta serve with ya. With yer unique qualifications and the Beta's strong recon abilities, ya both will be more than a match for the intense resistance the colony will certainly face."

Scion did not move or speak. He just stared at Michael's colossal belt buckle. The CHH letters on it swirled before his eyes into a blur. Nausea rumbled in his stomach.

"Scion, the Lord himself commands ya to this. He knows yer situation well. He loves ya more than ya know. He is counting on ya!"

"Ya start on the morrow, on Earth date, September 11, 1561. Reports are coming in of Spanish activity in Virginia. Send yer Beta right away to see what our Catholic saints are doing there. Is that clear?"

"Yes, sir. I will," Scion mumbled somewhat incoherently. Michael blinked in amazement at Scion's expressionless face. But he went on.

"Also, Scion, on December 20, 1606, the Lord 'as planned to send three English ships to plant a colony in Virginia. I want ya both to reconnoiter the future route of the three ships to make sure the enemy will not interfere with them. Do that on December 18, 1606. Got it?"

For a moment, Scion could not speak. His lips moved but no sound came out. Michael glanced at Mola. At last, Scion nodded his head slowly and stuttered, "Ya…ya..*yes*.., I d..d…do." Michael looked worried. Michael shook his head in disbelief and raised his voice to get Scion's attention.

"Look, Scion, I know you did not expect or want this assignment, but ya must do all ye can do ta protect that colony. The ruling spirit of that area knows the ships are a-comin' and he will fight ya fiercely. But that's not all. Ya will 'ave a brave and godly pastor named Robert Hunt—one of the Lord's favorites. His prayers will do ya much good. But the ruling spirit there, named Okeus, is stronger than most. He pretends to be a powerful reptile demon, but we know him to be a Dark Angel."

At that last phrase, Scion's stomach lurched and he grimaced and shut his eyes momentarily. Michael pretended not to notice and continued. "The natives worship Okeus as their god. Because they sacrifice enemy prisoners to him often, he has given them great power in their spells and incantations."

Seeing that Scion was struggling to focus, Michael quickly concluded, "Well, me laddie. That's all fer now. I will send other instructions later to yer Beta since she has superior communication abilities," Michael joked with a wry smile. But Scion just stared at the floor. Michael blinked in amazement at the silent angel hunched over before him. He was not used to angels responding like this to his orders.

Finally, Scion slowly looked up at him. His face was a kaleidoscope of swirling emotions, but one sensation rose above them all like a dark tower: terror—terror like he had never known since the Great Rebellion. His legs began to give out. His mind became mush. He almost passed out. Mola reached out and held him up by one arm.

Slowly and with great exertion, Scion announced, "I have to go now. I feel sick." With a surge of strength, Scion turned and stumbled down the hallway—toward the tall bushes in Moses Park.

CHAPTER 7

September 11, 1561

The storm-battered Spanish galleon lurched into the mouth of the dark river just as Angel 442 swooped in from heaven. Scion had sent her there to record what the Spanish were doing and to get as much data as she could on Okeus if he showed up. The petite angel checked her sensors' data display embedded in her left arm to confirm her location. As usual, she was right on target.

| Angel 442

Standing at fourteen inches tall, with bright rainbow-colored hair, sparkling purple eyes, and a deep beige, velvety face, Angel 442 was stunning to behold. When in flight, the multicolored tips of her trailing wing feathers twinkled to the beat of whatever song she was singing—and she sang a lot. Like most angels, she wore a tunic covering her arms to the wrists and her legs to her ankles. But the tight golden belt around her slim waist left no doubt that beneath that garb was a very athletic female body. Today, her tunic color was hot pink. She never wore white like all the Alpha male angels do.

Some had said that she was sassy. But she herself has only ever admitted to quirkiness, which she claims, simply goes with being a risk-taker. Some others have said that she thinks "out of the box." She prefered to say that she *lived* "out of the box." What is clear is that she is one of the most intelligent, innovative, and emotionally sensitive angels in heaven. She was the top Beta graduate in her class. Although she is a sensory detection marvel, as all Betas are, she loves human history. Her final research thesis was on the romantic lives of humans. She has always said that if she were human, she would have been a romance novel writer.

"BUT, ADMIRAL, THE WAVES . . . THEY ARE TOO BIG—"

"I don't care *a damn* about the storm!" the Spanish captain shouted. "I don't care if you all die! *Get him*! Don't you understand that we need him to convince his tribe not to resist our conquistadors when they arrive! If Spain is ever to rule here, we have to have him! He is going to make us all rich!"

The man who was responsible for guarding the entire Caribbean fleet of Spanish treasure ships had come to collect a treasure. But tonight, Admiral Pedro Menéndez de Avilés, Captain-General of the Fleet of the Indies,* had come for something far more valuable than a boatload of gold. He had come for *a boy*.*

Frothy black waves slapped the heaving hull like thousands of angry hands as it tacked north out of the immense bay they called Bahia De Santa Maria* into a river the natives called Pamunkey.* Smelling the earthy scent of land nearby, Captain Menéndez's sharp brown eyes scanned the eastern bank for their rendezvous point near the Powhatan village of Kiskiack,* in the land the Spanish called Ajacán.*

But Menéndez and his crew were not the only ones peering into the darkness. Fifteen hundred pairs of fiery yellow eyes squinted back at the Spanish ship. But no one on the ship saw the mocking demon eyes or the colored lights that flickered from their bodies when they were aroused to fight. Looking on from his perch high above the storm, a gargantuan dinosaur-like spirit also watched with amusement. Okeus was the ruling spirit of Ajacán—and he looked every inch the part.

His fourteen-foot body was covered with thick seaweed-green armored hide. Atop his muscular torso, a huge reptilian head with frog-like lips displayed a wide mouth full of six-inch, razor-sharp orange fangs. Beneath his formidable eating apparatus, two short but powerful arms ended in six-fingered claws that could wield a mighty sword or flick a foolish demon across the room with one claw-finger. His broad, short legs descended into a fearsome spiked tail that he plopped behind him when he sat on his haunches.

He was strong as a dozen oxen, and yet he could glide effortlessly for miles on forty-five foot, semi-transparent green wings like those of a flying fish. And speaking of fish, Okeus loved to eat raw fish, dead or alive. His breath and stomach gas usually reeked of rotting fish. The stench was almost overwhelming, even to the strongest demons who served him.

But his most impressive feature was his eyes—large, yellow orbs set in bright red sockets that communicated a cunning and cruel personality only surpassed by Lucifer himself. Every demon under his command feared him immensely—or at least that is what his assistant named Snookus always told him to curry favor.

Snookus was the bright yellow, obese octopus-shaped demon who usually hovered just three feet above the left ear of his master. As the strange ship drew closer to shore, Snookus pretended to enjoy watching the Spanish intruders. He always mimicked his master's moods—the better to avoid a beating—or *worse.* He had already lost three of his eight tentacles to the wrath of Okeus years ago. Unlike the octopi of Earth, his three severed arms would never grow back. Okeus used his dark powers to make sure they *wouldn't*. But despite his cruelty towards Snookus, Okeus enjoyed having the only *gas-powered* demon in North America. Because Snookus did not have wings, he propelled himself by shooting inky gases from a tube under the back of his head. His landings were awkward and thumpy, but no winged demon moved faster in the air than Snookus—a fact that always brought a devilish delight in his light-green eyes as he squirted past every other evil spirit in flight.

SUDDENLY, A SAILOR SIGHTED THE SMALL TORCH ON THE RIVERBANK about one hundred yards off the port bow. "There's the village chief, the werowance, *mi Capitan*! And I see the boy with his mother!" the sailor shouted out in a husky voice, barely audible above the rumble of the storm.

"Make for shore and send in the landing boat with my cabin boy, Raqīb," Menéndez barked. He wiped the cold rain from his dark, well-trimmed beard. "Grab that little Powhatan and set sail *muy pronto* before this accursed storm tears us to shreds— or the tribe spots us taking the boy."

Raqib looked a this tall captain and asked, "But what if the parents refuse to give us the boy as they promised us last week?"

"Foolish question, son. The father of that boy is as greedy as we are. He'll hand him over."

As soon the landing party approached the shore, hundreds of giant, dark-red, horned demons circled overhead. These were fearsome Guard Patrol demons Okeus had sent out to scan for signs of the Heavenly Host among the Spanish invaders. With monstrous bat-like wings, swords drawn, and bared orange fangs, they glided into the ship's hull to detect and challenge any angels hiding there. But they found none.

~

FINALLY, THE SIX SAILORS LANDED THEIR BOAT AND HID IT UNDER AN overhanging tree. Raqīb—a swarthy young man with a strange glow in his eyes—was their leader. "Let's go," he whispered to the Algonquian family huddled nearby. Then they quickly disappeared into the bushes to avoid being seen by other members of the tribe.

As the sailors handed over a small chest of beads, trinkets, knives, and copper to the native husband, Raqīb ran into the forest—supposedly to relieve himself. But as soon as he came to a towering oak tree, he knelt down to dig a shallow hole with his knife. Then, after looking around quickly to see if anyone was looking, the dark-complexioned man pulled out a beautiful silken pouch from a hidden pocket in his leather sea-jacket. With extreme care, he withdrew a small, black rock from the pouch and cradled it in his shaking hands it as if it were a family heirloom— or something *very* sacred. Once the rock was buried, he bowed his head to his knees and mumbled a few phrases in a non-Spanish language. Then, the young sailor hurried back just as the others were pulling the weeping boy from his distraught mother's arms. "*Vámonos, vámonos! El Capitan esta esperando*!" he ordered. "We have to leave now. The captain is waiting."

The boy screamed! His mother collapsed onto the beach—but her husband hardly noticed. His gaze was fixed on the large ship just offshore. As the crewmen dragged the wailing boy into the small boat, his father's eyes gleamed with a dark joy. *Do not cry, my son. You are going to make me famous and powerful one day.*

"Papa, Papa, I don't want to leave!" the boy pleaded once more. "Please let me stay. I'll be good. I *promise*!" But the father was already gone, leaving his wife in the bushes to pour out her grief alone.

Mercifully, beyond his mother's eyesight, her boy was hauled up the side of the ship with a rope around his waist like a captured animal. He still cried out to his parents, but the heavy winds muffled his voice. The small boat was finally cranked aboard, the anchors were winched in, and the sails slowly extended. As the whistling winds caught the sailcloth at the front, the great ship spun around so fast that the forward mast cracked a little. Every sailor heard it and winced. It was a *bad omen.*

OKEUS WATCHED THE SPANISH PLOT PLAY OUT FROM HIS USUAL ROOST IN the clouds high above the churning bay. Then he turned to Snookus. "Let them take the boy, the fools. They want that young man to help them conquer this land. Little do they know that that boy will one day conquer them! I know what to do when that boy comes back. What the stupid Spanish mean for their good, I mean for their evil. It's *so juicy,* I can almost taste it!" Okeus roared above the thunder, "How I love to deceive and kill! It makes me feel so alive. I was made for this!" Okeus bellowed right in the face of his bloated assistant. The octopus tried to smile, but that blast of wilting breath from his rancid reptile master made him gag badly.

After a moment of savoring his assistant's gasping for breath, Okeus looked below at the circling red hordes and shouted, "For the Dragon! For the Rebellion!"

Howls of agreement filled the stormy night skies as thousands of well-worn swords clanged out of their scabbards as they were raised high above horned heads. Okeus drank it all in like an intoxicating potion. Then, with a twirling flourish of his massive wings, Okeus spun westward to his throne in the Great Swamp just miles away. Tonight, he would celebrate with his royal court of demons. His "mouse trap" was set. Now he had to wait for the mouse to return.

CHAPTER 8

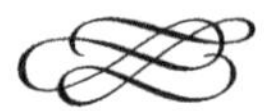

The tiny angel hiding in the densely forested shoreline saw it all. Her heart ached as she watched the native boy screaming for his parents with his terrified face thrust over the railing of the hulking Spanish galleon. Then the ship steered hard to port and the boy's pitiful cries grew fainter and fainter amid the growling thunder. As she watched as the dark storm swallow the fading shape of the heaving ship sailing west toward the churning ocean, her heart poured out a prayer, *Father God. Save that boy. Make him yours someday—and use him for your glory.* Then she remembered, *O my gosh! Scion! He's waiting for my report to give to General Michael!* Faster than a hummingbird's wing, she leapt into flight and rocketed heavenward.

Piercing the storm clouds at a thousand miles an hour, it took 3.43 minutes for her to reach the edge of space sixty-two miles above. After instantaneously accelerating to the speed of light, she covered the remaining 334,800,000 Earth miles in thirty minutes, which is the average transit time for trips between Earth and heaven.

With a snap of her tiny but mighty wings, she deftly exploded out of light speed just before bursting through the ceiling of Angel Academy and gliding up to the door of Scion's well-appointed headmaster chambers on the top floor. As usual, Scion was working late in the Headmaster's Office. Although it was sparsely decorated, a lavish golden frame on one wall held a beautiful watercolor of an unusual red symbol.

A somewhat startled Scion mumbled, "Well, *come in*, 442. I am glad you are back so soon. General Michael is eager to get your intel report. He wants your recon data of the Spanish landing before he plans his next steps to settle the saints there. Come closer. Let's get started."

With a smile as quick and bright as any in heaven, she rushed forward to hover slightly above Scion's enormous mahogany desk. But despite the urgency of the moment, her feminine curiosity had to ask, "Master Scion, why do you have that lovely painting on your wall? It's a symbol of a heart, I think. I've seen it used in England recently to communicate about romance." Then she looked at Scion with a dreamy face, "Oh, I *love* romance, don't you?"

Looking up shyly, Scion answered, "Yes—it is a symbol of love. I saw this one in our Great Library. According to the Librarian, an angel on patrol recorded this image in France around 1410 AD. It's part of a tapestry called *Le Don du Coeur*—"The Gift of the Heart." I liked so much, I had the painting made by one of my students."

"But the heart in your painting has a jagged, broken line down the middle, Master Scion. Why?"

Without looking at her, Scion whispered, "Let's just say it has a special meaning to me. Now let's get down to business. I picked you for this mission because your instructors said you were the best Beta they had. So, let's hear what you have."

Angel 442 giggled and then burst into a rapid-fire account of what she had seen and heard. "I thought General Michael just asked us to update him about that new Spanish exploration in Virginia. Wow! That place is buzzing with demons—hundreds of level-five, dark-red warrior demons—you know, the kind you taught us that are normally assigned to high-value locations. But there is nothing important there that I could detect. *Perhaps* Lucifer knows the Lord has plans for that area. At any rate, as we already knew, the Algonquians in that are are called Powhatans. I think I also saw their local god—the Dark Angel Michael talked about who calls himself Okeus."

Scion stared at her with a glazed look in his eyes for a long moment—and then nodded his head. "Please continue," he murmured.

"Yes, sir! Well, Okeus may be a powerful Dark Angel, but he looks like an overweight, fat-lipped dinosaur," 442 reported with a giggle. "And if that isn't weird enough, an octopus demon named Snookus seems to be his assistant. Snookus has a grotesque human-like face with the biggest green eyes I have ever seen on any demon his size. I also noticed he only has five tentacles. The other three look like they were torn off. Master Scion, you can't make this stuff up," Angel 442 snickered.

But then she got serious again. "Oddly enough, Okeus did not seem upset when the Spanish captured one of his Powhatan boys. I heard the Spanish captain talking about using the boy as a mediator to his tribe later on so the Spanish can plant a colony there. Surely, Okeus would be against any Christian colony in his lands. Why didn't Okeus send his demons to stop the abduction of the boy? It doesn't make sense."

Scion smiled. "Thank you, Angel 442. Good job. Can you show me some of your visual data? I'd like to know more details about Okeus."

"With pleasure," 442 gleefully responded. She loved showing males angels how effective her Beta sensor array was.

"You will soon see that this is no ordinary demon outpost. That settlement Jesus is planning to put there is in for some real battles. Here, let me play a few seconds of what my eye sensors recorded. I will download the entire footage into the War Room's records as soon as we're done so General Michael can analyze it further."

With a quick squint of her beautiful lavender eyes, a bright white light shone from her eyes into the darkened room, spreading out into a two-foot by three-foot screen, floating in the air six feet from her face. On it, vivid color images appeared of a large ship twisting at anchor in a storm not far from a small party of humans on the shore. One of the humans was crying out of control. Twenty feet above the ground, large, swirling clusters of amber-eyed, dark-red demons screamed curses into the darkness. Yellow, sulfurous breath chugged out of their gaping jaws filled with long, sharp fangs. Most of them held large swords above their heads with battle-scarred blades. Then the images panned upward above the storm where a huge dinosaur-like spirit hovered and gazed down on the chaos below. He looked like a demon, but the way he carried himself was different. Scion noted that Okeus seemed too confident, too aware, too much in charge to be just a demon. *Okeus is powerful and cunning—and he knows it. He is a Dark Angel, but which one is he?* Scion wondered with a shudder.

Angel 442 sensed Scion's gloomy mood and spoke up to change the subject. "I know I am not supposed to ask such questions, but what is General Michael's next step, Master Scion?" she asked meekly.

"I can't be sure. We need to be very careful . . . and *discreet*," Scion added with a pained look. "These matters are not to be shared with anyone. Is that clear? One slip of information about things like this can do more damage than you realize." Suddenly, his face darkened, and he looked almost sick. He turned his face away quickly to escape her notice, but she saw it.

"I need to consult with Michael before we proceed," Scion said as he cleared his throat. "I will also talk to Mola, my class assistant. He is a great listener and always seems to have wisdom for me. You may go now, Angel 442. Thank you for a job well done."

As the tiny scout moved toward the office door, 442 noticed that Scion's left cheek twitched repeatedly. She sensed fear boiling inside him. He looked like a volcano about to erupt. With a subterranean sigh, Scion stood up and quickly crossed the room to the gigantic window that faced God's Throne just north of there. His eyes flit above the diamond-like sparkle of the throne to the endless expanse of dark space sprinkled with billions of stars. Tears began to puddle in his eyes as he whispered to himself: "Dark Angels . . . my old friends . . . you are out there . . . *somewhere.* We used to sing together around the Lord's Throne. We played tag in Orion's Belt. How many times did we race each other home to heaven from the far edge of the Milky Way?" Scion's head and shoulders slumped forward. His hand covered his mouth. "Where are you now, brothers? *Who* are you now? And where is *Kai,* my beloved Kai?"

Scion was whispering to himself, but standing at the door, the Beta's super-hearing caught it all. She stood in silence, her eyes wide with shock. No student angel had ever heard Headmaster Scion grieve like that. Compassion welled up in her heart and tears in her eyes.

Finally, Scion turned away from the enormous window to see the little angel looking at him. They locked eyes for a second, each glistening with tears. Then 442 bowed her rainbow-colored head, turned, and ascended slowly through the hallway ceiling while Scion watched. It was a moment they both would not forget.

Soon, they would share much more than emotions and tears.

AS ANGEL 442 LEFT SCION'S OFFICE, CAPTAIN MENÉNDEZ PASSED between the twin capes of the Chesapeake Bay and out into the Atlantic, still fighting strong storm winds. He was fingering the image of King Philip II* of Spain on a copper jetton coin* as he smiled smugly at Raqīb. "This native boy will make me rich, Raqīb. King Philip will reward me generously for obtaining such a prize for Spain. That boy will be our bridge to his tribe and to the wealth of the New World there. Yes—Balboa and Coronado have all had their share of glory and gold. Now, it is *my turn* to make Spain the wealthiest and most powerful nation on Earth for generations to come. Soon, I shall feast on this land and digest its wealth for the glory of Spain! Mark my words, Raqīb, September 11, 1561, will go down in history as a new beginning. I believe we have started something tonight that will change the New World, starting here in Ajacán.

Captain Pedro Menendez de Aviles

"*Si, Capitán.* I agree. We have started something great tonight. But it is late. I'm going below now. *Buenas Noches.*"

Once below deck, Raqīb ducked into a small storage room where he often secretly worshipped his god—the god of *Islam.* As the ship rocked violently in the stormy waves, he grabbed a beam for balance. As he did, he looked out a small window as thunderous lightning exploded in the sky, washing the boiling sea with brilliant light. Raqīb threw his head back, drinking in the glory of the moment, then laughed and shouted, "Yes, September 11, 1561, is also *my* day of destiny! After almost one thousand years of jihad against Christian Europe, we Muslims failed to conquer Europe, but we will rule this new land one day! I have claimed this land with the black rock from the sacred, black *Kabba Stone* in Mecca—just as my imam commanded me. One day, this New World land with be ours! *Allahu Akbar!*" he shouted just as an other-worldly barrage of lightning and thunder shook the skies.

CHAPTER 9

September 6, 1606

With his upraised hands Scion knelt near the massive window facing the Throne of God. As he finished worshipping the Lord for about an hour, he prayed, "You are an awesome, awesome God! There is no one like you. You are my all in all—my God, my King, my Lord, and my Creator. I love you. I worship You! Jesus, are my greatest treasure. My greatest pleasure is to know I am yours forever. Amen."

A soft knock came to his office door. Scion leapt up with one powerful, fluid motion. "Come in." As the wide door slowly swung open, Scion was happy to see a smiling Angel 442 hovering there, her tiny body dwarfed by the enormous entrance.

"Welcome, Angel 442! Come in! Come in! I heard that you wanted to see me. Can it actually be *forty-five years* since you graduated from here? It seems like it was just yesterday. Well, it's always nice to see former students. I have heard so many great reports from Mola about your recon exploits. He says you helped the Alpha angels assist the English in their 1588 victory over the Spanish Armada.* Impressive. Mola also told me that General Michael considers you the best scout he has ever worked with, *Alpha or Beta*. That is quite a compliment—especially coming from Michael! And now Mola just told me how you uncovered a Muslim plot to wipe out a church in Turkey. *You go, girl!* I am so proud of you."

Angel 442 did a slight double-take, and her eyebrows arched. "He told you that? That's *odd*. Only the General and I knew about that mission."

"Well, 442, all I can say is that Mola is well connected. He seems to know things other angels are not aware of. He really is *amazing*—and my best friend."

"That's so good, Master Scion. I'm glad you have a close friend," 442 replied. "I will have to get to know Mola better. He sounds like a scout —like me."

"Come to think of it, 442, I agree. Mola seems to know everything that happens here in heaven. But enough of that—come over on my desk and tell me more about yourself. What's it like being a Beta out there with all the Alphas?

With her signature giggle, 442 gingerly landed on Scion's polished desk, sat down with crossed legs and began. "Master Scion, I feel *very* blessed to be a Beta. Yes—we are small and female—but we get the job done, despite some strange looks from Alphas. They are still not comfortable with 'Eve' angels, as they call us. But it's OK. I *like* being a pioneer. And since General Michael likes to use me so much, my Beta sisters are counting on me to prove to the Alphas that God did not make a mistake when he made Betas female. As they say on Earth, 'Come hell or high water,' I am *not* going to let my sisters down! One day, those Alphas will be *begging* to work with us!" she declared loudly, slapping her thigh with a *whack*.

Scion looked at her tiny, delicate face and chuckled, "Are you sure you are not really a *tiger* underneath that pretty rainbow hair?" They both laughed.

"Not hardly. Wrong fashion statement. I can't stand striped clothing," 442 quipped. "But are you sure *you* are not a Throne Room Angel? I heard you worshipping just before you opened the door. That's my favorite thing to do, you know."

"You heard me? Well, of course, you did with those special ears of yours," Scion chuckled with a grin. "Yes—I was just thanking God for the Anglican, Lutheran, Presbyterian, and Anabaptist churches that are on fire for God all over Europe*—despite the terrible Catholic wars raging against them. And now, just two years ago, God moved James I, the new king of England, Scotland, and Ireland,* to produce a new Bible.* Michael says that Bible will change the world. Yes, I am worshipping! Despite the many mistakes of men—and of angels—God is preparing all humanity for the return of our Lord Jesus! I cannot wait! One day, you and I will see the glory of the Lord covering the Earth like the waters cover the sea! It's beginning to happen now after so many centuries of pain and darkness in God's earthly family!"

Without warning, the petite angel leaped into the air, circling the room, arms raised high as she shouted, "Wow! Praise the Lord, praise Jesus! I worship you Father! Thank you, Father, for sending Jesus to save mankind! Thank you for your new Bible through King James! Thank you, Father, for *everything*!" she gushed until she was red in the face.

"Are you *OK*?" a smiling Scion inquired. "You worship so . . . *extravagantly*!"

442 took a moment to catch her breath. "I'm fine, Master Scion. It's just whenever I hear about the work of God's Spirit, my spirit leaps. I know I get a little wild; I can't help it. Praise just spurts from my mouth! In fact, one day, I had to leave my Earth history class early, so I could go outside and release some of this pressure to worship. It felt like a geyser inside me was ready to blast! Some of my friends think I am odd . . . but I *have to* worship—*a lot*," she laughed.

Scion laughed too, and noticed 442 giving him a quizzical look.

"Did you know that you are glowing right now, Master Scion? It looks like I'm not the only odd angel around here," She giggled softly.

Scion blushed, but you couldn't tell. "As you may know, 442, all angels of my generation glow in worship a little, but for some reason, ever since the Great Rebellion, I glow *way* too much in worship. Like you, I simply can't help it." Scion said while shrugging his shoulders. "I used to feel embarrassed about it. Angels would stare at me in worship and snicker. Some even complained to Michael that they had to shield their eyes from me in worship."

"I'll bet the Seraphim angels never complained," 442 added slyly with a big grin.

"No, 442, of course not. They cover their eyes with two of their six wings *all the time*. Now that's *really* odd!" They both laughed again and shook their heads.

"442, when we have time, maybe I will tell you how the Father used me as a very bright star for an important mission. Those same angels that complained about me suddenly became jealous!" Another round of loud laughter. Their eyes met again. He just stared at her and thought, *She's so small—and female! So different from me. But when she worships the Lord like that, it doesn't matter. I'd love to get to know her better. But how can we be friends— a fourteen- inch Beta and a twelve-foot angel. Angels already think I'm strange. O, well . . .* , Scion mused.

Just then, 442 flew right in front of Scion's glowing face. "I *have* to know. Please, please tell me?" 442 asked. "What star did God ask you to be?"

"Well, let's just say that some very wise men followed me for many miles."

The little angel's eyes grew wide. "That was *you?*"

"Yes," Scion smiled bashfully.

"Wow! And I thought all you ever did was paperwork and teach classes. Wow! Can I tell my friends that you led the Magi to Jesus?"

"I'd prefer if you didn't. I like being in the background, if you know what I mean," Scion grinned.

Just then, Mola poked his head into the open door. He seemed unusually tense. "Master Scion, I have a note from General Michael."

Scion saw fear on Mola's face. His body stiffened. "What did he say this time?" Scion mumbled with an ashen face. He knew that the day he had dreaded was here.

Deep compassion welled up inside 442 as she watched Scion. She already knew what was coming. The General had told her. She wanted to be with him when he heard the news.

Mola swallowed hard and continued, "He wants to remind you of your December 18 recon mission for the three English ships leaving soon for Virginia. They sail on December 20. He said not to worry about your duties at the Academy. They have already picked a headmaster replacement. You are now to serve was the Angel of Virginia as soon as you begin this recon mission."

Scion was visibly shaken. He stood up but his hand reached for a chair to steady himself.

For a long moment, no one moved or spoke. Scion's pain was palpable. When she could stand it no longer, 442 glided over to Scion. Reaching out with the smallest of angel hands, she put her palm on Scion's massive arm, but he did not see her do it.

"What in heaven...!" Scion blurted out as he pulled his arm away from an unknown touch. He was not used to being touched. Then, he realized it was 442. With a sigh as deep as the Pacific Ocean, he just stared at her. She looked . . . well . . . *angelic*. Her big purples eyes, wet with tears, were surrounded by a look of compassion Scion had never seen on *any* angel. He could not take his gaze off of her face. Her feminine tenderness drew him like a moth to a fire in a dark forest. It was the same look he remembered on her face forty-five years ago when he was grieving for Kai. His heart was beating rapidly now. His damp eyes twitched with fear. But inside—*deep* inside —something was moving. Something was slowly rising from a long-forgotten place in his heart that had been buried in fear: *hope.* As he allowed himself to focus on that hope, his brain fog began to clear. M*aybe I can do this —even if I do meet Kai. If she were by my side—I might make it*. It was a holy moment—even for heaven.

Finally, Scion was able to speak in a hoarse whisper. "Mola, tell the General that I will be . . . honored to fly that mission on the 18th with Angel 442. And tell him I . . . *we* . . . will do our best."

CHAPTER 10

December 18, 1606

Sweeping southeast across Scotland's dark, heather-covered glens at toward foggy London, Scion glided down the English Channel. He was *very* nervous: his first Earth assignment was finally beginning. After one hundred thousand years in heaven, the culture shock of being on Earth was overpowering over all his senses. In a few minutes, he would rendezvous with Angel 442 at just south of the Rock of Gibraltar at the southern tip of Spain a few hours before dawn.

There was *so much* to see. He had to look fast, especially at seven hundred miles per hour, just below the speed of sound at sea level. His eyes constantly darted back and forth so he would not miss anything. But the visual stimuli was almost too much. His heart pounded like it would jump out of his muscular chest. He slowed down and closed his eyes to pray.

"God, help me," he whispered as his wings tilted up to slow his descent. "I've got to do this *right*—and by *the book*."

His tall, golden body rippled with the muscles of a mighty warrior, but his brilliant blue eyes were filled with fear—the kind that little boys have when they think something is under their bed at night. The eight-foot scabbard that trailed at his waist kept reminding him that he was headed for something far worse than culture shock. Only the occasional sight of a church steeple in England or France brought a slight smile to his face.

As his twenty-four feet of feathered wingspan swished above the sweltering shores of North Africa, another angel streaked toward him —but he *heard* it before he saw it. This angel was singing loudly—and not in a normal way. It sounded like chanting—a flurry of words sung with only one note, just like the singing of monks in the British monasteries he had just flown over. Just as he turned his head to locate the source of the odd music, something stirred inside him. His face began to glow.

Suddenly, a blur of rainbow-colored hair and piercing vocals looped around Scion's head three times, finally hovering right in front of his startled blue eyes.

"Good morning, sir! Reconnaissance Angel 442 reporting as ordered." She tee-heed as she looped as fast as a falcon around his head. "Betcha *you* can't do that!"

Caught off guard, Scion stiffly replied, "Sorry, I don't do frivolous things like that. And could you please move back a bit? I will have *no* trouble hearing you with a voice that loud."

Scion grumbled in his thoughts, *So that's why Betas have their own worship section in God's Throne Room: deafening voices and very unique singing styles.*

Realizing that he had been too brusk with a friend, Scion smiled warmly, "442, it's *you*! I am so glad to see you! Betas really *are* different," Scion chuckled as she settled into flight formation with him.

"Yes—and we *love it*! Besides being the first female angels, we all have hair and skin color schemes that no one else in heaven has. I guess Father wanted to express his feminine, artistic side a bit," she snickered. "I was told that even Eve—Adam's super-gorgeous wife with the perfect body—was a little jealous of us. But hey, Eve always was a little over the top, right? She even joked with us about how she may not have eaten the forbidden fruit if God had made her look more like us."

"Yeah, right," Scion scoffed inwardly—*I'm glad Eve can joke about her colossal sin. I would still be hiding under a rock in heaven if I had messed up God's creation like she did . . . But—maybe I have , too— more than I know!*

Changing the subject, Scion said, "Okay, that's enough, 442. Let's finish that topic later. As you know, this is my first assignment on Earth. I cannot afford to fail. We need to get down to business. First, are you clear on your orders, Angel 442?"

"*Angelique*," she softly cooed.

"Angel-what?" Scion shot back with a perplexed glance at her.

"*Angelique*—that's my preferred name. All the Betas have given themselves a nickname. I think one of those old, male chauvinist angels in Michael's War Room decided it would be more efficient to give us gals numbers for our names. *Ha!* What woman wants to be called by a number? Please call me *Angie,* short for Angelique. All of my friends do," she said with her sweetest smile.

Scion gave her a confused look. "Look, I really like you—we are friends, you know that. I am also immensely grateful that you are on this mission with me—but I cannot treat you like a friend on an assignment like this. I am your Mission Commander and your former Academy Headmaster. This is not like those parties you angels have when someone comes to the Lord. This is *serious* business. We must follow the rules and procedures, or we may make a mistake. Do you understand? We cannot act like friends right now," he repeated firmly, expecting her to back down submissively as most angels did when he rebuked them.

Without a second thought, Angel 442 flew directly in front of Scion's face, flying backward. Scion instinctively sucked in his breath and stared at her in astonishment.

Angel 442 looked directly into his huge sky-blue eyes and calmly said, "Master Scion, I get it. The Headmaster of Angel Academy is not supposed to make friends with student angels. But you are *not* the Headmaster anymore! You are the Angel of Virginia and I am your scout. *See?* We are now free to be friends! Don't you want friends? Life is so boring without them. Please! Just call me Angie on this trip. We can just say it's a *code name* or something if you get asked. *Please?*"

Again, he felt something powerful and good inside him move. But his brow furrowed as his mind wrestled with her request— *I can't call her Angie. I've never addressed any angel by a nickname. Good God! What have I got myself into? I have to focus.*

Without looking at her, Scion spoke sharply as he began his climb, "Let's go, *442*! Time is short and this is a *critical* mission. Michael wants us to reconnoiter the entire route the three English ships will take in two days. Your assignment is to record the audio and video data of anything important along the way. From that, we will reconstruct a four-dimensional map with notes that Michael can use to prepare his warrior angels who will accompany the three ships on their voyage.

"As you know, I like to do things by the book. We can talk more about the mission on the way to save time. Please assume a wing position two feet astern of my left wing and two feet below, as per normal formation flight regs. We will maintain thirty thousand feet until we turn west toward the Caribbean, and then we will climb higher. Is that clear?"

"Yes, sir, Master Scion,"442 answered meekly. "But how will we know when to turn west?"

“Well, if you must know—British nautical lore says that you head south along the coast of Africa toward the Canary Islands until the butter melts, and then turn west for the Caribbean* That’s where the northeasterly winds and ocean currents converge to give ships the biggest boost west. We don't have butter, but I have the turn-point programmed into my Angel Positioning System in my belt buckle. It's an older version of what you Betas have embedded in your arm, but it still works well enough. Thank God for it. Without it, many of my Alpha student angels would have gotten lost in space long ago."

"Ready when you are, Master Scion," the tiny angel shot back with a wry smile as the two of them banked their wings left and climbed south in the cool, pale pre-dawn sky toward the Canary Islands—and an adventure beyond anything either angel expected.

CHAPTER 11

After a few minutes of flight, Scion looked back at the tiny scout near his left wingtip. "To be honest, Angel 442, I am still getting used to how small you are."

"Well, on Earth, they say good things come in small packages, right?" Angie replied with a coy smile. "God made me small. I like it. I hope you are not disappointed. We Betas are definitely not like the big Alphas you must have worked with in heaven."

Clearing his throat, Scion said, "Actually, I have only taught angel trainees my entire life." Angel 442's eyes widened.

Seeing her shocked look, Scion went on, "It's true. I have served in Angel Academy ever since the Great Rebellion. It's been my life's work."

"Wow, I had no idea! But didn't you ever want to try something else . . . something more *exciting*? I mean, you are so gifted, so strong . . . so *big*! Didn't God offer you any other assignments in the last ten thousand years?"

"Not really," Scion admitted. "Let's just say that the academy best suited my needs."

"Your needs? Just what are your needs, Master Scion? If we are going to work closely together, I'd like to know so I can help meet them," 442 cheerily announced.

Scion sighed. He looked at her again. His face flushed with emotion as he recalled how she had wept for him just twelve days ago. Impulsively—and uncharacteristically—Scion decided to tell her.

"Angel 442, can you keep a secret?"

Almost bursting with curiosity, 442 fairly shouted, "*Yes*, of course! I am a recon specialist. I deal in secrets *all* the time."

Scion was biting his lip to fight his fears. After taking a deep breath, he said, "The primary reason I have only worked at the academy all my life is that I need to protect my identity. Only Mola, Michael, and Gabriel know who I really am. If other angels knew. . . well, my life would be a lot more . . . *complicated*."

Angie resisted the urge to prod, but she desperately wanted to know more. She could not take her eyes off of him.

Suddenly, Scion looked directly at her inquisitive stare. He opened his mouth—but no words came out. His entire face was twisted and wrinkled, as if he were in great pain. Then, like a dam bursting, he shouted, "Angel 442—*I am Angel 24*."

For an instant, time seemed to stand still— *both* angels were in shock. Then, 442 shot into the air above Scion, spinning like a top and shouting, "*Holy Cherubmatzi*! I can't believe it. I can't believe I'm talking to the twenty-fourth angel! Holy Hannah, I am so glad I came on this trip!"

Diving again right in front of Scion's face, 442 sputtered, "You are the *legend* I've heard about for the last one hundred years, Master Scion! I can hardly believe it. What an honor to meet you. What an honor to fly with you."

Then, looking more somber, she looked at him closely. "But wait. I can understand why archangels like Michael and Gabriel would know your secret, but why is Mola the only other angel who knows who you are?"

"Well, Mola is my best friend. He's the only other angel I fully trust. He may be the only angel who fully *trusts me*. It makes sense, I guess. The angels who survived the Rebellion became hypersensitive to any hint of deception by another angel. When they realized that I was the *only one* of Lucifer's students who did not leave with him, they wondered why.

"I've heard the rumors. Some even say I was left behind as a *spy*. Anyhow, most angels doubt that I can be fully trusted. So, now that you know who I am, *please* keep it a secret!"

"Master Scion, that will be my sacred honor," 442 eagerly responded. Just as she said that, an idea popped into her head that made her smile. "Master Scion, as your new confidante, I have just one request."

"Sure, what is that, Angel 442?"

"Well, since I am committed to conceal your real identity and just call you by your assumed persona, I wonder if you could call me by my assumed name also?

"What in heaven are you talking about, 442?"

"You know—*Angie*—the name I prefer. We could use it only where no one else can hear us. Back in heaven, I will be 442 again. How about it? *Fair trade?*" She quipped with with a cheesy grin."

Scion huffed under his breath. Feelings of betrayal began to rise in his heart as his mind raced. *I can't believe it! That little Beta is trying to leverage her secret knowledge of me to get a favor.* Part of him wanted to tell her off. But then, he looked again at that gentle face with the dancing lavender eyes staring at him. Again, he felt the rigid walls around his heart softening in a way he had not felt in ages.

Another big sigh—but this time it was followed by a smile. "Okay, *you win*. While we are on this trip, you can be Angie. But as soon as we return to base, it is *Angel 442*. It's our little secret. Got it?"

"Got it, boss," Angie yelped as she spun around his head in a blur of rainbow-colored hair and blinking wing lights, shouting "Hallelujah" over and over.

"O, one more thing, Master Scion—did you notice that we have something else in common besides secret names?"

"What's that?" Scion asked.

"Neither of us wears shoes. Of course, I don't because it makes me feel —well, you know—*free* to be *me*!" she laughed. "But I thought all male angels wore shoes."

Scion pursed his lips tightly and then spoke without looking at his petite sidekick, "Right. Male angels do wear shoes. I don't. Please don't ask again. One secret is all you get today.

"Activate your recording sensors now. We have work to do," Scion barked as he cleared his throat. "The Canary Islands are just ahead. Stay close and keep your eyes open for anything unusual. Let's do this *by the book*, understood?"

Noticing that they were passing Morocco on their left side, Scion called out to Angie, "Check out that coastline before we head west out to sea. There are Muslim pirates in Morocco that often prey on European ships."

"On it! It's only sixty-two miles away, so my sensors can still pick up voices and body-heat signatures," Angie called out in a professional tone. "I have a one-hundred-mile range for audio, visual, and heat data."

Scion heard the pride in her voice. They both knew that only Betas could do that.

"*Impressive*! Alphas only have a one-hundred-*foot* radius for scans like that."

"Sir, I am just bursting with joy to be on this journey with you—one of the 24! I am so honored and thrilled and excited and—"

"That's enough!" Scion smiled more warmly now. "I'm glad you are here— but let's keep focused on the task at hand so we don't drop the ball. Heaven is watching, and the birth of a new Christian settlement in the northern New World may depend on how well we do our job today. Besides all that, I *cannot* afford to fail. Please remember that, too" he added.

Angie furrowed her brow. "Of course, Master Scion. I will do my utmost for his glory—and for you. Together, we can do a good job, I am sure."

"I believe you. Something about you gives me more confidence than I should have. And this mission means more to me than you realize. Thank you, 442 . . . uh . . . I mean *Angie*," Scion warmly concluded.

Angie felt like she could hardly contain the bubbling giddiness inside her. She turned her head left— supposedly to scan the steamy African shoreline— and her face exploded with pure joy! "Holy hallelujah," she whispered wildly. "I get to help the legendary Angel 24 change the course of history for an entire continent. And I thought *heaven* was heavenly!"

CHAPTER 12

10,000 BC

Deep in a frigid cave on Ganymede—one of Jupiter's moons—Scion and Kai finally located him. Lucifer, the former Headmaster of Archangel Academy, had done something terrible on Earth. Eden had been violated and corrupted by a sin Lucifer had instigated. All humanity was about to live under the curse of that sin. The Lord quickly reprimanded him and relieved him of command at the academy and over the choir of heaven. In a rage, Lucifer fled from heaven, spewing curses at General Michael, who had brought him before God for discipline.

When Lucifer did not return to heaven that day, no order was given to search for him. Michael said that the Lord would wait for Lucifer to come back when he was ready to repent. But Scion and Kai decided they had to find their beloved friend and mentor, even though this would be an unauthorized mission. If General Michael knew about this, they could face stiff discipline themselves. But they were determined to find their beloved Headmaster—and, to their great relief, they *found* him!

As the two approached the murky rear of the cave, Lucifer stood and faced them. Like all of the 24, the three of them usually looked just like brothers. They all stood twelve feet tall, with huge shoulders draped by platinum-blond hair and massive arms bulging out of their white robes. But today, Lucifer did not have a white robe. He wore a one-piece, full-length leather suit. The color was dark—like his *eyes*. As his two visitors saw him more clearly, they shuddered. Their former headmaster just stood there like a cold statue with fists clenched at his sides. "What do you two want?" he growled.

"Brother Lucifer, please come back. Kai and I came here to tell you that the Lord is willing to forgive you. He knows we all make mistakes. All he wants is some real repentance from you," Scion pleaded.

"So, the dirt-man and his woman sinned. *So what?* It was only a *little* sin," Lucifer shot back.

Scion stepped forward and looked Lucifer right in the eye. "With all due respect, Sir, deceiving Eve was *very* wrong, and you know it. You tricked them into rebelling against God. How *could* you? The Lord was enjoying them so much in the garden. You hurt him! Surely you believe that he doesn't deserve that after all he has done for heaven . . . and *for you*."

Lucifer's deep, raspy laugh echoed in the cave. "*Ha!* He'll get over it. He always does."

Kai moved closer, too. "How did you do it, Master Lucifer? How did you become an earth creature that talks like a human?"

"I like to experiment," Lucifer said with a sly smile. "Wasn't hard. I just entered the snake's body and took control."

"*Wow,*" Kai whispered in amazement.

Scion took a step forward, trying to show that he wasn't intimidated —even though he was. He'd never imagined that any angel would talk like that—especially an archangel. "Master, *please* repent and come back to finish our training. We assured the other twenty-two that you would return with us."

Kai inched closer and whispered, "But what did that *feel* like, Master Lucifer . . . you know, being in there and taking control? I'd like to know more about that."

Scion's eyes grew wide. *What is happening to Kai,* he thought. Lucifer has just caused irreversible damage to the Lord's earth children, and Kai just seems interested in *how* he did it!

"It was *fantastic,* Kai. I enjoyed it immensely," Lucifer replied with a hideous laugh. "I wasn't sure it would work, but it did. You should have seen the look on Eve's face when I spoke to her through the serpent! *She loved it*. I could *feel* her pleasure. It was like nothing I have ever experienced in heaven. I felt like she was *worshipping* me."

Scion grabbed Kai by the arm and pulled him back. In a stern voice, Scion said, "Please, Master Lucifer, you have broken heaven's laws. Now, please don't break our hearts. We all love you so much. The class wants you back. Many other angels do too."

Lucifer laughed scornfully and then snarled, "*Really*? The class wants me back—even after this? I would think that everyone hates me now."

"It's true; most of the angels are very upset with you," Scion admitted. "All of heaven is in turmoil over this. But the 24 wants you back! We know God had to discipline you, but the class still wants you back. We are like a family, and you are the father. Please, don't leave us. Come home to heaven with us. Please, just repent to God and come home with us!"

"*Repent?*" Lucifer snapped, his voice echoing in the cave. "For what? Those pitiful creatures would have eaten the fruit someday anyhow. I just made it happen sooner. We all know what happens when creatures have free will. Just look at *me,* you fools!"

"But you heard the curses God put on the man and woman. They and their descendants will be paying a steep price for thousands of years, all because you incited them to rebel. You have been a good and wise angel for eons, Master Lucifer. Surely what you have done now is not who you really are. Surely, you see your mistake now," Kai retorted.

"Cursed for thousands of years? *Huh*! Serves them right! The lazy, good-for-nothings everything handed to them. We do all the work in heaven, and those two got to walk and talk with the Lord in the cool of the day, just like old friends. I've served him for millions of Earth years, but God has never *once* walked with me just to talk about my life and my work. How dare God treat humans better than angels! It's *not fair*!"

The giant angel paced back and forth. His neck muscles swelled and his mood grew more menacing with each step. "And he is going to bring those human vermin to heaven to judge angels! I'll be *damned* before I let that happen to me! Humans overseeing angels! What a cosmic joke! What ingratitude! Here I am, the most powerful angel in heaven. I have served him for untold millennia. I have led worship around his throne millions of times. I was the Headmaster of Archangel Academy. But now he wants *me* to one day submit to smelly water-bag creatures like Adam and Eve?"

Scion interjected, "But God really loves you, Brother Lucifer. He has honored you above almost every angel in heaven. You know that. He loves you deeply like a son."

"Well, if he loves me so much, why does he plan to make those hairless bipeds rule over me one day? That *is* the plan! You know it, don't you, Scion? You told me yourself, didn't you? And you were not supposed to, *were you*? No rebellion in you, huh? Does Gabriel know you broke your promise to not to tell anyone about God's creation plans?"

Scion's cheeks burned hot. He had shared that secret. What if Lucifer were to tell Gabriel about this? A nauseating wave of fear began to rise inside Scion.

"I thought that since you were the head of the Academy and the main worship leader of heaven, those plans would stay secret with you. I . . .

I am *so sorry*. It was a terrible mistake. I didn't know it would make you so angry. It's my fault. All *this* is *my* fault . . . I feel so ashamed . . ." Scion's voice broke as he tried to hold back tears.

Lucifer suddenly turned away from them with a disgusted look on his face. "Look, friends, you are wasting your time here. I am *not* going to repent no matter what you say. I have made my choice . . . *forever,*" Lucifer shouted fiercely.

Like a powerful black panther, Lucifer leapt upon a large volcanic rock in the cave. Scion and Kai stumbled backward as Lucifer unfurled his twenty-four-foot wings to full extension and yanked his eight-foot sword out of the scabbard with a loud clang. He stood there, sword high above his head, and shouted with fury in his voice.

"I, Lucifer, the Bright and Glorious One, shall stop God's plans for humans. One day, all the angels of heaven will thank me for keeping those foul, malformed creatures out of heaven! They will *not* rule in heaven. *I* will rule over them in *my* way, in *my* kingdom!"

Hot tears gushed from the corners of Scion's eyes. He was in total shock. Kai was aghast and trembling with fear.

"I will *never* repent! Do you hear me?" Lucifer shouted until his neck veins bulged with rage. "I will never submit to them—or him—again! I'll be *damned* before I do!"

"Lucifer, don't say that! You are scaring us," Scion cried out.

"Master, who will lead us? Who will train us? Who can we look to if you are not with us?" Kai pleaded.

Lucifer jumped down, sword held high, to within three feet of his visitors. Scion and Kai instinctively backed up and drew their swords.

"I could kill you both," he growled like a crouching lion. *Go away!* All this talk of repentance and how good God is—it just fuels my hatred. This is not yours to fix. This is between him and me."

Shocked senseless, the two angels could neither speak nor move. Lucifer eyed them like a hungry beast.

"Remember, I can *kill* you. Only Michael and one of us can kill one of the 24. What have I got to lose by killing you? Now get out of here before I do something I might regret," Lucifer viciously shouted.

"You wouldn't! You love us, as we love you!" Scion shouted as he backed up farther, choking on his words with tears rolling down his cheeks.

Lucifer stiffened. The loyalty and determination of Scion and Kai to win him back was a powerful force against his rage. For a moment, he was perplexed. He knew others from the class would eventually come and make similar appeals.

Finally, a cruel smile crossed his thin lips. He felt like a shark when it detects blood in the water. He gently put his sword back in the scabbard as he laughed lightheartedly and shook his head as if he suddenly realized he had been mistaken about something.

"Well, gentlemen, I guess you *are* right. There *is* a deep bond between us. Why don't you join me? Stay here with me. We will build a new life together in the cosmos. Then we would *always* be together."

Scion was still in shock but but he was able to respond, "I could never do that, Master. I would *die* for you if I could help you, but I cannot forsake my Lord."

"What about *you,* Kai? You were number one in my class. I could use an angel like you. You and I could rule galaxies. We could be our own gods and enjoy more than we ever could in heaven."

Lucifer slowly sauntered over to Kai until his face almost touched his student's trembling face. "Kai, my friend, I have *felt* what God gave humans—flesh and skin to cover their spirits. Besides being in that snake body, my spirit entered those two humans while they were mating one night. Let me tell you, they have *pleasures* we've never known—incredible pleasures God has never offered to us. We just have to get inside of their bodies *through their sins.* Then, we can have the mind-numbing feelings they have. What do you say to *that,* my brother?"

Kai crumbled to his knees in tears. His heart was in a great conflict. With the cunning of a deadly predator, Lucifer moved in for the kill. He knelt over Kai and gently placed a hand on his heaving shoulder. As he did, a medallion on a gold chain fell out from behind Kai's collar. Lucifer reached out to hold it.

"Oh, what's *this*? An angel wing medallion. How special. But it's only *one* wing. I wonder where the other wing is," Lucifer's asked as he slyly looked over at Scion. He knew of their deep relationship. Everyone in the Academy did.

Lucifer gently pulled Kai's face up and looked him straight in the eye. With a deep, guttural, hypnotizing voice, the rebel angel bent down and whispered, "Kai, *come* with me. *We* can have it all. You can rule with me. Come now, or come later. I'll wait for you."

Kai tried to speak. "I d-d-don't . . . th-th-think . . ." His eyes were wild and wide—like an animal suddenly caught in a trap. Lucifer's mesmerizing stare held him motionless like a live moth suddenly wrapped up in a spider's strong web. But Lucifer saw Kai's hesitation.

"Okay, okay, you win, Kai. I think I spoke too quickly—and too harshly. Perhaps you are right. Perhaps I should go back to heaven for the sake of the class. After all, we have a special bond together, don't we? So, just do this one thing for me," Lucifer pleaded.

"Yes, anything you say," Kai responded weakly."

"Please ask the rest of our class to come and meet me here. I have something important to ask them. If I were to come back to heaven, I would need their help."

Scion and Kai looked at each other with amazement. "Yes, of course, Master. We will arrange the meeting. This is wonderful news," blurted out Scion.

"We will tell the rest of the class as soon as we get back. I am sure they will be more than willing to help bring you back to heaven and to the academy. Until then, may the Lord be merciful to you in every way, Master Lucifer," Scion yelled out joyfully as he and Kai shot into the endless light-years of darkness toward heaven with hearts aflame with hope.

BUT THE FIRE OF THAT HOPE DID NOT BURN FOR LONG. JUST ONE thousand Earth years later, heaven exploded as Lucifer and Kai led the remaining 22 in the Great Rebellion.

As the fighting began, General Michael intercepted Lucifer and his forces in the third heaven. He offered each angel the Lord's forgiveness if they would repent and lay down their swords. But Lucifer roared, "Better to reign on earth than serve in heaven!"

Lucifer lost that war in heaven but now his war on the saints of Earth had begun.

CHAPTER 13

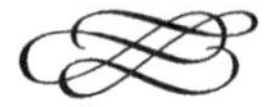

December 18, 1606

The dragon-like spirit floated slow and low over the hazy-blue spine of mountains bristling with spiky spruce forests until its massive wings banked east toward the glistening sea.

Visible only as an eerie, transparent shimmer in the Indian summer air, this ancient spirit descended toward the wiggling ribbons of river just west of the ocean. His large yellow eyes never tired of gulping in the grandeur of his realm. This was the land of Okeus, Principality of the Great Bay, the god of the Powhatan Empire.* For two millennia he has ruled this vast primeval wilderness—a land awarded him for exceptional service in the Middle East long ago as a Dark Angel. Masquerading now as a demon, Okeus has cleverly enslaved the native Algonquins to do his bidding for the Prince of Darkness.

The land of Okeus is magnificent. The forests are rent with rivers, deep and long, pouring into the Great Bay.* Between the rivers, sassafras and pine forests delicately scent the air with their earthy fragrance. The virgin woods teem with deer, black bears, wolves, foxes, raccoons, rabbits, and other creatures. Above the tall trees and sandy beaches, the skies dance with every imaginable kind of bird: robins, crows, hawks, majestic eagles, herons, seagulls, and flocks of pelicans silently skimming the waves in perfect formation, wingtip to wingtip. The waters of the rivers and bay teem with life. Fish, oysters, crabs, and clams are everywhere.* The natives even brag that they can walk across the rivers on the thick oyster beds.

"Beautiful, isn't it, Snookus?" Okeus grunted with a thick-lipped reptilian smile. "My Chesapeake, my Shellfish Bay."*

A floppy creature clinging to the reptile's neck with long, thin arms enthusiastically responded, "Truly befitting a great demon such as you, Lord Okeus. And don't forget your two portals, O Great One! Not only has Lord Lucifer honored you with one of his seven War Portals to the Abyss, but he has also given you that mighty divination portal near the sea. When your shamans worship you on that beach, that portal gives them more wisdom than any native priest has for a thousand miles."

Okeus nodded with pursed lips. *That's why I keep you around, you ugly slimeball. You flatter well—and I love it.* Then, pointing toward the War Portal with a regal flourish of his stumpy front claw, Okeus burped and commented, "Yes, but I love that one the most. It's a direct connection to the Abyss. The aromas of hot, burning flesh coming up from there are simply luscious. I *live* for that. Sometimes, I can almost hear the screams of the damned," Okeus snorted jovially. "Today, before we left camp, I detected a hint of Middle Eastern flesh coming from the portal, but mostly just Asians and Powhatans sizzling together. It makes me think I am home below with the Master—instead of being stuck in this boring hole full of putrid, gullible natives."

Looking over his shoulder to the west, Okeus gazed lovingly at his War Portal. It was his secret weapon deep beneath the yellow waters of the Great Swamp: a massive thirty-five-hundred-mile spiritual shaft that ended near Earth's molten center in a vast network of fiery caverns crammed with millions of demons and billions of the damned. The primary purpose of all war portals was to allow the armies of hell to move quickly to the Earth's surface to fight any major attack by the angelic Host of heaven.

Clinging to his master's scaly, green neck with all five tentacles, Snookus whispered in a fawning voice. "Yes, Lord Okeus. Your realm is beyond compare. You are truly magnificent—one of Lucifer's favorites, to be sure. And to think that you are only a demon—like all of us— and not one of those cruel Dark Angels who usually get the choice assignments like this one. Great Okeus, you cannot imagine how many demons in other places are jealous that we have a demon master and not a hated Dark Angel over us. You make us proud, Master Okeus! *Very* proud. We serve you willingly because you are one of us."

The obese monster belched again and looked back at his ingratiating assistant with feigned irritation. "*Harrumph*! Your flowery praise makes me suspect you want something. And perhaps you *can* get it someday—that is, if I don't have to chop off any more of your arms. You *do* have talent. I have told Lucifer about you."

"Ah, yes, Master—from your lips to Lord Lucifer's ears. May it be so one day. And, if I may say so, the name the natives gave your realm —*Great Shellfish Bay*—really suits you. I must say that you do have a hellishly good smell about you today. Been harvesting in the oyster beds recently?"

"No, actually, I was on a short cruise inside a passing whale last night. I'm not fond of plankton, but it goes down easily."

Then, as Okeus arrived at the sea, he wheeled around and hovered as he held out both of his short, dinosaur arms.

"Snookus, look at this land. I shall make my legacy here. Here is where I will prove that I am worthy of my Master's eternal affection." Then he coughed in a mocking, guttural laugh. "Or is it eternal *affliction*? No difference!"

"Yes, Master. His affection *is* cruel—not like yours," Snookus groveled with a forced smile.

"The natural is often a shadow to the spiritual, Snookus. My Great Bay is a womb for millions of water creatures. One day, the land around this bay will be a womb for a new nation. As you know, Lucifer told me that the Councils of Heaven had chosen my land to birth a new weapon against us—a nation that closely follows the hideous Lamb. But they must not succeed! We will stop them!" Okeus was so excited that he choked a little and held his throat for a moment. "In fact, we must stop them, or we are in great danger. You remember, don't you? You were there."

"Yes, I do remember. I was afraid for you, my Great Leader."

Okeus winced in pain as he remembered that visit to Lucifer's throne room fifty years ago. It was a moment he would never forget.

EVERY DARK ANGEL FEARED LUCIFER GREATLY. HE WAS LIKE NO OTHER Dark Angel. Lucifer had transformed himself right after the Great Rebellion. Using incredible evil powers no other angel possessed, Lucifer now stood twenty-seven-feet-tall, with enormously powerful hands and arms. Twelve-inch razor-sharp spikes were embedded on the leading and trailing edges of his sixty-foot, dark-red wings.

His face was fearsome.The once-handsome hero of heaven had changed his glowing golden skin into thick, dark-green hide. Slimy gray, tangled hair framed an angry face with a sharp, pointy nose just below dark, malevolent eyes which constantly flitted to and fro. No Dark Angel or demon ever dared look him in the eyes.

"You must crush them!" Satan had screamed at Okeus from his throne of human bones and skulls. "The Enemy's forces have invaded our New World in the south. Fortunately, they sin well, so they are not much of a threat to us so far. But soon, the Enemy will try to establish a new and deadly foothold in your land. He plans to attack us all over the world from that place. You must deeply corrupt the colony by sin. Plant every possible sin in them—pride, selfish ambition, jealousy, lust, deceit, divination, hatred, violence, murder, division and strife!"

Grabbing a handful of tarnished gold coins at his feet, Lucifer flung them at the gaggle of Dark Angels cowering around his throne as he bellowed, "Above all, we must addict them to the *love of money*. But be subtle. We must allow them to think they are doing what is right in seeking riches at all costs. If you do this *well,* we will not have to destroy them. The Enemy himself will destroy them—as he did to his infamous chosen people long ago because of their sins! *Sin* is the key! It always is. It worked in the Garden. It worked in Israel—and it will work in the New World. The old fool will never get what he wants as long as humans sin." Then Lucifer cackled loudly, got up, and moved toward Okeus. A shiver went up Okeus's spine. Snookus quickly slid away from his master into a corner, hoping no one would see him.

"Thank that old fool in heaven for sin, Okeus! Without it, we would be powerless. With it, all things are possible. Nothing and no one—not even the almighty—can stand before sin. Sin must be punished. His own laws demand it." Satan laughed hideously. "Sin will be your greatest weapon against his plans to settle in your land."

Okeus cowered in fear. "Great Lord Lucifer, Master of the Abyss, how much time would you give me to do this? You gave me eight hundred years to corrupt the Jews. Can I have at least six hundred years to ruin this new colony?"

Satan grabbed Okeus's thickly scaled throat with a hand that was several times larger than Okeus's own. With a rage every Dark Angel feared, Lucifer flung Okeus to the cave floor, cracking his ribs and fangs as Okeus slammed against the far wall in a heap. Every power, principality, and authority in the room cringed in fear. They had never seen Lucifer abuse a Dark Angel like that, especially one who had been his favorite for so long in heaven and on Earth.

Then Lucifer bellowed, "Listen to me, Okeus. Either you corrupt them within four hundred years of their arrival, or I will personally rip your eyes out and escort you to the Abyss for the amusement of Abaddon and his demons! That future colony is the Enemy's Trojan Horse in our plans for this miserable planet. Either you succeed or you will wish the Enemy had never made you."

OKEUS SHUDDERED AS HE SNAPPED OUT OF THAT FRIGHTFUL MEMORY. "Snookus, has Morph checked in with you today? I sent him to Voudoc to make sure we are alerted any to enemy activity down there. I have heard rumors that the Host of Heaven is preparing the path for the invasion."

"No, sir, no word from Morph today. All seems fine across the eastern Atlantic right now."

"All except Morph," Okeus joked.

"Yes, Master. He gets beat up by Voudoc's sentries every time he meets them," Snookus laughed.

| Morph

"Serves him right. He's such a pathetic clown, always screwing things up. He is the worst demon I've ever met. He never does what he is ordered. Remember when I sent him to drown that warrior who refused to worship me? That little rebel is still alive. Morph said he tried to drown him, but the warrior was too good a swimmer. *Bat crap.* Morph is just a loser when it comes to real demon work. If it wasn't for his uncanny ability to sense the presence of angels at great distances, I would personally tear him limb from limb. Every master he has served has wanted to annihilate him. It's a wonder he is still alive."

"Maybe he has nine lives," Snookus joked obligingly. "He looks and smells like a mangy, alley cat nobody wanted—matted green fur, busted hairy wing, and deep blue eyes! No demon should have eyes like that. He's a freaking *freak,* if I ever saw one."

Okeus actually smiled at that quip—to the relief of Snookus. "Yes, Morph is a freakish fool. But every prince needs a whipping boy, right?"

"Right, Master," and then he thought with a sly grin, *Someday maybe Morph can be my whipping boy when I have my own realm. Maybe one day this realm can be mine.*

CHAPTER 14

December 19, 1606

As silent, dark waves lapped the western coastline of the Canary Islands, Scion started his climb to a cruise altitude of seventy-five thousand feet. "Catch up, Angie!" he shouted. "Land under my left wing and hang on. I am about to fly faster than Betas can fly."

Angie quickly tucked herself under his left wing in a pocket of soft, golden feathers. With a snap of his massive wings, Scion rocketed to the stratosphere fifteen icy miles above twenty-six degrees latitude, streaking southwest, fleeing the rosy-fingered grasp of the African dawn.

As Scion leaned forward into his climb, he breathed in the cool air whooshing by and felt the effortless power of his mighty wings. *Ahh, this feels so good. It's been so long since I could fly like this.* Without even thinking about it, Scion felt his body and mind shift into the angel he was created to be: a formidable warrior, able to out-fly and out-fight almost any opponent in the cosmos.

For a moment, all his fears vanished. His eyes were wide, gleaming with joy.

"Angie, this is a special moment for me. I haven't done this for two thousand years."

Angie smiled sweetly. Then she took a long look at the vast, empty Atlantic Ocean ahead of them. "Um, Master Scion, speaking of special moments . . . *I* have a *special* request."

"What is it, Angie?"

"I need a favor. I want to uncloak when we get midway across. I've always wanted to see my contrails. *Please,* just this once. No one will see me way out here."

"Permission denied. You know the rules. Exposing your shape in a physical form is not allowed without specific clearance from Angel Command. I doubt if General Michael would approve that on a sensitive mission like this."

"But no one will see me except the dolphins. I promise to cloak myself again well before we get to land. *Please?* Just this *once*. I may never get this chance again. My contrail would be very, very small."

"Sorry, no can do. Our sentinels will see you. I can't let you break the rules. They might report us. I know every angel wants to try uncloaking, but rules are rules, and I don't want to be blamed for breaking them. I've worked hard all my life to avoid blame, and I can't afford any now on my first Earth assignment. Understood?"

Hearing the fierce intensity of his denial, all she could say was, "*Rat poop*!"

"What did you say?"

"Uh . . . um, well . . . actually, I was thinking—"

"Spit it out, Angie. Don't play games with me. I demand honesty. What is it?"

Then it hit her! A silly grin crept across her scrunched-up face.

"But, Master Scion, aren't you and the other archangels going to do a Seraphim Starburst after we arrive at destination today . . . *uncloaked*? Thousands of natives and demons will see that. What harm can a little uncloaking by me do so far from land? Life in heaven has been so stressful the last few centuries with all the brutal New World conquests by the saints. I need a little fun."

"How did you know about that starburst?" Scion shot back angrily.

"It was in the orders, remember? The orders from the War Room said that the Seraphim Starburst is a flight maneuver specifically designed to mark new land for the Lord. I've only seen it done once when Christopher Columbus landed on that New World island. It also opens a portal to heaven so the saints can access more angelic support, as I recall. And—angels must *uncloak* to do the maneuver, the orders say."

Wow—she's good. "Sorry, Angie—I guess I got a little carried away. Yes, you are right; it was in the orders. I assumed you hadn't read them. So, okay, you can uncloak. We will call it an uncloaking practice drill in our logbook for today. But just for ten seconds. You can do it on my mark after we reach mid-ocean."

"Praise the Lord! Praise him in his highest heavens, for he is good!" the little angel sang so loudly that Scion had to lower his left wing over her slightly to muffle the sound. "O Master Scion, thank you so much for taking this small risk for me. You are the best! I'll never forget this!"

"And neither will Michael if he finds out," Scion grimaced as he rocketed up through sixty-five thousand feet in the icy stratosphere. "On my mark: three, two, one, go!"

With that, Angie shot out from under his arm. Instantly, she materialized into the fiery spear-point of a mile-long crimson contrail piercing the minus fifty-degree Fahrenheit air with a sonic boom that trailed behind her in the robin's-egg blue sky.

"Wahoo! Look at that contrail, Scion! If only my friends at the Academy could see me now. I can hardly believe it is true. It makes me want to worship!" And so she did—with great gusto. "Praise God! Praise the Lord! Praise him, all you heavenly hosts! He is the King of Kings and Lord of Glory," she belted out with all her heart.

Once again, Scion felt a stirring inside—but he repressed it. He was nervous about that contrail.

"*Time's up.* Re-cloak and rejoin me now. We are approaching the southern islands off the coast of the New World North."

"Amen, Master Scion. Coming back your way." She quickly flew back to Scion and took her place in his left wingpit. "Wow, that was beyond awesome! Thank's again, Master Scion!"

"I can see the islands on the horizon now—maybe 300 miles away. Let's head for Saint Martin. The three ships will probably stop there for fresh water and supplies. Our intelligence reports indicate that there is a clever Dark Angel ruling in that area named Voudoc who might oppose our ships. Thank God he is apparently not an angel I knew in heaven."

"Not to worry, Master. I will record everything I see and hear."

"OK. Just remember to stay on task. And *no* singing, is that clear?"

"Very clear, sir!"

As he began a sweeping, twenty-five-degree starboard turn over the blue-green Caribbean, Scion suddenly felt sad. *Voudoc is down there because of me.* Angie's keen eyes saw his mood shift and prayed. *Holy Spirit, please heal your son wounded heart.*

But other eyes were also locked onto the gleaming warrior. Their thoughts toward him were anything but kind.

Bam!

Pain seared through Scion's right wing. He had been shot with a demon dart, but from where? Demons were not supposed to attack an angel without just cause. Angie felt the jolt when Scion's wing was hit but did not realize what it was at first. Then she saw the orange and blue head-feathers of a Caribbean bird sticking out of a small dart stuck under his wing. Darts were the preferred demon weapon in the Caribbean. Although these missiles were just eighteen inches long, their heavy, six-inch barbed tip ripped deeply into angel bodies when pulled out. When thrown by a skilled demon in high-speed flight, the darts can hit a target two miles away.

"Why did they attack us, Master?"

“Not sure. Hang on, Angie. We are going to find out who does not like us being here." He pulled into a tight dive, squeezing Angie tighter under his wing as he picked up speed. "Don't worry. It's probably just a bored sentry demon. Demons aren't happy unless they are hurting someone."

He twisted his head around to scan some islands huddled together in a thick, gray haze directly beneath them. Then he *heard* them—deep, guttural, wild sounds. Demon voices were moving faster and faster toward him, screaming and howling in a language he had never heard.

Oh, no! We've stirred up a demon nest. Must be hundreds of them. They probably saw Angie uncloaked and thought we were challenging them to fight. Good Lord! How stupid can I be? I should never have let her uncloak.

He glanced at Angie with fire in his eyes and yelled, "I should have followed protocol! Now we're going to pay for it. How will I explain this to Michael? They've probably been watching us for miles after they saw that silly contrail of yours!"

Scion knew the demons could not kill him or Angie with their hand-thrown darts or swords—only an angel can kill another angel. But they could wound him or Angie so severely that he would have to abort their mission, losing valuable time to prepare for the voyage of the three ships. But how was he going to engage several hundred vicious demons at once? Angel Academy had not prepared him for anything like this.

FAR BELOW, IN THE THICK JUNGLE CANOPY OF A LARGE ISLAND, THE Holy Spirit awakened two older native women who were sleeping late that morning.

They both felt a strong urge to pray. Years before, a Spanish friar named Carlos had washed ashore after a shipwreck in a storm and had been saved by these two women. They found him unconscious on the beach. When the priest told them that the God of all creation is a loving Father who sent his Son to die for their sins and bring them to heaven, they quickly gave their hearts to Jesus. The joyful friar named his first disciples Maria and Juanita. They became fervent intercessors. God often spoke to them as they prayed. That morning, in two different huts, they heard just one phrase in their minds: *Scion needs help. Pray for him!* Without understanding who Scion was, the women immediately set out for the large coconut tree on the nearby hill where they usually met for prayer each morning.

"Juanita, my sister, you heard it too—about Scion?" "Is that why you are here?" Maria asked.

"Yes," Juanita replied. "The voice of the Lord is telling us to pray for some person named *Scion*. I have no idea who he is."

"Me neither, but let's obey the Lord," Maria said with joy. "Padre Carlos told us that God might do this someday when someone is in trouble. I am so excited to see what the Lord does with our prayers. Let's kneel and pray right now. I feel like something bad is about to happen at this very moment."

The Holy Spirit smiled as he covered the two daughters of God with his warm presence and led them in prayer for the invisible battle five miles directly above them.

CHAPTER 15

As Scion dove below thirty-thousand feet, a hail of demonic darts shot past him as he twirled and twisted to evade his attackers. His heart raced with fear. He knew there was no angelic help anywhere nearby.

"Jesus, help me!" Then he pulled out his massive, eight-foot sword for the first time in battle. He hated swords. Swords had killed thousands of former friends. For a moment, he wondered, *Can I kill them? Can I mow them down like my friends were slaughtered?*

Just then, a dart narrowly missed Angie, who was hiding in the shelter of his wing. Scion looked at her fearful face and then glanced at the approaching cloud of murderous spirits.

"Hold on tight, Angie. We are going to make them regret this attack!"

Angie gripped his feathers tightly and kept praying.

"Ready?" Scion shouted as he raised his eight-foot sword above his head.

"Jesus, Jesus, Jesus, *help us!*" Angie screamed as she closed her eyes and felt her body begin to shake uncontrollably.

But Scion never heard her screams. With courage he did not know he possessed, the twelve-foot angel snap-rolled onto his back, flapped his wings once and then retracted the twenty-four-foot wings into a hawk-like stoop, instantly accelerating to Mach 2. With his sword in front of him, the golden angel plunged toward the first wave of red-eyed spirits. "Jesus, we come in your Name. Let your glory come *now*!" he shouted at the top of his voice.

Scion had almost closed the gap between him and the screaming demons. He was now close enough to see their bared orange fangs with yellowish clouds of breath chugging out of their lizard-like mouths. These were large war demons, about six to eight feet in height. Each looked like a hideous horned reptile with blazing yellow pupils set in deep red eyeballs. Their black, scaly hide glistened with a dark ooze that flew off in globs in the high-speed climb. Big, bony claws, like sharp meat hooks, were fully extended as they threw dart after dart at him.

Seconds before the island demons engulfed Scion, something happened. The most beautiful worship Scion had ever heard was suddenly coming from Scion's left wingpit. It made the hair on the nape of his neck stand up—even in a *power-dive*. Without thinking, Scion began to sing with Angie. Then his body began to pulse brighter and brighter—faster and faster. The hot surge of God's presence swept over him. He knew what that meant. He threw his head back, closed his eyes, and worshipped the Lord with the total abandonment. It was coming. Nothing would stop it now.

It was almost imperceptible, like the inhalation of breath a lion takes before roaring. For a nanosecond, the mouths of the demons twitched as they all sensed something bad was about to happen to them.

And then *it did.*

A three-second burst of white-hot light blasted from Scion's body totally washed out the morning light above the sleepy islands in a blaze of heavenly glory. Watcher Angels all along the Eastern

Seaboard broke into spontaneous applause as they soaked in the afterglow of the anointed light.

"Scion must be close!" they all laughed with knowing glances at one another.

Maria and Juanita felt a surge of joy and looked skyward just in time to shield their eyes from the intense whiteout. Shudders ran through the caverns of hell as three hundred moaning demons tumbled from the sky, blinded by the light. Scion had glorified. No angel or demon who saw it would ever forget it.

CLIMBING BACK ABOVE A THICK BANK OF CLOUDS, SCION AND ANGIE were in shock. Neither could talk. They both struggled to understand what had just happened.

Finally, Angie peeked out from under Scion's left wing and confessed with tears, "O Master Scion, I almost ruined the mission. I caused you to be wounded. Please forgive me! I am so sorry. I had no idea that my uncloaking would put us both in such danger."

"Yes—that was a *big* mistake. I should never have let you uncloak. But I forgive you. I just hope you have learned a lesson: Rules are to be *obeyed*! You can't just do what feels good. Bad things happen when you break the rules! From now on, you *must* comply with standard procedures. Is that *clear*, Angel 442—I mean, Angie?"

"Oh, yes, Master. I will *always* follow the rules from now on."

With the attack over, the two angels relaxed again as they turned toward Spanish Florida. Scion looked at the tiny angel for a long moment and then said, "Angie, you did more than break the rules back there."

Angie flinched and scrunched up her face, waiting for another rebuke.

"Your worship triggered something in me I had not felt that strongly since the birth of Jesus. When you began to sing back there, a door in my heart opened for me to worship God *very* deeply. Whenever I worship like that, my body shines uncontrollably. I can't stop it. That's why God used me to guide the Wise Men to Jesus. He needed a bright star. All I had to do was worship God continuously to be that star. Michael calls it 'glorifying.' It has only happened that one time—and never in heaven. I guess I have to be on Earth."

"But Master Scion, you always glow when you worship. I've seen you."

"Yes, but not *like that*. I just want to say thanks. I have always been a loner. It was safer that way. I guess I am beginning to see the wisdom Solomon wrote in Ecclesiastes—'Two are better than one.'"

"'Because they have a good return for their labor,' Ecclesiastes 4:9. I told you I was tops in my class—even in my Bible class." Scion just shook his head and smiled.

"Angie, you and I are headed into the New World—just minutes away. But something new has already started in my heart. Thank you," Scion concluded with moist eyes. For a long moment, the two of them just stared at each other.

Suddenly, Angie saw something out of the corner of her eye. "Look, Master—two beams of light up ahead about one hundred miles apart. I also hear angels singing in both locations!"

"What incredible sensors you have, Angie. I've lectured about this location many times in some advanced classes you haven't had yet. Those beams mark the Huguenot Martyrs," Scion replied. "Their blood still cries to God from the ground of Spanish Florida. See that inlet down there? The Spanish call it *Matanzas*, meaning 'slaughter.'* That's where the Spanish Captain Pedro Menéndez slaughtered over five hundred French Protestant Huguenots back in 1565.* Huguenots were French Protestants.* They came to Florida to escape the Catholic executions of Protestants in France.* Menéndez executed two hundred and fifty Huguenots even after they surrendered. You can read about it in the Great Library.

"You probably remember Menéndez. He is the same ship captain who picked up that native boy in 1561* you mentioned in your first scouting trip for General Michael. Those angels you see down there are from the Honor Battalion. They are assigned to stand guard over land made holy by the blood of martyrs.

"But enough of all that. Hold on tight now. I'm picking up speed so we can surprise whoever is waiting for us up north."

"Holding on— for a little *payback* for this morning's rude welcome," the tiny angel giggled.

Scion laughed. He felt a growing confidence that he might not fail after all. *I have a new friend—and an amazing one. I guess opposites really do attract each other—and wow—are we opposites!*

CHAPTER 16

"What was that?" Okeus mumbled to himself. Although his lair was located in a vast swamp, the screams of Voudoc's demons shook the spiritual web of the dark world. But he quickly dismissed it. He had received no communication from his scouts about any emergencies. Quaking in the satanic web was common when demons fought amongst themselves—which was *very* often They were bred to fight for power and pleasure—the very things their Lord Lucifer lusted for.

Fifteen hundred miles to the south, deep inside the Blue Mountains of Jamaica,* Voudoc, Principality of the Caribbean Islands, paced back and forth. He and his wounded demons had retreated there to recover from their recent encounter with Scion.

Like Okeus, Voudoc ruled his realm disguised as a demon— a monkey demon, in Voudoc's case. Although he was only five feet tall, his sinewy greenish-beige body was fast and agile. He looked like one of the cute white-cheeked vervet monkeys that a Spanish treasure ship had brought to the islands on its way to Peru.

As it turned out, the native Taíno people* loved Voudoc's monkey appearance when he uncloaked during their worship of him. Voudoc's demons, however, thought he looked too attractive. All of his demons were ugly. They despised any spirit with eye appeal. It just reminded them how disgusting they looked. Still, they obeyed Voudoc. He was a demon like them—or so they thought. Besides, not obeying always led to serious punishment. Voudoc was *very* sensitive about being disrespected—something Okeus had often exploited with great enthusiasm.

Voudoc looked around the cave full of his warriors—all temporarily blinded by that sudden blaze of light. He was so embarrassed by their total defeat by one angel that he decided not to warn Okeus about the intruder—even though Okeus had just demanded such a report.

"Do *not* send any alert! Let that pig-headed bully deal with that flashy angel himself. Okeus thinks he is so important because he is a "Continental Principality." I remember his taunts. "'Oh, you are so cute, you little island god,'" Voudoc roared in a squeaky voice, mimicking Okeus. "'Why don't you enslave all your island monkeys and show everyone how powerful you are: Voudoc, King of the Monkeys!'"

"I am just as good as he is—and *twice* as clever," the monkey-god shouted. His wounded demons nodded dutifully.

"Just because he is the Master's pet. *Ha*! We'll see who Lucifer's favorite is in the days to come! I have a strong domain full of seasoned Spanish sinners and thousands of natives and African slaves who do my bidding faithfully. I own San Juan Bautista, the gateway to the Caribbean. The Spanish could not possibly enslave the mainland natives and steal their gold without my help. I have made Lord Lucifer proud! And I have a spy in the court of that fat dinosaur buffoon. A clever spirit named Morph. One day, I will have my revenge in full."

His demons groaned weakly in agreement. They were too wounded to say much more. It would be days before the natives of the islands would have to deal with the usual sicknesses, nameless fears, and strange accidents that normally harassed them. A strange time of peace and safety rested on the islands while the island's evil spirits recuperated from the overflight of two worshipping angels.

CHAPTER 17

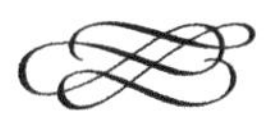

Scion was over the mainland now, streaking north toward Virginia below a dense cloud deck at seven hundred miles per hour—just under the speed of sound. To avoid detection, he flew just above the treetops. But despite the dangers, his thoughts were filled with gratitude to the Lord. He looked down at Angie snuggled in his wing pit and sighed with a joy he had long forgotten.

"Angie, I am beginning to see why the Lord had us work together. I think we are going to be quite a team."

"I have that same feeling. I am looking forward to using everything I learned in BADS."

"BADS? What in heaven's name is that?"

"Oh, just a name we Betas gave to your academy: *Basic Angelic Development School*. It sounds provocative, so of course, we liked that."

"Yeah, I can see why you would. *Lord, help me*! Okay, Miss BADS. Just hold on tight when we get there. We are going to hit the drop zone at high speed, and I am not sure if they are expecting us."

"They're not."

"How do you know that?"

"Just call it female intuition."

"Cut the jokes. How do you *really* know?"

"Remember, I can hear all communication—human or spirit—within one hundred miles. I heard a Dark Angel on the islands down there tell his scouts not to report our arrival to Okeus. That must have been Voudoc. Some kind of bad blood between them. So typical. These guys would slit their mother's throats to get ahead—if they had a mother. It's hard to believe they were once heavenly angels."

"Well done, Angie. By the way, did you know that this is only the sixth time General Michael has ordered this maneuver. It announces to the entire spiritual world that God's Kingdom is claiming an entire continent. If we do this right, it should hopefully frighten the bad guys in Virginia from attacking our colony as much."

Angie's stomach jumped as she thought, *I know what's coming. Orders are orders!*

"Here we go! And when we get on final approach to the target, we will do it *uncloaked*—both of us!" Scion shouted with a boisterous laugh and wink at Angie.

Angie thrust her tiny arm and fist forward and shouted back, "Uncloaked—for the Lamb!" Then, for a moment, the two of them just stared at each other, their faces aglow with childlike glee. *And I thought I'd never have a friend like Kai again,* Scion thought. But then he noticed a course correction coming up fast.

As the land north of Florida curved right, Scion banked left to intercept the bottom end of a two-thousand-mile mountain range that flowed northeast. He would fly low in the lush valleys on the western side. About halfway up the eastern seaboard, Scion banked hard right for their final leg into the Great Bay. The mountains had shielded their approach from sentinel demons and they would not expect angels to approach from the west since no Christians lived there.

As Scion turned northeast above the first valley, he shouted to Angie, "Here we go. I am about to accelerate to final approach speed."

Streaking now at Mach 5, Scion dove to five feet above the treetops. His heart began to beat wildly. A high-performance rendezvous with continental archangels was a completely new experience for the former headmaster. *O God, help me not to muff it,* he prayed silently.

"Did you give the five the right coordinates, Angie?"

"Yes, sir: 36 degrees north, 48 minutes, 9.6372 seconds latitude and 76 degrees west, 11 minutes, 39.8862 seconds longitude. Got that straight from Michael."

"Good. We have to be spot-on. That location is critical to the Lord's plans to impact many nations for the Kingdom."

"Got it, boss! Remember, this is my specialty—recon and intel."

"I was also a top student in my class, and I still made *serious* mistakes—but enough of that. It's time to do something you'll like."

"*Uncloak*!"

"Just be alert. It could get ugly. Remember, if I am hurt and can't get back right away, report back to Michael as soon as you can."

"Hey, you'll be fine. I'll be watching you from the ground below and taking good notes."

"Sounds good. The six of us have to face thousands of angry demons, and you'll be taking good notes. *Ha*! Maybe you want to change jobs someday?"

Just then, Scion's huge wings snapped hard to starboard as he climbed over the last mountain ridge fully uncloaked at five times the speed of sound. Below, all hell broke out as demon sentries fell over in shock, fumbled and cursed as they tried to sound the alarm. But it was too late.

One of heaven's most magnificent, prototype angels was streaking toward them—*fully visible*! Twenty-four feet of shimmering, golden wings sliced through the air at fifty-six hundred feet per second above a vibrating white robe. At the tip of this frightening image, every demon eye saw a shock of platinum-blond hair streaking straight out behind Scion's golden face and burning blue eyes. In front of that face, they saw a frighteningly large fist thrust forward like a battering ram. The angel's other hand held the jeweled handle of his massive sword in its golden scabbard.

In the same instant—or slightly before—Angie uncloaked under his left wing. She glanced wide-eyed at her rainbow-colored hair vibrating violently in the fierce wind. With a burst of laughter, she thought, *If only my friends could see me now!*

Screaming west across the Atlantic Ocean horizon from five continents, the incoming archangels suddenly appeared. They came to claim Earth's last continent for the Lamb and for his Church.

Tens of thousands of demonic eyes along the eastern coast of the New World were glued to the contrails of the five archangels. As the five came within 100 miles of the bay, they moved into formation, with two rows flying in the shape of an inverted "V"—except the top slot in the right row was empty. Every demon in the Great Bay area rushed to the ocean beach, mesmerized and frightened by this unusual angelic maneuver. Okeus quickly mobilized his personal guard demons. Giant dark-green, lizard-like warrior demons with blazing red eyes hovered in the air, growling and cursing as they waited to intercept the incoming angels whisking across the ocean at incredible speed.

But no one noticed the angel from the west. "Drop now!" Scion shouted, as Angie released her grip and swished to Earth.

"See you at ninety thousand feet above Bermuda in ten minutes," she yelled.

With a powerful flip of his wingtips, Scion accelerated to Mach 10. With trees and fields flashing past in a blur, Scion exploded into the Great Bay area just nanoseconds after the other five archangels arrived and hovered at twelve thousand feet, just above the target location, which was about ten miles west of the ocean. Every demon pretended to be ready to fight— with swords drawn and mouths frothing with yellow slime dripping through their bright orange fangs. But most were simply in shock. Even Okeus was stunned and silent as he watched from his swamp throne room.

Suddenly, Scion's twelve-foot uncloaked body reached the target and slammed onto the Earth in a kneeling position with one leg bent up. Angie recorded it all as she glided into a tree a few miles away.

Scion checked his position one more time on his belt locator. *Yes. This is it: 36 degrees north, 48 minutes, 9.6372 seconds latitude and 76 degrees west, 11 minutes, 39.8862 seconds longitude,* he noted to himself.

Then, with a loud twang, Scion pulled his eight-foot platinum sword from its sheath, leaped into the air and flew seven times around that spot in a tight one-hundred-foot circle, holding his gleaming sword over his head. As he did, he chanted two verses of Psalm 24:

> Lift up your heads, O ye gates; and be ye lifted up, ye everlasting doors; and the King of glory shall come in. Who is this King of glory? The LORD strong and mighty, the LORD mighty in battle.

Immediately, there was a loud cracking sound in the skies above, like a colossal castle gate opening on massive, rusty hinges. Every demon visibly cringed as a heavenly trumpet blared a victory note over and over. The ground heaved. Trees shook. Large rocks broke apart. Then, it happened.

A one-hundred-foot-wide shaft of pure golden light shot down from heaven like a lightning bolt to a spot just inches from Scion's knee. The burning beam crackled with fearsome energy, flooding the land for miles around with a light brighter than the sun. Then, with a three-note trumpet blast, the beam vanished. The air seemed to leave the forest. A holy silence captivated every living thing. Instantly, a roar of anguish erupted across the entire region as demons felt the surge of God's glory blind and burn them like no fire in hell ever could. But before they could attack Scion and the five, he shot upward in a blur of speed to join the five archangels on the top right of their inverted "V" formation.

As six angels arrived at twenty-four thousand feet, their uncloaked, gleaming bodies hurtled heavenward in a vortex of light and sonic booms that made men and demons fall to the ground—*stunned.* Spinning wildly into the stratosphere above the bay, the six split into a starburst of multicolored contrails that extended far beyond the horizon in a canopy of heavenly glory that lingered and shimmered in the sky for hours— like a rainbow of Northern Lights.

Angels cheered until they were hoarse. Dark Angels and demons groaned for days. They all knew what had just happened. The six had just opened a two-way portal from heaven to Earth!

Within moments, all hell shook with the roar of rage from Lucifer—a heavenly portal had been opened without even the slightest opposition from Okeus or Voudoc! Both principalities had to sacrifice sixty thousand of their best demons in horrible deaths to appease him. But high above the Great Bay, the mood was far different.

"Mission accomplished!" Scion shouted as the six reached the top of their climb, sixty-thousand feet above Virginia.

"Well done, brothers! That was more than amazing," Scion beamed. "All I have ever been was a school administrator and teacher. Wait till I tell my assistant, Mola, about this. Will he ever be jealous!"

The gigantic, black Archangel of Africa named Nabili spoke up, "Well, maybe the Lord thought you could instruct those yellow-eyed demons down there with some proper manners when receiving angelic visitors." Then, Nabili playfully shoulder-bumped Scion so hard that he almost fell over.

But not before the lightning-fast grip of a tall, pale-yellow angel named Amdo held Scion steady. "Master Scion, Angel 442's intel brief said there are two demonic portals in this region. One is just for divination. But the other one is a very dangerous War Portal. What happened? Okeus didn't use it to call for reinforcements from the Abyss," the Archangel of Asia asked.

"What can I say, Amdo? They must have freaked out when they saw Nabili's big black body hurtling at them uncloaked. You know, they think all angels are golden guys like me."

At that crack, Nabili tried to give Scion a friendly whack on the back but Amdo deftly pushed the big African away so hard that he spun into the air like a top. Loud laughter erupted at the sight of Nabili's huge smile and twirling body above them. Then Nabili snap-rolled and dove into the five angels with a loud *Yaaaah!*

In the next instant, angels bounced here, there, and everywhere as the five archangels and Scion deliberately rammed and wrestled each other—*just for fun*. Like most men, they enjoyed being pushed, hit, and knocked around by good-natured friends. Scion pulled away from the frolicking fray for a minute and just marveled. *Look at them: the five most powerful creatures in the Earth's atmosphere are horsing around like a bunch of teenage humans. O God, I need more of this!*

After it was over, the five stood in a circle hugging one another as they said goodbye. It was all Scion could do not to stare. Then he had to turn his face away. He couldn't let them see his tears. *O God, how I have missed times like this. How I miss those times in Archangel Academy just goofing off with the 23 after class in the park. Times with Kai. But these angels are different from the ones I know in heaven. These actually seem to accept—and like—me. Maybe it's safe for me to make friends again. Perhaps someday I can find Kai, and maybe, just maybe, God might forgive him—and we can be together again. Perhaps...*

Turning back to the five, Scion yelled, "I've got to go, guys. I have to meet Angel 442 and get her intel report to Michael."

"Okay, Master Scion," Nabili shouted back. "Just don't let us see you with any pink spiked hair or sparkles on your wings the next time we meet. Those Betas are clever— but weird! I hope it works out for you."

Amdo quipped, "Yes, my Tibetan people are small—but not fourteen inches!"

"One day, you may eat those words," Scion shot back with a grin. "That little 442 is bigger on the inside than she looks on the outside. Remember, King David was the runt of his family too." More laughter and five thumbs up.

With that parting remark, Scion's big wings snapped open and yanked him forward, climbing south to meet Angie high over the Bahamas. As he did, he re-cloaked himself to be invisible again. It was time to relax.

Hidden in a thick cloud bank near the coast, a small, twenty-four-inch, dark-green, cat-like spirit with unusual blue eyes stared at the departing angels forty thousand feet above him. *What was that all about? Is this a sign about The One?* Morph mused.

Then Morph turned and flew back to the Great Bay. Even with a gimpy left wing, he was able to avoid bumping into the screeching demons that were flying erratically all around him. But Morph didn't care. *What does it matter? Until The One comes, nothing will change anyway,* he thought. So, he went back to his rotten tree trunk to curl up and rest. *I wish I had never been spawned. I am a total failure. I wish—I wish I was dead.*

A few miles away in the big swamp, his master Okeus was far from sleeping. The war he knew would come had finally arrived.

Tomorrow, he would call a War Council. It was time to unveil his plan. *If it worked in 587 BC in Judah to defeat the Jews, it will work here,* he pondered as he settled into his putrid-smelling haunt in the Big Swamp about twenty miles south of the Great Bay. He would not sleep tonight.

CHAPTER 18

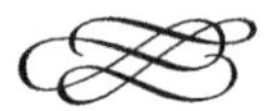

| Algonquin village*

December 20, 1606

Just after midnight the next day, Okeus dispatched Snookus to appear in dreams to Powhatan's main shaman, Mongo and to his eleven lesser shamans. Mongo was the thirty-four-year-old younger brother of Chief Powhatan. He was short, with small darting eyes and long, unkempt black hair framing his weasel-like face that twitched nervously most of the time. He always seemed to be looking over his shoulder for an attack or muttering to some unseen presence.

In the twelve dreams, Mongo and the other shamans were all summoned to an emergency Shaman Council with Okeus at dawn near Werowocomoco, on the west side of the Pamunkey River at exactly 3:23 a.m. This was the tribal headquarters of Wahunsonacock*, the Great chief of the Powhatan confederacy.*

Wahunsonacock was also called Powhatan* by the fifteen thousand subjects of his united thirty tribes.* Wahunsonacock, Mongo, and a fierce warrior named Opechancanough* were the three sons of Paquiquino—the eleven-year-old boy taken by the Spanish in 1561.

"But Master, why 3:23?"

"Simple, my little fish-blob, 3:23 is the verse in that awful book they call Genesis where God ejects the two vermin out of Eden. I think that time is rather fitting as get ready to repulse English vermin from our Eden," Okeus intoned with a mock British accent.

As soon as Mongo awoke, he hastily invited his father, Paquiquino—whom he called Father Paq—and his twenty-seven-year-old younger brother Opechancanough, whom he called Opie, to the Shaman Council. Both brothers readily agreed. They knew something big was coming. Why else did those powerful and mysterious spirits fly over yesterday? And what did that bright light mean that made Mongo so afraid?

The youngest son of Powhatan had a very handsome face, long raven hair and manly physique that made him a favorite with the maidens. And for awhile he played the field, breaking many feminine hearts in the process. But his real passion was to be the ultimate Powhatan warrior. He had to win every tribal contest and dominate his opponents at any cost. He raced to this rare meeting of shamans like a shark smelling blood.

As the twelve shamans and two guests arrived at the desolate clearing in the woods, each of the witchdoctors suddenly grabbed their heads in pain. Paquiquino and Opechancanough just watched in shock, clueless to what was happening.

A growling, screaming voice violently pounded in the minds of each native priest, "Call upon me! Invoke my name! I am tired of your whining about what happened yesterday. Worship me so I can show you what to do. Am I not the great Okeus, Ruler of the Rivers, and the Bay, Dark Lord of all this land?"

At first, the twelve shamans just stood there in a tight circle, stunned and trembling. But soon, their sweaty faces shook off the daze of terror that had immobilized them moments before. Their naked feet began to move in rhythmic stomping, giving a thumping staccato counterpoint to a rising hum of sacred chants.

Boom-bah-bah, boom-bah-bah, boom-bah-bah, the twenty-four calloused soles thudded together in the red dust and rotting leaves of the ancient clearing. Like a chugging freight train gaining speed, the twelve twirled and pumped their arms as they circled in a counterclockwise dance around the altar. Birds screeched. Owl hooted. In the distance, wild dogs barked as if under attack. Every animal sensed the gathering spiritual gloom. Even gnats and mosquitoes kept a respectful distance.

They danced with a violence that was incredible to behold. The cloud of dust from their jackhammering feet rose higher and higher. A choral roar of rage and anger filled the forest. Shouting and screaming, they flung themselves into the air, landing on the ground with crushing thuds, only to spring up again like antelopes frisking in the field. Drenched in sweat with glazed, dark eyes, the shamans flew around the clearing in a panting frenzy of worship. They felt invincible, powerful, wicked, and fearsome. They felt like gods—precisely what Okeus wanted them to feel—the same feelings that drove Lucifer from God's side in heaven.

O-ke-us. O-ke-us. Come to us, O-ke-us.

Ruler of the Earth, fall upon us now!

O-ke-us. O-ke-us. Come to us, O-ke-us.

Ruler of the Earth, fall upon us now!

They chanted to the mesmerizing rhythm of their dusty stomping. Then the crescendo of the chorus:

Come now and fill us!

Come now and meet us!

Come now among us!

Come, Lord O-ke-us!

Come, right now!

The last words exploded like cannon fire from their upturned mouths just as their feet slapped the ground one last time and froze in place. No one twitched. No one breathed. Their neck veins bulged in fear. Their stomachs squirmed with nausea.

They felt him.

He was moving.

He was coming . . . closer and closer.

Then, with the speed of a frightened deer, the dancing shamans spun on their heels, reversed the direction of the dance, and continued to chant, stomp, and whirl around. They entered a deep trance. With each revolution, their minds slipped deeper into a wavy, woozy, dreamlike state to the point of almost passing out.

Without their noticing it, the temperature in the small clearing dropped ten degrees. An eerie stillness filled the musty air of the dark forest glen. Pungent, choking smells of rotten flesh and animal waste seemed to escape from the slightly vibrating ground as a beehive of snarling, level-five guard demons rose out of the dirt.

"Okeus is here," a shaman whispered in fear.

They could feel him in the pit of their guts. An inner trembling simmered deep within their heaving diaphragms. Then an intoxicating combination of terror and evil pleasure quickly submerged their consciousness into mush. With a hideous, guttural sound no earthly creature could make, Okeus slowly opened his large, dinosaur mouth, releasing an undulating green haze of wispy tentacles that attached to the heads of each priest. Like a twelve-armed octopus, Okeus was locked onto their minds to fully possess their bodies.

"Ah, yes, that's it, yield to me. Now you are completely mine . . . again." He possessed them—body, soul, and spirit—as he had so many times before. "Oh, I love it. It is delicious. Give me more!" he greedily hissed as he drank in the prized submission of their wills and the luxurious aroma of their sins. He was feeding on his subjects, and he would not be rushed. "Come deeper, my precious Paq. Let me drink of your anger and self-hatred. And you, Opie, son of Paq, pour out your cunning ferocity to me. I desire it. Your wicked heart refreshes me. Only the worship and loyalty of your brother, Mongo, pleases me more. You three sons bring much honor to your father, Paq. He has done well to instruct you in his hatred of whites."

Okeus slobbered and smiled, imbibing the adulation of his subjects with sensuous delight. Finally, after a long moment, he uncloaked himself and slipped into their view like a gigantic liquid shadow looming above them. His dark glory pulsated through the forest in waves of evil. Everyone instantly knelt on the ground in terror.

A few yards away, hidden in a dense pine tree, Angie peered at the hulking form of the Algonquian god. She was recording the scene frame by frame in her mind, but fighting nausea from Okeus's stench and the heavy demonic oppression all around her.

Suddenly, Mongo, the high priest, began to shudder and twitch. The pupils of his dark eyes rolled back into his head. His body quivered like a tuning fork, his every muscle vibrating like taut piano wires playing a fortissimo chord. Okeus was possessing him totally. Mongo lost consciousness. He was little more than a puppet now— inhabited by his master.

With a head-tap on Mongo with his claw, Okeus levitated the enchanted shaman ten feet into the air. "Tell them!" Okeus commanded. In a scratchy, guttural voice that was not his own, Mongo sputtered out the thoughts of Okeus.

"Long ago, before the Great Emancipation in heaven, Lord Lucifer knew the Enemy's plans to establish a major base on our land to infect the world with his senile droolings. Yes, the pitiful followers of the Lamb are coming here again—this time from England. Listen to me. Make no mistake, the Lamb may be the called the Scourge of Hell, but we have driven out his Spanish followers, and we shall drive these cocky English slimebags back into the sea from whence they come."

Fear gripped the shamans, and Okeus sensed it. He squeezed the throat of Mongo with his dark powers and made him roar this message with the ferocity of a cornered lion:

"But do not be dismayed. For hundreds of years, I have known this was coming here. Our main weapon is sin. We will sow seeds of sin into these invaders. When these seeds become a dark harvest, we will not have to destroy them. The old fool, our Enemy, will do it himself."

Even with their eyes closed, the shamans bobbed back and forth, grinning drunkenly with relief. Their master had a plan. He always did.

Angie winced in fear. She knew it could happen that way.

Then Okeus roared a wicked laugh and he was gone. Mongo fell to the ground with a thud, and the eleven shamans immediately toppled forward and blacked out. Moments later, they awoke, grateful to have survived another meeting with their dread master.

As the shamans awoke, Paquiquino and Opechancanough decided it was safe to get up. They began to walk back to Werowocomoco, to tell their brother, Chief Powhatan, what had just happened.

But as Paquiquino stepped over some rocks, pain shot up his leg. "Ouch!" he yelped. His foot was bleeding. A small object glinted in the black dirt. It looked like a small branch encrusted with mud. After he bent over and picked it up, the old warrior rubbed the dirt off the long edge of what had pierced his heel. *This is strange. It is smooth like a seashell or stone, but it is not from the sea—or from the forest.* As he turned it over, his heart froze. A man's figure was carved on it.

Terror contorted his face as the Spanish crucifix fell from his shaking hands. Fueled with dark emotions he had not felt in decades, Paquiquino ran wildly for miles through the forest that day, tripping and falling on the tangled vines that covered the floor of the woods. A gaggle of guilt and shame demons heard his shouts and they dashed to feast on his misery. For hours, the crazed native crashed through the darkening woods, crying over and over, "No! No! I didn't want to do it. They made me do it. They made me do it."

Angie had followed and watched the demon feeding frenzy on the distraught native. Sensing that this was important to their mission, she recorded the entire scene through her eyes to share with Scion later. She knew her recordings would be somewhat blurred. She couldn't stop crying.

CHAPTER 19

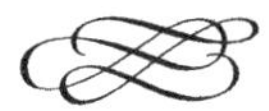

Later that day...

Angie alighted on the cirrus cloud just above the Bermuda islands—a small island chain six hundred miles southeast of Virginia. They were named after Juan de Bermúdez*, a Spanish sea captain who landed there in 1505 *and then lost some of his swine on the islands.* Herds of snorting wild pigs and the eerie night cries of the Cahow bird on the largest island caused sailors who arrived there later to call it the Isle of Devils.*

Ironically, since the islands were never inhabited by humans, no demons were ever stationed there. As a result, the spiritual atmosphere of the islands was altogether peaceful. This made it a favorite rendezvous for angels passing through the region since their movements and communication with each other would be more secure. Although no angel would admit to it publicly, many eagerly jockeyed for assignments to reconnoiter the area—for *one* reason: Bermuda's gorgeous, pink sand beaches and its brilliant, cerulean blue ocean waters. Heaven had neither. Those scouts always seemed to "get a little lost," and most returned to heaven a few hours tardy. Michael knew all about it. He just smiled when the angels checked in late from a mission over that area.

"Report," Scion ordered as Angie checked her sensors.

"Good news, Master. I was able to record the entire briefing Okeus gave to his shamans and a couple of tribal leaders. I didn't think I could get close enough, but then I remembered that rock the Spanish sailor had planted years ago under a tree. Well, guess what—that oak tree was right next to the meeting location. That black stone emits an intense red light only visible to spirits, so I was able to hide behind the rock's strange glow. The only problem was the unnerving presence of evil in that rock. It almost took my breath away. It buzzed and rattled like a snake getting ready to strike. But I *had* to use it. Okeus and his demons never saw me. Even his demons seemed to shy away from that spot."

"Good job. We'll deal with that weird rock later. What did you find out?"

"Well, of course, Okeus plans to attack the colony with sickness and native attacks. We expected that. But his ultimate strategy is to sow multiple sins in the colonists—like tares among the wheat. When enough sin take root in the settlers, Okeus predicted that God would eventually pull back his protection from them and then the colony would fail."

In a pained voice, Scion dropped his head and agreed, "Yes, it's a classic strategy—and it even worked against Israel. When God's chosen people ignored his calls to repentance for hundreds of years, the Lord abandoned them to the cruel Assyrians and Babylonians. The Lord hates to do things like that. Isaiah even called it the Lord's *'strange work'.*

"But we *can't* let that happen, Angie! If this new colony fails, who knows how long it will take to start the missionary nation the Lord wants to birth there. Thousands or millions of people could go to hell before another colony is successfully planted there—that's what Michael told me face to face just before I left heaven. Honestly, Angie, I'm *scared.* What if our colony fails? What if we fail? What if *I* fail?

The tiny angel gasped with relief. "*Wow*—I thought I was the only one fighting fear. I'm just a scout. I don't want to be responsible for something this important. Now I kinda wish that Michael had picked a different Beta."

"I get that completely. I never wanted this assignment. I wish I could quit now, but I can't. Most angels don't trust me now. It would look *awful* if I refused to fight a Dark Angel in such a critical assignment."

They both silently stared at the loose, pink sand beneath Scion's toes and Angie's shoes. For a long moment, their confidence seemed as wobbly as the shifting sands beneath them. Then Angie remembered something.

"Master Scion, my sensors picked up a demon flying very close to the six of you just after the starburst maneuver. I thought that was odd. What evil spirit wants to risk getting close to archangels—especially five of them. He must have been lost."

"Yes, of course, he's *lost,*" Scion smirked. "He's a *demon*!"

"Ha, ha! Good one, Boss. But I wonder what it feels like to be *eternally* lost—especially for a Dark Angel like Okeus who used to live in heaven. Sometimes I wish they could somehow be redeemed and brought back to live with us again."

Scion looked at Angie with astonishment. *That's what I just thought!*

"Well, is it time to go home, Master Scion?"

"Yes. Let's surprise Michael by coming back *on time*— from Bermuda," Scion chuckled. "I am anxious to get back to report to Michael."

"Okay, but first, can we take one more slow turn over the islands. It's so beautiful here," Angie said as she tucked herself into his soft, feathery wingpit. Scion smiled and complied with a lazy, left-hand glide over the brilliant blue waters ringing the pink beaches. Then, the twosome bolted into the heavens into a blur of speed and unknown adventures.

CHAPTER 20

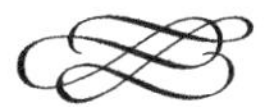

*December 20, 1606**

Three ships set sail from Blackwall Dock in London* on a cold, rainy morning on December 20, 1606,* with 105 male settlers and 39 crew members.* Famed explorer Bartholomew Gosnold* was Captain of the *Godspeed,* John Ratcliff* served as Captain of the *Discovery* and Christopher Newport* was Captain of the *Susan Constant* and the Admiral of this fleet.*

The trinity of ships had a royal charter from King James I to found a colony in Virginia.* Sir Walter Raleigh had named that land Virginia in 1584* in honor of The *Virgin* Queen, Queen Elizabeth I of England.* The queen had given Raleigh a similar charter* to "discover, search, find out, and view such remote heathen and barbarous lands, countries, and territories . . . to have, hold, occupy, and enjoy."* So, he did.

Starting in 1585,* Sir Walter Raleigh helped create two colonies in a place they called Roanoke Island,* but both failed.* The second settlement of 1587 was called the Lost Colony.* Over one hundred colonists simply disappeared when the next supply ship returned in

1590.* Now, this third British attempt to plant a New World colony was sponsored by the Virginia Company of London,* a British stock corporation that had been organized by London merchants.* They sold stock* to raise the money for the colony, promising a sizeable financial return to the investors who purchased the stock.

To protect their investment through sound leadership, the Virginia Company sent a sealed envelope* with the three ships containing the names of seven colonists* who would form the ruling Council for the colony after they landed.* As the three ships set sail for Virginia that December, no one on board knew who the seven would be.*

Neither did anyone know how difficult the voyage would be. The 105 passengers and 39 crew* members would have to endure an unusually long, four-month* transatlantic journey on small, cramped vessels. Seventy-one* people were aboard the *Susan Constant,* captained by Christopher Newport, admiral of the fleet.*

This man was a national hero in England.* As captain of three ships—the *Little John,** the *Margaret,** and the *Golden Dragon**– Captain Newport became one of the most successful and famous privateers England had ever seen.* He made the Crown and his financial backers rich from his raids against Spanish and Portuguese treasure ships in the Caribbean.*

He was a fighter in every sense. As a young man, Newport had sailed with Sir Francis Drake in the attack on the Spanish fleet at Cadiz* and took part in England's defeat of the Spanish Armada in 1588.* In 1590, during the Anglo-Spanish War, Newport lost an arm* while capturing a Spanish galleon*—a loss that made him even more acclaimed as a hero of England. Few men of his time commanded the respect of all British people as Newport did.* Everyone agreed that he was the best choice to lead this important expedition.

Fifty-two* more were aboard the *Godspeed,* captained by Bartholomew Gosnold* and twenty-one* aboard the *Discovery,* the smallest ship, commanded by John Ratcliff.* The ships held all men and boys—no women.* But plenty of invisible spirits—both good and bad—were also aboard.

Besides a dozen angels sent to serve the Christians on the ships, a sizable party of angry, bickering, and lustful spirits also joined the voyage. Scion glared at them, but he knew they had permission to be there because many crewmen and passengers had been drawing demons into their lives for many years through persistent sins. To keep the evil spirits at bay, Scion ordered the twelve angels to keep the saints occupied with prayer, hymns, Bible reading, and good works. The angels agreed to try, but they were doubtful it would work for very long. They was a rough lot.

Difficulties came early in the voyage. Just as the three ships sailed beyond the mouth of the River Thames, the wind completely died. For the first six weeks, the small, cramped vessels never moved out of the large anchorage called the "Downes"* near the county of Kent in southeastern England.*

The wind may have stopped, but tornado-like tempers flared as they all endured forty-five days on cold, damp, foul-smelling ships drifting within sight of their homeland. One settler even fell ill and died. The precious food rations stored aboard for the long journey were quickly being depleted.* Day after day, the 144 shivering men and boys stared at the high, white chalk cliffs of the Kent headland* just a few miles away.* The angels gave up trying to get anyone to read the Bible and pray. It was nautical misery of a high degree. Curses and foul oaths deepened the gloom of almost every passenger—all except one: *Chaplain Hunt.*

It was a depressing start to a difficult journey—almost as if someone or something did not want them to leave England. The settlers all sensed it. In fact, a comet had zipped across the sky one night.* They took it as a bad omen. Scion had tried to intervene and get the winds moving, but the powerful English weather demons who had becalmed the ships quickly reminded Scion that he had no authority there. "You are the Angel of Virginia. And this *ain't* Virginia, mate."

Scion and Angie could only watch from above and wait. Halfway through this agonizing stall, Scion leaned over to Angie and said, "Now I know why the Watcher Angels say that this kind of duty is ninety-five percent pure *boredom* followed by five percent pure *terror*. I am sure the five percent is coming."

Angie just looked at him and huffed her irritation. She hated to be still. *Fast* was her favorite speed.

Later, Scion would find out that Okeus had called in a favor from the Dark Angel, Lord Pict, Principality of London, to have the winds stilled. Such is the web of collusion in Lucifer's kingdom.

Finally, the *'adventurers'*—as they were called—made it to the Canary Islands,* where they stopped briefly to take on more supplies.* Afterward, Admiral Newport tacked his three-ship flotilla to starboard, heading southwest over the shimmering horizon toward the vast uncharted lands beyond. As the 104 men and boys stared at the smoldering sun directly ahead of them, their hearts wrestled with an emotional cocktail of excitement, fear, regret, and determination. But two men on the *Susan Constant* felt even *stronger* emotions—Captain John Smith and Lord Edward Wingfield.

Captain John Smith was a well-known soldier of fortune—a bold and cunning mercenary who had won distinction in many wars across Europe.

His appearance was startling. A shock of tightly-curled, bright red hair and carefully trimmed beard framed a continual facial scowl. He was short and very muscular, with a thick, suntanned neck jutting out of the stiff white collar of his neatly tailored blue uniform. A sharp knife always hung at his side in a weathered leather scabbard. His entire demeanor shouted, "Don't mess with me"—except for his *eyes*. They possessed a rare beauty and calmness that seemed out of place in such a man. Women were drawn to him like moths to a flame.

Edward Maria Wingfield had been a British soldier for a time, but he looked every inch the aristocrat everyone knew him to be.

He was tall, with creamy white skin that looked pampered and almost flawless despite his age. His closely-set green eyes, narrow lips and thinning brown hair topped off a slender, wiry body always clothed in the finest shirts, trousers and leather shoes London could provide. A smile from him was rare. A friendly word with anyone below his social status was even rarer. He was respected— but *not* liked by most who met him.

Each of these two very different men was destined to shape the colony's future. But today, they just wanted to *reshape* each other's faces.

"Look, Smith, I will have no more of your poppycock slurs upon my character," Lord Wingfield roared. "Either you stop slandering me, or I will have you put in irons. Is that clear? I don't care if we are only in the Canary Islands. You will rot in the brig until we land if you do not cease to stir up trouble among the men. I know you were invited to join this venture because of your military experience, but you are not indispensable. I was once a soldier, too, don't forget."

Scion heard the argument from his sentry position one hundred feet above the ship. He shot through the deck to see these two stubborn leaders face off in a nasty argument.

"Oh, no! Not already, Scion silently fretted. *The colony needs these two leaders to get along. Oh, please don't sin. Please protect this mission the Lord has sent you on.*

Captain John Smith shot back, "Wingfield, I don't give a damn if you have been a soldier, a member of Parliament, and are the largest financial backer of this voyage. The truth is the truth, and you know it as well as I do. After six weeks in the Downes and another week getting this far, I am sick of your little sermons to the men that this is a mission for *God*. 'A chance to bring the savages to salvation,' you say. *Ha!* Ever since we sailed, you have given me indigestion with your false words about religion to the men."

"They are not sermons!" Wingfield protested. "I am no priest. I just want them to be properly motivated. A lot is at stake here. These men are Anglicans. Men like them will die to please God—and they may *have* to."

"I hate duplicity, and you are full of it," Smith snorted. "If you wanted to win souls, why is there only *one* priest among the 105 who set sail with us?"

"Are you impugning Reverend Hunt's abilities?" Wingfield snarled.

"Of course not!" Smith snapped. "Hunt's probably the best man on this voyage, plus Captain Newport. But one priest cannot serve all of us and hundreds of savages at the same time. Any fool can see that. And how will Hunt speak to the savages? He doesn't speak Powhatan. But *I* do!"

Wingfield blanched, taken by surprise at Smith's last remark. "Whatever do you mean, Smith? No white man knows that language."

"Wrong again, Sir-knows-all-things. Have you heard of John White?* He's a famous artist and mapmaker* that Sir Walter Raleigh sent to Virginia to help establish the Lost Colony.* White had previously helped Greenville* found the Roanoke settlement in 1585.* As a result, White knew Powhatan better than any Englishman.

A few years before he died, I met the old man in an Irish pub in London. After downing a couple of pints together, he agreed to teach me to speak Powhatan. I had a hunch I might go to Virginia someday. And here I am! So, if you are going to talk to the natives about God, I'm the one who can do it. But I won't—I am not a preacher—and neither are you. So, stop all this talk about winning souls among the heathen. It won't happen, and you know it.

"And while we are talking— just who do you think is going to do all the hard work once we get there? Sure, you have carpenters, a blacksmith, a mason, a tailor, a goldsmith, a barber, two surgeons and a few soldiers,* but half of our ranks are gentlemen* dandies like yourself! None of your kind could grow a bean or catch a fish, if their life depended on it. I guess you gents all think the rest of us are going to wipe your noses and feed you like your wet nurses at home. But in Virginia, a plain soldier that can use a pickaxe and a spade is better than five knights like you," the captain spat out with an angry grimace.

Wingfield shot back, "Well, your *father* didn't think so. Didn't he rent a farm from Lord Willoughby in Lincolnshire? Your father raised you on that farm. Don't you have any gratitude for what Willoughby did for your family? Or are you just jealous of his money and want to overthrow all the lords and ladies so you can have it for yourself, you ambitious upstart?

"Rich gents, are we? Yes, there are fifty-nine gentlemen* on this voyage— and you are one of us, aren't you? I hear you made a fortune in piracy and by fighting other people's wars for them.* Who are you to blame me for having money and wanting to earn more? At least I will do it honestly and not as a low-life pirate."

"Now wait a minute, you bastard," Smith growled. "Yes, I have been fighting rich men's wars since I was sixteen. Yes, I was rescued by French pirates after a shipwreck.* If I had not joined them, they would have killed me. That pirate money I earned enabled me to fight the greatest foes of Christendom—the Muslim Turks* in the 'Long War'*—while you were probably sitting on your duff in some castle listening to chamber music all day while your hired men slaved in the fields for a pittance. That's how it always is with your kind—take, take, take."

Shouting louder now, Wingfield bawled, "Listen, you foul-mouthed mercenary. The Virginia Company has given these men a chance to get a fresh start in the New World. What's so wrong with that? We've even given them free passage in exchange for their service to the new colony. If you ask me, you are just jealous you did not have the same chance when you were younger. Ha! Maybe if you had a chance like this, you wouldn't have that ugly scar on your face."

Smith's rage boiled over. He moved closer to Wingfield, shouting, "Jobs? Yes, let's talk about jobs! You and your kind have made it easy to recruit men for this voyage. Who can get a job in England? The poorhouses are overflowing with men and their families unable to pay their debts.* Sure, just dangle the promise of gold and land, and what idiot wouldn't sign on to this voyage? But will they ever see any money? Not until they work for years to pay off the cost of this passage.*

But, if you fat-assed gentlemen do not pull your load, those men may not even make it back alive. This voyage is in great danger, if you ask me. One of us has already died of sickness. All the men talk of is finding gold and getting rich. Who will build the fort, grow the crops, hunt the deer, catch the fish, and run this colony? Do you know how to live in the wilderness? I do. I know war. I know men. If we are, as I suspect, comprised of half laggards and dandies like you, we'll all be dead before the year is out. If I had known all this before we left, I never would have sailed with the lot of you."

Scion was joined by Angie now. She, too, looked worried. "What can we do, Master? Maybe they will decide to calm down after they have vented their anger for a bit. That would be fine, don't you think?"

"That would be fine. The Bible says to be angry, but don't let the sun go down on your anger. If they end this by forgiving one another, there's no harm done. But if they don't . . ." Scion just furrowed his brow in worry.

Just then, Wingfield smiled slyly. "Smith, finally we *agree*. You should *not* have sailed with us. Perhaps that can still be arranged."

"What do you mean, Wingfield? Do you intend to maroon me on an island? I was once imprisoned by the Muslim Turks, but I escaped. If you cast me ashore somewhere, I will find you, and when I do, you will live to *regret* it."

"Oh, I am so frightened," Wingfield feigned. "Smith, I know you are famous for being wily and dangerous. That's why my cousin,*

Gosnold, asked you to come on this voyage. And, yes, I've seen your coat of arms with the heads of three Turks* you killed in hand-to-hand combat.* To be honest, I do admire your swordsmanship. I understand the Turkish army surrendered that fortress after you bested their three champions in duels.* So, are you going to lop off my head like you did those Turks? I don't think so, Captain Smith. I do think that the days of the Great Braggart of England are soon to be over."

Smith got right in Wingfield's face. "Look, your holy highness, I signed on to help establish a colony for the Crown. I know it's about money and power. It always is. The problem is you. I just can't stomach hypocrisy. I never could.

"It's why I left England years ago. I love God, but religion is rubbish in England. All form and no substance. When my mother died, all the parson wanted was money for the service. Money runs the church and the government. All that babbling by Parliament about saving the world by planting colonies like the Spanish and Portuguese—it was all bloody rubbish.

"England just wants to be rich like the Spaniards and Portuguese. We want gold, silver, land, power, and fame just like they do.* In fact, I happen to know that the Spanish have already tried to claim the same area we are headed to.* They sent priests to pave the way for their soldiers to follow later.* But, thankfully for us, the natives killed all the priests.* Newport himself heard that from a Spanish sailor he captured some years ago.

"Look, Wingfield, one last time: just tell the men the truth and stop using religion to cover your real motives. This colony is about money. If you say otherwise, you are a fraud, just like all those fat-ass whiners in Parliament."

Scion winced. He knew Smith was speaking a lot of truth. *O God, let this colony be different. Let this Christian colony turn from the love of money, and instead, have your motives to found the colony.*

Wingfield sneered at Smith with raw contempt. Then, he motioned to a nearby soldier as he glared at his pugnacious opponent. "Smith, you may understand war, but you underestimate me. I did not get elected to the English Parliament by putting up with the likes of you. You, sir, are just a mercenary*—a sword for hire. You are going to the brig. Maybe a few weeks on bread and water will soften your tongue. At the least, the men won't have to listen to your mutinous slander anymore.

"Guard—*take him away* and lock him up in the brig until further orders from me."*

CHAPTER 21

March 27, 1607

As a brilliant dawn broke over the Caribbean, Captain Christopher Newport turned to his right-hand man, Edward Wingfield, on the bridge of the *Susan Constant.* "Well, there it is. *Oualie*—the Land of Beautiful Waters*—as the natives call it. I can feel the warm island breezes already. Good God, I think we are *all* ready to go ashore for some relief after three months at sea."*

Scion and Angie were circling above the three ships, feeling good about the successful crossing of the Atlantic. "One more month, and they will be there," Angie exclaimed with excitement. "I can hardly wait. Soon Captain Smith will be set free from that awful brig. I feel so sorry for him."

Scion nodded. "When we get there, let's you and I do a small Seraphim Starburst ourselves—only *cloaked.* We can't afford to draw any more attention than we already will. The demons know we are coming—that's obvious from the issue with the winds in the channel. They just know *when.* I am so tired of just hovering over these ships. And I thought being Headmaster of Angel Academy for thousands of years was tedious," Scion laughed.

Angie cheered,"Starburst! *Whoopee!"*

~

"I RECALL THAT COLUMBUS NAMED IT SAN MARTIN,* CORRECT?" Wingfield commented to Newport.

"Correct. But we British sailors like to call it *'Dulcina,'* Sweet Island.* The water there will take your breath away, and the fruit will melt in your mouth. We have to be careful, or the men may never want to leave it." Newport grinned as he sipped hot tea from a large mug shaped like a boot.

"Well, I suggest we allow one man to do just that, Captain—stay *here."*

Scion drew in his breath. Angie cringed.

"Good Lord, Wingfield! What can you mean? If we left one here, they *all* would want to stay. This is paradise compared to England and perhaps to where we are going. You *can't* be serious."

"I'm dead serious, Captain. In fact, I want John Smith to be left here to die—*or* to be hanged! That infernal loud-mouth is a threat to the success of our colony. He is rabble-rouser among among the crew—and he has attacked my character and that of the Virginia Company. The man is a mercenary, for God's sake. All he knows is self-preservation and domination of anyone who gets in his way—including *us.* He wants the gold and the glory, and he will try to destroy our reputations to get it. He *has* to go!"

"But Sir Edward, isn't forty-five days in the brig on bread and water *enough* punishment? Have you seen the brig—or should I say, have you *smelled* it? A pig could not live under those conditions. The man has suffered. I hear he's been seriously ill for two weeks. Why do more than that?" But Wingfield's angry face did not even flinch.

Newport shook his head slowly. He knew he could not easily oppose the most powerful man in the Virginia Company and a former member of Parliament.

"If Smith stays alive and ruins this colony, I will hold you personally responsible," Wingfield shouted. "Are you prepared to pay the investors the thousands of pounds we will lose if Smith continues to divide the men against us?"

Then, he lowered his voice and looked at the captain with an evil smile, "You know, Newport, you are right. It would not be wise to leave him here. Others would be jealous. *Hang him,* I say!"

The tall sea captain lowered his head in defeat. He knew the Company would crucify anyone who got in the way of their profits.

"*All right.* You can hang him. We'll charge him with incitement to mutiny. We will land on the beach today and replenish our water and food supplies. You can string him up before we set sail again on March 29," Newport concluded with a hangdog look.

"You are a most reasonable man, Captain Newport. I shall personally see that the Company knows of your great cooperation in this matter. I'm sure they will reward you handsomely for protecting their investments."

"How can you be so *selfish* and *stupid?*" Angie shouted in frustration just above the heads of the two men who could not hear her. Scion grimaced as his own anxious thoughts swirled in his head.

Smith had not tried to lead a mutiny. He'd spoken to no one about his anger except Wingfield. He just wanted to blow off steam. We haven't even arrived at Virginia, and already one leader has conspired to unjustly kill another. If that behavior continues, this colony will never get God's complete protection and blessing. O God! Please don't let this colony— or me— fail!

As Scion fretted about this, months of boredom and stress finally got to him. He had to get away to clear his head. "I'll be back," he shouted to Angie as he shot into the stratosphere.

As he leveled off in the frigid air at fifty-five thousand feet, it suddenly came to him. *Hunt! Of course! Chaplain Hunt could still save the day. Wingfield is probably going to choose the crew members today who will hang Smith tomorrow. I will speak to one of them in a dream tonight to alert Hunt about this plot. The Chaplain will know what to do.*

CHAPTER 22

March 28, 1607

"May I speak to you, Master Wingfield?"

"Of course, Chaplain Hunt. Come in. You are always welcome."

Wingfield smiled. He admired the spirit of this forty-year-old short, slender man who was always neatly dressed in black. Hunt's lively grey eyes, bushy brown eyebrows and wide, boyish grin always made others feel at ease.

"Sir, it is about Smith. I hear that you have convinced Captain Newport to build a scaffold on the shore. One of the crew told me about it. You plan to hang Captain Smith tonight. Is that true?"

Scion and Angie both smiled. "Angie, I love planting thoughts in the minds of good people. That crewman was easy to influence. He has a very tender relationship with Jesus. God loves to use people like that to do great things—like what is about to happen."

Wingfield winced with fear. He knew Hunt had close friends at the court of King James. "As a matter of fact, yes. I wasn't going to tell you. I know how fond you have become of our little mutineer when you nursed him back to health while he was in the brig. I can't say I enjoyed seeing him survive by your hand, but I admire your motives, in any case. You may be the only Christian aboard who actually lives what you say you believe. You have earned my respect, Chaplain Hunt."

"If I have, sir, may I appeal to your noble character to spare Smith's life? It is my certain opinion that God has put Captain Smith on this journey for a purpose we have yet to know. I sense he has a destiny with us, despite his odd and often vexing ways. I think we dare not ignore what God may yet do with Smith, to our great benefit."

"To *hell* with his destiny, if you will excuse my phrase! The man is a menace. He only knows what is good for him and will take it by force if he must. *No,* he must die. There is no other way, I'm afraid."

"Well, since you will not consider my appeal, my esteemed friend, I will have to report this decision to my superiors in the church when I next communicate with them."

"You *wouldn't*!" Wingfield gasped. "Those small-minded clerics would crucify me. They have no idea of what mutiny is all about. Did you know I have already been accused of being an *atheist** by some obnoxious scallywags on this ship because I do not have a Bible with me?* How can I help it that it got lost when we loaded this ship? *Please!* Don't let this obnoxious mercenary ruin my reputation. He *has* to go! For the *Lord's* sake, Chaplain Hunt, be reasonable!"

"I am, sir. Smith is an Englishman and an Anglican. He deserves a full trial before he is condemned to death. There has been no trial, not even any calling of witnesses. This is not how we should begin England's first colony. This is not how civilized Anglicans should act. How can I ignore this when the blessing of God may depend on how we deal with Smith? He is our brother, and he has confided to me his sincere intentions to make the colony a success. He just has a rather sharp view of ruling nobles like yourself, and his tongue is even sharper, as we all know. But this is not the stuff of mutiny, and you know it. Hanging him would disgrace all of us, and it might bring God's judgment on the colony."

Wingfield stared at the deck for a long time, his face taut, his jaw muscles bulging. Finally, with fire in his eyes, he looked at Hunt, "All *right*, then, Chaplain. Have it your way. Smith will live . . . for now. But if he even looks the wrong way at me again, I'll have him shot. I cannot tolerate insubordination!"

Beaming with relief, Chaplain Hunt shook Wingfield's hand. "Lord Wingfield, I never have been prouder of you. I know how difficult this has been for you and how much you want to see this colony succeed. Even at fifty-six, you came on the voyage. You have my respect, sir. I know you will never regret this decision. God will surely bless you for showing such sagacity and mercy."

"Enough flowery talk, Chaplain. I'll see you on deck in the morning. We sail at first light."

LATER, ON THE DECK OF THE SHIP—

"O, Captain Newport—may I have a word?"

"Of course, Chaplain. How can I help you?"

"Master Wingfield has just graciously agreed not to have Smith hanged on this island. May I use the wood you set aside for the scaffolding as an altar? I want to celebrate the Lord's supper with the men tonight."

Newport looked stunned. He could not speak for a moment—and then the old, rough-faced sea captain broke into a toothy smile.

"Parson Hunt, I'll be keel-hauled and drink a bucket of bilge water if you are not the truest Christian I have ever met. You actually got Wingfield to change his mind! Thank God Almighty! You and I may not always see eye-to-eye, but no one has my respect more than you.

Yes, *of course.* Hold the service as requested. Just don't invite Smith. Wingfield might…,well, you know," Newport grimaced.

"Aye, Captain. As you wish," Hunt shot back with a warm smile

Rev. Hunt celebrates the Lord's Supper with the settlers

And so it happened. The first Protestant service honoring the death of Jesus for condemned sinners was held that night under a glistening sea of stars and on the planks of a would-be scaffold. Angie and Scion stand silently nearby—in awe of the symbolism the Lord had provided in the Land of Beautiful Waters.

CHAPTER 23

*April 26, 1607**

After four months of thrashing through the thick waves of the stormy Atlantic, the three sea-battered ships dropped anchor. They bobbed in the water a few hundred yards off a glistening white beach in a new, mysterious world at the mouth of what the local natives called *Chesepioc**—The Great Shellfish Bay*—that dominates the southeastern shores of Virginia. Rising sharply above the foamy, surf-soaked beach, fifty-foot sand dunes topped with short scrub pines and heavy brush gleamed in the morning sun. To the 143 weary, homesick British men, the creamy-white dunes looked like dwarf versions of England's white chalk cliffs of Dover that they had seen so much of when they were stuck in the "Downes" for six weeks.

"We made it. Land at last! Virginia!" the sailors shouted to each other.

Scion and Angie shot skyward, shouting praises to God in a Seraphim Starburst vortex! But Okeus and his army of demons on the shoreline didn't notice the two angels shoot heavenward.

Every evil eye was glued on the invading followers of the Lamb, the two six-foot angels assigned to help Reverend Hunt, and a small flock of English demons belching forth from the belly of the ships. Several of the immigrant demons squawked loudly and waved at their New World counterparts, relieved to finally be off the small vessels.

From just above the glistening beach, Okeus smiled wickedly as he thought about the cheering men below. *Poor human scum. If only you could hear the curses and jeers of my demons circling right over your heads now. Your cheers will soon be be tears.*

Floating next to him, Snookus managed a courtesy smile, but inside, he was shaken. Despite the momentary amusement, Snookus knew that the war for the colony was about to begin—and he would be the whipping boy for Okeus if things did not go well in the war.

But as Scion descended and flew into view of Okeus, the giant dinosaur froze in shock. No one had told him that *Scion* was sent to protect the colony. He had not seen Scion's face in over ten millennia. *I wonder who he thinks I am? I hope I can defeat him without revealing my identity. It will be easier that way,* Okeus thought nervously.

From a distance, Scion saw the giant reptile staring at him, and he returned his gaze. *Who are you, Okeus? Do you remember me? Were we in the choir together? How many of my friends did you kill in the Rebellion? Somehow, I will find out now that I am finally on Earth—no matter what it costs. You are going to tell me what I need to know!* Scion vowed silently.

As the two big angels warily eyed each other, Angie flew back to the ships from their starburst high above the beach. She had an impish grin from ear to ear as she twirled exuberantly in front of Scion like a spinning top. "Wow, Scion, it's so cool to finally be here and fly with you like that! I can't wait to tell my sister Betas all about this!"

Scion looked at her with a firmly. "Not now. Okeus is here."

Angie followed his gaze and saw the enormous dinosaur spirit staring at him. She sucked in her breath.

"He is sizing us up for the kill, Angie. He knows these Christians are about to plant a colony that will greatly threaten his rule here. That's why there are thousands of demons circling us. The clash of heaven and hell is about to begin for this colony—and for the nation God wants to birth here."

Like birds being released from a cage, thirty bearded men whooped and hollered as they splashed ashore to check out the land. Some of the younger men jumped overboard and swam ashore. Most got into small boats and chanted over and over, "We made it! We made it!" like giddy schoolchildren on the last day of school. One hundred forty-four days on cramped, foul-smelling ships with sick and angry people was more than they had bargained for.

In his iron-barred brig, John Smith peered out a tiny porthole and saw land. "*Damn* these chains!" Smith shouted. "Somebody let me out! Tell Wingfield that I am no threat now. I never was. We're *here* now. Just get me out and let me help. For God's sake, let me out now!" he shouted.

Two decks above, Reverend Hunt heard Smith's cries and prayed, "Father, you are close to the brokenhearted; please be with John Smith now. Please set him free, not just from the brig but also from those things that torment his soul. He's a good man. He just needs your Fatherly love."

AT THE SUGGESTION OF OKEUS, SNOOKUS FLEW DOWN TO INSPECT the *Susan Constant* more closely. He looked at Smith with disgust. He and Okeus had heard about Smith's military exploits against Muslim Turks from London's Dark Angel, Lord Pict— an old friend who had sung tenor with Okeus in a heavenly choir. Snookus spurted back to his master and reported Smith's presence.

Okeus sneered and farted. "He's no problem. We can use him for our purposes. His insecurities and pride have served Our Master Lucifer before. They shall again."

Then Okeus launched his first attack. "I'm going to give the invaders a reality check," he bragged.

As soon as the men stepped ashore from their small boats, native arrows flew at the English landing party, leaving a few men wounded on the shoreline.*

Snookus let out a war-whoop of triumph and waved his five fat tentacles above his bulbous head as his demons prodded the natives to fight.

It was over quickly. The warriors felt relieved. They knew it was foolish to attack the whites with so few warriors. "What if they had used their loud fire-sticks like the Spanish did many moons ago? Thanks be to Okeus that they did not stay to fight."

Scores of large, deep green warrior demons descended upon the retreating men in the boats, red fangs bared. The largest demon was yelling orders. "Sting them with fear, anger, and confusion! Get that oarsman. I'll take the wounded one. He's easy." Okeus watched with growing satisfaction.

Sliding up to the big dinosaur, Snookus cooed, "Master Okeus, you will be pleased. The English are already seething with anger against the natives."

"Well done, Snookus. Your job will be easy as long as you keep them full of resentment, unforgiveness and hatred. Those sins are powerful weapons for us."

"Yes, Master. Of course. It is always my pleasure to serve you," Snookus cooed.

"Oh, get out of here, you sniveling sycophant!" Okeus blustered with a slap of his spiked tail against Snookus—followed by a sneering laugh and a loud, parting fart.

CHAPTER 24

Back on their ships, the exhausted advance party was frustrated and furious. Their nerves were already raw from months of living in cramped, dark spaces hammered by the incessant pounding of cold waves. Now they had been attacked by people they never saw. Many cursed. A few wept. Most were just silent and bone-tired.

To calm the men, Captain Newport called for the scouts to come aboard his flagship. Within thirty minutes, all the men had rowed over to the *Susan Constant*. But before the captain could begin, a short, swarthy man called Jehu Robinson from the Discovery spoke up, "By the God of heaven, give me a musket and I'll go ashore and teach those savages who is boss. I'll hang their filthy carcasses from the yardarm by sundown, or my name isn't Jehu Robinson." Yelling down into the hold where the brig was, Jehu shouted, "These animals only understand force. Right, Captain Smith?" Smith banged on his door in agreement.

Scion and Angie looked at each other. Something had to be done. Scion quickly flew into the angry mob to whisper to one man—a man in black.

Okeus was also near the side of the ship. He heard what Scion whispered to the Chaplain and shot Scion a hateful look, but one also laced with fear. *Can he see through my disguise? Will my voice give me away when I talk?*

Scion saw the look but pretended not to notice as he silently fussed, *Fat boy, if I had time now, I would love to deal with you personally. We will "parlez" later, as the French say. But not now!* Meanwhile, Angie recorded the scene from the roof of the captain's cabin.

From the back of the cursing, churning mob, a man with a black topcoat stepped to the front to address the captain. The crowd quickly settled down. Most took off their hats in respect. Then Chaplain Hunt spoke softly.

"Captain Newport, your men are sorely tired and are greatly perplexed at the turn of today's events. If we are to accomplish King James I's intentions in our royal charter, we must go ashore as Christians *first* and as soldiers and settlers second. Could we not take three days to rest and seek the Lord's help before we begin so great a task for God and King?"

Newport, sensing the silent approval of his harried men, quickly responded, "Good Chaplain Hunt, as usual, you seem to have the mind of the Lord— *and* of the men. I agree. We'll have three days to rest, just like Jonah in the whale's belly, before we go ashore again. We'll order extra rations for all, to include *double* grog at night."

A cheer erupted from the men.

Hunt smiled. "Ah, my dear Captain Newport, your leadership now betrays the reason your men and your king admire you so. But may I also suggest that to seek the *greatest* help from our God, we set aside each noon meal for a voluntary fast to seek God, repent from all sin, and pray for the grand adventure onto which we are now to embark. We must all *repent*, especially from any anger in our hearts, and to be reconciled to one another."

The men shuffled their feet and whispered. They did not look happy. Okeus snapped his attention to Snookus sitting on the yardarm and shouted, "*Do* something, you idiot. They are about to repent."

Snookus looked terrified. He knew that once a person decided to repent, stopping them was one of the hardest things for any demon to do. His mind raced. *And now, they have a man of the Lamb instructing them! O, Great Lucifer. What can I do? Okeus will beat me unconscious if I fail.*

Then, turning to the men, Hunt went on, "You men are destined to change the course of human history by what you do on these shores. Surely, God has more grace for us in this great endeavor if we earnestly seek him for such help."

Scion and Angie grinned. Okeus gulped. *That little slug is a real Christian. I'll have to make short work of him, or else hell's to pay.*

There was a long silence as the men pondered Hunt's words. Finally, a sailor said, "Parson Hunt is right. These savages are wily and dangerous. We must have the power of God if we will win. I say that we do the fast for God and king."

The men shouted, "For God and king!"

Okeus almost fell off the ship's railing when he heard the men cheering for a time of repentance. *I am going to kill that little man in black if I have to do it myself. If this prayer and repentance crap keeps up, we will lose this colony, and Lucifer will make me pay a price I do not want to pay.*

And where is that blubbering idiot Snookus? He's no help. I might as well have sent Morph to stop this. We've lost this battle—but I have just begun to fight. I will ambush them when they seek a place to start the colony. Then they will begin to feel the power of my foot on their souls.

As the men shouted their agreement to fast and repent, Newport grinned at Reverend Hunt. He had never seen a ship's crew and passengers agree to such a proposal before. *Surely God is with us for such a thing to happen,* he thought.

Hunt smiled and nodded his head. "Captain, what the enemy has meant for evil, God meant for good . . . *again*!"

"Three days, gentlemen, and then we'll get out of this "whale" and go ashore!" Newport declared.

Cheers again, only much louder. The sound frightened natives for miles around. But if they could have been heard, the victory shouts of Scion and Angie were even louder—especially those *from Angie*. The twelve guardian angels on the ships laughed and put their hands over their ears.

As the cries of joy died down aboard the ships, Scion and Angie did another Seraphim Starburst—only this time at just fifty feet above the water. At a speed that made even the guardian angels dizzy, the pair looped the ships seven times, spinning their bodies lengthwise at three revolutions per second. Some demons followed them, but they were quickly out-lapped by the angelic duo who playfully bumped their pursuers into a heap of squawking bodies.

At that sight of that demon doggy-pile, Angie and Scion threw their heads back in laughter. They felt the pleasure of God all around them that night—and it was *so* good.

Meanwhile, on the *Susan Constant,* Newport shook his head in disbelief. "Reverend Hunt, you amaze me. I can see why Reverend Hakluyt,* your dear friend at the king's court, put so much trust in you. You really are God's man for this adventure."

"Thank you, Captain. I certainly sense God's grace on me for this colony. In my heart, I know we are all doing more and better than we should because God is with us. And since the Lord is being so kind to us, may I also ask for more kindness for our Captain Smith? Could we not give him some time on deck to see this new land and enjoy some fellowship with God and man again?"

Newport gritted his teeth. *This holy man is relentless,* he thought. "Of course, Chaplain. I'll deal with Wingfield if he objects. See you at evening prayers."

That night, after a nourishing dinner and prayers, Newport and Hunt sat in the captain's cabin. After sharing some pleasantries, Newport unlocked the strongbox with the sealed orders from the Virginia Company and handed them to his Chaplain who quickly scanned the document. "Great God in heaven!" Hunt murmured.

With wide eyes, Chaplain Hunt read the names of the seven-man Council: Captain Christopher Newport, Edward Maria Wingfield, Captain Bartholomew Gosnold, Captain John Ratcliffe, Captain John Martin, Captain George Kendall, *and* Captain John Smith.

"Captain, thank God you spared Smith's life in the islands. Apparently, we are all going to hear a lot more from this mercenary soldier. Wingfield will be furious, of course, but he will yield to the Company's wishes. Once we find a place to plant the colony, he will have to release Smith from the brig for good."

Then, looking intently at Newport, Hunt asked, "What do you think it means, Captain, when one of our principal leaders comes here in chains? The Bible says that 'a house divided cannot stand.'"

"Only God knows," Newport said. "Thank God we are already praying, but I fear it will take more than prayer to see this colony through to success. This house is already badly divided. Only God can save us, to be sure."

"To be sure, Captain! We are not off to an auspicious beginning. And yet, in my heart, I sense God's powerful purposes and presence in what we are doing. Remember Israel? God founded Israel to bring forth the Messiah, who saved the world. But God used an unruly group of stiff-necked, rebellious Jews to begin that nation. Most of them were so hard-headed that God wanted to execute them in the desert on the way to the Promised Land—but God changed his mind when Moses intervened. Smith can't be much worse than those stiff-necked Jews. When God decides to do something, he will use *anyone,* even a donkey, to do his bidding. Remember Balaam!"

They both shared a hearty laugh. "Is God really that good, Chaplain?"

"More than we could ever imagine or deserve— or even understand. The goodness of God defies mortal minds to comprehend. The Virginia Colony will live and see the mercies of God—not only *because* of us, but perhaps also *in spite of* us. God will do it for *his* glory. As I have prayed on the voyage here, God has convinced me that this colony is destined for great things— but they will not happen easily."

"I like your spirit, Hunt. You remind me of my mother. Her faith in God was the anchor our family clung to in the storms of my childhood. We had no one else. My father was a drunk.

So, I guess I'll agree with you in this: God is doing a great work through us all—and perhaps even through someone like Smith. Your words and your actions seem to make that more real to me. Thank you, Chaplain Hunt—and good night."

CHAPTER 25

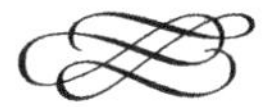

*April 29, 1607**

Three days later, purified by prayer and fasting, a dozen men in small boats rowed ashore far from where they had been attacked on April 26th.* Captain John Smith had finally been released from his chains to watch from the deck of the ship.

Captain Newport and Edward Wingfield decided to call the place Cape Henry*, named after King James's son, the Prince of Wales.* Four of the dozen men carried a large wooden cross* that they made from a spare mast.* Wearing the robe of an Anglican bishop in a representative fashion, Reverend Hunt led the men up the sandy dunes to plant the cross as they dedicated the land to God and his Kingdom.*

As the party climbed the high dunes with the cross, Okeus glared and sulked while he watched from high above his Great Bay about a mile to the north. Scion and Angie circled above the dunes. They could not stop smiling. Scion could not remember when he had felt so happy. With her hyper-sensitive ears, Angie thought she heard deep, beautiful laughter. It sounded like *Jesus*—but she couldn't be sure at that distance from heaven.

As the last man reached the top of the dune, the fourteen angels who came on the ships joined Scion and Angie to form a royal honor guard just above the cross. Meanwhile, hundreds of demons hid in the scrub pines five miles south, waiting for the command from Okeus to strike—but *none* came. The scene was too holy—and Okeus knew it.

Today, there were no spiritual weak points in the settlers or crew for an attack. They each had repented of all their known sins and forgiven each other—*and* the natives who had ambushed them. Every man's heart was right with God and with each other—or, in the case of Smith and Wingfield—*almost* right with each other.

Finally, under the glare of a cloudless, azure sky, with seagulls swirling overhead and with a dozen heads bowed around him, Reverend Hunt prayed. "Almighty God, we thank you for sending us safely to this New World. We come now to dedicate this land we now call Virginia to Jesus Christ, your Son, and our Savior."

Taking out his well-worn Anglican 1559 Book of Common Prayer,* Reverend Hunt read the scriptures for Morning Prayer for April 29: Psalm 29, II Kings 11, and Acts 26.*

"Lord God, you spoke to your servant, Reverend Richard Hakluyt, and gave him the vision for this colony, a vision now described in one of today's readings from Acts 26:17–18:

> To open their eyes so that they may turn from darkness to light and from the dominion of Satan to God, that they may receive forgiveness of sins and an inheritance among those who have been sanctified by faith in me.

Hunt suddenly felt the Presence of the Author whose book he was reading. Choking with emotion, he raised his trembling hands to heaven and prayed, "From these shores, the Gospel shall go forth to not only this New World— but also to the entire world.

"Father, we pray the only prayer that Jesus ever asked his followers to pray for others: that you would send workers into your harvest all over the world. As Jesus said in Matthew 9:37–38, 'The harvest is plentiful but the workers are few. Ask the Lord of the harvest, therefore, to send out workers into his harvest field.'"

The air was suddenly unusually still. The gulls still glided silently in a tight arc above the motionless clump of men around the tall, weather-beaten cross. The surf behind them continued to pound out the same rhythmic beat on the soggy sand. It seemed that nothing had changed. But Okeus felt a subtle shift in the spiritual atmosphere. One that he had felt before—and hated.

Snookus threw his five tentacles over his head and cowered when he heard his moody master begin to groan as if he was in deep pain.

High above the Earth, where men cannot see or hear, all heaven broke out in thunderous applause as the Son of God stood up and shouted a victory shout that reverberated throughout the heavens and shook the gates of hell.

"*Victory for Jesus!*" the heavenly hosts sang at the top of their lungs.

"*Victory for the Lamb*!" the 24 elders shouted as they fell before him.

"*Victory for his Kingdom*!" the cloud of witnesses repeated.

The air was electric with the Presence of God. The honor guard of angels came to attention. Scion and Angie just stood above the cross, weeping for joy and silently glorifying God.

Suddenly, Hunt spoke. "My brothers, I am amazed, but God has just spoken to me! I sense he is saying that this is a day of conception. The seed of the Reformation Gospel has now been planted in the New World. Out of this colony, God will one day birth a new nation to complete the Great Commission of Jesus in Matthew 28:18–20 to make disciples of all the world. Men, God says this land is a *womb*—and it is now pregnant with the Kingdom of God!"

Hunt threw his hands into the air and shouted, "*Hallelujah! Hallelujah!*"

The men cheered.

Okeus groaned—*louder*.

Demons trembled. Some evil spirits shook so violently, they dropped their swords. Others began to slink away in fear.

But a deep peace enveloped Hunt and his small entourage as they slowly descended to the beach. They all knew something wonderful had just happened.

But in the invisible world, war had begun for that land. Okeus and Scion both knew it.

Moving quickly, Scion alighted on the top of the cross, looked to the heavens, raised his mighty sword over his head, and shouted, "For the Lamb and for those for whom he died!" As he shouted, bursts of invisible, heavenly rainbow light cascaded across Chesapeake Bay, washing up all the way to the bluish mountains two hundred miles inland.

Not to be outdone, Okeus leaped high above the mouth of his Great Bay and roared, "Blood, death, and victory—for the Dragon!" In response to the Principality of the Bay's war cry, jagged red bolts of light shot up from one of his portals on the beach just south of the cross.

For a moment, Scion expected an attack. But then, he realized the hellish red beams were coming from the divination portal. The War Portal—wherever it was—remained quiet. But every spirit there knew their lives would soon be far from quiet.

The battle for Virginia had begun.

CHAPTER 26

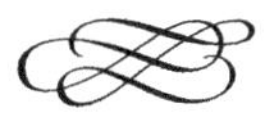

*May 13, 1607**

Captain John Smith's 1612 Map of Virginia's Chesapeake Region*

After planting the cross on April 29th, the three English ships turned northwest on April 30th into the mouth of the great bay that the Spanish called Bahia de Santa Maria.* Spanish explorers had come there fifty years earlier, looking for a northwest sea passage to India. Every nation in Europe ferociously coveted a new sea route to the Far East after 1543 when Muslim armies conquered the Christian city of Constantinople.* From that strategic position between Europe and Asia, Muslims controlled the land and sea routes to vast commercial wealth that came from selling spices like cinnamon, cassia, cardamom, ginger, pepper, and turmeric from Asia. Spain sent Christopher Columbus to find an alternate westward route to that wealth in 1492.* England quickly followed suit, sending John Cabot in 1497.*

Finding such a route was also assigned to the 1607 Virginia Colony by the Virginia Company.* Their second mission was to find gold.* The colony's third mission was to discover what happened to the Roanoke "Lost Colony" of 1587 that had disappeared without a trace.*

But every colonist knew that this Virginia settlement was really about England's fierce battle with Spain for control of the New World and its vast riches. Spain had become rich with gold from the central and south of the Americas.* The English Crown and the ships' English investors wanted their share of New World wealth.* To claim the entire east coast of North America, they had to plant a colony there before the Spanish did. And so, in 1606, wealthy English businessmen paid all the expenses for the three ships and the 105 men they sent to Virginia. Every colonist knew that they were required to make a handsome profit for the businessmen who had financed their voyage and the colony.

With all of that in mind, Captain Newport began to explore suitable locations around the bay to establish the settlement. The Virginia Company had instructed him to settle far up a river away from the bay to escape notice by Spanish ships that might pass by.* The orders also stated that the location should be easy to defend against possible Spanish attacks.* After two full weeks of searching for a suitable spot, Newport tacked his three ships northward into a large river that emptied in the bay.*

Sitting on the prow of the *Susan Constant* that day, Angie was recording everything that was happening as the ship sailed up the river. She was alone. Scion had decided not to show himself yet to eliminate any unnecessary agitation of local demons who would not appreciate the presence of a huge warrior angel. He would follow the ships from fifty feet below the river bed.

That was fine with Angie. She had more time to admire the muscular, young men who came to Virginia. She fixed her gaze on one handsome man in particular named Jack. He was not like the others. Jack was always singing as he worked. Today, the lad's bright red hair flopped across his bare back as he heaved heavy grain barrels across the deck. When he occasionally looked up with soulful, brown eyes and a bright smile, Angie felt a little dizzy. *Now, if I were a human, that man would certainly be someone whose attentions I would encourage. Why do humans have mates but not angels? I'll have to ask Michael that one day. Doesn't seem fair,* she pouted.

Suddenly, Captain Newport noticed a half-submerged island protruding into the river channel.

Snookus looked down from the line of pine trees on the hill above the island. He had been waiting for the ships to arrive. He slapped a small, furry demon next to him with one of his tentacles and yelled, "Get down there, Morph, and foul the rudder on the flagship with some driftwood! The *Susan Constant* must not pass. Lord Okeus has decided that the ships must land here."

Angie heard Snookus bark a command to a demon to halt the ship. Instantly, she scanned the river to intercept the demon.

Stung with wounded pride, Morph finally got up and slowly flew toward the ship's stern, fuming silently. *Someday, that bastard Snookus will get what he deserves.*

As Angie saw a feline-looking evil spirit head toward the rear of the ship, she quickly deduced that he was the one assigned to stop the ship. At her size, she knew she could not stop him. But hoping to distract him, she flew right in front of the evil spirit as he dove into the water.

But Morph batted her away with a swipe of his powerful right claw. "Get out of here, whatever you are. You're not going to stop me!"

Angie had expected that, but as the demon dove deeper into the river to find driftwood, she thought she saw a faint light in the dark water where the demon had gone. *How odd. Now, what in the world could that be?* she wondered. She decided to find out.

Angie plunged into the murky, silt-filled water of the river bottom. As she turned to look over her shoulder, a yellow, rope-like arm with grabbed her neck and threw her to the surface so hard that she penetrated the ship's hull and landed in a dark bilge area, dazed but unhurt. Snookus had secretly followed Morph to the river bottom to make sure the job was done right. Snookus knew Okeus would make him pay dearly if it wasn't.

When Angie regained her senses, she squealed, "Oh, no! She had accidentally uncloaked, and the bilge was filled with brilliant, rainbow-colored light. Instantly, fifty rats that had been feeding on decaying grain ran for cover.

A drunken settler who had been half-asleep in the darkness awoke with a start, "*Fairies* . . . I see fairies. Oh, on me mum's grave—they are real," he gasped and hiccupped. Angie blushed and quickly re-cloaked, hoping Scion did not notice.

From his perch in the tall pine tree on the west bank of the river, Okeus watched his circling horde of level-five, assassin demons above the river—awaiting his command as the three ships crept closer to a spot Okeus had chosen months ago. *This is it, he thought. This island is the place where I will destroy them . . . from the inside out.*

CHAPTER 27

But there was something on the lead ship Okeus definitely did *not* like.

As the ship sailed closer to his position, Okeus felt a shaking in the web of dark energy he lived in. He could sense the presence of a few angels, but this was different. This—whatever it was—made the thick green scales on his humped back bulge with fear. *Where is that coming from?* he snorted anxiously.

Then he saw him. A short man dressed in black, standing on the deck near the stern, hands clasped together and eyes closed. He was *praying*.

"Father, God almighty, guide our good captain to the right place to plant this colony. We need a fair land blessed with freshwater, good soil, and a place where we can defend ourselves from the Spanish should they come nigh to harm us. Gracious heavenly Father, lead us to our promised land as you did your beloved people, the Israelites, long ago."

"*Idiots!*" Okeus screamed at his demons all around him. "Why was I not warned! Planting the enemy's cross is bad enough. But Great

Lucifer—that Anglican pastor is a *man of prayer*! If he keeps that up, he will draw more of the Kingdom of Heaven here."

Sensing the demon-numbing weight of God's glory radiating from the ship, Okeus blared to his demons, "Take him out! Shut him down. Stop that infernal praying! His prayers must not strengthen the captain's mind to move away from this place I have chosen for them."

Five of Okeus's giant demons bolted into action. Two of the largest ones tackled Hunt's two angels who were standing behind him. All four spirits fell into the river in a fierce wrestling match. With the angels gone, a spirit of confusion landed on Hunt's back and drove sharp claws deep into his brain. Another demon flew in front of Hunt's closed eyes and spewed a dark, red cloud of paralyzing breath right into his face. Then he put his sticky reptile mouth close to Hunt's left ear and chanted over and over, "*It's too late*. Newport will not find the right place. No need to pray. No need to pray. It's too late."

Hunt reeled with dizziness and almost fell over. Newport saw him stagger. "Hunt, are you okay?" Then Newport shouted, "You men, take the chaplain below and see that he gets some water and rest."

Okeus also saw Hunt's distress. "The wall of prayer is down! Time to strike!" Okeus roared.

Before the sailors could move Hunt, a hideous war cry filled the air! A demonic feeding frenzy erupted as hundreds of ferocious, bare-fanged evil spirits fell upon every human on the ships. The twelve, unarmed guardian angels were no match for the huge onslaught. They fled for safety.

Suddenly, fights between the settlers broke out everywhere. Tempers flared. Curses filled the air. Others dropped to the deck with sudden stomach or head pains. All three ships exploded in a cacophony of curses, yells, and agonized cries. Hell had come to earth.

Just then, Angie swung over the ships. "Boss, get up here. The ships are under attack and no one is praying! Even Hunt's prayer shield is down. The demons are trying to stop the ship here. It's *a trap*."

"Angie, I can't show myself yet. Do what you can until I figure something out."

"Aghhh! No prayer!" Angie cried. "When will humans learn? They have to pray— and not give up if they really want to do God's will. But enough pouting. I think I will do something Beta's are not supposed to be good at—use a *sword*!"

Then the tiny angel dove into the demonic fray, singing to the Lord and swinging her mini-sword at every demon she could reach. Her tiny body moved moved so swiftly, it looked like a momentary blur. Demon eyes could not focus well on something that small, at that speed.

Within a few seconds, dozens of thick-necked, yellow-eyed spirits froze with confusion. Their attacks on humans also stopped. *Where was that painful, angelic singing coming from? And what are that tiny pricks in my neck as the awful sound spun by them?* they all wondered.

The invisible singing-stinging combination was like nothing they had ever experienced. For a full sixty seconds, the demons could only grunt and curse, swiveling their scaly green necks in vain to see the source of this heavenly distraction.

Just then, the *Susan Constant* suddenly lurched to starboard toward the eastern bank of the river. Every angelic, demonic and human eye turned to watch the shoreline suddenly draw closer to the ship. Beneath the ship, Morph had entangled the rudder with a large tree branch he'd drug up from the muddy bottom, pointing the ship toward the shore. The wind would do the rest. Angie just stared in disbelief.

"Captain, the rudder's afoul. I need to pull into shore to clear it," the ship's helmsman shouted.

At that remark, maniacal laughter erupted from hundreds of demons. A deep, grunting "*ha, ha, ha*" came from Okeus as he called his horde back from the trio of ships.

Scion secretly popped up out of the riverbed where he could not be seen and quickly scanned the eastern river bank where the ship was headed. He winced. *I was afraid of this. This island is toxic to humans. It's too low and swampy to be healthy.* And look at all the mosquitos.*

Then Scion scooped up a handful of water from a stream on the island and tasted it just as Angie alighted next to him. "It's *awful*, Angie. The water's got salt in it. This is tidal water from the bay.* It will never be drinkable.* We have to keep them from settling here at all costs, Angie!"

Jamestown Island

Captain Newport didn't like the looks of the low island either, but his rudder was fouled. He swore under his breath and reluctantly gave the order to head for the island to clear his rudder. Suddenly, the thought came to him: *Why not check this place out more closely? Perhaps it might work. But that made no sense to him. It looked too low—like a swamp. It might flood easily. And what if the natives attacked from the higher ground above the island?* But then he thought, *it is far out of sight of any Spanish ships that might prowl the bay. And from this island, we could see ships sooner because the island allows us a long, clear view of the river downstream.*

Newport was suddenly conflicted—and confused about *why* he was conflicted. The normally astute captain could not see the small lying spirit clinging to his neck. He called for a deckhand to bring Captain Smith up from the brig. Within minutes, Captain Smith appeared on the deck. He saw Wingfield standing near Newport but pretended not to notice him. Wingfield did likewise. They both knew it was not a good time to start another war of words.

"What do you think of this place, Smith?" Newport asked, not looking at the bedraggled prisoner next to him.

John Smith was unsteady on his feet from his long confinement. He grabbed the railing with both hands and breathed deeply for a few moments while he studied the land. "I'd take it, Captain. It's protected on three sides by the river and marshes. We have the force of arms and plenty of men and cannon if we need to drive back attacks from the natives. We will need to make sure the water is good, but I've survived in worse places. I've been a farmer, a soldier of fortune all across Europe, a pirate, and even a slave to Turks. We can do this. Just give me a chance, and I'll show you how to make this colony successful."

Newport huffed. As much as Smith was hard to get along with, he was an experienced leader—and Newport knew it. "Smith, you may be right about our ability to defend it. All of this is new to me. I'm a sailor, not a soldier. But it's only thirty-five miles upriver, not the one hundred miles from the bay as the Virginia Company suggested. I was planning to sail farther upriver. What I do know is that the men are desperate to get off this ship, and I don't blame them," Newport sighed, "but, to be honest, this island looks like trouble to me."

Just then, another shout: "Captain, The water is deep, really deep here!* We can pull the ship right up the shore and tie it to the trees!" the forward lookout on the Discovery bellowed. "We've got six fathoms right now."

Upon hearing that, Jehu Robinson ran to the quarterdeck of the Godspeed, stood beside Captain Bartholomew Gosnold, and shouted, "Come on, men! We can unload right onto the shore from the ship. What could be easier?"

Cheers erupted across all three ships. Gosnold, easily the most experienced explorer of this expedition, shook his head at Newport, who was looking to him for approval. That response strengthened Newport to not land there.

"Snookus, *do* something!" Okeus demanded. "He is wavering!"

"No problem, my Master," Snookus slobbered out of his bulbous mouth. "I already have a dozen demons stationed on the shore to make sure the ships stop here. I suspected we might have to use our usual tricks," Snookus proudly snickered as he blasted into the air, trailing a dark plume of vapor behind him.

"Get below decks, Jehu, before I throw you in the brig, too!" Gosnold ordered. "Don't ever do that again. I'll decide where this ship lands, and this island is not the right place. I smell death all over it."

"But, Captain," Jehu argued, "I know land like this. I've seen it before."

"Shut up and leave me, you impudent fool, and get below where you belong. I know more about exploring the New World and founding colonies than you ever will. Where were you in '02 when I named Cape Cod and Martha's Vineyard?* Just because you're older than me doesn't make you smarter."

"Wow, look at all the demons following that guy, Scion," Angie muttered as she watched Jehu head for the hatch to go below. "No wonder he tried to get the ships to stop. He's surrounded by several strong demons who are doing the bidding of Okeus. Then she looked closer at him. Her eyes went wide as she scanned with heat sensors. Wait a minute. He's not just anxious to go ashore like the rest. His brain temperature is very high— but not in the area associated with pleasure. His brain is burning up with energy, where I usually detect rage. And he has clenched teeth. Wow, this guy is seething with anger —but for whom? Something about him gives me the creeps.

Jehu walked toward the hatch that would take him below decks, muttering to himself, "We'll soon see who knows more about these woods!" At forty-nine, he was older than most of the settlers. His thin build was not impressive, but he was as strong as men twice as young. Oddly enough, even in May, he looked deeply tanned. Pasty-faced gentlemen envied him for that. But his weasel-like face, framed by prominent, dark eyebrows above thin lips, made him seem a bit sinister. Most avoided him. He seemed to enjoy that—almost as much as he liked a good fistfight when he got bored.

Just before Jehu entered the hatch, a crewman shouted, "Captain, look! *Deer!*"

Herded by Snookus's demons, a large ten-point buck scrambled to safety away from the river. One hundred hungry men gaped in awe and shouted so loud it hurt Newport's ears. "Deer . . . meat . . . victuals!" The men were now delirious with anticipation of getting ashore.

"Captain? Are we cleared to send a landing party ashore?" the first mate yelled above the jubilant noise.

Newport bit his lip. "No, I don't trust this island," he replied with an angry look. Something is not right here, but I can't put my finger on it.

Snookus cowered at the growing anger he could sense in Okeus across the river. It could prove fatal if he did not act quickly. "Time to release them," the frightened, yellow-headed octopus muttered as he spurted off to activate his final, desperate trick.

CHAPTER 28

Scion saw that look and shot into the sky to see what Snookus might do next. There they were: twelve native women hiding in the bushes just off the river bank. As usual, the Powhatan women were naked above the waist. Six demons were guarding them and staring at Snookus for a signal of some sort.

"Oh *no,*" Scion gasped. "Angie—come quickly. Stop those women before the men see them! I'll get their guards."

The twang of Scion's eight-foot sword made the six guards flinch and reach for their swords as Scion dove to the river bank. But the guards were too late. Flying at seven hundred miles per hour, eight feet above the ground, Scion's outstretched sword became a decapitating sickle. The headless guards vaporized into red smoke just as Angie reached the frightened ladies. As Angie sang a psalm over them, the frightened women suddenly relaxed, smiled and did not move. Angie smiled too.

High above them, Snookus saw the red vapor trails of his dead demons. He had to improvise. But *how*? Scion would kill him or any spirit who tried to intervene. He suddenly remembered something he had seen Okeus do long ago.

Just as Newport was about to order the ships to sail farther north up river, the bushes near the shore rustled and out jumped one of the half-naked women looking terrified. She had heard the growl of an angry bear nearby and got spooked. She was young and beautiful with dark hair braided down her bare back to her waist. Then, she suddenly bolted back into the forest.

That ought to do it, Snookus thought with much relief. *I always wanted to growl like that.*

Pandemonium broke out on all three ships as 104 men saw her. Two men—one of them Jehu—jumped overboard into the river, swimming feverishly toward the shore while many others cheered.

"We can't leave them, Captain. Let's moor here. *Please,* Captain," Newport's first mate pleaded.

Newport looked at Wingfield, who had been silent until now. In that same moment, the lying spirit that had been unsuccessful in influencing the captain to stop the ship decided that the other man might be easier to convince. Like a giant flea, the spirit jumped on Wingfield's head and sunk a sharp claw deep into his brain.

"Captain, I hate to admit it, but Smith may be right . . . this time. This place affords excellent defenses from shore and water. I say land here."

Smith heard that. A secret smile crossed his face when Wingfield was not looking.

"But it's low land, Master Wingfield. The water may be salty, and who knows what kind of food can be easily acquired there. I'd like to keep looking upstream a little more for higher ground if you don't mind."

Standing as erect as he could, the former member of Parliament declared, "I *do* mind. I have decided that we will land here. Please bring your ship about to land, Captain Newport. We've been searching for many days already. The men can't wait any longer. This island will do for now. We can always move to a different place later. Let's just try it!"

In the treetop, Okeus smiled. "I love it when the humans say, 'Let's *try it.*' Yes, don't sin. That would be terrible. But just *try it* a little," he gargled a throaty laugh.

Snookus also laughed on cue—but nervously. "I told you, Master. I told you I could do it," he sniveled in a squeaky voice, trying to sound confident. As usual, when he was pleased, Okeus farted his approval. Snookus smiled through the haze of the pungent flatus, but his mind was not smiling. *One day, Master, one day, you will wish you had treated me better.*

Back on the *Susan Constant,* Newport felt helpless. Two dozen men were already ashore chasing the woman in the forest. His crew was exhausted and hungry. Their eyes begged him for relief.

Smith just stood at the railing, looking angry. He knew he had to return to the brig now.

Finally, with a deep sigh and a sad face, Newport turned to the crew and shouted, "Prepare to anchor and unload the ship!"

Scion groaned loudly. Angie put her hands over her mouth and cried. Okeus roared and gloated with a rare joy few had ever seen. Hundreds of demons also screamed their evil approval overhead, but the men only heard their own hearty cheers as the captain's order was relayed to the other two ships. Gosnold and Newport looked somber— as if they knew something they would rather not say.

"Look out below! Lower the anchors!" came the order as the mammoth iron anchor splashed into the river near several sailors swimming to shore. Soon, heavy rope hawsers were tied to nearby trees. The colony had landed. It was May 13, 1607.*

Scion hung his head. "I can't believe it. They chose the worst place on the river to land. Well, Okeus has definitely won this round. They sailed right into his trap. Like you said, Angie—if only the saints among the crew had prayed more, we might have been able to steer them to safer ground. God always wants to help, but he often waits to give help until someone prays and asks for help. Without such prayer, men fall into many traps Satan has laid for them."

Angie's keen eyes detected a change in Scion. "Scion, you seem really sad. Are you are thinking of the rebellion again?" Angie asked.

"Yes. Lucifer led my closest friends into a trap—one they can never escape from. I'll never forgive him for that."

Angie gently touched his hand. "Scion, that's why we're doing this. We are going to fight for this Christian colony so that Lucifer doesn't trap anyone else that God loves."

The lookout on the *Susan Constant* excitedly called out, "Look, oysters! They could have pearls!"

Immediately, more men hopped over the side to search the large oyster beds sticking out of the river.* Opened oyster shells flew everywhere as the men scrambled to find their wealth in the New World. One discarded oyster flew over the rail and hit Smith square on his steel helmet, sprinkling him with river mud.

"You always seem to draw the fire of others, don't you, Smith?" Newport chuckled.

Brushing the dirt off his uniform, Smith replied with feigned frustration, "What shall we call this place . . . *Oystertown?*"

Newport laughed. "Oh, I don't know. We've already used up two names on the two capes, Prince Charles and Prince Henry. Let's name it after our King. How about James Colony or James City or James on the Thames? We could name this river New Thames, or—"

"How about James Fort?" Smith suggested.

Newport nodded. "Yes, that will do fine. James Fort it is.* It's time for you to go back to the brig, I'm afraid. I am so tired. Let's all get some rest. Colonizing the New World takes a lot of energy, especially for an old sea-dog like me." As he headed for his cabin, the weary captain turned and said, "I'll stop by to bring you dinner in your cell after a short nap, Smith. Maybe then I can face Gosnold. I know he is furious that we choose this spot. May God help us. I have a feeling we may live to regret this choice yet."

"*Alea jacta est,*" Scion sighed.

"Alea—what?" Angie asked.

"That's what Caesar said as he crossed the Rubicon River before he attacked and conquered Rome. It means 'the die is cast.'* There is no stopping them from settling here now. Okeus has won this battle, but wait until Reverend Hunt gets that church up and worshipping. God's Presence will come, and then we'll see what the Algonquin god can do."

CHAPTER 29

The west side of the oval lake where Okeus had his base slowly bubbled with a stench like rotting fish. Black bear and deer were abundant, but no humans came to hunt in the massive swamp. The pine forest surrounding the lake was unusually dense, making travel difficult. More importantly, rumors of evil spirits kidnapping and eating natives kept all but the most fearless away. Okeus had commanded the shamans to spread that myth among all the tribes. He liked solitude.

Okeus ruled his domain from here in what the Powhatan natives called The Great Swamp. Near the lake's grassy shoreline, his personal guard demons built a throne for him. Okeus secretly hated it, but he pretended to love it since it fit his demon disguise. It was a throne only a demon would enjoy: decaying black bear hides and deer antlers embedded atop a mound of animal bones and putrid mud. To top it off, flies, ticks, spiders, and giant roaches filled every crevice of the hideous heap. He sat on his throne now just after he and Snookus returned from watching the English ships land.

"Well done, Snookus. Your recent plan to use Mongo's all-night incantations and human sacrifices has released my power well to snare the English. The bird is in the cage. Now, all we have to do is slowly close the cage door, and the foolish English bird will soon be ours to devour."

"Thank you, Master." Snookus's blubbery body quivered with delight at such a rare compliment from Okeus. "Mongo works well with us. He is our best ally among the natives," he squeaked. "His father Paq also hates the whites, which serves us well. His brother, Opie, is even more allied with us. His venom for Europeans knows no bounds. One day, Opie must replace his spineless brother, Chief Powhatan. We may have to eliminate him soon, Master, if we are to destroy this colony."

"Not so fast, my little slug," Okeus smoothly retorted. "Powhatan can be useful to us now. The other tribes trust him. Opie is only twenty-seven and too hot-headed to be chief yet. Powhatan may be too eager for peace, but his father Paq has taught him well how to use alliances against enemies, just like the whites do in Europe," Okeus slobbered with a toothy smile. "The Spanish have done themselves and us a great favor. What they taught Paq will now be used on their enemies, the British. But for now, send a message to Paq that he is to watch the man named Hunt. I may need to use him as an assassin again. Hunt worries me."

"I also planted the cursed Spanish bones on the island, as you suggested, Lord Okeus," Snookus giggled, always wanting to curry favor with his master.

"Oh yes, the bones," Okeus remembered. "Are you sure you got the right ones?"

"Yes, my Master. Mongo showed me the very spot where Paq's raiding party killed the Spanish priests. One skull still had a Spanish ax in its head. I took some of the biggest bones and cursed them with a death curse last month."

"Good. So, we have death curses, a long drought, bad water on the island, our Powhatan slaves to harass them—and did I mention that Prince Beelzebub, Lord of the Flies, has come from Africa to help us?

His power to use flying insects to deliver death is unrivaled. When summer comes, the water will have enough salt in it to weaken them. Then, his mosquitoes will finish them off, one by one—if they don't starve first!" They both laughed. Okeus was feeling confident. "Snookus, if this works, we won't have to infect the colony with sins after all. Disease and starvation will wipe them out quicker! Lord Lucifer will be pleased—and I will be safe," Okeus added with a relieved look at Snookus.

Snookus could tell that Okeus was in a good mood, so he thought he might gain some valuable favor by amusing his prickly master.

"And how about that Morph fouling the rudder?" Snookus asked with a high voice. "That may be the first time in his miserable life he did what I told him to do without screwing it up. I think I might reduce his beatings to only three times a week now," Snookus joked nervously, hoping Okeus would be pleased.

Okeus only looked at his obsequious assistant and grunted—and then he lifted his colossal rear and passed terrible gas. Snookus pretended not to notice, but finally, he gagged and coughed loudly several times. Okeus laughed! It sounded like a big animal choking on something in its throat—but it was a laugh, nonetheless. Then, one of the dinosaur's huge paws slapped Snookus's squishy yellow head so hard that he squirted a large cloud of black gas. Without looking at his master, Snookus meekly smiled.

The floppy octopus knew he could rest easy tonight. He had actually made Okeus pass gas and laugh. Those were the best terms of endearment he could ever expect.

CHAPTER 30

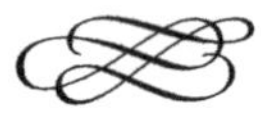

May 13, 1607: Later that day.

Seventeen miles east of the James Fort, at the village on the Pamunkey River* called Werowocomoco,* Wahunsenacawh* the great chief of the Powhatan confederacy listened carefully to what his scouts told him. He was commonly called Powhatan*—the primary ruler of thirty tribes, each with its own chief called a werowance.* The confederacy covered about ten thousand square miles* mainly on the west side of the Chesapeake Bay.* The Powhatans called their land Tsenacommacah,* which means "densely populated land."*

"They have come, Great Chief Powhatan. Just as your prophets said.* People from the East have come to take away your throne."* Then they gave him a full report about the three ships landing, the number of men, a description of their weapons, and how much food they had brought ashore.

Powhatan nodded gravely. He was thirty-six, taller and more muscular than most warriors. Premature flecks of gray were sprinkled in his shoulder-length black hair, but his large brown eyes still sparkled with hawk-like alertness.

Despite his primitive lifestyle, he had the bearing and dignity of a great and wise king. His courage was legendary. Many battle scars covered his face and arms. But he gave his father, Paquiquino, credit for his wisdom as chief. Paquiquino had tutored each of his three sons in what he had learned in his nine years with the Spanish: how to converse in Spanish, French, and English; how the Spanish organized their soldiers; how "their big canoes moved by catching the wind in big, white skins"; and how they made and used metal weapons. The three boys were fascinated with his tales about what they called fire-sticks—guns that can kill with a small piece of metal. Most of all, Paquiquino taught his sons not to trust any whites. "We must hate them! Never allow them to come here. They will only bring death," Paquiquino warned them severely. As a boy, Powhatan agreed with his father, but he also dreamed of having metal weapons and tools to help his people become more prosperous and mighty in battle. Now, as chief, he might have that chance.

Wahunsenacawh finally spoke with great solemnity. "Yes, even with thirty tribes in our alliance, this is terrible news. These *tassantassas,* these strangers, can do us much harm or much good. I hope that they come in peace. But we may never know. Perhaps they will just die from lack of food since our land still suffers from such a bad drought."*

His favorite daughter, Matoaka,* was sitting at his feet. Wahunsenacawh had many wives and many daughters, but it was no secret that the chief favored Matoaka above all his other children. She was very mature in their thinking—an eleven-year-old going on twenty-two. Spunky, bright, kind, athletic, daring and full of fun—Matoaka was all of that and more. Everywhere she went in the tribe, she brought joy. That's why her father, the chief, nicknamed her Pocahontas—"Playful One."*

She was a delight to look at. Atop her four foot eleven frame, her face of creamy brown skin glowed with joy when she talked or sang—which was *most* of the time. Her waist-length, coal-black hair flew around her face and deep brown eyes as she skipped, ran, or twirled. A rapid series of wild cartwheels was her specialty. She even seemed to bounce a little when she was standing still. Her body did not know the meaning of *stop.* "Playful One" lived up to her name every day. But she was also quick to give her opinion about anything—even to her father.

"Father, the long drought that started last year may cause them to leave when they cannot grow food. But you always wanted to know more from whites. We should give them corn, so they stay longer. Maybe they will share some weapons with us if we treat them kindly."

"You know me well, Pocahontas. Yes, I desire their weapons.* Our enemies would dare attack us if we have such things. But first, we must win their favor—and soon—before they have no food—and leave our lands. My brother, Mongo, says these whites have not brought women with them. He thinks we should send many girls to their camp to lie with them. After all, it is our custom to share maidens with guests.* Mongo says Father Paq thinks this is good plan to weaken them. Father Paq says sleeping with maidens will offend the god of the whites. Then the whites lose favor with their god. How strange. White god is so different from Okeus. My friends who visit us would not like white god's rule," Powhatan laughed.

"Will I sleep with whites someday, Father?" Pocahontas asked sweetly. "I will be old enough to marry soon."

"No, my child. You are chief's daughter. That is not for you."

"But Father, what if I marry white man? My white husband can teach me about his weapons, and then I can teach you," she impishly suggested.

Her father laughed again and patted his raven-haired, daughter. "Pocahontas, only you would think foolish thing like that. No white man would want to marry one of our girls. They think they are better than us."

Gently grabbing his beautiful daughter by her shoulders with both of his strong hands, Powhatan looked into her upturned face and said, "Matoaka, you are eleven.* You are my playful princess, my little Pocahontas. Dealing with whites is for Mongo and me and father to decide. You need to stay in village with grandfather for now. Perhaps I can talk with white skins and make friends with them. If they choose not to be friends, then I will do all in my power to make sure that the whites do not hurt you or our people."

Clenching her tiny fists at her side, Pocahontas quickly shot back, "But *nohsh,* my Father, I cannot play in village while my father faces new enemies," she announced, with her arms folded tightly across her chest. I am brave and strong—like you. Please let me help! I am a princess, with heart of a warrior—like your heart."

"My Pocahontas, I love you more than all my children.* Our great god, Ahone, has given you to me when I am old. You are too precious to lose. Stay here with your grandfather, Paq. Our tribes are safe. We are fifteen thousand braves strong, and whites are but a few."

But Pocahontas stomped her foot and said, "No—I must be with you, Father."

Dropping his hands from her shoulders, the chief looked his feisty child in the eye and sternly declared, "This is not a request, my child. You will stay with your *numohshomus,** your grandfather, so the whites will not know you are my *nuntanuhs,** my daughter. That will protect you. If we are not careful, we may go to war. These invaders have fire-sticks and hard war-skins that our arrows cannot pierce"

Pocahontas seemed to back down a bit when she heard that. Then the chief squatted down to get eye-level with her. "Playful One, I know Father Paq has taught you many white man words and white man ways. Learn more from him. Later, if whites become our friends, you can help me talk to them. I will need you then."

At that proposal, Pocahontas smiled, "I would love that, Father. I will ask our Creator god, Ahone, to help you. He is kind—not like cruel god, Okeus."

"Pocahontas, I know our Creator speaks to you. I have seen this for many moons now. I know he will help you. Go and play now. Do many cartwheels for me!"

"Yes, Father! For you! Maybe someday, I can also turn the plans of invaders upside down!" she giggled.

Then she tossed her body toward the dusty ground in a perfect cartwheel—right through Scion and Angie, who had been listening just outside the chief's hut. As Pocahontas flipped upright again, she felt something in her spirit. She looked around in slow motion for a moment. Even Powhatan sucked in his breath. He felt it, too.

Scion and Angie looked up and saw the heavens opened above the girl. "My Lord and my God," Scion and Angie spoke in unison. Scion's entire body began to glow. The Lord's Presence had come.

Sensing that the Great Spirit was near, Chief Powhatan's eyes teared up. He bent down and whispered, "Come here, my child." Pocahontas flew into her father's waiting arms. For a long moment, he held her—wondering what kind of child he was embracing. *Pocahontas—The Great Spirit must love you more than even I do.*

"The Great Spirit, Ahone, is here, Father.* He can feel him. I want to know him more."

"When you see your grandfather, ask him about Ahone. He can tell you much about him."

"I will, Father. I will go to Papa Paq now." Then, she put her small hand on her father's scarred cheek and said, "I'll bet Ahone is a lot like you, Father."

Wiping a tear from her own eyes, Angie said, "Wow—who would have thought that God would pick someone so young and small for his amazing work here?"

"That's what I thought when I saw *you*, Angie," Scion smirked. "Keep your eyes on her. I think she is more important to the future of this colony than we thought. Go with her now and record everything she and her grandfather talk about. Before I left heaven, Michael told me that God would use an old native called Paquiquino to bless the colony. And he is her grandfather."

"I'm on it. This will be a pleasure." Angie smiled and then thought, *Wow, God. You are so kind! Even though these people have been worshipping evil Okeus for thousands of years, you have been planning to bless them—and you have revealed yourself to them as a good Creator God named Ahone. What a great God you are!*

CHAPTER 31

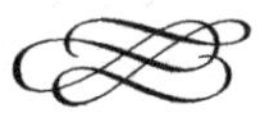

Long shafts of golden sunlight pierced the fragrant pine trees as Pocahontas approached her grandfather's hut.

Morph was half-asleep next to Paquiquino as the old man slowly stirred an earthen pot over the flames of a flickering fire in the center of his warm, dome-shaped home. It was crude but effective in construction: birch saplings bent and tied together to form a shell with a round top, covered with woven mats of birch bark with a hole in the center to let the smoke out. Angie stayed outside, hidden behind an outcrop of rocks behind the hut—not wanting to alert the cat demon to her presence. She assumed he was the assigned guard demon for Paquiquino, and he would oppose any angelic contact with his human assignment. *Let sleepy demons sleep,* she decided.

"Papa Paq!" Pocahontas shouted as she bounded into the open doorway.

"Matoaka! Good to see you," Paquiquino replied with a long-toothed smile. By Algonquian standards, he was old at fifty-seven but still spry and sharp of mind. "What brings you here, my child?"

Drowsy Morph saw her out of one blue eye and yawned. *Excellent—this brat will keep the old man busy for a while so I can rest some more.*

"Father sent me to stay with you a while," she responded. Pocahontas leaned over the boiling pot, sniffed deeply, and smiled. "Oh, that smells so good!" Paquiquino's eyes returned the smile.

Pocahontas grew serious. "Father does not want whites to know who I am. He thinks that will protect me. But I want to help Father make friends with whites so he can have weapons like whites to protect our people. Father says that I can help him talk to whites, but I must know more white man's words. Please teach me, Papa."

Morph's head suddenly snapped upward and looked up at the princess with alarm. "Oh, batcrap! She wants to make friends with the whites. Snookus will be furious if I allow this talk to go on," he muttered to himself.

Gazing at his clever, young granddaughter with a twinkle in his eye, the aged warrior soberly replied, "Do you know whites love to capture and torture our kind?" Morph saw his opening. He leaped onto Paquiquino's back.

Then, as if suddenly remembering something, a dark mood washed over Paquiquino's face like a solar eclipse. A tomb of dark and dangerous memories was unearthed in his mind. Morph saw the pain on Paquiquino's face and smiled as he pulled his talon out of Paquiquino's mind. For the first time in a long time, Morph felt good about himself. Good job, Morph, if I do say so myself. What an opportune time to poison the chief's favorite daughter against these Christians—and using her own grandfather. Wait until Snookus hears about how I handled this. I may get a promotion after all.

Just then, an odd thought came to Morph—one he had never had before. *I think I'll go and tell Snookus now. He will understand why I left my assignment here so I could report this good news. And while I am gone, Paq will infect that little wench with his hatred of whites. Perfect!*

Morph zipped off, unaware that his last thoughts had *not* come from his own mind. Just behind him, a tiny angel smirked. *It worked. He took the bait,* she silently gloated.

Angie was in the hut now, and she was determined to protect Pocahontas from whatever that demon was hatching. Now that he was gone, she could intervene more easily.

Pocahontas saw the dark anger sweep over her grandfather's face. "Papa, are you angry at me?"

Paquiquino clenched his wrinkled hands and stood up quickly. He paced the small dirt floor without speaking. Then he yelled, "I hate them! I know whites. Stay away from them! They only come here to steal our land and hurt our people, just like Spanish whites did to our people in south. I teach my sons—your father Powhatan and Uncle Mongo and Uncle Opie—how to conquer whites. Opie learn the most from me. He is very clever. Opie hate whites as I do. Opie know the cruel ways of white man better than anyone except me. That's why I give him a new name when he became warrior: Opechancanough. It means 'he whose soul is white.' You must think like your enemy to defeat him. Opie know how to think like a white man—and if we have to fight whites, Opie will win," the old man shouted with obvious anger.

Taken aback by her grandfather's outburst, Pocahontas sat for a long moment and pondered what she had just heard. She loved her grandfather and knew he was the wisest man in the entire confederacy. There had to be good reasons for his anger, but she had never heard them.

Scrunching up her courage, Pocahontas sat down at her grandfather's scarred, calloused feet and stared at his face. Her big brown eyes danced in the glimmering flame of the cook fire.

"What is it?" Paquiquino grunted angrily. But when he saw the compassion in her eyes, he hung his head in shame. *She is not to blame. I am. I must tell her—to protect her.*

"Tell me what happened to you, Papa Paq. Many moons ago, you said you would tell me your story. You are the most famous warrior in our tribes. You know more about whites than any warrior. Father tell me that some whites take you far away when you are a boy. What did they do to you that make you hate them so much?"

Paquiquino huffed in frustration. "My brave Matoaka, your father want the help of whites too much. He want peace so whites can give him their weapons. But he is wrong. We must destroy whites before they destroy us!"

As Paquiquino waved his arms, one hand touched the hot pot on the fire. "Ouch! Do you see how this upsets me? I cannot control myself. I don't like talking about this."

Gazing into the flickering fire with sparks flying out, Paquiquino suddenly saw the flames of Mexican villages and the flashes of Spanish guns slaughtering hundreds of innocent natives. He had been there. The gruesome memories made him tremble.

Pocahontas gently touched his knee and whispered, "I love you, Grandfather. I hurt when I see you hurt. What did they do to you? Please tell me. My heart is tied to your heart for as long as there are moons. You are like father to me. When Papa was busy for many summers, you cared for me. Please, Grandfather, tell me your secrets. I need to know. Please do not deny me. I am Powhatan princess. We may be at war soon. I need to know about whites, so I can help our people."

Paquiquino stared at his pleading granddaughter, then looked away. Tears formed in his eyes. *I can't tell her. She is just a child.*

"My father tell me that you have another name."

Her words hit Paquiquino like a tree trunk falling on him. His mind went to mush. Pain shot through his hands and knees. His stomach turned into knots of fear and anger. He felt himself hyperventilating, trying to stay focused, trying to remain conscious. It was like a giant hand had grabbed his head and was squeezing the life out of it. Don't fall into the fire, he thought. He was losing control, and he couldn't stop his terrifying freefall into dark memories that were drowning him in a whirlpool of confusion and pain.

"Grandfather! What is it? What's happening? Please say something!" Pocahontas screamed.

Paquiquino was speechless. The wooden spoon fell from his hand to the dirt floor. His face was frozen in agony, gripped by hideous feelings and memories long suppressed. Slowly, with glazed eyes, Paquiquino fell off his stool onto his side in a fetal position. He lay there motionless. Pocahontas had never seen any warrior act this way, especially the greatest warrior in the Powhatan Confederacy. As Pocahontas put her arm around her stricken grandfather's shoulder, he was mumbling about killing someone. Then she noticed that his skin was cold and clammy. White foam bubbled on his lips.

"Grandfather, you scare me. Are you sick? Do you want Mongo to say incantations for you?"

No response—just his heavy breathing. Pocahontas screamed for help. But no one heard her through the double-thick, deer-hide walls. Paquiquino could not hear her either. His mind was far away—tumbling in a dark labyrinth of memories spawned in Mexico long ago. But as the acrid smell of the smoky fire wafted inside his nose, a new, dreadful scene arose in his consciousness— that terrible night around the fire with the tribal elders.

CHAPTER 32

October 31, 1570

Just a few miles south of Powhatan's throne in Werowocomoco, a small village on the west side of the Pamunkey River sat nestled near the shoreline, lined with tall, green pines and wide oak trees laden with brown, autumn leaves.

John Smith's map of the Kiskiack village area

This was Kiskiack,* Paquiquino's village.* Twenty-year-old Paquiquino had just been returned to his homeland by the Spanish.* Seven Jesuit priests,* three teachers called catechists,* and a ten-year-old altar boy named Alonso de Olmos,* also came back with him. They nicknamed him Aloncito.* After a few days of walking in the woods, the priests had built a small camp in a mossy glen not far from Kiskiack. They had come to establish a church.* But Paquiquino went back to his village to reunite with his family and tribe.*

His surprise arrival in the village was one of the greatest events the tribe had ever remembered. The tribe thought he had died. His parents also believed he was dead, and they had died without ever seeing him again after that rainy night in 1561. For a few days, hundreds of warriors and squaws had celebrated his return. They killed many deer to hold many feasts in his honor. They made him feel like a hero to have survived nine years with the dreaded whites and their terrible weapons.

At first, Paquiquino felt loved and honored. But his life was not his own. Everywhere he went, children and adults stared at him. Day after day, week after week, they asked the same questions about fire-sticks, horses, the white man's box that told time, the white man's big villages, and what their lands were like. It was a happy time, but Paquiquino was growing tired of the fame. He just wanted to live a normal life again, to start a family and settle down. He had been treated like a freak for years by the Spanish—and now his own people saw him as someone different.

FINALLY, ON A COLD NIGHT IN JANUARY 1571, THE LONG-LOST BOY WAS summoned to tell his tribal elders what had happened to him. The twelve old warriors sat cross-legged in a large hut filled with smoke from a small fire and waited for him.

Okeus and Snookus followed Paquiquino to the meeting. They floated just above the top of a tall pine tree. "Watch this, Bubblehead," Okeus snorted. "That young dirtbag is about to fall right into my trap. This is why I let the Spanish pigs take the boy long ago. They were fools to keep him and train him for nine years. They have doomed that boy to something worse than death. And after this is over, the Spanish will never dare come back. *Watch*! I've seen this before—it works like a perfect curse."

Just then, Paquiquino arrived. He bowed to the sitting tribal council and also sat down cross-legged next to the oldest warrior in the group, who gave him a faint smile. "So, this is the famous Paquiquino everyone talks about," the old man announced. "Let us hear him tonight and see what must be done."

The young brave looked slowly around the circle, nodding at each stern face. Then, he cleared his throat. He was nervous—but he knew the elders would be pleased to hear how he had suffered bravely during his captivity. He was also proud and excited to tell them things that they have never heard before. When I am done, they will probably want me to teach many braves what I know. I am ready! And so, Paquiquino began to tell his tale—one that no Powhatan had ever heard before.

"When I had seen eleven summers, Spanish white men trick my parents and take me from my village of Kiskiack. The Spanish say they will keep me until next summer to train me like a great warrior. Instead, they keep me nine summers, like a prisoner.* When soldiers take me from my family, they put me in big white man's canoe that belong to white chief called Menéndez," Paquiquino recalled. "His canoe bigger than fifty huts. Winds push the canoe with big white skins on bare tree trunks. The canoe goes across many waters to where white men live in a place they called Spain.* In the language of British white men, the name of that place sound like their word for suffering: pain. Spain mean 'pain' to me.

"I was treated like animal at first. They lock me in a room and chain me to soldiers when I travel. Along the way, white people look at me —like I am evil man. I cry many tears for my family and for my tribe, but I could not escape to come home. Later, they take me to a land called Cuba.* It very hot there. Later, I go to a place they called Mexico,* where they have many soldiers and many native slaves digging for what white man calls gold.* It look like some rocks we have here, but different. Almost every white man will do anything—

even very evil things—to find gold. No one cared for the natives—they just care about getting rich with gold."

The faces of the elders grew even more severe, as Paquiquino described how the natives were treated.

"Yes, I saw it with my own eyes. Spanish soldiers treated the native people like animals—even worse than animals.* They made them carry heavy bags with many gold rocks for many days in the mountains. If a native fell down, the soldiers would beat him. If native could not get up, they just kill him with a long knife and push his body off cliff for animals to eat. Once the bags of gold rocks arrived at the sea, the natives would load them on big canoes going to Spain. Even women and children were slaves. Many died from such work. Many more died from catching a white man's sickness."

Paquiquino also told stories about some Spanish who were kind to him. One of them was his teacher, a white woman called Sister Gabriella.

"I was put into a large, stone lodge with many rooms. I meet an old Spanish woman, Sister Gabriella, who lived like Mongo, always worshiping her god and reading from her god's carvings—small pictures on something like thin tree bark, but sewn together. They called it a book—a Bible. Gabriella become my teacher. She covered her body with a black robe with white under her chin and a black and white hat on her head. The only skin you could see was her very white face and hands. She also had reddish cheeks and big, brown eyes like us. She looked like a woman shaman. But she treated me like a son, and soon I loved her like a mother," he said with obvious affection.

He told them that in Mexico, Sister Gabriella tutored him every day for five years. She taught him the words and the ways of the white man. The tribal leaders were stunned to learn that Gabriella had taught the young brave to speak and write in four white man's languages: Spanish, French, Latin, and English. They listened closely to this young man as he described how their fire-stick weapons kill and how they ride big animals they call horses. Puffing out his chest, Paquiquino bragged, "I can shoot their fire-sticks and ride a horse just like a white man."

Several leaders smiled. They hoped to get such weapons and animals one day. But the oldest leaders in the circle began to grow more anxious. No native in their thirty tribes knew what Paquiquino knew —not even the wisest of their chiefs.* What if this young brave challenged them as leaders? They wondered. What if the Spanish shamans that brought him here had fire-sticks? How could they protect themselves from such a formidable opponent if he turned against them?

Oblivious to the growing fears in some of the tribal leaders, Paquiquino continued. "Sister Gabriella loved native people. She hated what the Spanish soldiers did to the natives. There were many rapes, murders, and much slavery. She said money make the Spanish like wild animals. They live for money, not for their god. She said her god angry with the soldiers for all this evil. She said her god will punish them if they not change their ways. She pray to her god that they change."

Paquiquino went on to tell the leaders about the white man's god. Okeus and Snookus quickly flew away. "Let's get out of here, Snookus! It makes me queasy to listen to that Bible crap. We'll come back later for the good part."

"Sister Gabriella tell me about her god—a god who loves to give mercy. I could not believe at first. No god could be so good. Even better than Ahone. Her god sacrifice only son and make him die in terrible way so everyone—natives and Spanish—can be forgiven for all bad things they do.

"No god or chief would do that, I thought. And it very foolish to kill only son to help others who deserve to be punished." With a faraway look in his eyes, Paquiquino continued. "But when I saw how she treat others, I begin to believe such a god can exist. She act like her god she spoke of. I feel loved and safe with her. I see in her eyes what I see in eyes of my mother. My heart was warm and I feel mercy even for Spanish killers. I long to know this god who make people like that. One day, her people put me in water to say I am a child of that god. It feel very good."

The tribal leaders listened closely. Their eyes were alternately wide with amazement and then narrow with fear. At one point, they asked him, "What about white man's shamans—their priests—are they cruel like soldiers? Do they use spells and sacrifices to hurt natives—like our shamans do to fight our enemies?" Paquiquino shook his head vigorously. "No, priests are different from soldiers. Sister Gabriella tell me of Spanish priest they call Bartolomé de las Casas.* De las Casas love native people and try to protect them.* The eight white priests and boy who come back here with me are good people like Sister Gabriella and de las Casas. My new friends, Father Segura and Father Quiros,* wait at camp nearby to meet all of you. They call camp Ajacan Mission.* They will help us know their god—who is better than Ahone. His name is Jesus."

As he said that, a cold shiver went through the elders. Finally, Paquiquino mentioned that a high-ranking Spanish government official in Mexico had treated him like a son. The official was Luís de Velasco.* Luis loved Paquiquino so much, he gave him his own name: Don Luís de Velasco.* Looks of shock swept across the faces of the elders as they realized: Paquiquino has *a white name*. Their admiration of Paquiquino began to dissolve into suspicion. Just how "white" had he become? Was he more loyal to the whites and to their god or to our god and us? None of the leaders could escape such thoughts. What if he is a spy for the whites so they can come here and conquer us as they did in Mexico? Like a dam bursting, all the elders began to pepper Paquiquino with questions about his loyalties and beliefs.

Finally, the oldest warrior who sat next to Paquiquino raised his hand to silence them. Turning to the frightened young brave next to him, the old warrior probed Paquiquino with very direct questions.

Okeus and Snookus flew in just as the elders were shushed. "Listen, Snookus. That little wet turd is about to seal his fate—just as I anticipated."

"Who is your god now?" the oldest warrior asked with a hint of sarcasm in his voice.

"Ahone *and* Jesus," he replied. The tribal elders frowned and murmured. Paquiquino felt fear rising in him.

"Who are your people—whites or this tribe?"

"This tribe! But I have some white friends."

More frowns. Paquiquino winced.

"If you must kill a white, can you?"

"Of course. Spanish soldiers are cruel. They deserve to die if they come here," he replied with forced confidence.

"But what about your white friends—the priests? Can you kill them if we tell you to do it?"

At that question, Paquiquino began to stutter and tear up. "I . . . *no*, I cannot kill them. They love me and protect me many times from bad soldiers. They are innocent men with no weapons. They will do no harm. It not our way as Powhatans to do such things, my father tell me long ago."

For almost thirty minutes, they continued to examine him about his relationships with whites and their god. Then, they dismissed him. "You have done many things well, young Paquiquino, but your heart seems to be half-white. Go to your hut. Let us discuss this alone now. We will call you back soon."

In the hour that followed, the tribal leaders finally decided that Paquiquino's loyalty would have to be tested very seriously. After another fifteen minutes of agitated chatter, they came up with a plan that would change the young warrior's life— and the lives of countless others for centuries to come.

CHAPTER 33

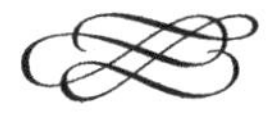

The campfire in the hut was slowly dying as Paquiquino was summoned back to the group. He was sweating under his bearskin robe, even on a cold January night. He had heard the angry voices of the leaders from his hut, which was not far away. As he sat down with them again, an owl screeched in the treetops and a cloud slid across the large moon above them. Everyone felt the tension in the air as the young man sat cross-legged, facing the twelve, stony-faced elders.

Okeus began to slobber. He punched Snookus in the head, "Watch this. That boy is dead meat. Our demons are about to have fun with this fool."

And then, the oldest tribal leader stood up to speak. "Paquiquino, we agree it is not right to ask you if you can kill now. You are one of us, but you left us before doing *Husquenaw* ritual* that all boys must do to be a warrior.* Become warrior first, and then we talk again about your place in the tribe."

Paquiquino was shocked. He knew that every boy in the tribe was required to do this when they were thirteen to prove their willingness to suffer in battle.* But it was a dangerous ceremony. Some boys died while doing it.*

"But why now? Haven't I proven I am brave warrior, after all I endured with Spanish?"

"You are man now, stronger and wiser than boy, and you have seen many things," the elder said. "But this is the Powhatan way for every boy. There are no exceptions. If you want to stay and be member of this tribe, you must do the Husquenaw ritual. The medicine we give you in the ritual will strengthen you to be strong in battle for your people."*

The more Paquiquino thought about it, the more it made sense. He was desperate to prove his loyalty to his people, and every other boy in the tribe has had to do the ritual. With a sigh of resignation, he agreed. "I'll do the Husquenaw."

The elders decided that the ceremony would take place the next day at dawn. All the elders smiled, and Paquiquino thought it was a friendly smile . . . but he couldn't have been more wrong.

The next day, Paquiquino went deep into the forest to live alone for seven days. Before he left for the Husquenaw ritual, he was fed the customary potion of poisonous roots and the dried flowers of what English settlers later called Jamestown Weed.* The usual effect of the potion was temporary madness!* He could not think normally. He felt like a wounded bear. All he wanted to do was fight and kill. Okeus sent spirits of terror to torture him every night with horrific nightmares and visions. His body was wracked with unrelenting pain in every joint, like a hot knife stabbing his bones.

At the end of the ritual, the young warrior somehow managed to limp back to the village—*barely* conscious and not quite sane. His stomach was empty, but his body was full of demons, writhing inside, screaming for blood to be shed. When the elders asked him again if he would kill the priests, he stared straight ahead—stuttering and foaming at the mouth—and then shouted, "Death to the invaders! Death to the enemies of Okeus and the tribe!"

The elders shouted back with a war-whoop while Okeus belched out, "We got him!" as he grabbed Snookus by his head and beat him playfully in the treetops nearby.

Finally, on February 9, 1571,* Paquiquino led a war party of fierce braves and went to the camp of the Jesuits they called St. Mary's Mission.* It was a rare and beautiful place where moss clung to almost every tree and rock in a small clearing nestled in the middle of low, rolling hills. The priests named it Valle de Musgo—Moss Valley. Most of the ten Spaniards were sitting on a small log listening to a reading from the Bible during their celebration of Mass. "Unless a grain of wheat falls into the ground, it remains alone. But if it dies, it bears much fruit," the reader intoned. The leader, Father Segura, was sick that day, but he was listening as he lay on the damp ground on a warm, wool blanket.

Virginia's first Christian martyrs*

Paquiquino and his war party crept in unnoticed. Then, they silently grabbed the axes and shovels of the Jesuits.* In an instant, they pounced upon the unarmed Christians during their celebration of Mass.* A few pleaded for mercy. No one resisted. Father Segura lifted himself up from his sickbed, looked into the crazed eyes of Paquiquino and whispered, "I forgive you, my brother," just as Paquiquino buried a hatchet in his skull. Father Quiros* blessed another attacker just as that warrior cut off the priest's head with an ax. One by one, Paquiquino's gentle, innocent friends were slaughtered like defenseless animals. But Paq felt nothing. The elders had forced him to eat more of the mind-altering Jamestown Weed just before the raid. The hallucinogenic potion and the evil spirits inside him owned his soul that day.

Suddenly, Aloncito* came running out of the forest when he heard the priests crying out. "Stop! Stop! What are you doing? We are unarmed!" he bravely cried out.

A warrior saw the frantic ten-year-old and moved quickly to silence him with a knife. But Paquiquino caught the warrior's movement out of the corner of his eye. The boy's cry momentarily awoke Paquiquino's mind with images of his own boyish cries for help from the deck of that Spanish ship. With speed that surprised him, Paquiquino tackled the other warrior just in time. "No, he is a *boy*. Leave him!"

"But he will tell the Spanish."

But Paquiquino only tightened his grip on the legs of the thrashing brave and shouted, "Run, little man! Run for your life!"

In that moment, the pinned warrior flipped over and sliced open Paquiquino's cheek with a sharp flint knife, causing Paquiquino to release his him. Then, he got up, spat in Paquiquino's bleeding face and ran after the boy— but to no avail. The boy was gone.*

For a long time, Paquiquino just sat staring at the carnage in shock. He was grateful that Aloncito was gone—but—to his *horror*—his mind had *returned*. All around him lay the bloody, black-robed figures of men who had loved him like a son and protected him many times from the taunts and cruel ways of Spanish soldiers in Mexico.

"No . . . it can't be! *Noooo!*" he moaned as he stood up on wobbly legs. Then, as he backed away from his massacred friends, he tripped on a wooden altar with a crucifix sitting on top. As he fell, the crucifix tumbled onto his chest. He screamed, his vision blurred, and then he passed out. Later, some of the other warriors found him and carried him back to the village. For two days all he could do was lay in his hut, in and out of consciousness, sweating and groaning, "*No! No!*"

When he finally came back to his senses, Paquiquino told everyone, "I have killed innocent men. I killed friends. I am *cursed*. I must kill myself!"

But the shamans came quickly and chanted over him. They offered him spirit guides so he would not kill himself. One of the spirits was a monstrous spirit of hate that possessed his mind. "Whites are enemy. You must hate whites. *Kill* whites. This is your purpose," the spirit murmured over and over into Paquiquino's tortured soul.

It worked. Paquiquino's deep hatred for whites caused him to forget what he had done. Since then, he has lived to hate whites. Eventually, he taught his three sons to hate white people like he did. This was his demonic calling, and he was faithful to fulfill it. He *had to*. That hate was his only defense against suicide.

What Paquiquino and his war party did that Friday, February 9, 1571, became a turning point in American history,* and in the spiritual history of Virginia. The blood of Virginia's first Christian martyrs* had consecrated Moss Valley as holy ground*

High above, in the throne room of God, the nail-pierced hand of Jesus pointed to that blood-soaked Virginia soil and decreed, "*There* is where I will plant my church. There is where I will raise up a nation to glorify my name throughout the earth."

Instantly, all the saints and angels fell down and worshipped, saying, "Worthy are you, O Lamb, to receive glory and honor and power, forever and ever! Amen!"

LITTLE ALONCITO WAS EVENTUALLY RESCUED BY A SPANISH SHIP WHO came by to check on the Jesuits.* He had been hiding with another tribe.* The ship that came was captained by Pedro Menendez,* the very captain who had whisked Paquiquino away nine years earlier.*

After that, Spain never returned.

Neither did Paquiquino's sanity.

CHAPTER 34

May 13, 1607: That Evening

Just then, Paquiquino coughed several times and began to wake from his trance-like state—still in the arms of a very distraught Pocahontas. Finally, he could sit up next to her on the hard ground covered with trampled brown straw.

"Oh, Papa Paq. Are you *sick*? I thought you were dying."

"No, Matoaka, my body is fine," Paquiquino coughed, "but my heart is sick."

"Why, Papa? Pocahontas asked.

"Playful One, I cannot tell you now. Only elders and our family knows. It is great secret. Long ago, I did something very evil. This is why white men have come upon us. I have brought a curse on our people." For a moment, Pocahontas was speechless and in shock. Finally, she spoke.

"Is this why our shamans tell of a people coming from the east to take over Father's kingdom?"*

“Yes, my evil deeds have caused this. I tried to forget, but now all tribes will suffer. O Great Spirit, merciful Ahone, please forgive me and do not punish my people.” Paquiquino bowed his head and sobbed. Pocahontas threw her arms around her grandfather’s neck and wept with him.

Unseen to them, the room began to fill with a shimmering, rainbow-colored light as Scion and Angie knelt in worship. Spirits of self-hatred, guilt, and insanity who lived in the trembling warrior squealed in pain. They shot through the roof to alert Okeus to their victim’s dangerous prayers and the presence of angels in his hut. Scion and Angie saw them go, and they both shouted at once, “Hallelujah!”

Then Scion stood and spread his golden wings over the kneeling native and prayed, “Thank you, Holy Spirit, for beginning to set this tormented man free from decades of self-hatred. Thank you for helping him repent. He does not know you yet, but his heart is waking up. Reveal yourself to him more!”

At that exact moment, Morph returned from telling Okeus what an excellent job he was doing. Okeus had mocked and kicked him out of his presence, as usual.

As Morph landed near Paquiquino’s hut, he crumbled to the forest floor, blinded by the heavenly light pulsating from the longhouse. *Oh no! The glory of heaven is here! Great Lucifer! Okeus will pull me limb from limb for this if he finds out!*

He dashed into thick bushes near the hut, covered his terrified blue eyes with both paws as he moaned softly, “If any demon finds out about this, I’ll be deader than the deer that the English will get tomorrow from the tribe.

"Why, does this always happen to me? Every time I think I’m gonna do a good job, something like this happens. I must be jinxed or cursed. Lord Lucifer, help me! I am so tired of being treated like a freak. Maybe I should just do something *really* stupid and let Okeus kill me and get it over with. Maybe I should..." But his voice gave way to heaving sobs.

Angie had heard it all. She stopped worshipping in the hut and stared at the downcast demon just yards away. He was pulling out his fur with angry yelps, beating the ground with his paws, and rolling around as if in pain. For reasons she did not fully understand, she felt a sudden chill run down her spine. "Now that's weird! I feel . . . oh my gosh . . . I feel *sympathy* for him! Demons are our sworn enemies, but that's one I'd like to know more about."

As the tiny angel turned away to rejoin Scion in worship, she did not see Morph suddenly look up and stare at her. His sharp cat eyes had seen Angie watching him. He had seen something on her face he had never seen in any spirit: *compassion.* The, he made a dangerous vow.

If I ever get a chance to see her look at me again like that, I will take it—no matter what the cost.

CHAPTER 35

May 18, 1607

Within five days of their arrival at the island, as the last hogshead of food was heaved ashore by sweaty colonists, a long procession of Algonquian warriors wound down the hill toward the new settlement like a snake sizing up its prey.* An old man with greying hair, a large hooked nose and slightly stooped shoulders led the delegation. He looked frail but his eyes sparkled with intelligence and he had the bearing of a king. Paquiquino was among white people once again. "This time," he whispered to himself, "I will not be their victim! Whites have come to take our land. This time, I am ready."

Hundreds of demons in the surrounding treetops heard that whisper and roared their approval. They remembered what Paquiquino had done to the Spanish years ago.

Paquiquino sensed the darkening spiritual atmosphere and smiled. He knew that most whites were no match for the powerful, demonic powers of his tribes. Just then, a shout went up from the fort.

"Captain Newport, come quickly. Savages are approaching!" a sentry nervously yelled. "About two hundred of them."

Newport ran from his hut toward the sentry's voice as heavy muskets and long swords began clattering into the hands of nervous settlers. They remembered Cape Henry.

"Ready the forward gun!" Wingfield barked to a sailor on the Susan Constant, who was manning the first dogwatch.

Circling slowly above the island like a hungry vulture, Okeus sneered. "And so it begins, my little grubs. Now you shall see how well prepared we are for the likes of you and your foolish lord of heaven. You will soon dread the day you stepped on my domain."

Muskets cocked, swords drawn, fifty British men moved quickly uphill toward the undulating column of natives descending toward James Fort. As their most experienced soldier, Captain Smith was allowed to lead the armed procession, with Captain Newport right behind him. The other two ships' captains brought up the rear. Scion and Angie watched it all from the deck of the *Susan Constant*. Every spirit and human knew that history was about to be made.

"Company halt!" Smith called out. The English froze in position. The Algonquian column also stopped. A long, tense silence ensued while both sides sized each other up.

Finally, a brawny Scottish sailor called Big Jim swore under his breath, "For Gud's sake, Captain Smith. Ken ye nae dae somethin' b'fore me wee heart explodes? Dae we kiss 'em or kill 'em?"

Then, with his head held high, Paquiquino walked slowly past Smith and stood proudly before Captain Newport. Newport looked at the wizened old face before him with the big scar across the left cheek. The famous, one-armed hero saw something in those fiery, brown eyes that shook him—a look of *recognition*. Newport felt an unsettling mixture of fear and respect for the older man. He did not know if they would soon be friends or enemies. Then, with a low bow, the old warrior held out his hand to Newport and said in perfect English, "Welcome, sir."

"Did you hear that, Smith? He greeted me like a bloomin' Englishman! *Extraordinary*!"

Smith whispered to Newport, "This is no ordinary native, sir. Perhaps he has met an English survivor of the Lost Colony and learned a few words. He could have walked that far. But let's just play along for now. We need to find out more before we can assert our authority here." But Paquiquino heard every word—and *understood* it.

Unbeknownst to Smith or Newport, the sailor who went by the name of Jehu Robinson was also fascinated by the old warrior. *Could that old man be him? He was so young when I last saw him. Will he recognize me—the little altar boy?*

Suppressing a snicker, Paquiquino turned and told his warriors to bring the presents for the English. Four large legs of venison appeared. "Come, you white fools, *mecher,* eat. Wahunsenacawh, our King Powhatan of the Tsenacommacah Kingdom, gives this to you as a gift so we can find out what you really want. We know you came to deceive us," Paquiquino said in his native tongue as he bowed again to Newport and turned to leave. But at that moment, he heard a sailor shout.

"Chief Wahunsenacawh is telling us we are fools," Jehu announced with a snort of anger. "I say, let's not trust their friendship." Newport shot Jehu a look of hot anger. Jehu quickly lowered his head. He realized he had gone too far.

Smith turned to Captain Newport. "Sir, unfortunately, what Jehu said is true." And then Smith gave a rough translation of Paquiquino's entire message to Newport, who smiled and shook his head in amazement.

Now it was Paquiquino's turn to be perplexed. *How do these white ones know our language? This is not good.* Fear rose in the old warrior—as he looked closer at Jehu. *Wait—that one looks like someone I once knew. But no—it could not be.*

Jehu saw the wily native looking at him closely. "I need to smoke this guy out more—and make up for my foolish outburst," Jehu whispered to himself. "If it is him, he will understand what I say and respond. Let's see what that Powhatan does with this." He pulled out his smoking pipe. "Well, if we are gonna eat venison tonight, I only wish I had some tobacco to smoke with it. Why, then, I'd be fit as a king." Jehu knew the Powhatan's often smoked tobacco.

All the sailors laughed. "Fat chance 'a that happening," the big Scottish sailor quipped.

There was another secret chuckle from Paquiquino, but no tobacco appeared. *Didn't work,* Jehu concluded. *Guess it wasn't him after all. I need to kill the right man.*

Just then, there was a small scuffle on the starboard flank of the British group. A native was trying to steal a hatchet from a sailor.* Natives and whites began to yell and curse. Suddenly, a knife slashed into the side of the native, mortally wounding him. Just as quickly, an arrow sang past Smith's head. Then a musket fired. Within a moment, they were at war.* Screams of pain and musket smoke filled the air. But within two minutes, the battle ended. The thunderous blast of a ship's cannon scattered the warriors back to the forest above the island as frightened colonists scurried to the safety of their ships. All that caused Okeus to laugh and slap Snookus hard on his blubbery head. "Told you so, Snookus! These English are doomed!"

"Now what, Master?" Angie moaned. "This is a terrible start for the colony." Scion just shook his head and grimaced at the puddles of English and Powhatan blood seeping into the ground—together.

"I don't know, Angie. I don't know. I instructed angels for 10,000 years. But no one ever taught me how to handle things like this. God help us all."

As the cries of wounded men ebbed away, Smith looked around from the deck of the *Susan Constant* and shouted to Newport, "I knew it would go like this! You can't trust the natives. Look at us—two killed and ten injured! If this ship had not fired its cannon,* more of us might be dead already. Those savages only know one way to treat us: at the end of an arrow or spear!"

Newport spat into the dark river and stared at the brackish water, "This is a bad omen, Smith—just like that comet we saw while we were becalmed in the Downes. We must be cursed! What will the end of us be if the beginning is like this? We are almost out of food, the natives are already against us, we have not planted any crops, and winter will be upon us before we know it. We might as well be shipwrecked. I've got to return to England to get more food and men."

Peering from the low ridge above the silent battlefield below, Paquiquino's mind was tumbling with emotions he dared not voice. *The war has begun—and it's my fault. This is the curse I brought on our people. They will take our land and rape our crenepo, our women, just like Spanish n Mexico. We must stop them. But how?* Then he turned and walked east to see his son, the chief. They had much to talk about. His son had hoped for friendship with the English, but now blood has been shed. Paquiquino knew more of the same would come. It always did.

MONGO WAS KNEELING IN HIS DARKENED HUT, CHANTING PRAYERS TO Okeus to drive out the English. Suddenly, Snookus arrived and wrapped his five long tentacles around the head of Mongo.

"Mongo, Lord Okeus congratulates you on a job well done," Snookus gushed. "The British have tasted their own blood already. Your spells and incantations are working well. Soon, we will show their lord that we are not so easily devoured by his people or his angels. But first, we must kill the man they call *Hunt*. Hunt prays too much. He is dangerous to us."

Mongo slowly rose, his eyes glowing like burning coals. He raised both hands above his head, looked upward, and began to pray,

"Master Snookus, I am grateful for your trust in me as Chief Shaman for Lord Okeus. Please tell him I am his faithful slave and that Hunt will die soon. Tell Lord Okeus that my father will kill Hunt—just as he killed the Spanish priests for us!"

Snookus cackled with joy as he released Mongo's head. Then, with a pungent blast of ebony gas, he shot into the air to visit James Fort once more before reporting to Okeus.

CHAPTER 36

As the crimson sunset washed across the blood-stained ground just outside James Fort, Captain Smith and Jehu Robinson searched the battle site for personal items lost by their men. Just before returning to the ships, Smith saw something glint in the dying sunlight. He bent over and picked up two small objects half-buried in the dirt. Snookus flew over at that moment and dove closer to see what the two were doing.

"Look, Jehu, icons of history: a quartz arrowhead and a silver sixpence with the bust of bonnie King James I. What irony—just lying here together in the dust of battle."

Smith gazed at Robinson intently for a moment and then stood up with a faraway look in his squinting blue eyes, "Mr. Robinson. We are witnesses: the clash of two civilizations has begun. Both sides came in peace, but peace was not to be."

Jehu just grinned and then picked the items from the soldier's hand to view them better. "Hah! I wonder what your favorite author, Machiavelli,* would say about today, Captain? What kind of trickery would he come up with to deal with these savages?"

"Oh, you remember me telling you about my admiration for him,* do you? I had too much grog that night on the ship. Don't tell the others. They already fear my loyalty to them. Well, I don't know what Machiavelli would say, but what I do know is this: I have not fought people all over Europe only to come here and be defeated by a bunch of illiterate, half-naked savages. This fort shall *not* fall on my watch. If the rest of the Council will listen to me, I can help them defeat these natives and establish this colony on a firm footing."

"I'm with you, Captain Smith," Jehu quickly retorted. "These wretched creatures must submit to us. They are cruel and can never be trusted. I hate them as you do."

Snookus heard Jehu's remark and chortled wickedly, "Oh, listen to that! This is good news for my master."

"Actually, Jehu, I don't hate them for being who they are. I just despise them when they resist our British Empire."*

"But you hated the Muslims that you fought, right?" Jehu countered coyly. "I've seen your military crest with the three Muslims on it."

"Yes, I killed those three, and many other Muslim Turks, but I don't hate them. I feel sorry for them."

"You do? How can that be? Muslim armies have ravaged Christian Europe for almost a thousand years in unprovoked attacks.* They have slaughtered tens of thousands of Christians and Jews in the process.* Remember the huge Muslim siege of Vienna in 1529?"*

"I certainly do. Some of my Austrian friends lost their grandparents in that siege. But I see it like this: Muslims are wonderful people—just like you and me. The real problem is their holy book, the *Quran*. It forces them to attack and kill Christians and Jews. Did you know that there are one hundred and nine war verses in the Quran promoting violence against non-Muslims, especially Jews and Christians?*

"According to a university professor I met in Vienna, the Quran the only holy book in the world that calls for war against Christians and

Jews.* Their founder, Muhammed, lived what he taught in the Quran. He led many military jihad campaigns himself against civilian caravans.* He even had five hundred Jews decapitated—*after* they surrendered to him in Medina."*

"I didn't know that, Captain. I guess you learned a lot, fighting them all across Europe."

"Yes—experience is the best teacher, Jehu. The Quran is the problem —not Muslim people. Actually, Muslims are the biggest victims of Islam. It has forced so many of them to die in battles for Islam. I'm not very religious, but I hope they'll come to know the God of the Bible someday. I hear that he is a lot nicer than their god." Both men laughed.

"But, Smith," Jehu interjected with a sly smile, "Muslims claim that their god is the God of the Bible."*

Snookus smiled and snickered. *If they only knew how false that was.* But Snookus did not smile for long.

"Nothing could be further from the truth, Jehu. Look, I'm a foul-mouthed bastard, but even I know that the Christian God commands his people to love others—even their *enemies*. The god of Islam would never say that. But you claim to be a Christian—and yet you hate these natives. Why? Where did all that hate come from? You know, while in a Muslim prison years ago, I met a man you remind me of. . . . He was an assassin."

"Oh, really?" Jehu murmured as he turned to look across the river.

"And by the way, is Jehu your actual name?"

"Why do you ask, Captain?"

"O, just curious. Jehu was the name of an assassin God sent to kill the household of a wicked king* in one of those Bible stories my mother read to me long ago.

"I'm impressed, Smith. For a mercenary, you know the Bible better than I thought. Yes, Jehu is my nickname. My real name is John. My friends back home call me Jehu because I like to fight the enemies of God," Jehu said forcefully with a chilling smile. Smith saw it and grimaced.

Snookus grinned again. *Oh, I really like this one. We must help him kill many here.*

"I believe you, Jehu. I've seen that smile on many men I've fought in hand-to-hand combat. They were hard to beat. Hate is a powerful weapon. And to be honest, Jehu, I'll tell you something I do hate: the killing of Protestants by Catholics all across Europe."

"Yes, quite terrible, isn't it?" Jehu agreed blandly.

"I've seen it with my own eyes as I've fought in several countries. But, hey—when this colony grows, Protestants will have a place to call their own right here where we stand. That's good news, right?" And with that, Smith slapped Jehu on his chest, laughing.

"Ahh!" Jehu yelped in pain. "I broke my collarbone when I was a boy, and it never healed right."

"How'd you break it?" Smith asked.

Jehu looked away again. "It's a long story."

"Oh, more secrets, huh?" Smith chuckled. "Yes—I have a few of them myself. Well, let's get back aboard those rancid ships and sleep safely while we can. Hopefully, we can build a decent stockade on the island soon to protect us because Newport is taking our two biggest ships back to England for supplies on June 22.* And he's taking all that iron pyrite—*fool's gold*—the men have collected.* I told him it was all worthless. And you know what? He agreed. But he said, 'We have to show the Company that we are trying.'" The two men laughed again—both relieved that there was something they could laugh about before they parted ways to their berths.

But as he approached the gangplank, Jehu had to stop. He was breathing heavily—but not for physical reasons. The pain in his collarbone had triggered a flood of painful memories. As he hurried into the belly of the ship, he was overcome with emotions that had haunted him ever since he fled Virginia in 1571.

BACK AT THE SWAMP BASE OF OKEUS, SNOOKUS ALIGHTED AND screeched, "Master, I found a man they call Jehu who really hates the natives!

Okeus looked at his bulb-headed assistant and farted loudly. "That's good. Any man who hates well is a friend of ours. What else have you learned today?"

"Well, was the Master aware that Muslims have tried to invade Christian Europe for a thousand years? Do you think they might try to invade our lands, too?"

"O, shut up, you dolt. Don't you know anything? Don't foxes and raccoons piss on things to stake out their territory? Heaven made Hunt plant that hideous cross to claim this land. The Muslim spirit, Jibril, had that boy hide a sacred stone in the ground when the Spanish came here. Same thing. One day, Snookus—count on it. They *will* come."

CHAPTER 37

May 26, 1607

Thirteen days after landing on the island, the weary settlers erected a crude fort with stockade walls in record time.* After that first skirmish with the Algonquins, every man and boy worked as if their lives depended on it! With that measure of safety in place, Captain Newport prepared to sail to England for food supplies.* The men ate most of their food on the unusually long voyage.*

Before Newport sailed, a meeting was called. Everyone was to meet in the fort that night at seven sharp. After a sparse dinner of beans and rice, everyone came off the ships and sat on the ground in a half-circle around the newly appointed president of the colony, Edward Wingfield,* who stood on a stump, smiling like he had just conquered the entire known world.

"Quiet now. Settle down. Please take a seat where you can, gentlemen. I am calling us to order. This is the first public meeting of the Virginia Council in our new colony. To honor our good King James I for sending us here, we have renamed this river. Captain Smith says the natives call it the Powhatan River.* But we will now call it the James River."*

Cheers erupted from the dirty, unshaven men. Wingfield, however, looked every inch the quintessential English nobleman dressed in his finest military uniform and wearing insignia to show his previous membership in Parliament. He also had powerful friends in England. Few dared to oppose him, even in trivial matters—except for Smith.

Okeus and Snookus hung in the air just above the river to monitor the meeting. Scion and Angie sat nearby on the mainmast of the *Susan Constant*, watching for any demonic interference. The two pairs of spirits exchanged hateful looks now and then just to warn each other not to try anything.

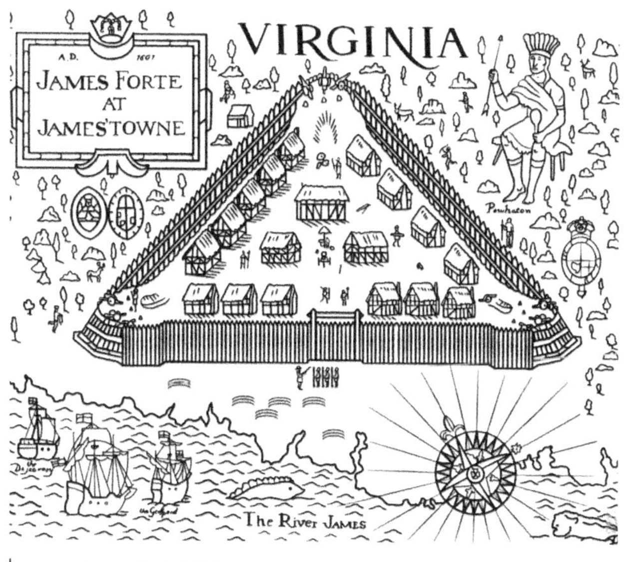

Jamestown Fort, 1607

Wingfield continued. "I want to personally thank all of you for working so hard to make our new fort so strong against future native attacks. The ten-foot walls are impressive, and the gate is massive. But the triangular shape of the fort is just brilliant. With our cannons on each of the bulwarks where the walls meet, we should have an excellent field of fire against intruders, be they Spanish or Powhatan. My congratulations to all!" Cheers of approval rose from the listeners again—only louder.

"And a double portion of grog tonight, perhaps, to celebrate, my lord?" Jehu Robinson shouted over the applause.

Wingfield smiled broadly, "Of course, laddies. Tonight, we will tip our cups of kindness together. You all certainly deserve it. And we have a lot to be grateful for. We only lost one man on a four thousand mile voyage and we only have a few wounded from that recent scuffle with the natives.

"Now, on a weightier matter: I recently opened the sealed orders from our sponsors. We used to call them the London Company, but since we are in Virginia, we shall henceforth call them the Virginia Company. Tonight, I wish to announce whom they have chosen to be your leaders in this glorious adventure for God and for England."

More cheers.

"As some of you already know, your new Council has elected me as president on May 13th for a one-year term. Let me introduce the rest of your Council. First, my dear cousin, Captain of the Godspeed, world-famous explorer and Vice-Admiral of this voyage, Captain Bartholomew Gosnold.* He is the man who has done more than any to establish this great colony. Then, we have Captain Christopher Newport, Captain John Ratcliffe, Captain John Martin, Captain George Kendall, and—" Wingfield winced and cleared his throat, "Captain John Smith."*

At that, all one hundred and three men and boys stood and clapped.

~

Above them, Okeus grunted. "Too much harmony here. Not good," he muttered.

Snookus quickly interjected, "No worries, my Lord. That demon they call Mammon who came here on their ships is already hard at work. Did you see the English leap from the ship and start looking for gold and pearls as soon as they landed? And in the evenings, Mongo has arranged for native women to visit the fort. Heh, heh, heh—gold, glory, and girls. It works every time on men like these—just as you said, Master," Snookus snickered nervously.

Okeus belched loudly and then barked, "Not good enough! What else?"

Snookus cowered. "Well, we also have *sickness*. The mosquitoes we control are ready to swarm as soon as the heat comes."

"*Bugs*!" Okeus roared. "It's disgusting that with all of our mighty powers, we rely on insects to do our work!"

"Yes, it is a humble means, my Lord—but a clever and strong one. Even our Enemy in heaven knows it," Snookus quipped, trying to lighten things up. "He calls Lucifer the 'Lord of the Flies—*Beelzebub*.'"*

"Shut up, you fool! Don't remind me. The Enemy just uses that name to insult Lucifer," Okeus huffed. "I know we need their crusty little bodies to propel our weapons. In fact, I have big plans for our sickness arsenal.

"Ha! Remember the native scum in Roanoke who welcomed the whites to their shores? Their brown native eyes bulged with curiosity when the invaders read from the Enemy's book. A few weeks later, their eyes bulged with *fever*—just before they died. *Ha-ha*. Our bugs down there made sure the diseases of the whites* were carried right into their villages. Lucifer is a genius with sickness."

"And we have had this wonderful drought now for several years,"* Snookus said. "Food will be scarce. And when the summer comes, they will get thirsty and drink the foul water near the fort."* He clutched his throat in mock terror, followed by a devilish grin on his bulbous, flaxen face. "Mongo's curse on the water will work wonders on them. They will be like clay in our claws."

"True," Okeus conceded, "but something about this group still bothers me. There is a faint glow in the fort. Where the hell is that heavenly light coming from?"

"No worry, my Fearsome One. Probably only the filthy residue from their worship and prayers at the cape. Once we remove Hunt, few will remember to do anything like that again."

Okeus burped and farted his agreement as Snookus flashed his usual ingratiating smile in return. But their smugness was about to be tested again— by Chaplain Hunt.

CHAPTER 38

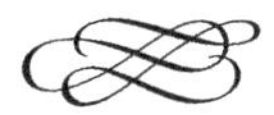

As the cheering and clapping slowly died down, Wingfield called Captain Christopher Newport to the stump to address the men. More cheers erupted. Newport was a national hero to every English sailor.

"Tell us about how you captured the *Madre de Deus*!"* someone shouted from the back. More cheers.

"You are right!" Wingfield replied with evident pleasure. "Who could forget the plunder of that one-hundred-and-sixty-five-foot Portuguese treasure ship?* It was the largest haul of New World wealth ever captured by an English ship in the entire sixteenth century*—I think it was five hundred tons of spices, silks, gemstones, and other valuable goods."*

The crowd roared even louder as Newport took the stump from Wingfield and smiled at the assembled men.

"We *made it*—thanks to all of you! You've done bloody well despite a very, very long voyage."

"I thought we were going to colonize the bloomin' Channel," a sailor chimed in, much to the amusement of everyone.

Newport joined in the laughter and concluded, "I congratulate you all. I leave in about a month for England. I hope to return within four months with fresh victuals and fresh workers for the colony." With that, he waved to the crowd and stepped down to give Wingfield the stump again.

Wingfield cleared his throat. He wanted the men to hear this part well. "Now that we are here, I want to congratulate you on being part of this historic adventure for God and Crown. It is no small matter, as you may know, that this is England's newest colony in the New World. Roanoke didn't make it, poor souls, but *we* will.

And isn't this a grand place to plant our colony? Captain Smith just told me that 'Heaven and Earth never agreed better to frame a place for man's habitations.' *As you know, Smith and I disagree on some things, but I heartily concur with my fellow Council member on that."

More cheers from the weary travelers.

Okeus was tiring of all the good cheer. "Just wait till summer, my ignorant jackasses," Okeus snorted to himself. "Have your fling in the spring. Have you not heard of smallpox? Influenza? The bloody flux? These and more await your putrid bodies, dear Christians—we rule the swamps in summer."

"Maybe it needs not to be said, but you all know we have a debt to pay," Wingfield reminded them. "Each of us has come here with our passage paid by investors of the Company.* While it is true that his Majesty's charter to us does command us to convert the local savages, we have to put first things first. If we do not begin to show a profit soon, we may all have to return to England with a heavy debt over our heads."*

The crowd groaned and whispered among themselves. A sly smile crossed Okeus's mouth, and Chaplain Hunt began to squirm a little.

Wingfield held up his hand to silence the crowd. "Now, if the Spanish and Portuguese can haul tons of gold and silver home to their countries, why can't we? As for me, I am tired of our ships raiding other ships for gold. Let's get *our own,* I say!"

More cheers. Okeus looked at Snookus. They both smiled.

"Aye, Lord Wingfield, we've already been looking for pearls in the oysters all around us," a sailor shouted. "But there twern't any."

A murmur of disappointment rose from the men.

"All right, all right. Don't be discouraged. We just arrived, and this is the New World. Anything is possible. There has to be gold here, just like there was for the Spanish down south. As you know, we have brought several assayers with us to help us find the best gold and silver here. You have already found a bucket of what looks like gold, but starting next week, Captain Smith and a small detachment of armed men will go with those assayers to explore for more gold deposits."*

Sounds of approval rumbled through the crowd.

Then, as Wingfield stepped down from the stump, Chaplain Hunt rose to speak. Wingfield smiled and said, "Chaplain, what would say to us tonight?"

"My esteemed President, it is certainly true that good King James has given clear financial goals to the colony God is planting here. But surely, since the King is also head of the Church of England, he must have a deep interest in seeing the natives become Christians, as he mentioned in his charter to us. With all due respect, sir, may the Council also encourage the men to pray for the conversion of the natives and do what they can to present a Christian witness to them? Perhaps one day, when we learn their language, we can tell them more of Christ if we have first tried to show them Christ in our actions toward them."

"Well put, my good parson," Wingfield responded. "I will bring this matter up at the next Council meeting. I can assure you that we all feel as you do in this regard. It is just a matter of time before we do seek their salvation. But Newport must leave soon, and he needs to take back some evidence of the wealth here to our financial backers. Remember—they paid our way here to make a profit for them. Therefore, finding gold must be our first concern. I am sure you understand, Chaplain Hunt."

Hunt nodded his head in appreciation. "I assure you that God wants this colony to prosper, or else he would not have brought us here. My concern is that we plant this colony as God would have it done. There is no greater warning in scripture about money than the one Jesus gave us when he said, 'You cannot serve God and mammon.'* If the men think that making money is our main goal, they may end up loving money more than loving God. Surely God can make us prosper if we seek first his Kingdom, can he not?"

Wingfield and Hunt were smiling, but everyone felt the growing tension between the two leaders.

As the crowd was dispersing, Captain Smith saw the deep disappointment in Hunt's eyes. In a very rare gesture, Smith walked over and placed his brawny hand on the chaplain's shoulder. "Don't fret, Chaplain. There is still much good you can do here. Over time, with your help, the men will do God's work among the natives."

"I hope you are right, Captain. My heart tells me that what we do now as we start the colony will decide its fate for many years to come. God is watching. He wants to bless and protect us, but we have to do it his way."

Smith smiled. "I've never met a man who believes the Bible like you do. It's as if you actually know the author personally," Smith laughed.

"I do, my friend. That's why I am so concerned. When we close a door to God, it opens another to the devil. Who knows what that fiend may bring through that door into our colony?"

Captain Smith looked directly at the sad-faced chaplain. "Sir, no one I have ever met commands my respect more than you. When I was unjustly condemned in the ship's brig for three months, it was only you who came to my defense and brought me fresh water and extra victuals each day. Even from my cell, I saw how you soothed men's souls who were wont to fight and steal from each other on the long voyage. You are truly a saint, sir, and no one can deny it. I would fight them to the death if they tried."

"Captain Smith, you make my ordinary actions too large for truth," Hunt humbly responded. "I would have done that for any man."

"Exactly my point, parson. Your life bespeaks of a fellowship with the Lord that few could ever hope to have. But listen—you know full well how much I despise the president, but in this matter, Wingfield is correct. The men must be driven to work hard to find wealth here, or all is lost. Making money must be their first concern, not God," Smith said. "As a soldier, I've learned that practical matters must often take priority over spiritual goals. We must be practical, or we will be forced to leave or to die."

Hunt looked at Smith with fatherly affection. "Captain, we all have to respect you for your strength and courage in fighting for what is right in many places. Yet, I have to disagree with you on this. Were it not possible for men to seek first God and love him more than money, God would not have commanded it. God does not wish to constrain our work. He demands to control our hearts. He wants our hearts for himself, above all else. Whatever captures our hearts captures us. 'For where your treasure is, there will your heart be also,' Jesus spoke. If we teach the men that money is their greatest treasure, then money will rule their hearts, not God."

Smith was smitten to silence by the love and logic of Hunt. The two men just stood there and looked at each other. Each so different, yet each so appreciative of the other.

Smith and Hunt finally parted—with a friendly nod to President Wingfield. They noticed that he had been watching them talk. As the slender English parson in the black coat trudged back to his new cabin in the fort, Wingfield mused, *Hunt may be right, but my job is to keep the investors happy. We were sent here for gold, not God.* God forgive us.*

Flying away from the scene, Okeus and Snookus both felt relieved. "Thank Lucifer, those pathetic slugs have no idea how right Hunt is," Okeus snorted contemptuously. "The gold, glory and the girls. I love them all. Men love them all—especially the gold. And these waterbags came for *gold*. Praise Lucifer! Soon, this is going to be another "Lost Colony!""

CHAPTER 39

December 1, 1607

The colony suffered deeply that summer and into the fall. Semi-salty well-water caused numerous stomach problems.* Hot, humid days with little sanitation brought flies, mosquitoes and sickness* they called "the bloody flux."*

Each night, the pitiful wails of men dying horrible, slow deaths kept most people awake. The suffering was so great that even Algonquin warriors stationed near the fort felt sympathy for them.

By fall, food supplies were critically short.* Most of the healthy men had been too busy looking for gold or pearls to plant crops last summer.* If the Powhatans had not brought the colony multiple, large donations of corn and venison, the settlement would have collapsed before January.* By winter, over half the colony was dead.*

Scion was aghast. He never expected disease and famine to decimated the colony so quickly. He felt helpless to save it—and Okeus knew it. He sent word to Lucifer that the English invasion would be destroyed by the spring of 1608.

Angie's monthly reports to Michael were hard for Michael to read. He was very disappointed and wondered if he made a mistake to send Scion there. His messages to Scion were always the same: "I'm a' praying fer ye, laddie. Dunnae give up!" Scion's eyes always grew moist when Angie relayed that part of the General's message. Scion also knew he had to do something different to save the colony—*but what?*

One day, as Scion was praying for the settlers, he remembered that Gabriel had spoken to Joseph in a dream about traveling to Egypt to protect Jesus. So, the next night, Scion planted an idea in Captain Smith's mind through a dream. Smith dreamt that he should go hunting to get food for the fort. He awoke that morning and recruited two men to accompany him. They knew they would have to trespass on Powhatan lands to hunt—which might lead to conflict—but the starvation of the men more than justified the risk.

So, in the frigid, gray dawn of December 5th, Smith and two nervous soldiers stomped into the dense forest to hunt deer.* High overhead, Scion could see that the fort was being watched day and night by native sentries dressed in thick bearskin clothes. As soon as Smith's brown leather boots crunched the icy snow outside the main gate, the threesome was spotted and tracked. Within the hour, Opie and a dozen warriors ambushed them. The two soldiers were quickly killed by a flurry of arrows,* but, miraculously, Smith survived.* No spirit or man had seen Scion dive like a lightning bolt and deflect three arrows that would have easily killed the surviving soldier.

The warriors were shocked. "The Great Spirit must be protecting this man. Our arrows should not miss when enemy is so close," one attacker gasped. But Opie just cursed and said, "The real reason is you men shoot like women. Bind him. Let's get back to our village."

After binding his arms tightly with vines, twelve warriors took turns pulling and pushing the armor-clad soldier for three hours by foot and by canoe to face judgment by Chief Powhatan at Werowocomoco.

Opie sent one warrior ahead to alert the Chief that they had captured the white warrior who spoke their language. The news spread like wildfire. Everyone at Werowocomoco hurriedly gathered to see what no Powhatan had ever witnessed.*

Algonquin warriors*

Two dozen tawny, Algonquian warriors clad in deerskin waist flaps, leather leggings, and bearskin robes, gathered around a smoky fire in front of the wide entrance to Chief Powhatan's throne room. Like most Powhatan longhouses, it was constructed of bent saplings covered with tree bark and woven mats. But this *yihakans*—longhouse—was draped with large black bearskins and brown deerskins on all the interior walls. Long white and brown eagle feathers were attached along the entire interior frame of the entrance.

Powhatan's father, Paquiquino, and his younger brother Mongo had seats of honor on the chief's throne—a large, log platform, eight feet wide by twelve feet long and three feet above the ground, facing the entrance.* The platform floor was strewn with multiple layers of skins from black bear, red fox, raccoon, and deer. Powhatan's throne was made of two dozen massive deer antler racks woven together with pearl-studded leather straps. The rugged antler racks were softened with a thick bearskin rug, covered by the most exquisitely woven blue fabric whose corners were festooned with dozens of beautiful turkey and eagle feathers.

Tomocomo sat directly behind Mongo's seat on the platform. Tomocomo* was an assistant to Mongo and married to Matachanna,* the sister of Pocahontas.* Several of Powhatan's many wives and children sat silently at the rear of the long room on the ground, straining their necks to see all they could. But one child did not have to struggle to see. Eleven-year-old Pocahontas stood to the left of her father's royal seat, looking beautiful and wise beyond her years in her fox-trimmed deerskin dress and long raccoon-skin robe. Her big brown eyes danced with so much excitement that her body actually vibrated and made her long, raven hair bounce slightly as she rapidly scanned the crowd. *Finally, I get to meet one. I wonder what he looks like up close. I hope he is handsome . . . and not married,* she imagined with girlish glee.

After all the leaders were in place, Powhatan arrived and took his seat on his throne as every head bowed low in honor of their great chief. With his tall headdress of eagle, hawk, and osprey feathers and his powerful build and regal bearing, Powhatan looked every inch the paramount chief of the thirty tribes. As he sat down dressed in his finest black bearskin robe, an audible sigh of relief could be heard in the crowd. The entire tribe knew that one of the British invaders had been captured and was being brought to their camp. Fear was on the face of almost every person. The tribe dreaded what might happen to them if more harm was done to the white people who have powerful weapons—weapons their warriors fled from in the May 18 battle. But every Algonquin who gathered in that dusty clearing trusted their great Powhatan to rule wisely in this tense moment.

However, no one could have anticipated that what happened next between the chief, his favorite daughter, and the soldier would become the stuff of legend—and the root cause of what saved the Jamestown colony from certain doom in its first two years in the Virginia wilderness.

Suddenly, the nervous serenity of the crowd was rent asunder by the sounds of a scuffle with cracking branches, and loud cursing—in a language the village had never heard. Several wild-eyed warriors burst into view, pulling a very angry British soldier in full uniform—but stripped of his sword, musket, metal helmet, and breastplate.

As the war party arrived, Scion swooped onto the roof of a nearby hut to join Angie, who had been watching over Pocahontas since she arrived an hour earlier. Scion came to protect Smith—at all costs. General Michael had told them that Smith was essential to God's plan for the colony. Okeus and Snookus saw the big angel alight. He just glared at him from the blazing firepit near the throne room. But a gaggle of towering demons quickly slinked backward when they saw the twelve-foot angel land.

The soldier was still blindfolded and bleeding from superficial wounds on his head. Opie entered the royal longhouse, dragging Smith behind him, and then knelt before the chief. Smith was shoved to his knees by a muscular brave. He just stared at the ground, seething with anger. Suddenly, Opie turned and grabbed the soldier's blood-matted, auburn hair and yanked his head back with such brute force it made the squaws suck in their breath.

"My Chief, my father, and brothers, look! We captured this white devil near our Chickahominy River. He says that he and his two warriors were just looking for food. But they fought us when we challenged them for being on our land. We killed two of them but captured this one. He speaks our language a little. He also has things we want. Look, he has shining bark for his chest that no arrow can pierce." The crowd let out a gasp as Opie held up Smith's breastplate and struck it with a flint knife. The blade broke.

"He deserves to die, my Chief. He is one of white warriors our father, Paq, told us would come someday. He has come to kill us and steal our lands, as the Spanish did in Mexico—just as our father Paq has taught us."

Chief Powhatan took a deep breath. "My brother, Opie, you have brought great honor to our tribe today by defeating the whites and bringing one here. But as Chief, I must decide if he will live or die. Unmask him." One of the braves ripped the blood-stained blindfold off, causing Smith's head wounds to bleed more.

Smith opened his mud-caked, blue eyes. He'd been bound and pulled with a rope through the woods for miles. Now he was face to face with the Algonquian chief who would decide if he lived or died. He looked weary and wary, but not afraid. Then, still kneeling, he smiled, bowed low, and in perfect Powhatan said *Meegwetch**—thank you. The crowd gasped again. No prisoner had ever acted like that—and this white one spoke Algonquin!

Just then, Powhatan heard a small whimper behind him where his favorite daughter was hiding. He sensed her concern for this white man, but he did not know why.

Powhatan looked at the strange, smiling prisoner and said in his native tongue, "You have come to the throne of the Great Powhatan at Werowocomoco. You have come with fire-sticks and sharp blades that we do not have. Why?"

Captain John Smith*

Smith stood up slowly.

"He has hair like a fox," one brave whispered. But, in a world of brown eyes, Powhatan could not stop staring at Smith's eyes. They were sky-blue! They seemed to float in a pond of pink flesh nestled above a bushy red beard and mustache.

But the visual spell on the chief was broken as Smith began to speak. Using hand gestures and his rough knowledge of Powhatan, the twenty-seven-year-old soldier explained that he'd come in peace.

"Forgive me, Great Powhatan, for causing this problem. We have no food in our village, and I was told to find deer to feed our people. Many have died of sickness, and all of us grow hungrier by the day. Please have mercy on us. We meant no harm," Smith implored with much sincerity.

Paquiquino leaned over and whispered to Powhatan, "I think he is telling the truth, my son."

Pocahontas heard that and nodded dramatically in agreement toward her father. Powhatan looked at Smith again. Perhaps he is more useful to us alive, the chief thought. He decided to spare him.

Smith scanned the crowd. Men, women, and children gawked at him, unsure of whether to hate him or admire him. But one of them stood out—a young girl near the chief. Her eyes shone with kindness and compassion—and something more, which made Smith somewhat uncomfortable. As their eyes met, Smith smiled at her and bowed his head slightly.

Angie sighed deeply as Pocahontas blushed and pulled her raccoon coat over her face a little more.

Okeus poked Snookus and demanded, "Get your lackeys speaking, you idiot! Can't you see Smith is a charmer?" In an instant, Snookus was inside Opie and Mongo, in succession.

"Kill him now, brother!" Opie shouted. "His head on our spear will show the English who they are dealing with. Do not appease them, or we will all live to regret it." Shouts of agreement began to be heard from the half-circle of older braves.

Okeus burped with satisfaction. Snookus looked relieved. Scion's hand twitched toward his sword, but Okeus and Snookus missed that micro-movement. They were salivating for blood.

"Your brother, Opie, is right, Great Powhatan," Mongo quickly added. "We cannot trust white men. I say slaughter him as an example. Father Paq says whites are like a bear robbed of its cubs—very dangerous. Whites never give up, unless met with force." War-whoops of approval shot up from the assembled warriors. Snookus whooped with them. Okeus gave him a rare but weak grin.

Powhatan looked around at his angry, cheering warriors and sighed. He could see the futility of going against his most trusted leaders and braves. Finally, with regret, he commanded, “Bring the stone. The white man must die. He will be a sacrifice to Okeus.”

CHAPTER 40

No sooner had he said it than six braves leaped up to move a large, ceremonial rock they carried by using large vines wrapped around it. They set it in front of Powhatan with a thud. Just as quickly, Mongo appeared with a large, metal hatchet—a Spanish hatchet he had found years ago in a mossy part of the woods. Smith's head was forced down on the stone by two braves. They held him there by his hair and feet, his body dangling in the air horizontally. When he saw the hatchet, Smith kicked and twisted his body violently to get loose—until one warrior hit him on the head with a heavy wooden club. Dazed and weary, the seasoned soldier realized it was useless to resist, and his body went limp.

Okeus drooled green, sticky slime down his chin. He loved killing. And human sacrifices to him were like a sweet dessert. He could feel his dark spirit feeding on the crowd's hatred for Smith and their worship of him as they began to chant: "O-ke-us. O-ke-us"—over and over. Even the demons nearby joined in, intoxicated with bloodlust.

Scion stood up slowly while Okeus was distracted. He had a plan. But Angie's eyes were glued to Pocahontas. Somehow, she sensed that the chief's daughter had a part to play here. Suddenly, Angie saw what no man could see—a rainbow of light piercing the darkened sky. It struck the little princess right above her heart.

Pocahontas almost fell backward. She sat down and put her hands over her face. She couldn't believe what she was hearing in her head—or what she was feeling. Her heart was pounding. Her head was spinning. Ahone was speaking. *Save him.* Her eyes got wide. How could she? Her two uncles wanted death for the prisoner. She knew her grandfather hated white soldiers. The braves were cheering for his death. Her thoughts raced as she stared at Smith.

This white warrior only defend himself to hunt for food. His people sick and starving. He is strong warrior who can teach us many things—maybe help Father get fire-sticks. This white one even speak our language and show us respect. And . . . he looks very good to me. Then she looked around quickly to see if anyone saw her gazing at the prisoner... and blushing. No human noticed.

But a hyper-alert female angel did. Now Angie knew why the light of heaven had touched the princess. With the quickness of a frightened hummingbird, Angie darted right next to Pocahontas and frantically whispered, "Go now! Tell your father to spare him!"

As if pricked by a pin, the little Algonquian girl jumped up and threw herself into her father's arms crying, "Father, let him live! For me, please. I know not why, but my heart and Great Spirit tell me to save him. Please do not kill him, Father— for my sake!"

The surprised chief smiled and looked into his daughter's soft brown eyes brimming with tears, "My dear Pocahontas, how can I resist you? You bring me much joy with your laughter, your singing, and your happy cartwheels. I want to spare the white warrior, but your uncles have much wisdom—and my braves demand his death. They are right to call for his death. He is dangerous to us."

Angie stood up, flew right in front of the chief's face, and with her tiny arms akimbo, she shouted at Powhatan, "You're the chief! You can do whatever you want! Listen to your daughter!" She knew he could not hear a word of that. But it made her feel better. Then Angie wept. *It's just not right—and I can't stop it,* she groaned inwardly.

Okeus belched at the sight of the tiny angel crying over Smith. Snookus followed suit.

Pocahontas also cried hot tears and put her head on her father's shoulder. *Why did I even try,* she thought? *Of course, Father is right. My uncles cannot be ignored. They are mighty warriors, respected by all the villages. And they are brothers of the Chief. I am foolish girl to ask.*

Meanwhile, with demonic fury in his black eyes, Mongo raised his sharp, blood-stained hatchet above Smith's neck, waiting for the signal from the chief. Okeus and Snookus froze—transfixed by this glorious moment. Angie held her breath as Pocahontas buried her face deeper in her father's broad chest. She could not watch.

But a sudden, metallic clattering broke the palpable silence. Everyone flinched. Warriors reached for their clubs and spears. The war party had stacked the muskets, swords, helmets, and breastplates of the three soldiers in a pile against a tree trunk nearby.

For some strange reason, the pile of weapons was tipping over. Just as the last sword fell, the blade hit the trigger of a loaded musket. Terror filled the heart of every person in the crowd as the weapon fired with a deafening explosion and an acrid blast of gray smoke. The musket ball shattered the handle of the hatchet in Mongo's hand before burying itself into a nearby tree. Men, women and children fell to the ground. The braves holding Smith dropped him as they ducked low. Only Paquiquino and his three sons did not flinch. *Was this the work of an evil spirit?* they all wondered. For a long moment, no one moved or spoke. No such weapon had ever been fired in a Powhatan village.

Finally, Chief Powhatan stood up and asked Mongo to bring him a musket, sword, and breastplate from the pile. He studied them for several minutes in silence while everyone looked on, transfixed by what just happened. An obviously impressed chief looked down at Smith. Then Powhatan turned to his two siblings, "Brothers, if our people could learn from the whites, we could have weapons like *these*. With such fire-sticks, we would never be afraid of other tribes. If we were friends with the whites, they might help us."

Okeus was furious. He had seen Scion kick over the pile of weapons moments before. Scion just stared at Okeus with a grin as big as a crescent moon.

"But, Great Chief—" Opie and Mongo said simultaneously.

"*Silence,* my brothers. You are great warriors and beloved brothers, but our wise father believes this white man tells the truth. Father has never trusted any white man except the priests. But our father says this man tells the truth. I trust our father in this matter. And my daughter hears from Ahone. I believe Ahone has spoken to her to save this man." Many in the crowd knelt down in homage to Ahone at that last remark. Some began to chant.

"Yes, Pocahontas, perhaps the gods have spoken to you after all," Powhatan said as he pulled her close for a hug.

Angie smiled and caressed the head of the princess. "Congratulations, girl. You just made history."

Powhatan stood as everyone bowed before him. He leaned over to Pocahontas to whisper in her ear. She quickly dashed to Smith and motioned for the braves to pick Smith up from the ground. She spoke to him in simple Powhatan. "Smith, Father want two great guns and big grindstone. You give, and he let you go."

Smith nodded his head. As he did, Pocahontas jumped for joy and smiled at her father. Then she did something no one expected. The beautiful young princess took off her heavy raccoon robe and raised her slender arms and hands above her head in a graceful arc. Then, with an agility and skill beyond her years, she twirled her body seven times as she danced and lept in a circle around the smiling soldier. No one moved or spoke. It was a magical moment—a dance no one had ever seen her do before.

But the angels and spirits also saw something far more amazing: heavenly streams of rainbow-colored light spinning above the head of the jubilant princess as she danced. Angie squealed with delight! Scion grinned and slapped his thigh.

"Pocahontas, my daughter, what was that dance?" the amazed chief asked.

"It is my *victory dance,* Father. Whenever I am alone in the forest, listening to Ahone, I dance this dance for him because he makes me victorious in all I do."

Powhatan shook his head and smiled proudly, "My little Playful One. You are so much more than I can understand." Pocahontas giggled, ran to her father and kissed him. Then Powhatan stood up and shouted, "Release the prisoner.* He will now be friend of the tribe."

Mongo was thunderstruck. "My Chief, this man will betray us. He must die, or we will."

Opie was livid. "My brother and Chief, do not dishonor Mongo, your chief shaman, or me. Please listen to your brothers."

The warriors around the fire did not speak, but their crossed arms and angry faces showed their agreement with Opie and Mongo.

Raising his war-scarred hand to end the discussion, Chief Powhatan spoke firmly but gently, "You all hear my decision. I, Powhatan, Chief of the Thirty Tribes, have spoken. Let it be done."

Grumbling rumbled throughout the crowd as Captain Smith's bonds were cut by an irate warrior. He made sure he 'accidentally' cut Smith on the wrist as he sliced the leather thongs. Smith just smiled at him as he put pressure on the small wound. Compared to a bashed cranium, that cut was nothing, Smith chuckled.

The chief turned to face Pocahontas again and hold her by her shoulders. "Matoaka, you are the light of my life. I give you this man's life as gift. But, I warn you, if he become our enemy—and he may—I will have to kill him. Understand?"

"Oh, Papa, he will not. I make sure of it. Thank you, Papa! I love you so much!" Then Pocahontas shouted with joy as she jumped off the raised throne and cartwheeled around the hut to the amusement of the gathered warriors, women, and children. Many boys quickly followed suit, trying to out-cartwheel the chief's favorite daughter. They soon gave up. Pocahontas was victorious again!

Opie and Mongo could not smile even if they tried. Seething with anger, they looked at each other as if to signal something sinister. They walked outside the longhouse for privacy. Opie stood in the frigid darkness, his face darkened with rage as he silently cursed his older brother.

Little brother—that's all I am to you, aren't I, Powhatan? As oldest, you always steal the glory. Father Paq always favor you, and now you are chief. Even Mongo has honor of Chief Shaman. I am nothing to you!

Okeus twitched with delight as his talon stirred the deep well of hatred in Opie's mind. "That's my boy. Feel that rejection. Embrace your rage. You were never given the attention you deserved. You were cheated by your older brothers. Your father never loved you like you deserved.

"You need to make a name for yourself, my little grub. Do something dramatic. Something bold and dangerous that your brothers would not do. That will show them who you really are. Then you will get the respect you deserve. Drink deep of your hatred. You bring much glory to me as you do. Drink deep. This is your hour. This is your destiny. Drink deep . . ."

Opie drank deep. A wicked smile crossed his face as he contemplated what to do.

Yes, little brother will show who is best. Father is old and has soft heart now. I, Opie, will avenge our people. I, Opie, son of Paq, will drive out these

English! I will deceive and kill them like white man deceive and kill—just like father Paq teach me.

Meanwhile, back in his hut, Mongo winced and squirmed in his bed as Snookus threatened him with malevolent whispers in his mind: "You fool, you idiot, you foul-smelling bag of rancid swamp crap! I will make you pay for this mistake. You will rue the day you allowed John Smith to live. I hold you accountable for this. You are the chief's shaman, but Powhatan ignores you because of that silly little girl. You will pay—and one day, *so will she.*"

CHAPTER 41

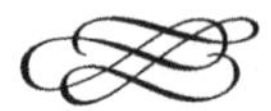

December 6, 1607

The following morning, John Smith awoke to see a bevy of giggling girls peeking inside his hut and then running away. Despite his many bruises, he had slept well on the soft bearskin rug with a double layer of deerskin covers. As the rugged soldier stepped outside into the frosty air to clear his head, his breath billowed out in small white clouds.

He noticed two sleepy guards on either side of the entrance, their heads covered with multiple layers of raccoon fur. And then his nose crinkled with disgust. *Good God, what is that awful odor?* he thought. Then his drowsy mind caught up with his nose: *the stench was him*! His uniform was caked in mud, his face unshaven, and he reeked of urine, sweat, and stale blood from his head wounds. But *he was alive*—and for that, he gave thanks to God—something he had done many times throughout his years as a mercenary soldier all over Europe after a battle.

The scene before him seemed surreal. Here he was, an English soldier, watching the normal life of a Powhatan village—something no white man had seen since the lost Roanoke Colony of 1587.* But the village was too busy to notice him. Morning chores were afoot. Women in deerskin moccasins and opossum-skin shawls scurried about the snowy ground with armloads of wood and skins of water. Brown, scantily clad children laughed and talked nonstop as they swept out their family's huts with dried cornstalk brooms.

But the children's laughter was soon drowned out by shouts from several women as a dozen braves entered the village. They had just returned with fresh rabbit and raccoon slung over their shoulders on leather cords after an early morning hunt. Soon, a procession of curious children and hugging women surrounded the happy hunters. The women clapped their hands and made strange, high-pitched sounds to celebrate the meaty breakfast to come. The entire village acted like one big family—and a very merry one at that.

Smith leaned back on his hut and took it all in with a sigh. *When was the last time I ever saw a morning like this?* he mused. *And we English soldiers think we are the civilized ones!*

A loud squeal of delight brought Smith out of his reverie. He turned to see Pocahontas darting across the clearing, carrying a bowl of hot, cooked corn mush and a skin of water. Breakfast. *Maybe getting captured by these folks isn't so bad after all. The men at the fort would kill for a meal like this,* Smith thought.

"Why, thank you, princess. This smells wonderful," Smith pronounced in his best Powhatan as he gratefully accepted the steaming food. *Thank God for John White's Algonquin lessons!* he added to himself.

"You very welcome, Chief Smith," Pocahontas replied in her best English with a cute laugh. Smith was dumbfounded.

"You speak English? Who could have taught you? This is . . . incredible!" Smith sputtered out with such force that he almost dropped his breakfast bowl.

Raising herself up to her full height of four-foot-eleven, Pocahontas proudly declared, "My grandfather, Papa Paq, teach me. He great warrior. Spanish teach him many tongues."

Smith almost choked as he spat out his mush. "He what? The Spanish did what?" Smith's mind reeled with questions. Then it hit him. "Oh, that must have been your grandfather who seemed to know who our leader was when your warriors brought the deer to us last May. And he shook our leader's hand like a white man. Incredible! Bloody incredible! Never seen the like of it. Wait till I write about this in my book about Virginia!"

Pocahontas's eyes glowed with joy as she listened to this mysterious and handsome stranger talk about her grandfather, even though she could not understand all the words. She could see Smith was impressed. Then, as Smith leaned back to stretch, she saw a drawing on Smith's forearm. It had four sections, and in two of the sections, the heads of three men were depicted. She was intrigued.

"Chief Smith, may I ask question?"

Grinning from ear to ear for the first time in a long time, Smith said, "Any Powhatan who can speak English like you can ask me anything!" Then he did something that surprised them both. Smith put his hand on her head and ruffled her hair playfully, like a father would.

Pocahontas blushed and quickly looked down to hide her emotions. *Oh, what a handsome man you are, Smith, she thought to herself. My father say you are a gift to me. Oh, Smith, you are a gift I want to keep,* the eleven-year-old gushed silently.

"Chief Smith, who are three men on your arm? Are they friends or brothers?" Pocahontas asked.

"Oh—my tattoo! First, let me tell you how I become a soldier. Like you, I once lived in a small village and helped my father plant crops."

And for the next hour, Smith wove together some Powhatan words, some English words, and lots of creative hand gestures to describe how he left home at age sixteen, after his father died, to fight on the battlefields of Europe. Smith told her of his hero, Sir Francis Drake—an English sailor who sailed his big canoe to many other lands no one had ever seen. Then, Smith squeezed mud from the hut floor into a ball and cradled it in his palms. Pocahontas was mesmerized as the bearded captain explained that God made many lands in many places to look like that mud ball, surrounded by great waters. With a flash of a smile, Pocahontas pretended to understand so Smith would not be offended.

"Oh, Chief Smith, I want to go in white man's canoe to many places on the mudball—like my Papa Paq did. But I want to go with you," she giggled again.

Smith smiled and then pursed his lips as he whispered, "I don't think so. I have a lot of blood on my hands. I have been a soldier, a pirate—I stole many things from the white man's canoes. I have been a slave who killed his master. I attract trouble. I would not want you to get hurt, little one."

Then, Smith's face grew serious. "You asked about the three heads.* Six winters ago, I fought Muslim Turks in a land called Transylvania, in a white village called Alba Iulia.* Muslim Turks follow a god that makes them fight against my God and my people,* who are called Christians. A big battle began there, but no one could win. So, the chief of the Turks said to our leader, 'Our man will fight your man, and if your man wins, we will go home. If our man wins, you surrender to us.'" *

Capt. Smith fighting Muslim Turks*

And with great relish, Smith proceeded to tell the wide-eyed princess how he killed three Turks in three separate hand-to-hand combat matches.* As a result of his three victories, Prince Zsigmond Bathory of Transylvania granted Smith the right to wear the three Turkish heads on his shield.*

Captain Smith's Coat of Arms*

"And that's why I have three heads on my arm and on my chest shield,"* Smith proudly concluded.

"Chief Smith, you are mighty warrior!" Pocahontas exclaimed loudly. "But my uncles do not like you. My grandfather make them hate all white men—but you are a brave warrior like my uncle Opie, I think. Maybe if you stay here, they make you warrior in our tribe. My father want you to stay and help protect our people. If you stay, you can marry and become a great chief someday. Please stay, Chief Smith," Pocahontas pleaded with tears in her eyes.

Smith looked at her and thought, *Young one, you are not the first girl who has said that to me when I was her captive. If you only knew how that first story turned out, you would not be quite so eager to have me stay. I really hurt that girl. I didn't mean to, but I did. I still hate myself for that.*

"Princess, I am honored by your words. Long ago, another young woman asked me to stay with her people so I could marry her, but I had to leave her." Pocahontas looked shocked—but not defeated.

Smith looked away to hide his pain and thought, *Charatza,* where are you now? I hope you found a good man to love you. I am so sorry I could never be that man. And please forgive me.*

She was a young, beautiful Muslim—and Smith was her slave—found almost dead after a vicious battle with the Muslim Tartars in Crimea on the border with Asia.* He was a gift to Charatza from a Turk who'd bought him in the slave market.* Soon, she'd fallen in love with Smith and wanted to marry him,* but Smith knew it could never work out— nor did he want it to. He was not the marrying kind. So, one night, the wily soldier escaped from Charatza. In the process, he had to kill her brother.* He never saw her again.*

Turning back to Pocahontas, Smith grimaced and pushed the painful guilt out of his mind. He had to do that often in his eleven years as a soldier of fortune. Just then, a grazing doe and her two fawns at the tree line caught his eye. A group of laughing children stopped running to gaze at the gentle deer family, too. As Smith looked at the peaceful surroundings, a thought pulled on him. *Maybe it would be good to stay awhile.* Finally, he took a deep breath and turned back toward Pocahontas. She was staring at him. "You are lucky, Pocahontas. Your village is so restful. Your father loves you much. One day you can marry any handsome warrior in your tribe. I had to leave my home to find my life, but your home here is so good. I can see why you want me to stay, but I cannot. I have to help my people stay alive in our village. They need food, and many are too sick to find food."

"Oh, Smith. I want to help you. If you stay with us a little longer, I can ask Father to send food to your village."

Smith eyed her closely. He suddenly realized that he probably could acquire more food for the men at the fort by staying here than he could by leaving to hunt game by himself.

"Well, ah, yes, I'm sure you could," Smith agreed. "I will stay twenty-five sunrises, and then you must send me back. They will think me dead if I do not return by then."

Pocahontas let out girlish war-whoop and jumped up to tell her father the good news. She started to run and then stopped, turned, and pointed her finger at her attractive captive. "This time, you must not run from girl who capture you," Pocahontas laughed. "Stay here. My father will give you anything you want. Even marriage to his daughter!" she blurted out with a blinding smile.

Smith laughed, waved his hand at her and shouted, "Go, you silly girl!" *But if you were older, and I was not who I am right now, I might have found it hard to leave you,* the wistful captain thought as the charming little princess pranced away to the big longhouse of her father.

CHAPTER 42

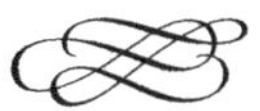

December 16, 1607

A tired and gaunt man got up before dawn to pray. *But where can I go?* Chaplain Hunt wondered. The fort was small and every cabin was already overcrowded. Some settlers even slept in the cold stockade yard to avoid the sick who seemed to be coughing behind every door.

If only I could go into the woods, he sighed. *The forest is so lovely and quiet, draped in soft, new snow.* He knew the woods might be a dangerous place to pray, but he was desperate. *I've got to get alone with the Lord—away from this morbid fort,* he thought to himself. *The men's pitiful cries day and night are wearing me out. Besides, the native sentries have not been seen since Captain Smith left to go hunting on December 5th. I must go. The Lord will protect me. It's worth the risk. I'm no good to men if I cannot stay close to the Lord.*

Morph saw the man in black leave. He watched the preacher traipse into the woods above the triangular-shaped stockade. After a few minutes, Hunt stopped in small clearing near a stand of thick bushes that gave him a measure of privacy.

Morph flew closer to investigate just as the parson raised his hands and began to worship God. As Hunt praised God with deep emotion, Morph instinctively jerked back a few yards. Unbeknownst to the little demon, Angie was recording the entire scene from a distance on her multiple sensors for evaluation later by Scion and Michael. After sighting the small evil spirit near Hunt, she focused her telescopic vision on Morph.

Hey, wait a minute. Isn't that the same spirit I saw beneath the ship when they first came here? He's the one who had a light with him in the water. I'd still like to know what that was, Angie thought as she studied him.

"Our Father, who art in heaven, hallowed be thy name . . ." Hunt prayed. Hunt's face was so full of love and joy that it made Morph wince in pain. Such public displays of affection toward God were highly offensive to demons. Usually, wholehearted worship by Christians drove demons far away, but Morph did not flee.

"Thy kingdom come, thy will be done on earth as it is in heaven," Hunt went on.

Morph winced from the increasing presence of God's glory. He had never been around a real, praying Christian before. He was intrigued. A terrifying tingling crept over his body. He was tempted to escape, but then he decided to see where this feeling was going. *Why not? he thought, If it is painful, it can't be worse than living here with the cruelty of Okeus.* So, he continued to stand fast just a few feet from Hunt—that is until he began to lose his balance. Soon, the cat-like spirit was on his claws and knees on the ground, too weak to stand. His furry green body shook a few times, but not in pain. His blue eyes were now soft and peaceful. After a few more moments, he collapsed on the damp forest floor and lay so still he seemed to be dead. Because his face was turned away from Angie's position, she could not see that his mouth had on it what no demon was ever supposed to wear: a sweet smile.

Angie was fascinated. "A demon who chooses to be in God's Presence! Fascinating! This is great stuff for my paper in *Advanced*

Reconnaissance among Demonic Lifeforms," she said out loud to herself. "I'll bet no angel has ever seen anything like this. I would love to interview him," she giggled.

As she focused her thermal imaging sensors on Morph, she picked up a strange reading in the thick fur under his left wing. "This can't be right," she mumbled. "I've got a thermal burst on this little cat-bat that only comes from intense light. But how can that be? His fur is as dark as a green tree python."

But then she saw it. A groggy Morph rolled over on his back toward the praying Hunt. As he did, his left wing was lifted slightly into the air.

"I don't believe it! There is *a light* under his wing—the same light I saw on him under the ship! It's coming from *his body,*" Angie said in awe. She was almost beside herself now. No demon had ever shown any ability to radiate light.

I knew it! Angie thought. *I knew if I came to the New World, I might discover something we have not cataloged in heaven. Holy Cherubmatzi! I may have found a new species of demon! No doubt about it—I am going to find out more about this demon. But that means I'll have to talk to him at some point. Wow—I'm not sure that's legal, but, oh well, I have to try. This strange, light-emitting demon could give us vital intel to defeating Okeus and his forces here. I'll be famous! Little Beta girl angels will not be disrespected by the "big boys" in heaven anymore! This is one opportunity I am not going to pass up. Maybe they'll name a star after me or something. That little demon doesn't know it, but he will be followed and recorded a lot in the days to come.*

Then her heart sank as the thought hit her, *But what if this is some type of clever demonic deception? Demons can be very tricky.*

Just then, her sensors jumped. Morph's left wing heat index was off the charts as the intensity of his wingpit light increased tenfold. Oddly enough, it happened just as Chaplain Hunt began to sing praises to the Lord. "Just like Scion!" Angie whispered excitedly to herself. "I have got to tell Master right away. He won't believe it! But wait! First, I need to get a close-up picture of that light."

Just as Angie hovered above him, Morph opened his eyes and saw Angie looking at him with shock and admiration splashed all over her face. They both froze. Then, in a moment that seemed to move in slow motion for both of them, Angie reached out her hand to help Morph get up—which, in retrospect, seemed silly— since Angie is half the size of Morph. But she did it anyway, without really knowing why. Instantly, something like an electrical charge passed between their hands, and Angie jumped back in the air. But Morph never took his cerulean blue eyes off of her.

They both just stared at each other—the twenty-four-inch, dark green cat demon with furry wings and the fourteen-inch, rainbow-haired, golden-skinned angel. Then, Morph whispered with an almost childlike tone, "Can I talk to you someday? You have something I have always wanted."

"I . . . I . . . I do?" Angie stuttered.

"*Compassion*. No one in my world has that."

"Well . . . I don't know. It's really not allowed . . . well, ah, let me get back to you on that," Angie managed to whisper with great effort. Her emotions were frightening her. She felt like she was about to explode with feelings she could not control—or even understand. She had to leave.

Angie shot straight up into the air faster than a lead ball from Captain Smith's snaphance musket. Flipping over onto her back at ten thousand feet to level off, Angie then arched her back and flipped over again, heading southeast toward the big Christian cross at Cape Henry—breathing very fast the entire way, trying to calm down.

Ten seconds later, Angie sighted Scion standing above a small cloud, guarding the cross. She snapped her wings straight out, slammed to a halt next to the cloud, and shouted, "Master Scion, have I ever got news for you!"

"Not so loud, Angie. The demons have ears, you know. I've been watching them all day here. They are trying to get the natives to tear down the cross. What do you have for me?"

Breathlessly, she began, "That demon you told me to watch—the one assigned to Paq—well, he does something no other demon has ever done, as far as I can tell. He has a ray of light under his left wing. That's the wing I thought was maimed. When he flies, that left wing doesn't move far from his body. I think he is deliberately doing that to hide the light from other demons. I am sure he would do a lot to keep the other demons uninformed about his . . . condition. We may have some leverage here to exploit him for Kingdom purposes. What do you think, Master? Can we approach him for some help?"

"Angie, you never cease to amaze me with your creative ideas, but this could be a waste of time—or worse, a trick. You need to investigate more. I'll check with Michael about lights on demons. In the meantime, just don't let this little demon distract you from our mission here to protect the colony. And do not try to talk to him. It's too dangerous. You know the rules: no angel is to talk to any demon. That was in your first class at Angel Academy, remember?"

"Yes, I remember. I won't try to talk to him," Angie responded, but her heart sank to say it. She was dying to find out about that demon's light. And, as crazy as it seemed, her heart told her that she had to see him again. She just needed to find a way to reconnect with him.

"Oh, Scion, in my excitement, I almost forgot to tell you—that light under his wing grows brighter when he hears worship of God."

"He what?" Scion blurted out, almost choking on his words.

At that response, Angie smiled slyly and thought, *Well, now you are impressed. So, maybe talking to that demon is not such a bad idea after all, is it, Master Scion?* Then, Angie flew right in front of Scion's perplexed face. "Like I said, that little demon has a light under his left wing. It glows with a light that comes from his body somehow. Isn't that totally awesome?" Angie laughed with excitement.

"Impossible! They are creatures of the darkness. I've never heard of such a thing—and I've taught classes on demons at the academy. Your sensors must be malfunctioning—or it's a trick of some kind to distract you. Look, I've got real demon issues to deal with now. Please don't bother me about that anymore."

After a few moments of studying the disinterested look on Scion's face, Angie made a decision she hoped she would not regret: *I have to interview that demon. But Scion is not wired to break rules. It's no use asking him for permission. But if that demon is a new species or just an anomaly, we have to know. Either way, General Michael will eventually thank me—rules or no rules. We have to know all of our enemy's strengths and weaknesses if we are to defeat him. That's what they taught me in Intel Class. And besides —I really like that little green cat!*

As she turned to fly away, Angie looked up toward heaven and whispered to herself, "Sometimes it is better to ask for forgiveness than for permission. O Holy Spirit, guide me. I believe you want us to know more about this strange demon. Everyone knows I think out of the box—but now I am about *to live* out of that box. I am going to ask a demon for an interview."

CHAPTER 43

January 1, 1608

After finishing his twenty-five-day sojourn with Pocahontas,* Captain Smith said goodbye to the clinging, pouty princess. His clothes were clean, his belly was full, and his face was set like flint to help the colony survive the bitter winter.

After two slightly clad, shivering braves paddled him across the Pamunkey River,* they released him to walk west back to James Fort. Scion and Angie flew above him to make sure he made it. Three hours later, tired and wet from plodding through snow-covered underbrush, Smith emerged from the woods just above the whitened wall of the fort. As he strode down the slope, a cry went up from the sentry on the rear point of the triangular defenses.

"It's Smith! He's alive and alone!" And then, with a painful cry, the guard added, "—and with *no food*!" Curses and groans spewed from the small, frozen fortress as they rushed to open the gate.

The first man out was big and angry—but that was normal for Jehu Robinson. But today, he was furious—and even he did not know why. But Scion saw why: Snookus had just jumped onto Jehu's back and was whispering into Jehu's mind. Scion leaped into the air and sped toward Snookus to stop his mischief. But just then, the hulking shape of Okeus appeared into the sky across the river. One hundred demon warriors came with him. Okeus just hovered and glared at Scion. The giant angel backed off. He knew he could not win that fight.

Meanwhile, Snookus kept planting thoughts in Jehu. Smith must die. *Smith is a friend of the Powhatans. That's why they did not kill him. Smith must die!*

"Captain Smith, where have ya been for more than three weeks?" Jehu shouted to the weary man everyone already distrusted. "Looking fer food for all of us, of course?"

"You know that, Robinson. I had to," Smith tersely yelled back. Sarcastic snickers billowed up in the mob behind Jehu.

"And what, pray tell, did ya bring back for yer starving mates? I don't see any bags of corn or legs of dried venison." More sneers—this time darker and more threatening.

Robinson moved closer to Smith with clenched fists. "Did ya know we've been starving here fer the past three weeks while ya were gone? There's only thirty-eight of us left out of the bloody fools who came here last spring.* Most of us are sick—and damned hungry. We came here for a new life, and all we got is starvation and disease. The well water's bad, our supplies are almost gone, and the blasted savages kill anyone who leaves to find food. But sickness is the worst of it. We had ten more die of bloody flux last week. All Chaplain Hunt says is, 'Trust the Lord and pray often.' Lotta good that does!

"And what has our wonderful Council done fer us?" Raucous jeers and curses exploded from the haggard crowd. "Nothing that feeds us! Captain Gosnold died of the flux in August.* Captain Newport left for England over five months ago.* Only God knows if 'e'll come back. Then, our dearly beloved President Wingfield hoarded food for 'imself.* We put 'im in jail.* And then there's Captain Kendall*—another fine member of the council. Of course, ya remember that we executed 'im for plotting against the colony.* To top it off, Wingfield's successor, President Ratcliff, wants us to build 'im a bloody governor's palace out here*—while we starve! Have ya all gone daft? Or ya just don't care about the likes of us? Ya all are the leaders from hell! This place is cursed with the likes of ya, and so are we!" Whoops of agreement and racking coughs pierced the frigid air. "But Smith here looks like the fattened calf. Ate pretty good with the natives, did ya? How many girlfriends did they give ya? Yeah, run off and take care of yerself. That's yer style, isn't it, Smith?"

"Look, Jehu. I took the risk to go hunting on their land—to feed all of you. But we were ambushed. My two men were killed and I was taken prisoner. They just now released me. I was almost killed trying to get some victuals for you ungrateful louts, and now you curse me like a dog!" Smith angrily shouted and started to enter the fort.

But angry voices, darkened eyes, and weapons met Smith as he approached the gate. Even though he was the best swordsman in the colony, he was outnumbered. Smith knew he could only win with words—but today his words were not working very well.

Robinson suddenly moved in front of Smith, shouting, "And two of yer men were killed, but ya have nary 'ave scratch! How convenient. Did ya betray them to save yer own precious skin? And what did the savages give ya in return fer giving them yer muskets? Are ya hoarding Powhatan food somewhere like Wingfield did here?"

In a flash of anger, Smith reached for his sword. "Listen, you bastards. I was surrounded, with a dozen drawn arrows aimed at me, so I surrendered. So would you! And yes, Wingfield is a selfish man—like most nobles I have known—and a coward. I am not selfish! And if you want to find out if I am a coward, meet me tonight in the field with your choice of weapon," the cocky soldier challenged as he pulled out his well-worn sword with a flourish.

Another man shouted, "Listen to the proud peacock, will ya? First, ya desert us for weeks, and now you insult us. Maybe we should shoot ya like we did that deserter, our esteemed Council member Kendall, last September?"

"No, too easy. I say we string 'em up in the morning!" Jehu shouted above the crowd. He's not on our side. He deserted us to feed 'imself. He's worse than Wingfield. If we killed Kendall fer deserting, I say we kill Smith fer leaving us to feed 'imself. He's probably made a deal with the Powhatans to finish us off by starvation, and then they will reward 'im with food and ladies. Let's finish what Wingfield started on that island in the Indies. Get the chains that were taken off Smith last September."

Hearty cheers erupted. Before he knew it, thirty-eight sick and smelly men jumped on Smith, clawing to get a piece of him. The mob beat and kicked him fiercely with the little remaining strength they had. Irons appeared, and within minutes, Captain John Smith was back in shackles—the same rusty ones he wore for almost three months coming to Virginia. Smith looked at his chains and the vicious faces all around him. Hmm, he thought, wincing in pain. *And I thought the natives were my enemies! Maybe Pocahontas was right about staying with the tribe, after all.*

Circling above with Snookus, Okeus bared his fangs with a devilish smile. "Ha! Their best leader in chains. Snookus, you have done it again. The quickest way to their anger is through their empty stomachs. And I thought we might have to have the natives kill them. Hunger, anger, and disease are so much better. What a seedbed for sin! You are a true sin farmer, Snookus!" the giant reptile exclaimed with a loud fart.

Okeus was in a good mood for once—but Snookus was ready to rid himself of his moody master. The crippled octopus demon often dreamed of overthrowing his cruel master by getting him in deep trouble with someone even more irritable and vicious— Lucifer. *One day...one day, you foul-winded lizard, I will avenge my lost tentacles! But now I wait,* Snookus mused with a crooked grin.

To cloak his plans, he had to convince Okeus that he was not personally ambitious. "Lord Okeus, to be honest, Mongo helped a lot. He got his shamans to put special, cursed poisons and many dead squirrels in the water. Last July, he also forced several spirits from a passing Spanish ship to plant sicknesses from Cuba in the summer bugs and water around the fort. English bodies have never dealt with all that. It worked, as you can see, Master. Mongo deserves so much credit for all that," Snookus reported with great, feigned humility.

"Finally, we get to make white invaders sick," Okeus gloated. "My partners in the south lost millions of followers to Spanish sicknesses. That pig Pizarro bragged that he could not have beaten our Inca empire without smallpox.* It's our turn now."

In the small Anglican chapel, Scion and Angie sat with sad faces as swarms of demons throughout the fort celebrated the imminent death of Captain Smith. The starving men planned to hang Smith in the morning. "Death to the deserter!" they shouted as they threw him into the chapel and locked the heavy door.

"We have to do something," Scion said. "I know how it feels to be wrongly accused. He's innocent, and we need him to protect this colony."

Angie smiled. "Scion, you underestimate a girl's crush on a man. Didn't I tell you about the deal Pocahontas made with Smith? She has a huge crush on him."

"Yes, but she's only eleven. She can't get them any food. Remember, the chief's two brothers and most of the warriors want to annihilate this fort—crush or no crush. We have to think of another way to save Smith."

"Oh, Master Scion, you sound just like a man. Can't you just be romantic for a moment?"

Beta females, Scion groaned and thought. *What hath God wrought? Heaven, help us! Now we have to consider girlish romance as a tool to defeat the enemy. What will Angie think of next?* Aloud, he said, "Well then, Miss Romantic—where is our prayer cover? Would you please tell Michael that we need more prayers from the saints in England to protect this colony? This is too much for me. No angel can do his assignment well unless someone is praying for that assignment. This is hard, Angie. Too hard. Sometimes I feel like the colonists: I just want to go home."

CHAPTER 44

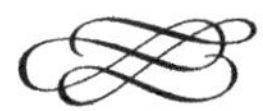

The following day, as a hazy sun rose over the frozen James River, Pocahontas and two other women stood at the gate of the fort, their arms loaded with corn.* Behind them stood six worried warriors, each carrying two legs of cooked venison.

A startled Scion saw the food parade from his post above the gate. Angie smugly winked at him. A demon guard nearby whispered to his partner, "The tribe must be punished for this." He rushed away to alert Okeus. But he never made it. Angie detected the whispered threat. Instantly, Scion rocketed into the sky and sliced the demon into a putrid, red mist with a flick of his massive sword. The other demons watching the fort just nodded sheepishly to Scion as he returned to the gate. They motioned to Scion that they had no plans to go anywhere now.

"Impressive, Master Scion, but won't that anger Okeus?" Angie quipped.

"He'll never miss that little twerp. I am tired of my colony getting beat up by the likes of them. I also needed to blow off a little steam. It's been stressful. I'm okay now," Scion confessed with a slight grin.

"Look! They have corn and meat!" the sentry shouted hoarsely to the groggy men in the fort. Shouts of "Hallelujah!" and "Praise the Lord!" were heard from several cabins as the news spread. Angie looked over at Scion to see his reaction.

Scion sat on the gate, watching and looked a little bored. Angie smiled and said nothing at first. Then, she couldn't hold out any longer and almost shouted, "Master Scion, I couldn't help but notice that little Pocahontas was in that group bringing food to the fort," she sarcastically announced with heavy, mock surprise. "And I thought that little girl would be home feeding her pet raccoon—like most eleven-year-olds this time of day. She is so unpredictable. You just never know what that girl is going to do." Angie just stared straight ahead—waiting patiently for his male retort.

At first, Scion pretended not to hear. But then, just as Angie was about to get angry because he was ignoring her, he burst out laughing. She looked at him and thought to herself, *Well, look at you! And I thought you were not capable of cutting up. Angel Scion, if I were more your size and angels could have mates, I might choose you! You can actually be fun!*

Soon, the gate flew open. Ten scruffy and scrawny men piled out to grab the food from the waiting natives. The two women and six young braves dropped the food and ran home as the raucous herd of hungry men approached. Pocahontas also ran—right into the fort to find the handsome gift her father gave her: Captain Smith. Angie flew into the fort five seconds ahead of the young girl—and she knew exactly what had to be done. As the Powhatan princess looked frantically for her man, Pocahontas heard someone shout that Smith should stay locked in the church and not get any of the newly arrived victuals. Too late—Angie had already unlocked the door to the chapel. Soon, Pocahontas was at Smith's side in the darkened chapel. Smith was bruised and bloodied from the beating the men gave him yesterday, but she was relieved to see him alive.

Smith looked at her sternly. "Pocahontas, we should not meet again."

She was shocked at his words and pulled back from him, tears already in her eyes.

Then he smiled, "Every time we meet, I am bleeding," Smith winced as he laughed with swollen rib muscles.

She also burst into laughter—and then cried to see him bound and in pain—again. But she quickly became serious. Time was of the essence. If she were found there, her own life might be in danger. She talked as fast as her limited English would allow. She wanted Smith to know that her father had given permission for her to bring food from the tribe—as long as Smith would protect the tribe from English attacks. Food for the tribe was scarce due to the long drought, but her father agreed to share anyhow. He wanted peace—and he wanted to make Pocahontas happy.

Smith listened closely. *It's working again,* he thought—*God has given me another fair maiden to save my life* and the lives of others. My grandmother's prayers are still protecting me. Maybe someday I should get to know her Jesus more. Perhaps I was wrong about religion. But for now, I have my wits, my sword, and God-sent girls of mercy to fend for me. It is enough,* he concluded with a wry smile that Pocahontas thought was for her. He made her blush again—and she loved it. But she had to leave.

"I've got to go. Father will miss me. He doesn't know I came here with the food. I will come back soon, Smith."

Smith gave her a casual salute with his hand and said, "Goodbye, my little friend. Please come back—with more food."

She beamed back a ravishing smile that should have melted his heart —but he was afraid of close relationships. Being a detached loner was the only way he has known to deal with his emotions. No woman, let alone a mere girl, could change that now.

But something was about to change. Something that would once again save John Smith from hanging at the hands of the colony.*

The next morning, January 2, 1608,* the sentries sounded the alarm as the white sails of two ships came into view sailing up the James.* No one knew if they were Spanish or English. Several had already decided that they would surrender if the Spanish came. At least they would get fed and be taken away from their "death colony." Everyone just wanted to go home. Soon the sentries called out, "They are British! It must be Newport with the First Supply!* Some cheered. Others groaned.

Later that morning, Captain Newport arrived with one hundred new settlers.* Within a few hours, he released Smith. No one really cared about Smith now. The ship's hull was packed with food and new friends to help work in the fort.

"Whew, that was close," Scion said to Angie. "I don't know how long these colonists are going to make it at this rate. Okeus has Mongo's witch doctors still praying and fasting to make the men sick. It also looks like Smith's days here are numbered. He is brilliant—but always looking for a fight. We have got to get him away from these desperate, angry men so he can do some good with all of his amazing leadership skills. I know—let's lead Smith to go exploring the Great Bay region.* Maybe he can make some contacts with other tribes who might be willing to help the colony with more food."

"Sounds like a plan for the summer, Master Scion. In the meantime, we have another problem: General Michael just sent me a message yesterday that the prayer cover for the colony is weakening back in England. Many Christians were praying for the colony at first, but now they have stopped. The demons can sense it. More and more of them are gathering around the men, who are extremely vulnerable now. It's beginning to be a demonic feeding frenzy."

"Did Michael say why the people are praying less?" Scion asked.

Angie grimaced, "Believe it or not, it's about money.* Michael said that the Virginia Company is telling their investors that the colony is doing great and making real progress converting the 'savages' as they call them. The Company has even instructed its ship captains to secretly censor anything negative in the colonists' personal letters to home. Basically, the Company is lying to keep the investors happy, so they will invest more money in the 'successful' colony.* So, the investors have stopped praying."

"This is terrible news, Angie! How can God bless a colony founded on the lies of its leaders? What a mess!"

"But there is also good news, Master. Michael said that the Holy Spirit already has Captain Smith writing the truth about the colony. You know how Smith hates hypocrisy of any kind. I saw him writing in his cabin last night with many pages stacked next to him. He looked agitated. I'll bet he is working on a book."*

"Let's hope so, Angie. But for now, I am going to visit Chaplain Hunt when he prays this evening at bedtime and suggest that he preach from Psalms 127:1 this Sunday: 'Unless the Lord builds the house, the builders labor in vain. Unless the Lord watches over the city, the guards stand watch in vain.' Maybe we can get the men here to pray more until the Christians back in England rejoin the prayer battle. I'm not sure we can adequately protect this colony unless the men here pray more—and turn from sin," Scion concluded with a sad look. "The colony has to make it . . . and I have to make it."

Angie flew over and put her tiny hand on Scion's massive forearm. They both sat there on top of the James Fort gate with heads bowed. Neither said a word. They didn't need to. Then, Angie began to hum a worship tune. Scion joined her. A soft glow began to form over the gate. Demon sentries nearby began to squirm. As the humming continued, the air grew electric with God's Presence. The soft glow became a ball of light so intense that the demons screamed, cursed, and dove into the ground. They didn't emerge for several hours—even after Scion and Angie had left to seek a quieter place to pray for the rest of the day.

CHAPTER 45

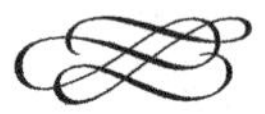

January 6, 1608

Soon after Captain Newport released Smith from his chains, he conducted a short investigation and determined that the charges of desertion against Smith were baseless.* Upon hearing of Smith's long and cordial visit to Powhatan's headquarters, Newport asked Smith to set up a meeting with the chief to make a peace agreement.* Smith happily agreed, and so did Powhatan when he was asked by Smith on January 10.

"Let us meet as brothers in the morning on the day the moon does not shine at night," the old chief suggested.

"Yes, Chief. That will give us time to prepare. We call that moon a New Moon. Let me see...," as the soldier flipped open a small book from his vest. "Yes, according to my almanac, that would be seven days from now on what we call January 17." With a flourish of his hand and a low bow, Smith and his companions turned and began their trek back to the fort.

As the jubilant Englishmen walked back from their meeting with the chief, Scion and Angie spun overhead in dizzy victory spirals, worshipping God at the top of their lungs. "Somebody must be praying," Scion shouted! Angie whooped and grinned like a schoolgirl how just aced final exams.

When Okeus heard about the truce plans, he flew into a rage. The two closest demon guards were ripped and chewed to pieces by the powerful, six-fingered claws and six-inch fangs of the crazed, fourteen-foot dinosaur. A faint red mist was all that was left of them.

"War! This is war!" the enormous reptile roared. "Snookus—get everyone up on high alert!"

"Everyone, my lord?" a half-asleep Snookus whined. But after one glance at those six-inch bared, orange teeth and the eight-foot sword still dripping with demon slime, Snookus shot out of there with a choking blast of black gas that blinded everyone long enough for the floppy octopus to flee and awaken the troops.

ON JANUARY 20TH, THE DAY BEFORE THE ENGLISH PLANNED TO MEET with Powhatan, Snookus saw his opportunity. An inebriated colonist was sleeping next to a burning candle in the storeroom. Snookus woke Mongo and led him to the place on the stockade wall where the storeroom was located. Snookus gave Mongo supernatural strength to leap over the ten-foot wall.

Within a minute, Mongo had tipped the burning candle over into a pile of dried, crushed corn. The corn began to burn instantly, and the flames rose quickly toward bottles of cooking oil on the shelf above. Mongo was over the wall and running into the woods just as the drunken colonist began to cough violently from the smoke. He lurched for the door and yelled to awaken the men—but it was too late. In just an hour, the entire fort was burned to the ground.* Hunt lost all his sacred books, even his personal Bible.* The chapel was gone. Their cabins where the colonists slept were reduced to ashes. Almost all their food stores were burned. Everything was gone—and the worst of winter was just beginning. Okeus, Snookus, and their demon workers celebrated for days over that attack.

But Pocahontas again intervened with her father to get emergency food to the suffering colony. To her great delight, he agreed—even though tribal food supplies were also meager. Powhatan hoped that such displays of kindness would hasten the peace process. His decision saved the colony.* With the multiple shipments of corn and meat from the Powhatans, James Fort survived the loss of their buildings and food in the dead of winter.* It was a miracle.

Hope for peace was in the air on both sides. Indeed, peace was all the shivering men talked about on those long, cold days. They knew they would die in James Fort if the natives ever attacked them. Finally, on January 21, the day arrived for the peace talks to begin.

As Scion and Angie flew to Powhatan's village that day, it all seemed too good to be true. Peace with the Powhatans would all but ensure the colony's survival. Scion would be vindicated in heaven and honored as the new Archangel of Virginia. Peace in the settlement would also vindicate Angie's vital scouting work with Scion. The doubts of male angels about the effectiveness of female Betas would be dealt a severe blow. Millions of her Beta sisters were counting on Angie for that. Today, hopeful men and angels would find out if peace was possible.

As the people gathered that afternoon, Chief Powhatan sat in full regalia on his throne in Werowocomoco and scanned the crowd with great interest. He knew this was a historic meeting—the likes of which had never taken place anywhere in his domain. He rubbed his hands together quickly to warm them. The air was frigid, and so were the looks of many native warriors and soldiers from the colony. Fear and anger floated like a dark cloud just above the heads of everyone—except Pocahontas. Her full attention was captivated by a certain handsome man with flaming hair and mesmerizing blue eyes. *If only he would look this way,* she fussed silently as she tried to squeeze closer to her father.

Powhatan's two younger brothers were there—looking very hostile, as usual, along with many village chiefs from several other tribes in the confederacy. Paquiquino stood close to his son, the chief, to translate into English. But he was disguised. He was fearful that a revengeful Spaniard might be hidden among the whites men.

Okeus and Snookus drifted just above the crowd, looking for targets of opportunity to tempt or harass. They paused to stare at Pocahontas. She was flashing secret smiles toward Captain Smith. Several shy teenage girls noticed and giggled at her attempts to catch Smith's eye. But Okeus's was enraged. "That girl has to go. She's responsible for all this. I will kill her someday," the spiked-tailed dinosaur vowed.

The meeting began with a procession of colonists carrying gifts for Powhatan that Newport had just brought back from England: a feather mattress and bed frame and beautiful English clothes.* Baskets of copper items were also brought to trade for corn. The Powhatan crowd clapped. Then, Powhatan raised his hand to silence the gawking villagers who had never seen such things. As Powhatan spoke, a disguised Paquiquino translated his words into perfect English—much to the astonishment of every Englishman there—except Smith.

"Thank you for coming, Chief Newport. You are a great warrior of the great waters. You honor me with gifts from your king. Thank you, Smith, that you bring Chief Newport.

Newport quickly responded, "Great Chief Powhatan, please allow me to give you two more gifts. May I present you with this thirteen-year-old boy, Thomas Savage, as a personal servant to you?* I have also brought this beautiful crown.* It is from my king to show that you are the king of this land under our King James.* If you will kneel here in front of me, I will crown you king of all this land."*

Paquiquino was shocked. He knew what would happen if he told his brother exactly what Newport said. But he did. He had no choice.

When Chief Powhatan understood that he was being offered a kingship under King James, he looked at Captain Newport with a fierce gaze that suddenly made Newport nervous.

"Chief Newport, you offer me something I already have. I am king of this land. I do not need your king to make me king. I cannot take your crown. I will not kneel to you."*

The English visitors were visibly shaken when the translation was given to them. Seeing the fear in their eyes, Powhatan quickly made a counter-proposal—a European tactic his father Paquiquino had taught his sons.

"Chief Newport, we see a good heart in your gifts. Your people see my good heart in the food we send. Your people are on my land. So, let your people be my people. We want peace with you. We help you. You help us."

He paused for effect. Every native and Englishman strained to hear what the chief's said next. Then, Powhatan stood and slowly scanned the faces of the most unusual group to ever gather in Virginia. With the regal bearing of a great monarch, he spoke in a deep resonate voice as Paq translated for the English.

"Listen to me, my werowances, my commanders. Today, I, the great Chief Powhatan, decree that white people living here are friends. We must be kind. We must be brothers to them. They gave me a young boy to serve me. Now, I give my servant Namontack* to them as a sign of brotherhood. We must share so each people can enjoy the land the Great Spirit has given us. We must help our white brothers, and they must help us. The white man's village has burned. When warm days come, we must help them make a new village."

Instantly, Okeus and Snookus dove inside Powhatan's two brothers. Okeus took Opie. They knew Powhatan's peace offer had to be challenged immediately. No one was better suited to do that than Mongo and Opie. Scion and Angie saw the demonic possession occurring, but they could not intervene. The two brothers had given permission to Okeus and Snookus to enter them many times before.

"Did you hear that, Mongo?" Opie whispered. Veins in his neck suddenly bulged in anger—and yet his mind was unaware that his powerful rage was coming from Okeus inside him. "What is our brother doing? Has he been smoking Spanish Thorn Apple* again? That plant always makes me act foolishly when I smoke it. He is acting crazy to accept white invaders as brothers. I never thought I'd hear him say such a stupid thing. Okeus must be very angry with our brother right now. Okeus knows that white people come here only to betray and destroy us, just like father Paq has told us all our lives."

Mongo, equally provoked by Snookus inside him, nodded. "Yes, Opie. Either Powhatan is losing his mind—or he is deceiving the whites so he can get their fire-sticks and long, sharp knives. He always talks of that."

"Yes, that is a good point," Opie said pensively. "Maybe our brother is not so weak after all. He knows what our prophet said: 'People from the east will come to take our lands.'* Maybe he's just pretending to be friends so he can trick them later." Okeus did not like that thought. He poked Snookus to make Mongo refute it.

"But we can't be sure what our brother is doing. I hate not knowing. If only the fire I started at their fort had made them go away," Mongo said. "Did you see the fear on their faces when they woke up to see their huts on fire? Even their priest, Hunt, lost all his belongings and books, just like Okeus ordered." Mongo smiled at the thought. He and Opie had watched from a distance—the screaming, the crying, the ashes falling from the sky.

Opie smiled as he remembered that night as well. But one image from that event still bothered him. While everyone was running around half-clothed and crying out in fear, Hunt was outside the gate on his knees with his head bowed in prayer. "I hate Hunt," he said. "Okeus told you that Hunt is the most dangerous one of the whites. He has powerful magic from the god of the whites. Okeus told you that he must be eliminated if we are to defeat the whites. Why are you waiting? Curse him, Mongo, and send someone to kill him. You are the Chief Shaman. Okeus will do it for you."

Okeus and Snookus smiled with relief. They had turned the conversation in the right direction now.

Mongo looked around hesitantly at the crowd of natives and English onlookers. "Lower your voice, Opie. Smith may not be the only white who knows our language." Mongo moved closer to Opie, bent over, and whispered, "Hunt's angelic guard is too strong. Most whites have one angel to guard them sometimes. Hunt has two all the time, and they are big. But Okeus has shown me how he wants Hunt to die."

Okeus heard it all. His six-inch fangs gleamed in a gruesome grin. He was proud of his plan.

"Poison? Sickness?" Opie asked with a wicked smirk.

"No, my brother—better. *Father* will do it. Just like he did to those Spanish priests."

"Father will refuse," Opie said quickly.

Mongo clicked his tongue. "Yes, but he will do it. We'll use root medicine again on him. His mind will be ours long enough for me to send a spirit of murder into him for the kill."

Snookus looked to Okeus and obsequiously nodded his approval of the plan.

"What if Father fails? What if Hunt's angels are too many?"

"Hunt likes to help the sick. If Father fails, I can make him sick—especially if others are sick and he gets too busy to pray, then maybe . . ."

Opie's heart raced at the thought. He was eager to end the whites' invasion of their land once and for all. Then, his eyes fell on his niece sitting next to her father. She was swaying to the beat of the peace drums and softly clapping.

"Mongo, we also must stop Pocahontas from asking Powhatan to help the whites. She's a big problem for us."

Both men grimaced at the thought of hurting their niece in any way, but they knew the future of the entire confederacy was at stake. They had to stop the food shipments Pocahontas was instigating. Neither spoke for several minutes as they contemplated that.

Finally, Opie whispered, "For now, we must do work in secret. Keep making sacrifices of captured enemy warriors to Okeus. Okeus releases great power to us when we do that. Keep sending women to the white men at night. This will weaken the angelic protection around the fort. Hunt is very sad about the men sleeping with our women. He warns them that their god forbids that, but they don't listen."

The two men laughed hideously, not aware that their snickering was in perfect sync with the cackling of Okeus and Snookus inside them.

CHAPTER 46

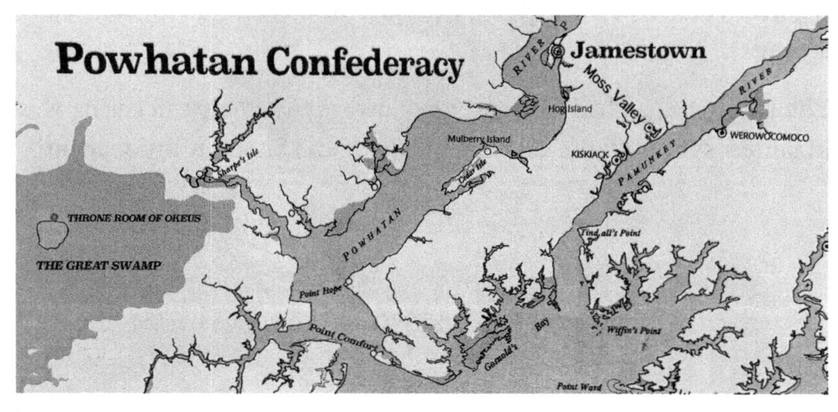

| The Great Swamp

January 23, 1608

Morph looked around the vast swamp about seventy miles southwest of James Fort. Thick, dark mud bubbled and oozed brown, sulfur-smelling water from deep reservoirs of rotting vegetation in the ground. Few natives ever ventured in there. It was too easy to get lost. The swamp was thirty-five miles long from north to south and half as wide. In this vast, liquidy wilderness, black bears and deer were everywhere, as well as thousands of large cottonmouth snakes and millions of the most voracious mosquitoes in Virginia. Okeus loved the location. He had his hideout in the middle of the swamp on the shore of the large, oval lake, which looked from above like a giant evil eye bulging out of the surrounding dark pine forests. Morph usually felt safe there from prying angel eyes. But not today.

Today, Morph felt anything but secure. Crouching under a large bush, he trembled with terror. Angie had contacted him secretly last week when he was cruising by the fort around midnight. She had shot past him so fast he thought it might have been a flaming native arrow. But the "arrow" stopped and waited for him to investigate further. He did. She led him into the fort chapel where no other demons would linger. Just as he flew through the chapel wall, the furry, green cat demon screeched to a halt and almost head-butted the petite angel as she hovered inside.

"You said you wanted to talk to me," Angie whispered nervously. "Well, I want that too. But promise me you will never tell anyone about our meetings! I am breaking multiple heavenly rules to talk with you. Promise!" she demanded.

Morph looked at her with wide, soft eyes and thought she really likes me that much? He smiled and agreed. Then, she asked to meet him in a secure location the following week. She said she wanted to get to know him better. He readily agreed to that. They parted in different directions and left at staggered intervals to avoid detection.

Now the day had come for the meeting she wanted. But he felt so conflicted. He desperately wanted to be with her, but his fear of being discovered was making him nauseous. *If Okeus ever finds out about this secret rendezvous with an angel, a dozen demon swords will vaporize me before I can blink. But here I am about to meet with not just any angel but, according to Snookus, a spy angel. I must be crazy—but I have to do this, even if it means death. What have I got to lose?*

Angie was a jumble of nerves as she flew to meet Morph. Her head told her not to do something that could really embarrass Scion—and maybe make him angry with her for disobeying a direct order. But her heart told her this was the right thing to do. In the end, the spunky little angel went with her heart. *Hey, wake up, Angie. I'm a recon angel,* she suddenly thought. *The Lord designed me to sneak around behind enemy lines and investigate things those big male angels don't know,* she concluded with a girlish giggle and a sly smirk.

Filled with confidence now, she glided down toward the rendezvous point while turning on every one of her sensors to ultra-high-definition mode. She knew she was making history, and—if this turned out like she hoped it would—future classes of angels would study her three-dimensional videos in Angel Academy for millennia to come. Fortunately, Morph would be unaware that his every movement, sound, and heat signature was being recorded. At the last minute, after double-checking all her sensor settings on her arm's built-in control pad, she turned off all the sensor monitors so she would not be distracted by the continuous data reports. Morph would not even see the control pad on her arm. She wore a very feminine, decorative armband over it.

At first, Morph struggled to speak. "I . . . I . . . I think we are safe here," he stuttered. "It's totally deserted. No angels or demons will think to look for us in this part of Okeus's swamp. Most demons and angels want to be where people are—and there ain't none here," he quipped, trying to relieve his tension.

Angie nodded. She saw the fear flickering on the demon's face and knew why: he was risking his life to meet with her. For a moment, she felt foolish for putting him and herself in this situation. *Maybe this is a big mistake. What if we are discovered? We both might die out here in the middle of nowhere.* But then she remembered what this meeting might mean for the colony—and for herself as a Beta intel angel. After taking a big breath, she put on her game face and began to speak. Morph curled up on the ground under a dense bush with his tail twitching constantly. Angie hovered near him about two feet off the ground to be at eye level with him.

"Okay, thank you for agreeing to meet with me. I know you are taking a dangerous risk to do this. So, let's do this quickly. First, what do you call yourself?" Angie hesitantly asked.

"Morph—my name is Morph. And you are called Angie? That's what your big angel calls you, right?"

"Yes. That's my name. Now, forgive me, but let's get down to business before we are discovered. I want to know more about demons and especially about you because you seem to be different from other demons I have seen or heard about."

Morph had not expected that kind of question. He squirmed for a moment, wondering if he could do this. Finally, he responded, "What do you already know about demons?"

"Not enough," Angie said. "We angels know Dark Angels are not demons. The Bible never equates fallen angels with demons. Of course, we know that demons serve Lucifer. God certainly did not create demons. So Lucifer must have made them. But how? Can you tell me?"

Morph looked around again quickly to see if any demons were near, and then nodded. "Lucifer's first strategy was to send gangs of Dark Angels to Earth to get women pregnant so they could make a warrior race of giants called the Nephilim to defeat mankind."

Angie's face twisted in a grimace of perplexity. "But Lucifer had at least sixty thousand powerful angels. Why didn't he use them to attack humans? Why use surrogate creatures like half-human giants?"

Morph suddenly looked disgusted and scoffed louder than he should. "Are you kidding? You really don't know those rebels. Those monsters live and breathe arrogance and pride. It's beneath their dignity to do the dirty work of deceiving and tormenting puny humans. Can you imagine the shame they would feel if a human got the best of them, like David did Goliath? They can't afford that kind of humiliation. *Poor things.* They lost Paradise, and all they have is their false identity as big-shot Dark Angels. Besides that, your Lord was creating millions of humans, and those sixty thousand would have to work really hard to manage so many victims. Work is a four-letter word to them. So, when little David defeated Goliath, Lucifer realized he needed to invent another life-form to fight men. So, he create a new slave race to tempt, torment, and deceive humans. That's us—demons."

"Wow," Angie gasped. "But how could Satan make demons? I thought only God could create things?" she asked.

CHAPTER 47

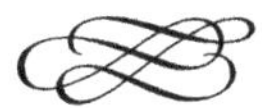

Morph crouched down as if he were afraid someone might hear him. "It's a well-kept secret. No one really knows how he did it. Humans make babies, so he can make demons, I guess. His powers are beyond that of any other Dark Angel. First, let me tell you a little more about us demons.

"All demons are male. Some are small like me, and some are really big, like Okeus. Most cannot fly, but some can. Some more powerful demons do have wings so that they can do combat with angels. But even the most powerful demon is no match for a Dark Angel. Lucifer made sure of that. He knew his demons had his rebel nature in them. He made us all weaker so that he and his dark angels could humiliate us constantly.

"We come in different shapes and colors. Most have scales or a thick hide. A few have fur—like me. But one thing we all have in common: extreme ugliness. All my friends know the stories of Lucifer laughing as he gave his demons some of the most disgusting faces and bodies in creation. Some of us look like insects, birds, reptiles, and even deep-sea marine life. Lucifer said our ugliness would help subdue humans through fear. Ha! But we all know better—and we all *despise* Lucifer for it.

"The only relief we get from seeing our own repulsive bodies is when we shift into another shape to trick humans. Even Lucifer does it. Long ago, he appeared on earth looking like a human with magical powers. As a result, millions of people in Asia now worship him as their god. It works. So, we demons do it too when we need to trick someone badly."

Angie was spellbound, but also impatient. "Fascinating, Morph—but how did Lucifer actually create all of you?"

"Well—Lucifer spawned us. I can explain the spawning process if you want—but I warn you, it's messy.

"It started with the Fifty. Lucifer chose fifty of his least favorite Dark Angels—usually those who complained a lot about leaving heaven. He took them into a secret chamber of his palace in hell and killed them by piercing their bodies five times with his huge sword, then knocking out all their teeth.

"After ripping out the insides of their abdomens, he inserted spawning organs into them. Then, Lucifer resurrected the fifty back to life and chained them in a special spawning cavern. An enormous Dark Angel called Vermixen was put in charge of Fifty. Lucifer had previously altered Vermixen's organs so that his pores could ooze a sticky, red gel that covers the floor of the spawning cave four inches deep.

"Each day—as humans count time—the fifty spawn slaves vomit about one thousand egg sacs out of their toothless mouths onto the floor where they are fertilized by the sticky slime. Every sac grows a demon in just three days. Within minutes of fertilization, five thousand sadism demons are assigned to kick the newly fertilized sacs hard five times a day. After each kick, they stab the sacs with what they call the *Lightning Spear.* The spear has three sharp points charged with high-voltage energy captured from lightning bolts on earth. There are no words to describe that pain. By the time a demon is ripped out of its sac, he is so traumatized he'll do anything the Dark Angels tell him just to avoid more pain. That's how the Dark Angels break any resistance to obey them."

"Oh, Morph! Those Dark Angels really are monsters!" Angie blurted out angrily—and a little too loud. Her big purple eyes were brimming with tears. "I hope they at least fed you well after all that."

"Not really. All I could eat was the thick, mucous membrane of my sac. I threw it all up. Later, I found out that the Dark Angels expect us to feed ourselves on the evil energy we get when we make people sin. But sometimes people refuse to sin, so we have to hunt and eat small animals, fish, insects, and . . . well, worse things too," Morph gagged, sticking out his purple tongue in disgust.

"Our favorite meals are what we call Leechy Meals. We suck a little blood when we are inside someone who likes to sin. Not a lot of blood, mind you. Just enough for a big leech—you know, those slimy things that live in water. The sins of humans are our main source of energy, but their blood is like a sweet dessert. In most places, we can get Leechy Meals often. But not in Europe. Your Lamb makes it hard to stay inside his people. They keep repenting, confessing their sins, and forgiving others. We never can stay in a person very long when they do that."

"Aghhhh! That all sounds so disgusting!" Angie winced. "And to think that former angels of heaven are forcing you to go through all that. So, what types of demons does that spawning process produce?"

"Well, out of about one billion demons spawned so far, most are just the normal ones that specialize in only one kind of sin, like lying, stealing, fornication, hatred, self-pity, and fears. I've met a few fantastic religious demons in my day. They are masters at masquerading as the Enemy Spirit of heaven. We love them. They are very effective in getting Christians to oppose and even kill each other."

"So demons can't kill humans themselves—they have to use humans to kill humans?" she asked as she checked her sensors to make sure all this was being recorded.

"No, we *can* kill humans directly— but it is not common. Apparently, Lucifer doesn't want his demons known as assassins. It might force humans to take us more seriously. *Secrecy* is our greatest weapon, you know. When we kill a human, Lucifer says we must shift into another shape so no one suspects a demon did it—*or else* suffer the consequences at his hand. It's a rule every demon knows *well.* Some demons in Africa shift into black panthers to kill the natives. Here in Virginia, when Okeus forces us to kill a human, we do it by shifting into a wolf or bear shape.

"Some of our best assassins were specially spawned by Vermixen to be bigger and more powerful. Okeus seems to be one of them. Demons like him have killed many other demons as as well as some humans."

Seeing the pain in Angie's face, Morph quickly moved on, "But by far, the most common type of demon Lucifer has spawned are demons that tempt people with the love of *money*. No other demon type has deceived people more effectively than they have. Some of the most famous demons of that type go by the name of Mammon.

And then there is Okeus. I'm not sure what type of demon he is. He's one of the most famous demons on this continent, I can assure you. I've even heard of demons in Peru bragging about Okeus. They all want to be like him one day."

"Morph, stop! I have to tell you something. Since you have been so honest with me, I need to be honest with you. Since I have come to Virginia, all I have heard from the demons here—including you—is that Okeus is a high-level demon. He isn't."

"He isn't?" Morph hissed incredulously. The fur on his back shot up.

"No, Okeus is a *disguise*. He is a Dark Angel. He has a humanoid form —like every angel God made. We don't know his angel name yet."

"Why that sniveling, farty, butt-faced reptilian fraud!" Morph growled. "He's lied to us for thousands of years. Then Morph mocked him in a squeaky voice. 'Oh, I am one of you. I am just a demon who rose through the ranks by working hard to please my Dark Angel. One day, I got a promotion from Lucifer himself when he saw how effective I was against the Jews long ago.' That's the pile of crap he feeds us. And you know why? He knows we won't turn against one of our own. He knows we *hate* Dark Angels. And he *is* one. Wow—wait till the gang hears about this!"

"No, Morph. Not yet. I need that to stay a secret. It would not be good if Okeus knows that I know that. And who knows, the day may come when you will need to protect yourself from Okeus by threatening to expose him as a fraud to his demons."

Morph's eyes got big, and he looked at the angel with a slight smirk, "Angie—you are thinking like a demon now. I would love to do that! I want to see the terror on his face. He will never touch me again!"

"OK—now let's talk about *you*," Angie smiled. "How exactly did you become you? You have a light under your left wing, and you seem to enjoy being around worship to our God. Are you a new species of demon? Are there others like you?"

CHAPTER 48

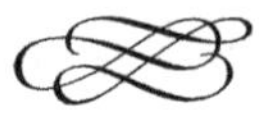

Morph was shaken. No one had ever asked him that. This was his darkest secret. For several long moments, he hesitated and just stared at the bubbling mud around his paws.

Finally, he spoke. "Angie, if Okeus finds out about this wing light and how it got there, he will probably rip my wings and legs off one at a time and then feed me alive to his guard demons. I really don't think I should talk about this."

But when he looked into Angie's face and saw that look of compassion again, he decided to tell her.

"*OK.* I will tell you what I have never told anyone—not even my closest friends," Morph whispered with a big gulp in his voice.

"On the very day I was being spawned, your Lord's Son was crucified on Earth. Even in the thick sac, I could hear a tremendous roaring and howling all around me. The sounds seemed to come from every direction. It sounded like every Dark Angel and demon in hell was celebrating. It went on for hours.

"Three days later, just after I had been yanked out of my sac, I was standing with millions of demons near Lucifer's throne room. Everyone had stopped their regular jobs so they could see what would happen next. The massive demon horde was quiet now. Lucifer paced the floor, looking very nervous. Suddenly, everyone froze in terror as they saw Jesus descending from earth toward Lucifer's throne room. All I could do was shake violently. I'll never forget what happened next.

"The one you call the Lamb of God arrived in Lucifer's throne room with a blast of light brighter than a thousand suns. Every demon and Dark Angel screamed, crumpled to their knees, and covered their eyes —including Lucifer! From the cavern floor, I squinted hard and glimpsed rainbows bouncing off the walls of hell. I saw hundreds of brilliantly colored angels circling overhead, blowing golden trumpets. It only lasted a few seconds, but the light was so intense that some demons just exploded. Lucifer tried to roar, but he could only cry. He just laid there in his own piss. It was the most frightening and the most beautiful thing I have ever experienced in the last two thousand years."

"Jesus came to hell?" Angie gasped. She could hardly believe what she was hearing. "Morph, I know our Bible says that 'after being made alive, He went and made proclamation to the imprisoned spirits,' but I never knew he actually visited hell itself. But what has all that got to do with the light under your left wing?"

Morph stared at the mud again before responding. His voice quavered as he spoke. "When Jesus appeared in hell, I raised my left wing to shield my eyes from his blinding light. But after a moment, out of curiosity, I lowered my wing just long enough to see Jesus pointing right at me with his finger. A white-hot ray of light exploded from his index finger and hit me under my left wing. Later, after Jesus had left, I noticed a faint glow there. It terrified me. Somehow, I knew no demon was supposed to have any light on its body.

"Then, Vermixen rushed into our cavern. He grabbed a demon who also had a similar spot of light on his chest. Vermixen bit his head off and ripped his body into shreds with a ferocious roar that shook the spawning cavern. Then, he raced around the cavern to hunt down any more demons who had any spots of light on them. Many others did. They died horrible deaths that day. I managed to slide into a deep hole in the cavern wall and hid. I stayed there for days until I was starving and had to leave. After escaping from hell, I eventually ended up here with Okeus."

"But how did you hide your light spot later?" Angie inquired.

"When I came out of the hole, I discovered that if I kept my left wing close to my side, I could walk and fly, and no one would see the spot of light. Holding my wing that way made me slower in flight, but everyone just thought I had a defective wing, which is common."

"And how has that spot affected your life?" Angie asked as she covertly checked her sensors to make sure all this was being recorded.

Blowing air out of his mouth in disgust, Morph responded, "It has *ruined* my life. I'm not sure why, but that light seems to cripple me from being fully evil. It has made me a failure as a demon. Everyone knows it, and everyone bullies me and laughs at me.

Whenever I am about to inflict severe pain on a child, make someone commit suicide, or infect a Christian with a fatal disease, I foul it up. The people never die. They never get really sick. Just before I strike my victim, I feel the wingpit light get warmer and brighter. It makes me lightheaded, and I can't think straight. Eventually, my head starts to swim, and my body goes limp," Morph whined.

"Lightheaded. Hmm. What a cute way to describe it," Angie chuckled.

Morph scowled. "Nothing cute about it! I live in constant fear that the light will be discovered by Okeus or other demons. Angie, I know you are an angel who does good, but we demons have to be bad. It's what they spawned us for. All my life, I've wanted just once to be a great demon like Mangel and show the others I can be as evil as they are—but *I can't*."

"And who is Mangel?" Angie asked.

"Just one of the greatest demons hell has ever spawned! Mangel's work is the stuff of legends. In Assyria, in 800 BC, Mangel influenced the Assyrian army to skin their victims alive* before roasting them in the fire. Lucifer loved it. And later, Mangel got promoted for something no evil spirit had ever thought of. It was incredibly cruel and grotesque. You see, he just..."

"Morph—please, that's enough," Angie interrupted, with her face scrunched in disgust. Thank God you could not follow his example. So, how have you avoided being killed for all the times you failed to fulfill your missions?"

"Easy answer: Every demon can lie, but I have become an expert at making up stories to protect myself. Some of our best lying spirits even envied me. Eventually, my Dark Angel masters discovered I was lying to them, but they still decided not to execute me. They discovered that I had a special gift they needed."

Angie looked perplexed. "What gift could you possibly have that would make them keep a lying, bungling demon?"

For a moment, Morph just stared at her and smirked. He liked this little angel. She seemed genuinely interested in his story. "I can sense the movements and plans of angels, even at great distances. It's like an instinct or something. I knew, for instance, that you and your big angel were coming here when you flew over Voudoc's islands. I can also sense when angels are watching. I saw you watching me for a long time, even though my masters were unaware of it. I thought you were targeting me for capture or attack," Morph chuckled.

Angie was stunned, but she didn't want him to know that. "So that's why they keep you around. Knowledge is power, isn't it? That's one reason I enjoy being a recon angel."

"I guess so, but even with my special powers, it doesn't protect me from all the Dark Angels and their pet demons. Everyone knows I am different. In hell, being different is like having a large target on your back. I am the clown of every Dark Angel I have served—the victim of every cocky demon looking for sport, a cheap thrill, or a way to show off. I've been beaten up, spat on, ridiculed, and defecated on so many times I can't even count them all. And all the while, the Dark Angels just laugh at me. Without my friends, I would have gone insane long ago."

"Tell me about your friends, Morph. They must be amazing like you."

CHAPTER 49

The sky over the great Swamp was getting darker as Angie's interview of Morph continued. He was relaxing now. He knew he shouldn't feel this way, but he was *really* enjoying talking to the little angel.

"The story of my friends is not a nice one," Morph whispered with a sad smile. "Okeus has maimed hundreds of us demons over the years. Some of the most damaged ones are my best friends—especially the twelve who have a knack for making us all laugh: Hopin, Scopin, Mopin, Flopin, Dunt, Fard, Snoozle, Og, Butz, Guano, Splatz, and Doltt. Hopin has no arms or wings, but he can dance better than most by hopping like a rabbit. Mopin drags himself around with just his arms, but he can really sing. He lost his wings and legs to Okeus when he failed to kill a small child. Snoozle had his nose cut off by another demon in a fight. He's a mess—but wc love him. He can sling snot and hit someone on the forehead up to one hundred feet away. And then there's Butz—he had his rear end cut off by Okeus for allowing a native to live after the native had cursed Okeus. Because of his deformity, Butz can fart continuously if he wants— and louder than anyone. Okeus used to challenge him, but he finally gave up. And the rest—well, they all have turned their broken bodies into something that makes us laugh. Believe me, we need all the laughter we can get. But it's never enough.

Morph hung his head. "You can't imagine how lonely it has been and how much I have wished I had never been spawned. Who needs a life like this?" He stared off into the dark night. "The only thing that keeps me going is a vision I had shortly after I saw your Lamb in hell. In the vision, I saw millions of demons taking revenge on Lucifer and his damned angels. All the demons I know would love to do that. My best friends said they would try it if they thought it might work."

Angie's eyes grew wide. "You mean you and your friends would try to attack Lucifer and his sixty thousand?" Once again, her voice rose in her surprise. Morph's eyes widened in fear.

"*Hush,* angel!" Morph whisper-shouted and looked around in panic. "I am not that stupid. I would have to get millions of demons to help me. I think it's possible. An older demon once told me how a Jew named Moses used millions of tiny gnats to defeat the leader of a great nation called Egypt. Those little gnats brought the most powerful man on Earth to his knees to ask for mercy from Moses. I figure we can cut a deal with 'his royal darkness,' Lucifer, for our freedom if millions of us 'little gnats' stood against him and his angels. There are over one billion of us. Let's say five hundred million joined up to oppose Lucifer's sixty thousand. Not bad odds, I'd say."

"Pretty clever, Morph. I'm impressed. And angels say I think out of the box. Wow—we may be more alike than we realize," Angie said with obvious pleasure. "I've never really considered such an idea. For that matter, I don't think any angel in heaven has."

Scrunching up his dark green face so that his indigo fangs showed, Morph responded, "Well, I don't try to think that way. I just do. It's part of my weirdness, I guess. Besides, I know it will never happen, but it helps me deal with this hellish life just to think such crazy thoughts. Even demons need a little hope, Angie. Otherwise, we'd probably all commit suicide sooner than we do. Many of my friends have already ended their lives. They just couldn't take the abuse any longer. If only they had continued to wait for *The One*."

"*The One*? Who is that, Morph?"

"Oh, yeah—I forgot to tell you. I figured it was too much for you to believe."

"Try me," the little angel said eagerly.

"Okay. Well, many, many centuries ago, there was a demon famous for his wisdom. He predicted that a special demon would one day arise to overthrow the Dark Angels. Everyone calls that special demon *The One*. Of course, most demons think the prediction is a joke or worse. My friends and I believe it, but we wonder if it will ever happen before we all get terminated in one of Okeus's foul moods. I think about *The One* when I feel discouraged—which is often," Morph laughed sardonically.

But Morph's grin disappeared suddenly when he heard a swarm of guard demons rapidly approaching—and headed directly for their position. He could tell from their voices that they were a rough bunch.

Angie heard them too, and at first, was confused. Why had she not sensed them coming sooner? Then, she froze with fear as she remembered she had turned off all her sensor monitors earlier. They both looked at each other and knew they were about to be discovered. Without even thinking, Morph did something no demon has ever done to an angel.

With his cat-like reflexes, Morph sprang into the air, snatched Angie to his chest with one paw, and crashed into the bushes on his shoulder before rolling over to cover her with his body. Instantly, the guard demons dove with swords drawn to investigate the source of the sound. The guard patrol came to a halt about twenty feet above Morph and began to laugh scornfully. "Oh, it's only that clown Morph. He's probably hiding from Okeus again. Let's go, boys. We can come back later to torment him if we have time."

As the thugs flapped away, Morph got up on all fours. Angie was lying face up beneath him on the ground, stunned but unhurt.

"I'm so sorry, Angie. It was the only way I knew to hide your angelic glow. Those guys are vicious. They would have cut you badly." Angie just lay there, eyes blinking but saying nothing. "Morph, you . . . you . . . you just *saved* me. You're a demon, and you saved me. I have no words . . . no words . . . I . . . well, thank you," the little angel squeaked with a weak smile.

"I think we should leave now," Morph whispered as he helped her up with a paw and a toothy smile. "Just promise me you will protect me and my secret," Morph pleaded. "And my twelve best friends, if you happen to encounter them. They are the official clown demons for Okeus. We stick together and watch out for one another."

Angie rose slowly to hover right in front of Morph's dirty, sad face. As she looked at him, her heart was filled with a strong compassion that surprised her—*again*. Then, almost without thinking, she put out her hand toward his face—then drew it quickly back. Neither spoke, except with their questioning eyes. After a moment, Angie slowly extended her hand again with regal gentleness to the mud-caked fur of a very startled demon. As her tiny palm connected with his face, their eyes locked. Neither moved for several moments. Morph thought he was going to faint. No one had ever touched him like that —or looked at him like that.

"Morph, I tell you this," Angie said very solemnly, "Your secrets and your life are safe with me. Go now and sleep, dear friend. Let's meet again soon. If either of us puts a gray whelk shell at the base of the big cross at Cape Henry, that will be our signal to meet here that night."

CHAPTER 50

January 24, 1608

Three days after the peace conference with Newport and Smith, Opie and Mongo met with their father. Paquiquino agreed to meet that night at Opie's longhouse, close to Powhatan's throne room. As soon as their aging father came in out of the freezing night air, he could see that it was going to be a difficult meeting. Paquiquino said nothing as he sat on a cold woven mat near a dying fire. Powhatan culture requires younger men to sit in the presence of older warriors. But both sons insulted their father by refusing to sit down. Opie could hardly talk. He paced the room, seething and grunting with anger.

Then, Opie spat out,

"Remember the Tlaxcalans,* Father? You tell us how Cortez conquered mighty Aztecs in Mexico with only six hundred Spanish soldiers by making friends with Tlaxcalan tribe and other tribes that Aztecs rule.* With those tribes and terrible sickness the Spanish bring, they defeat Aztecs.* Now, Powhatan has five loyal tribes: Pamunkey, Arrohateck, Appamattuck, Youghtanund, and Mattaponi. But what about other twenty-five tribes he rule? Will they stay loyal to us? Some tribes not happy with our rule over them. These English whites may use some of those tribes to attack us— like Cortez did in Mexico. We cannot allow whites to live near us, Father Paq."

Paquiquino remained silent. He knew he had taught them to think like that years ago when his rage toward all whites was fierce and unrelenting. But he was different now.

Mongo walked over to his father and got down on one knee in front of him. "Father, Lord Okeus has ordered me to kill Hunt. His prayers are too powerful. We cannot defeat the English until we kill him."

"No, my son, please do not talk of such a thing," Paquiquino countered with anger in his voice. "Powhatan thinks we can live with English, and they can help us with weapons and tools and wisdom that white people have. We can be stronger if they are friends. Don't you see that?" Paquiquino said, frustrated.

Mongo shot back, "No, Father. Opie is right. All of my shamans tell me that the spirits that serve them are very upset when Hunt pray. More angels will come to help English if Hunt continue to pray. He must go!" Mongo concluded with a quick nod to Opie.

Finally, Paquiquino stood up, looked at his two sons, and gave a long sigh. "What you both say is true about whites. They cannot be trusted. They always come to conquer and take our land. But Hunt is good and kind to our people. I watch him. He give warriors small tools, talk to us about his good god, and play with our children who come to the fort. I once know some whites like Hunt. Your niece, Pocahontas, also like him very much. He is not like other English. He is man of peace and his god is god of peace. Please, let him live. If we kill him, English will start a war, and they have fire-sticks! Many of our people will die."

At that remark, Opie's anger boiled over into rage. He stomped his foot on the ground and shook his fist in the air and shouted, "Yes, Father, but we have fifteen thousand brave warriors*! We can keep one hundred English in their fort until they starve—and they *will!*"

"Then let Hunt starve. I cannot kill him. He is innocent, unarmed man," Paquiquino wearily responded.

Mongo put his finger to his mouth to shush his brother's wrath. Then, he tenderly put his arm around his sad-looking father. "My dear Father, you must do this, Mongo pleaded. I know it is hard for you. Hunt must die. His prayers are worse than ten thousand fire-sticks against us. If Hunt stay alive, the English will stay, and then they will steal our land and our women—just as you see in Mexico. They will kill your sons and our sons. Father, you did this before. Now you must do this once more for safety of our tribes. No other warrior will kill unarmed priest. They know it is evil to do. But you have already done. I myself will prepare Husquenaw ritual medicine* for you and I chant the powerful spirit we call *Hate* into you again. You will not even know what you are doing when you stab him. Please, Father, we are all counting on you to save us from English."

Dark, soul-crushing, vivid memories flooded Paquiquino's mind. He heard the dying prayers of the Spanish priests and the war-whoops of his fellow braves as they slaughtered the Jesuits. But then he looked at his two sons in the room and thought about their children. He knew his son Powhatan would be one of the first killed in a war with the English—and all of Powhatan's royal children, including Pocahontas. He knew his sons were right. The English would conquer his people just as the Spanish defeated the Aztecs in Mexico.

With a cry of anguish, the old warrior dropped to his knees and covered his face with both hands, sobbing. A great battle of emotions now raged within him: deep sadness and horror at what he had done — and might yet do—and fear for his people if he did not kill Hunt. *What should I do? How can I live with myself if I do what they want—or if I do not do what they want?*

With great effort, choking out his words, Paquiquino muttered, "As you wish, Mongo. I will kill Hunt. But I… I wish there was another way."

CHAPTER 51

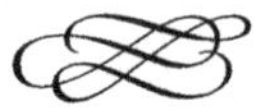

March 15, 1608

It was a warm March day. Small animals could be heard foraging in the damp, musty leaves beneath budding redbud trees. But the air was unusually still, as if the forest was holding its breath.

Deep in the forest, to the east of the burnt-out James Fort, a lone man stood at the edge of a small clearing. Pastor Hunt had left his tent very early and strolled into the trees, relishing the joys of nature along the way. The fort had not yet been rebuilt after the great fire, so he and most of the men were still living in tents along the shoreline. It had been a miserable winter. Now, with warmer weather, Hunt wanted some time alone with God in the beautiful woods.

High above him, Scion and Angie glided in slow circles as they carefully watched over the colony's most powerful intercessor. They knew Hunt would soon be in great danger, but they had made preparations for this day soon after Angie's long-range sensors heard Paquiquino agree to kill the godly pastor.

Yesterday, Scion had planted a thought in the mind of the praying chaplain that Moss Valley would be a great place to seek the Lord.

Scion knew the guard demons near the ruined fort would alert Snookus, who would probably send Paquiquino to follow Hunt when he left that morning.

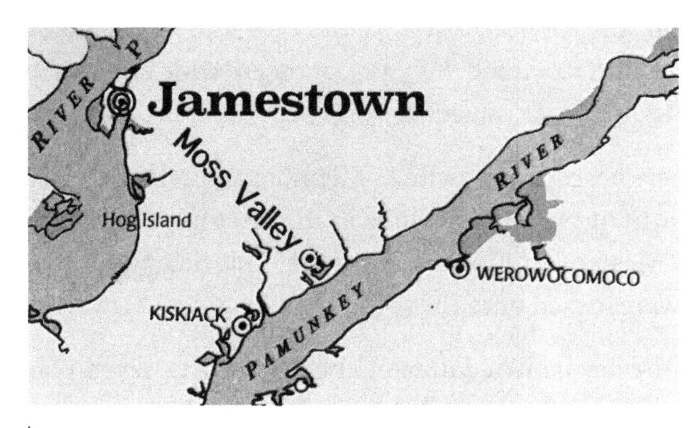

Moss Valley, southeast of Jamestown and southwest from Chief Powhatan's village at Werowocomoco

But, to Scion's surprise, demons assigned to Jehu awakened Jehu just in time to witness Hunt's departure and Jehu hurriedly dressed to follow Hunt. As the sailor left the fort, a small flock of very bored demons followed him to see what he was going to do.

Scion whispered to Angie, "Now this is really going to be interesting. We may have to uncloak to handle this."

An hour later, as the Anglican priest reached the tranquil meadow. *Ahhhh.* He sighed sigh audibly. "What a restful place."

The air was earthy, damp, and fresh. Before him stretched a carpet of spongy ground covered with deep green moss that gave the fallen trees, rocks, and land a soft, restful feeling. As his bony knees sank into the cushioned forest floor, the man in black began to pray. Unbeknownst to him, he was about to *become* prey.

Looking up through the tightly woven branches of tall maples brimming with new leaves, the weary chaplain spoke as if to an old friend. "Father, here I am again. Pocahontas brought me here last November. I felt your sweet Presence here. I long to feel that again."

You're right, two other people thought to themselves at the same time. One carried a Powhatan spear; the other clutched a big knife. Both had murder on their minds.

Paquiquino was about to kill a priest . . . again. His hands shook, his steps were unsteady, and his eyes dimmed with age, but the spirit called Hate and the Husquenaw drugs kept him fierce and focused.

When Angie heard the growling of demons in both of the armed men and the flock of mocking demons in the treetops, she poked Scion in the arm. "Master—this looks dangerous." But Scion did not respond. His eyes were locked onto the scene below.

This was the day Jehu had dreamt about for thirty-seven years—a day of revenge. He had followed Paquiquino into the woods as the old Algonquian tracked Hunt in his early morning journey. Normally, a seasoned brave could tell when someone was following them. But today, a mental hurricane of fear, shame, guilt, and hatred overpowered almost every other sense Paquiquino had.

As Reverend Hunt continued to pray, Jehu's mind boiled with anger. *Don Luis, you will die today, just as cruelly as your Jesuit friends died—killed by you— a friend they had trusted.*

Today, I, Aloncito, am the Lord's avenger. Today I fulfill my childhood vow to kill you. Then, I will pin the blame for your murder on the English. That will start a war with the Powhatans that should keep the English out of here for good. Then I will help Spain claim this land again!

As the husky Spaniard savored these thoughts, he imagined his knife on Paquiquino's throat. He saw himself look into Paquiquino's terrified eyes and say, "Don Luis, didn't you pledge your loyalty to the Jesuits who lie beneath us here? They taught you about Jesus. They protected you from cruel soldiers on the ship that brought us all here. They even shared their food and nursed you back to health when you caught the Spanish disease in Mexico that killed so many." Then, Jehu took great pleasure in imagining the look on Paquiquino's face as he sliced Paquiquino's neck open and watched the warm blood soak into the same green moss that was once covered with Spanish blood.

The demons of murder and revenge in Jehu sensed his furious hatred. They slapped each other's spiked backs with a satisfied growl. Revenge by humans always gave them a special thrill.

Angie gasped. "Master Scion, are you seeing this? A powerful spirit called Hate in Paquiquino wants to kill Hunt, and Jehu looks like he wants to murder Paquiquino. The demons in both of them are howling with delight. We've got to do *something!* I could pierce the ear of one of those demons with my sword and distract him. He could never catch me."

"Hold on, little one. Just give this some time. It's always better when humans work things out by themselves. They learn more. I have followed standard procedures in setting this up so far. Let's give this more time."

"Okay, but if that hate spirit so much as touches Hunt . . ." Angie hissed.

Scion looked at her tiny, drawn sword and shook his head. *How could such a small creature be so fierce?*

Paquiquino crept closer to Hunt, gripping his spear tightly so its aim would be true. He was fifteen yards away. Jehu also closed in behind Paquiquino. He smiled when he saw that Paquiquino had no other weapon but the spear.

Hunt pulled a small crucifix out of his pocket and held it tenderly in his right hand. "Father, I come to you in the mighty name of Jesus, King of kings, Lord of lords, and Lord of Virginia and all it contains. I come to you on behalf of our colony and the precious Powhatan natives who do not yet know how much you love them," Hunt prayed.

Paquiquino almost stumbled. Hunt's words stung him like angry wasps. He had heard words like that long ago. His breathing became faster. He felt dizzy. The spirit of hate in him cowered at the mention of Jesus and his love for the natives. But the Husquenaw drugs gave Paquiquino the strength to force himself closer to Hunt. *Now, I will kill him!* he thought.

But just then, Hunt got up and walked away to the edge of the clearing near a pile of decaying logs. Nature was calling Hunt's bladder. Paquiquino froze. Jehu cursed softly. Angie's eyes grew big. Demons growled. But Scion smiled and murmured under his breath. "I hope this works."

CHAPTER 52

As Rev. Hunt reached the edge of the small glen, sunlight glinted off something. Despite the need to relieve himself, Hunt was curious. After striding over to where he saw the gleam, Hunt reached into a mossy heap of rotting logs. His hand came out with a small, tarnished, silver box. The top was exquisitely decorated with an inscription in Spanish— *Mi Vida in Christo.*

Good Lord, what is this? Hunt wondered. "My Life in Christ," Hunt intoned softly. "Great God in heaven, the Spanish were *here,*" he whispered. Then, he pried open the thick lid and saw a small earthen bottle. It had an inscription: *Agua Bendita.* "Holy water," he muttered. He shook it. He could hardly believe there was still water in that old bottle!

But the other object in the box made him suck in his breath: a small leather book with a wide silver clasp and lock. The key was still in the lock. *My God,* Hunt thought, *the book is still intact.* Hunt's heart began to race. *I have got to read this,* he decided. To Hunt's surprise, his urge to pee instantly vanished.

With the box under his arm and the bottle in his coat pocket, Hunt quickly moved back to where he had been praying. As the Chaplain opened the silver clasp of the book, the demon in Paquiquino screamed. "Kill him now!"

Jehu also recognized that book— and his heart filled with grief. *It's Father Segura's diary!* His anger grew stronger.

Hunt opened the book. The leather cover was dry but still flexible and its pages still intact. Hunt gently flipped through the pages. "It's hand-written but readable" he murmured. "Thank God I took the time to learn some Spanish before coming here."

As he translated some of the pages out loud, the two assassins heard and understood every word. "Hmm, the last entry is on February 9, 1571."* That date hit the mushy brain of Paquiquino like the jolt of of the bucking horse he tried to ride in Spain. Images of warriors swinging hatchets, knelling men with raised hands—and the screams of a small boy flooded his mind. He lowered his head to his knees, overcome with shame and guilt.

Hunt continued to translate aloud from the diary.

> Buenos dias, Dios! This morning it is cold outside but warm in my heart to know we are here to bring the light of Jesus to these dear people who are lost in darkness.
>
> I am sick in bed while my brothers celebrate the death of our Lord today in Mass. Jesus, just as you laid down your life on Calvary so others could find eternal life in you, we also offer you our lives for the salvation of this tribe. You said in John's Gospel reading today that 'unless the grain of wheat falls into the ground and dies, it remains alone. But if it dies, it brings forth much fruit.'
>
> Lord, all of my Jesuit brothers have vowed to be grains of wheat willing to die here so that you may have a harvest of souls that you purchased on Calvary with your blood. In my heart, I believe that even

our little Aloncito also feels the same way, even though he is but a boy. May you be honored by all we do and say today, Lord Jesus. You are our very life.

And, Lord, please bring my beloved brother, Don Luis, back soon from his tribe. I miss him greatly. He must be detained in his village, getting enough supplies to bring back to us since there is so little food here for the ten of us. Lord, would you send Don Luis here today?

But wait, there is noise in our camp . . .

Dear Jesus, you answer prayer so quickly! I hear the brothers welcoming Don Luis back. Forgive this short time with you now, Savior. Later today, I will come to you for a much longer time of sweet fellowship.

This is my life in Christ today.

Your son and servant,

Juan Segura

As Hunt finished reading, a holy hush wafted down over the mossy dell.

“Now, Angie!” Scion commanded.

A piercing musical note rang out from her tiny angel frame, so high and so loud it was heard in the spirit world hundreds of miles in every direction. Every demon in Jehu and Paquiquino instinctively sucked in its breath, closed its eyes, and braced itself. The gaggle of taunting demons in the treetops shrieked and fled as the blinding light of a dozen magnificent angels suddenly arose from the mossy ground with drawn swords. A shift in the spiritual atmosphere was about to happen—one they had learned to dread. Angels in Florida giggled. Demons all along the eastern coast cringed. Hunt shouted, “Hallelujah!” without fully knowing why.

Sensing imminent failure, Hate instantly rose up inside Paquiquino and overpowered him. The old warrior yelled, as if burning alive. He ran toward Hunt to spear him, but before he could throw the weapon, his body slammed into an invisible wall and crumbled to the ground, screaming curses.

Hunt got up and went to the howling native. Without thinking, he exclaimed loudly, "Come out, thou foul spirit! I say, come out!" He scrunched his face and thought, *How odd. I've never said words like that before.*

Hate immediately screeched and jumped out of Paquiquino, trying to flee, but Scion's sword intercepted him, impaling him halfway up the eight-foot blade. The demon jerked to a stop, perfectly skewered, like a writhing snake on Scion's glowing blade just before he exploded into a putrid red mist. Paquiquino now laid motionless near Hunt's trembling knees.

"Good work, Master Scion!" shouted Angie as she flew around Hunt's head like a crazed hummingbird.

"Hang on, Angie. It's not over."

Glancing quickly at the remaining assassin hiding nearby, Angie flashed a brilliant smile and chirped, "Okay, I'll take Jehu," as she darted to the ground.

Just then, Jehu leaped from the thick bushes and charged Paquiquino like a mother bear robbed of its cubs. But he tripped on a branch that was not there a moment before, smashing his head on a large mossy stone that knocked him unconscious. Hunt was shocked to see Jehu suddenly appear—and with such violence— but he kept praying for the old warrior lying next to him.

Angie looked at Scion and smirked with a small curtsy. "It's the least I could do."

Scion nodded and smiled. "Now, the stage is set for God to do something extraordinary."

"I can't wait!" Angie bubbled with girlish excitement.

And so began one of the most glorious moments in the heavenly history of the colony.

CHAPTER 53

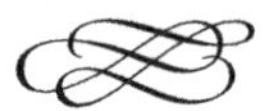

Scion and Angie watched in awe as twelve huge Watcher Angels arrived and formed an honor guard fifty feet above the three men below. The brilliantly bright angels hovered in a perfect circle with their swords pointing heavenward and their gleaming wings fully extended.

Instantly, a blinding, iridescent blue light unseen by humans shot down through the center of the angelic ring. The Presence of God blasted outward in all directions from the impact point. The scent of God's Throne Room incense filled the air. Scion and Angie bowed their heads. The Lord of Hosts had come.

"Sister Gabriella . . . Casas . . . Padre . . . Sister Gabriella . . ." Paquiquino mumbled.

Slowly, with great effort, Paquiquino lifted his head and turned toward the person he had come to kill. As he did, he saw a dangling object in Hunt's hand much like the one he had accidentally stepped on last year: a crucifix.

"Jesus . . . oh, Jesus . . ." Paquiquino choked out hoarsely.

Hunt was more than a little taken aback. *He says the name of Jesus! How unusual,* he thought.

"There, there, my man. It's okay. I'm not going to hurt you," Hunt whispered, not really expecting the native to understand what he said, but hoping his tone would convey the meaning.

"I am so sorry. I am so sorry," Paquiquino whispered.

"Good Lord, man, you speak *English*! Who in heaven's name are you?"

Silence. All Hunt heard was heavy, labored breathing from the mysterious Algonquian at his feet. Then, great sobs—body-wracking sobs—the likes of which Hunt had never heard from a grown man. Time stood still as the weeping turned into a prolonged wailing that frightened small animals nearby. Twelve golden faces above bowed lower with eyes shut as the Lord's Presence grew heavier and heavier in the scene below.

Angie stole a look at Scion, half-turned from her. He had a thousand-mile stare on his face. "Master, are you okay?" As he turned to respond, she gasped. "Master, there are tears in your eyes."

"Yes, I once felt like Paq." Then Angie remembered. She gently put her hand on his arm. Scion smiled as his ancient grief slowly melted away again.

Finally, Paquiquino's wailing stopped. The twelve above raised their heads just as a mysterious tingling sensation crept over the three men's bodies. They looked around to see what was happening.

Hunt was the first to speak. "My goodness! The moss suddenly looks so green. And the sky seems brighter and bluer—the bluest sky I have ever seen! And this feeling—I've felt it before but never this strong. The *Lord* is here!" The hairs on the back of his neck stood up as he knelt down in worship.

The Lord's strong Presence vibrated in every creature in the clearing. Birds, bugs, and a curious red fox in the tree line all felt it. And then, it was gone. The Lord had finished what He came to do.

At that same moment, Jehu woke up. With his long knife between his teeth, he tried to get up again, but a size sixteen invisible foot shoved his chest back into the mushy moss. "Not so fast, big boy," Scion barked. Jehu froze—with his eyes full of fear—an invisible weight was pinning him to the ground.

When Hunt saw that the violent sailor was somehow immobilized, he turned his attention again to the mysterious old warrior lying next to him. After getting down on one knee, Hunt asked him why he was crying.

Angie held her breath. *Lord Jesus, let him repent!*

Looking into Hunt's light green eyes, Paquiquino's dark eyes grew wide. "Your eyes . . . they just like Sister Gabriella's. You are one of *them*."

Hunt smiled, but then Paquiquino blurted out, "I come to kill you but I not want to kill you—because you are one of them."

"One of them? Who are you talking about, sir?"

"One who love their God—more than gold. One who love native people. Not like soldiers who hurt and kill native people. Padre Segura in Spain, Sister Gabriella in Mexico . . . they like *you*. They like Jesus she tell me about. Please, help me be like you. I no want evil Okeus or his spirits any more. I so sorry for bad things I do. I no more hate white people. I want soft eyes like you. I want Jesus. Please help me."

Hunt was stunned. For several moments, all he could do was stare at the desperate man next to him. His mind reeled with questions. *How could this be possible? Not only was he talking to a half-naked native who spoke English—but someone who also had traveled with the Spanish to Mexico and Spain. Who is this old man? And why would he want to kill me?*

And now, he wants to become a follower of Jesus! It was more than Hunt could take in, so he decided to focus on the main thing—the man's salvation.

"Why, sir, that is one of the most beautiful repentance statements I've ever heard. I would be honored to help you. Put your hand in my hands and repeat after me."

"Here it comes, Angie," Scion whispered. The two men prayed together. Paquiquino repeated Hunt's words: "Father God . . .I want Jesus as my Savior. Forgive me for all my sins, especially ones I just confess. I no longer follow Okeus and his spirits.

"I belong to Jesus. He now my Lord and God." Then, throwing his head back, Paquiquino shouted, "I belong to Jesus! He now my Lord and God . . . I will have *His* eyes!"

Hunt struggled to hold back his tears as he spoke. "Well, my friend. You are now my brother . . . *forever*. God is your *Nohsh*, your Father, and you are His son because you belong to Jesus, the Son of God."

Hunt placed his hands on Paquiquino's head to bless him. The newborn Christian looked up as joyful tears flowed from his sparkling brown eyes.

Paquiquino

"Good Lord! Your eyes—they are shining!" Hunt exclaimed with a big laugh.

Scion shot into the air with a snappy victory roll and shouted, "*Yes!*" Angie could not contain herself either. She flew a beeline to Scion's cheek and gave him a microscopic kiss on his cheek. He blushed with a shy smile. "Look, Angie! The Watchers are celebrating too."

Sure enough, the twelve angels were whirling in a circle just above the treetops, their arms interlocked and their flashing swords held high above their boyishly grinning faces.

But after a few moments of celebrating, every angel turned their faces to the men on the ground. The all sensed another miracle was about to occur.

CHAPTER 54

As Pastor Hunt helped Paquiquino to his feet, he asked, "You said you came to kill me. *Why?*"

"My leaders—my brothers—all afraid of you. You make strong prayers. Our witch doctors confused when you pray. Their spells no work. Tribe think that your people will take our lands. Tribe think your prayers are big enemy to us."

"I had no idea it was that sort of contest, but I am kind of glad it is. I know who will win," Hunt grinned.

"My sons, Opie and Mongo—they make me do it. They give me evil medicine and put hate spirit in me to make me kill." Paquiquino clutched Hunt's arm with his trembling hand. "Please, *forgive* me. I no want to be bad man."

"Not a bad man? Really? You are a terrible, evil man who does not deserve to live!" Jehu shouted as Paquiquino and Hunt whirled around. Jehu was still on his stomach, struggling to get up.

"Look, Jehu, if you will just hold your tongue, I will attend to you after I hear this old warrior's story. And why don't you get up? Are you hurt?"

Jehu spat and cursed, "I can't move! There is *something* . . . very heavy on my back!"

"How *odd*. Perhaps that bump on your head has addled your mind. There's nothing on your back, sir."

Seeing that Jehu was no threat, he turned to Paquiquino again. "My friend, let's take one thing at a time. First, who are you? What is your name?"

"His name is Paquiquino, and he is a murderer!" Jehu shouted. "He killed our priests. He deserves to die. Help me get up, and I will kill him for you!"

Angie zipped over to Jehu, looked him in the eyes, and placed her tiny hand on his sweaty throat. He struggled to speak, but only muffled, growling sounds came out. He finally gave up and face-planted back into the moss.

Scion gave Angie a quizzical look. "It's okay, Master," she said. "I saw Gabriel do that to the father of John the Baptist once. It is an authorized tactic," she smirked proudly.

Hunt shook his head and grinned at Paquiquino. "Amazing. You wanted to kill me, and he wanted to kill you. But now he can't move. Then, he bloody shouts at me, and now he can't talk. And I thought this was just a normal day."

Then he grew serious. "So, Paquiquino, why do you think that man wants to kill you?"

Paquiquino hung his head in shame. "I killed his friends . . . Spanish . . . priests . . . Jesuits."

"You *what*? But why would you do that? Surely, they did you no harm."

"No. They my friends. I love like brothers," the old Algonquin whispered with sad eyes.

"This is too much," Hunt huffed. "What kind of person kills his beloved friends? What in God's name would make you do such a terrible thing?"

At that remark, the veins in Jehu's throat bulged. Hunt and Paquiquino looked and saw Jehu writhing on the ground, trying to get the mysterious weight off his back. Then the sailor opened his mouth wide, but no sound came out. His face was a portrait of agony.

Hunt asked again. "Paquiquino, what led you to kill your friends?"

Paquiquino then told Hunt the story—how the Spanish had captured him as a boy and took him to Spain and Mexico, where he met his friends, the priests. But when the priests brought him home from Mexico,* the tribe drugged him and forced him to kill the priests to prove his loyalty to the tribe.

"We kill all of them. Only boy Aloncito lives." At the mention of that name, Paquiquino broke down in heavy sobs. "When I wake from drugs and see what I did, my shame and guilt almost kill me. Part of my soul die. My mind can only think about evil white man hurting our people in Mexico," he whispered as he rubbed a large scar on his cheek.

Hunt was dumbfounded.

But so was the mute sailor on the ground.

Scion winked at Angie. It was time for Jehu to speak.

As he lifted his foot off Jehu, Scion announced, "Okay, big guy, your turn." At the same time, Angie touched the Spaniard's throat once more.

Jehu slowly got up, looking shocked and ashamed as his tear-filled eyes locked with the eyes of Paquiquino. "I...I didn't *know*," he stammered. "I didn't know they made you do it. They drugged you!" And then Jehu began to tremble violently as he cried out in anguish, "I thought you hated us. I thought you had tricked us. I thought you had brought us to your land just to kill us. I have hated you all my life—and now I almost killed you—and *innocent* man! I have been so wrong! Paquiquino, *please* forgive me."

As Jehu moved closer, he saw the long scar on Paquiquino's face. "That was *you!*" he muttered in disbelief.

"Yes, one of my braves try kill you. We fight. He cut my face with knife."

"I remember," Jehu almost shouted. "He grabbed my hair and was going to cut my throat. Then, someone knocked him down, so I ran. *O Madre de Dios*! Paquiquino, you *saved* me. I owe my life to you."

Every human and every angel wept as the two men fell into each other's arms for a long time as blazing arcs of rainbow light danced around the two former enemies. A holy hush filled he forest.

After a few moments, Hunt knew he had to speak. "Paquiquino, you are right. The white man is guilty of so many sins against your people in other lands. It breaks my heart. Many who say they are followers of Jesus do not act like Jesus at all. Dear brother, on behalf of my white people, I ask your forgiveness for the suffering and death of your people caused by our white people. Forgive us also for the silence of our priests when they saw this happening. Our God is sad and angry when His children do such things."

The former Spanish altar boy lowered his head and bit his lower lip. He, too, had been to Mexico.

Paquiquino looked intently at the Anglican priest, as if searching for any trace of dishonesty. "I never hear white man speak like this . . ." Finally, with smiling brown eyes, the old man rested his wrinkled hand on Hunt's shoulder and spoke in a voice resonant with authority, "I, Paquiquino, father of Chief Powhatan, forgive all white men for bad things they do to our people. I ask Great Spirit, Ahone, to bless white man and make white man friends with my people, so we live in peace."

"Amen, my good man! Amen!" the Anglican pastor shouted as he and Paquiquino laughed jubilantly.

Scion and Angie stared with open mouths. "Maybe this colony *will* be saved," Scion exclaimed.

Angie looked up to see the twelve angels giving each other high fives. "Why are Watcher Angels stationed over this glen, Scion?"

"They are from the Honor Battalion."

"Oh, right, the Huguenot story," Angie smiled.

"I ordered this squad to wait a thousand feet underground so no demons would notice them. I figured we would need backup today."

Angie furrowed her brow. "How did you know what was going to happen?"

"It's all very elementary," Scion replied with a sly grin. "According to the Standard Operating Procedures for such things, you have to scout out places where the enemy will be at his weakest and prepare your setting for maximum effect. In this case, I came here earlier to get the silver box out of the ground and into a place where Hunt could see it when he needed to relieve himself."

"You mean to say that you had a hand in that, too?" Angie chuckled.

"As the good book says in Proverbs 21:1, 'God can move the heart of a king any way he wants.' I guess an angel can move the bladder of a priest when he needs to," Scion grinned.

Angie was undone. She dropped onto the green moss, holding her sides, giddy as a five-year-old.

Scion watched her with delight and then suddenly realized, *Good Lord! What is happening to me? I'm acting like Angie. Manipulating the bladders of humans is not in any of my Academy textbooks. Maybe thinking out of the box is not so bad after all,* Scion sighed. *As long as I don't have to have rainbow hair!* he snickered to himself.

CHAPTER 55

March 17, 1608

As the inky sky filled with brilliant stars, Angie glided toward the swampy forest just as Morph dropped out of the sky to meet her under the large bush where they had first met. The Great Swamp was quiet as usual—except for a loud Barred Owl singing her eight-note mating call in the darkened trees.

"Morph, I saw the whelk at the cross today. Is everything okay?

"I've been having terrible dreams," Morph hissed.

"About what?"

"Many years ago, I snuck a peek at a bible the Spanish priests brought here. I saw something your messiah said about Satan's kingdom. It frightened me back then. Now those words are giving me nightmares."

"What words?"

"He said if Satan's kingdom was fighting within itself, it would be divided, and it would fall.* Does that mean Satan's kingdom can really fall—like Pharaoh's kingdom fell before tiny gnats? I've got to know! Is your lord saying that if millions of little demons rebelled against powerful Lucifer, his kingdom could be divided and fall? I've *got* to know. It's driving me crazy!"

Angie's eyes bulged with excitement. "Holy Cherubmatzi! Matthew 12 and Luke 11! Oh my gosh, Morph, I've never thought of it that way!" She paced around in the smelly mud as she tried to wrap her head around what Morph had just said.

And then it hit her. "Maybe it is a *clue*!" she whisper-shouted. "Maybe what Jesus said in that text is connected to your light-spot—and your idea about the gnats, Morph."

Morph groaned. "Now, *you* are the crazy one. Why would the son of your lord have any plans for me but a death sentence in the Abyss?"

"But Morph, don't you see? You've been touched by heaven. That was no coincidence. Things like that never are."

"Angie, I am not getting this."

"Morph, Jesus does nothing by accident. I'll bet it means He has chosen you for something important. And it may be something connected to this colony. Maybe...*maybe* you can help us in some way," Angie suggested sheepishly."

Morph stared at her for a long time. No words would come. Finally, he shook his head violently and forced himself to talk again.

"Look, Angie, I respect you, but please do not talk to me of that again. I cannot deal with those thoughts. If I were to take them seriously, it would destroy what little sanity I have. *No* one in heaven or hell could value me that much. No one would trust *me* that much. No one would choose me for anything that important. I'm just Morph the fool, Morph the failure, Morph the butt of jokes, Morph the broken demon —not wicked enough, not good enough. Not enough of *anything.* Your smart messiah must be thinking of using someone else—not me!"

"But Morph—"

"Shut up, you fool!" he almost shouted. His claws came out, and his feline face contorted with an animalistic rage that sent shivers into Angie. "Leave me alone! At least I know who I am—and who I am *not.* Don't try to change that. It's all I have. My identity is all I have. No one can take that away from me . . . not even you!" he screeched with blue fire in his eyes as his shoulders rose, fur on end, ready to attack.

After a tense few moments, Morph's chest heaved, his shoulders drooped, his claws retracted and he let out a huge sigh. When he looked at Angie again, there was a deep sadness in her eyes. "Well, what are you staring at? Just tell me how different we are—me a damned demon and you a beautiful angel. Tell me what a creep I am and how much better I'd be if I were already mashed into the filthy floors of hell so I could escape an eternity with my tormentors in the Abyss. Go ahead. Get it over with. Just tell me."

Blinking hard to regain her composure, Angie pushed her long, rainbow-colored hair over her shoulders, looked at Morph'a tear-filled eyes, and tenderly said, "Morph, listen to me. You are *chosen.*"

Morph trembled visibly as she spoke those words. Fear washed across his face. *No, way, he thought. She's lying . . . again. Or is she? I've got to get out of here—now!*

And with that, he bolted into the night sky. He couldn't bear to have Angie see him cry again.

~

BY LATE MARCH 1608, THE COLONY WAS AGAIN DESPERATE FOR FOOD.* Captain Smith was exasperated with the factious, disorganized colonists.* He said, "These colonists were ten times more fit to spoil a commonwealth than to ever begin one."*

To acquire food, Smith led a raid on one of the Nansemond tribal villages where Opie was chief under Powhatan's Confederacy.* The natives refused to give up their corn, so Smith and his men burned their homes*. Then the tribe reluctantly agreed to give the English most of their corn supplies—even though that meant the tribe would not have enough corn to feed themselves for several months.* Opie was furious. The tribe was humiliated and wanted revenge. But Powhatan called for patience—and that patience saved the colony from extinction. The remaining settlers were too weak from hunger and sickness to fight a war—even with Smith in command.*

Smith captures the King of the Pamunkey while raiding his village for corn*

April 6, 1608

Only one short month later, after the burned fort had been rebuilt, Scion and Angie sat atop the new chapel roof, looking anything but happy. It should have been a time of celebration. James Fort had literally been resurrected from the ashes in less than two months.* Now it was called Jamestown. The new chapel was beautiful and much larger.* And it was Easter Sunday—usually a day to rejoice in the resurrection of Jesus. But both angels were overwhelmed with grief. Reverend Robert Hunt had just been buried after dying of the same sickness that many had succumbed to at Jamestown.* Against the advice of many, Hunt had worked too many nights tending the sick in their cabins.* Exhaustion and disease took their cruel toll.

"I just can't believe we lost Robert Hunt," Scion moaned. "The holiest man to set foot in Virginia so far. A man of prayer. O God, who is going to pray for this colony now? We are in so much trouble, Angie. How can we possibly save a colony with so few Christians who are living holy lives? Most are so distracted and weary by the daily struggle to survive."

Angie sighed. "I know what you mean. The colony is in great danger. I get messages from General Michael about every other week that the Lord is not sure this colony is spiritually strong enough to found the great nation he wants here. Master Scion, we are on very thin ice. What are we going to do?"

"I am not sure, Angie. I am doing my best, but it is obviously not good enough."

~

That April 10th, 1608, Newport sailed back to London for more supplies, taking the first book written about the colony by Captain Smith—*A True Relation*.* That book began to awaken England to the dire needs of the colony and the clever lies of the London Company who had been pretending all was well in Virginia.* As a result, more money, colonists, and prayers for Jamestown became available.

~

The following September 10, 1608, Captain Smith was finally made president of the colony.* The previous presidents, Wingfield and Ratcliffe, were both forced to resign for hoarding food.* Smith was the third president of the colony now, in just a little over a year since they'd first landed.

Scion fretted daily over the moral and physical state of the colony. Hunger and sickness made men desperate. Desperate men did desperate things—many sinful and foolish things.* Jehu Robinson, who had seen well-run Spanish colonies, said of this colony, "A more damned crew Hell never vomited." Okeus gladly agreed. His demons and shamans had done their jobs well to create havoc in Jamestown. Each month, Okeus grew more confident of the colony's demise.

To make matters worse, tensions with the native confederacy grew critical when the English raided Dumpling Island in the Nansemond River to the west of Jamestown*—where the Nansemond Tribe kept its valuables, such as pearls and copper ornaments.* During the raid, seventeen starving Englishmen absconded to a nearby Kecoughtan village to buy corn.* They were all killed.* Much blood from both sides was in the ground, and war was in the air. Opie was eager to fight, but Powhatan still wanted to make peace.

Okeus liked what he saw. As he watched the Kecoughtan village raid, he slapped Snookus hard on the back of his bulbous yellow head and crowed, "Thank Lucifer that the old fool Powhatan kept Smith alive when he had him prisoner. Smith is a '*survivor.*' Vermin like him will do whatever they can to live—even if others have to die. I can use of a man like that anytime."

And Okeus did just that. For almost another year, until September 1609, Captain John Smith led the colonists in a continual series of small battles with the Powhatans for food and dominance. Months of bloodshed and smiling deceits on both sides made life miserable for both Powhatans and Englishmen. It seemed like the conflict could not get worse.

But in the fall of 1609, just after the arrival of four hundred and fifty new settlers, the unthinkable began to happen.

CHAPTER 56

June 8, 1609*

Six hundred men, women, and boys crammed aboard nine ships in Plymouth, England to sail for Jamestown.* The flagship of the fleet, the *Sea Venture,* was captained by Christopher Newport.* This was called the Third Supply*—the Virginia Company's largest rescue mission for Jamestown.*

When Okeus heard of this from his Dark Angel allies in England, he put Snookus to work immediately. "Do whatever you have to—but stop those ships! Those six hundred vermin will infect the colony with hope. Drown them all at sea like rats!"

That very night, Snookus possessed Mongo and gave him strict instructions. "Capture and sacrifice three British men to Okeus tomorrow at midnight. That will give Okeus the power he needs to curse and destroy the enemy vessels."

And so, a great tempest arose in the path of the nine ships.* The storm bore down on the ships like a violent avalanche of wind and rain that made even seasoned sailors grimace in fear. The monster hurricane quickly sank one small ship, the *Catch.**

No one was spared. Screaming men, women and mooing cattle were tossed about like rag dolls in the churning and crashing waves. No one could eat or drink or even use the privy to relieve themselves. Death seemed to leer at them from the crest of each new wave.

But at the end of the storm, seven out of the remaining eight ships miraculously stayed afloat and were able to continue on together to Jamestown with four hundred and fifty people, arriving in Jamestown in August. The eighth ship, the *Sea Venture,* was blown far off course—a change that later altered the course of the entire Virginia colony.

But being separated from the fleet was the least of the *Sea Ventures's* problems. Thirty-foot waves had opened a large hole below its waterline, soaking everyone below decks to the waist as the ocean rushed into the ship.* One passenger later wrote, "We almost drowned within the bowels of the ship."* Every man on board took a turn with a bucket or bilge pump to empty the ship's hull of water. Still, the water level increased. Inch by watery inch, the ship began to sink lower into the frothy ocean.* Disaster seemed moments away. The wind howled so loudly that no cries or prayers could be heard. All hope was gone. Hell had come to the high seas.

Finally, on Friday, July 28, at the end of four days, convinced they were all but dead, several sailors broke into the grog stores to toast their last moments of life.* Others broke out in prayer again to surrender the ship's fate to God.*

As the ship slowly sank, a sailor called out, "Land ho!" Captain Newport immediately knew it must be "The Isle of Devils," or Bermuda as the Spanish named it.* Spanish sailors shunned the island like hell itself, but Newport had no choice. He had to get the ship to land. He called for sails to be hoisted and made for land before the vessel was completely awash. There was no safe harbor, so Newport decided to smash the ship between two jagged ridges of rocks that would keep it upright long enough to get the passengers off safely.* It worked. All one hundred and fifty survived.* Most onboard knelt on the beach and gave heartfelt thanks to God for a miraculous rescue from the storm.*

The island was a paradise. Breathtakingly beautiful, with good water, no inhabitants to struggle against, and many natural resources to live on. Even wild pigs—remnants of a former Spanish landing—roamed the island and provided a welcome source of delicious meat.* Several traumatized sailors decided to follow the example of the pigs and stay on the island. They ran off into the forest and were never found.*

But one man had different reasons for exploring the island. He was a curious and innovative farmer named John Rolfe. He knew Jamestown needed a dependable cash crop, so he scoured the fertile woods in hopes of finding a new plant species that grew well in the New World.

While he was busy with his research, his wife gave birth to a daughter.* They named her Bermuda,* in honor of the island that had given them a safe haven out of the deadly storm. One day, after months of searching, Rolfe came running back to the camp shouting, "I found it!" Rolfe discovered a tobacco plant that he thought might grow well in Jamestown.*

But his joy was cruelly punctured soon afterward by the death of his wife and daughter from a freak sickness. Rolfe was crushed. Eventually, he recovered from his deep grief and determined that he would honor their deaths by planting this Bermuda tobacco seed in Virginia. Little did the grieving farmer know that his discovery would be a major turning point for the Jamestown Colony.*

In the ten months that followed, the settlers were able to build two smaller vessels, the *Patience* and the *Deliverance,* using the tools and remains of the *Sea Venture* and local wood and oils.* However, the two ships would not arrive in Jamestown until the following Spring.

IN EARLY SEPTEMBER 1609, CAPTAIN SMITH SUFFERED A SEVERE BURN to one of his legs from a gunpowder explosion.* No one really knew how it happened, but Smith left for England on the next outbound ship on October 2nd.* When Pocahontas came to see Smith at the fort the next day, she was told Smith had suddenly died of sickness,* and they had buried him in an unmarked grave like so many others of the colonists. Pocahontas was grief-stricken for weeks. She was now almost fourteen—old enough to be married—and the man she most wanted was gone—*forever.* Her father soon sent his heartbroken daughter away to another village* to get away from the memories of the handsome soldier. It would be many years before she discovered the truth that her beloved John was still alive.*

But soon, many of Smith's fellow colonists would be gone forever.

BY NOVEMBER 1609, POWHATAN HAD RUN OUT OF PATIENCE WITH THE marauding English invaders. He secretly declared all-out war on the colony.* In early December 1609, just two weeks before Christmas, Powhatan struck the first brutal blow of war in a way that stunned the entire colony.

With skillful cunning, Powhatan invited the former president of the colony, John Ratcliffe, and fourteen fellow colonists to a peaceful gathering with some of his tribe. He promised the starving colonists that they would be given corn. It was a trap.* The colonists were ambushed, and Ratcliffe was tied to a stake— and burned to death.* One settler was released so that he would go back and tell the others at Jamestown what had happened.*

Terror seized everyone. No one dared to leave the fort—despite their desperate need for food.* Even George Percy, President of the Council, lost control of himself and cried out in front of the surviving men, "We're all doomed!" As the reality of their situation sunk in, moans of despair and screams of rage pierced the frigid air every night for weeks until the men became too weak to make any sounds.

THE SEAWEED GREEN REPTILIAN SHAPE GLIDED IN LOW, SLOW CIRCLES above the half-frozen men in the triangular fort that January morning in 1610. Okeus had come to gloat with his small entourage of guard demons, "Can you smell it? It makes my mouth water. Their fear. Their rage. Death all around them. Drink it in, my slimys! Behold—their blood is in the water now! Like sharks, we'll rip them into pieces soon enough!"

Watching nearby, Scion heard everything Okeus said. A sharp pain in his gut made him wince. Then his cheek began to twitch as his mind slid into a slippery, dark tunnel of thoughts. *He's right. This colony is doomed—and so is my reputation.* How *can I ever face heaven again? Some angels might even think I allowed this Dark Angel to destroy the colony. Aggggh! Why did I agree to come here? I feel so helpless! I've got to get away from here and clear my head. I can't take it anymore. Bermuda! That's right —I almost forgot—I have colonists there. I need some time to wait on the Lord in a peaceful place. I am exhausted.*

From a mile away, Angie's hawk-like vision saw the fear in Scion's eyes. She had a very unusual idea about how to rescue the colony. But she couldn't tell Scion yet.

I need to recruit Morph to help us, she decided as she snapped her wings open to fly. *But first, I need to do some research in the Great Library in heaven. If I can find some stories in the records of heaven where God used a demon to do His will, maybe Scion will agree to use Morph to help us. I just need one heavenly precedent for this—or—Angie giggled mischievously—perhaps I will have to just create a precedent,* the sassy little angel mused as she shot into the stratosphere.

CHAPTER 57

January 6, 1609

As the twelve-foot golden angel dropped from the clouds above the north coast of Bermuda, he smiled. The settlers were making good progress building two small ships to sail to Virginia. The men were floating long wooden boards and tackle from the shipwrecked *Sea Venture* to the beach while a few wives cooked several large wild boars over an open fire. He heard them talking about celebrating the Feast of the Epiphany* that night. *Wow—that pork smells really good. Well, at least part of the colony is eating well.*

But a few minutes later, Scion was sitting under a tall palm tree on a nearby beach. For long, mesmerizing moments, he just stared at the crystal clear, surf-fringed aquamarine waves in the shallows. The tranquility was broken only by an occasional seagull swooping down to feed on the small fish near the pink, sandy beach. Then, he would raise his tired eyes to look past the reef into the cerulean blue waters that gradually dissolved into a dark blue that stretched to the horizon under a cloud-flecked azure sky.

All this and heaven too, he thought. *Maybe I can get Bermuda included in Virginia's next royal charter from King James.* I love it here. But the way things are going, this may be my last visit!*

Just then, Angie zipped into view.

"Good day, Master Scion! I have good news. I just spent several hours in the Great Library, and I've discovered some incredible things that might help save the colony."

"Like what? Let me guess. Manna will fall out of heaven, and the colonists will not starve anymore. Or maybe Powhatan will wake up one day and decide to turn the other cheek—*again.* He'll forgive the English for robbing them of their scarce food, smoke a peace pipe together and let bygones be bygones," Scion sarcastically joked as he continued to stare at the dazzling ocean.

"Not exactly," Angie smirked. "But maybe even something better."

Scion turned to look at her now.

"I propose that we partner with that small cat demon, Morph, to help us protect the colony. He is no ordinary demon. I think God has planted him near the settlement to help us—as a spy.

"Now you *are* crazy!" Scion muttered and shook his head. "How can you be serious about this? It's insane. Heaven would never forget that I partnered with a demon to get my job done. That's exactly the kind of thing many angels have been accusing me of for millennia. It has taken me centuries to be somewhat trusted, and now you want me to bring a demon onto my team? Out of the question! I won't do it." Scion ran his hands through his long, blond hair in frustration.

"Please, just let me explain. I just know it could work. God may actually have planned all this."

"Oh, now you have really lost it! The holy God of the universe planned to use a wicked demon to further his divine plans for Earth? Now I know you are wrong. The Bible says you are dead wrong, for heaven's sake. How could you even think such a thing about our pure and holy God? We have to do this operation by the *book*—God's book and the Angel Academy Manual for Spiritual Warfare."

Pulling herself up to her full fourteen inches, Angie flew to eye-level with Scion and hovered there, arms akimbo, purple eyes flashing defiantly. Her mind was made up. *I have to convince him. I know I am right, but he is too afraid to bend the rules.* She knew how terrified he was of being wrong . . . again. She knew if this idea failed, many angels in heaven might never trust him again. She took deep breath.

"Master Scion, you are the wisest and most godly angel I have ever known, but you must listen to me one more time."

"All right, all right! But this is the last time we talk about this," Scion almost yelled as he jumped up and slammed his massive fist against the palm tree. As he did, a heavy coconut dropped right through his head. They both laughed.

"There are advantages to being a spirit," Angie quipped. But Scion quickly became moody again.

"Angie, you are very clever, very innovative, and I respect your courage to try new things. You are freer than I am in that regard. But what you are proposing cannot be done. In fact, according to everything I know about the Bible and angel training, it should *not* be done. I know you and that cat demon have become friendly. But what if this is all a trick that Okeus dreamed up? What if Morph betrays you, and we lose the colony? *No*, I tell you! I've been tricked and betrayed once already—at great cost to heaven. I cannot take the chance of that happening again."

Angie saw the pain in Scion's face. Her shoulders slumped, and she sighed deeply as she flew to his side. "Forgive me, Master, for being so pushy. You are right. I cannot force you to take a chance on something that could ruin your life forever in heaven. That's not fair to you. I was just so excited about this possibility—and I want to help Morph find a better life somehow. He's miserable doing demon work.

"I have an idea. Why don't we ask the Holy Spirit to speak to you about this? Jesus said the Spirit would lead God's servants into all truth. We are God's servants. Let's ask the Spirit what he thinks of allowing Morph to help us. I will comply with whatever the Spirit tells you."

Scion glanced at Angie, bit his lip, and furrowed his brow. "Well, if you really mean it—that part about settling this matter once and for all—well, then, yes. I will ask him."

Scion sat back down under the palm tree and laid his head against the trunk. Silently, he called upon God's Spirit to speak to him about this. The words of the young prophet Samuel in the Old Testament came to his mind, "Speak, Lord, your servant listens."

As he closed his eyes to focus, a deep peace came over him. His breathing slowed, and he felt as if he was lighter. Angie saw him begin to glow brighter. The Holy Spirit was near, waiting for Scion to speak.

Finally, Scion silently asked, Spirit of God, Spirit of Truth, lead me to know your will and ways. I need to know what you think of my objection to Angie's idea of partnering with Morph to help the colony. What is your perspective on that, Holy Spirit?

Scion's head gently bobbed once, and his closed eyes squinted as he suddenly sensed the Lord speaking. *My beloved son, did not God use an evil spirit to torment sinful King Saul?* Did God not use a lying spirit to confuse wicked King Ahab*? And did not God allow Satan to inhabit Judas* so Jesus would be arrested and sent to the cross for the salvation of the world?*

Angie watched in shock as tears begin to flow slowly down Scion's golden cheeks. She burst into tears too. She knew the Spirit had spoken to him. He opened his eyes and took a deep breath, and whispered, "*Okay,* Angie. Tell me what you have found out about this demon."

Angie's eyes flashed with joy, and her wings fluttered with excitement. She rattled off her research with obvious enthusiasm, "Two thousand years ago, when the glorified Jesus dropped into hell to announce his victory over Satan, the light of Jesus struck Morph as he emerged from his spawn sac. Morph is a flawed demon. He has something of heaven in him. He actually seems to enjoy the Presence of God. Why? Could it be that God planted that spot of light in him so that when the time was right, Morph could help build the Kingdom of God in some way?"

"Where is that in the Bible, Angie? Sounds pretty far out," Scion objected.

Angie had done her homework. She quickly answered. "In the Book of Acts, chapter 17, Paul noticed an inscription on an altar in Athens to an unknown god. Paul then preached to the Athenians that he came to tell them the real identity of that unknown god—the God of the Bible.* See? Many years before Paul arrived in Athens, God apparently had a pagan Greek man unknowingly 'plant' that clue in that inscription so Paul could use it to preach the Gospel to them!"

"Impressive, but maybe that is just an anomaly that is never supposed to happen again," Scion suggested. He knew he had to be very careful. His future life in heaven might hinge on how he handled this matter. He had to get more confirmation about working with Morph.

Angie smiled. She knew the facts she was about to share would carry a lot of weight with Scion. "Master, according to my research, there are at least ten large tribes in Southeast Asia who have been waiting for someone to bring them the long-lost book of their god.* Some of those tribes are actually waiting for a white man to bring that book.* Hundreds of years ago, God seems to have woven Gospel clues into their pagan mythologies to prepare them to accept the Gospel when missionaries arrived."*

"*Incredible*. Can you be specific? What tribes? I have never heard of them."

"Can do, Boss! In Southeast Asia, we have the Karen and the Kui, the Naga and the Kachin . . . all waiting for the book to come.* The Wa are waiting for a white brother with the lost book of Siyeh, their god.* The Lahu are waiting for their lost book of their god, Gwi'sha.* The Lisu still look for a white man to bring back their god's long-lost book.* Can't you see, Master Scion—it's just as the Bible says, 'He has hidden eternity in the hearts of men'—even demonized, idol-worshipping men."

Scion was visibly impressed. "That is amazing. I know Ecclesiastes 3:11 says that, but I never thought God would use pagan prophets to prepare their tribes to receive a missionary with our Bible. And now you think Jesus wants to use a demon to do something for our colony? Wow! All this reminds me of that verse, 'It is the glory of God to conceal a matter and the glory of kings to search it out.'"

"Exactly—Proverbs 25:2," Angie added. "And I guess we get to be the 'kings' in the case of Morph."

But then Scion suddenly stood up without saying anything and walked to the water's edge, with his back to Angie. He had to be alone. A great battle was raging inside him. He knew his entire future in heaven could hang on this one choice.

After what seemed an eternity to Angie, a very solemn-faced Scion slowly turned around. "Angie, if God Almighty can use pagan shamans and demons to do His will when it suits Him, then I guess a foolish and desperate angel like me can do the same. *Let's do it!* Recruit Morph and pass the word to any other angels in the vicinity. They must not harm or resist Morph in any way when they see him."

Angie wanted to shout and dance but, with some effort, she restrained herself. "Amen to that, Master Scion! You will never regret this decision. You know what they say, 'The enemy of your enemy is your friend.' I believe Morph will be more of a friend to us than we can imagine."

"I hope so, Angie. If we are wrong about him, we may spend eternity wishing we had never come here.

"And, Angie, do NOT tell Michael about this—yet."

With a wink and a smile, Angie soared upward into a blurring, vertical spiral, singing at the top of her voice, "Glory to the Lamb, who is worthy to receive all honor and glory and power!"

Scion stood there and watched her fly to Morph to tell him the good news just as a strong gust of wind blew across the beach. He looked up just in time to see five more coconuts fall right through his head into the pink sand squishing between his toes.

He chuckled. "Well, Lord, I hope things are falling into place with Morph like you planned long ago. I didn't see that coming any more than I saw those coconuts about to fall on me. I am trusting that Morph is a sign that You plan to rescue this colony. I know I can't."

CHAPTER 58

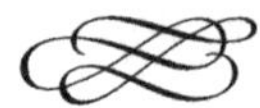

The Starving Time

While the Bermuda castaways were feasting in a tropical wonderland, Jamestown descended into scenes straight from hell. The infamous "Starving Time" had begun.* From November 1609 through May 1610, Powhatan laid unrelenting siege to the fort. Mass starvation and disease followed quickly.*

Powhatan's edict was cruel, but understandable. The English had often lied and had broken many promises.* Smith had told the chief on their first meeting that the English were only taking refuge from Spanish ships and would be leaving soon.* But then Powhatan saw the English build houses and a church. Even so, Powhatan tried to build a friendship with the colony, hoping to trade with them and learn from them.*

But later, hundreds of more people came and started farms along the river, taking native land without permission or payment.* Powhatan later confronted Smith about that. "Your coming is not for trade, but to invade my people and possess my land."* Smith just smiled and walked away.

Multiple English raids on Powhatan's villages for food quickly eroded the remaining goodwill of the chief for the settlement.* Even Pocahontas could not help the colony now. Her father was determined to make the English bow to his rule on his lands—or *die.* And die they did—by the hundreds.* It was total war.

The four hundred and fifty souls who had arrived in August with the remaining seven ships of the Third Supply quickly devoured the few rations they had brought with them.* The wrecked *Sea Venture* had been carrying the bulk of the food supplies for the entire flotilla as well as the new leaders of the colony.*

When the leaderless immigrants of the seven ships arrived in sweltering August heat, they found eighty men* barely alive in Jamestown—and the season for planting crops already gone.* Now, in January, hundreds died slow, freezing deaths mostly from starvation.*

In mid-January 1610,* George Percy, who replaced John Smith as interim president of the colony,* stood near a large oak tree in Jamestown and surveyed the scene. He could not believe his eyes. Dead bodies were everywhere. The gagging smell of death hung heavy in the air, choking the throats and hopes of every survivor.

"Oh my God, how have we come to this?" Percy moaned. He had been ordered to record the miseries of the colony for the London Company's records,* but he hated the thought of it almost as much as the foul smells that permeated the dying fort. But he had to follow orders, so he wrote a letter to describe the terrible conditions of the colony.* Percy hoped this would force the London Company to send help.

> To my esteemed friends in the London Company,
>
> We are experiencing a world of miseries deriving from our lack of supplies. Hell has come to Earth. We are food for demons. Many have lost their minds and do terrible things no sane man would do.

> Some have robbed our store, for which cause I had them executed. Others have fed on horses and other beasts such as dogs, rats, and foul fish to satisfy the cruel hunger. Still others succumbed to eating boots, shoes, or other leather goods. Once those were spent, they searched the woods for roots where many were cut and slain by the savages. The famine makes us all pale and ghastly in the face, making us do things which seem incredible, such as dig up dead corpses and eat them. Some even lick up the blood from their weaker fellows. No one can work. No one can leave. The drought here is severe. The natives have us shut up here to die. After all we have done to steal their food supplies, it is hard to blame them, but what they are doing to us now is beyond words.*
>
> As you know, Captain Smith left us last October due to a terrible leg wound caused by a gunpowder accident. He was not welcome here anymore by the colonists or the Powhatans. As we say, 'Some cause happiness wherever they go; others, whenever they leave.' Many rejoiced to see Smith sail out of here.
>
> Unless help comes soon, we shall certainly be like the Roanoke Colony that has gone before us.*
>
> George Percy

SCION SAT STONE-FACED IN PERCY'S CRUDE, LOG HUT AND WATCHED HIM write that letter. *O God, what can I do? We are losing the colony,* his tortured mind kept echoing over and over. Just then, Angie arrived from watching Pocahontas, who was still depressed and grieving the loss of Captain Smith. She saw Scion's blank expression, then gulped hard and took a deep breath.

"Scion, I have *terrible* message from General Michael. He says the Lord may have to abandon this colony because of their many sins. He says the colonists have abused the Algonquians and each other so much that they are disqualifying themselves from founding this new Christian nation."

Scion exploded in anger. "This is *exactly* what I feared would happen. These are some of the weakest and most sinful Christians I have ever seen. How could God expect them to start a Christian colony—not to mention a Christian nation? What was Michael thinking when he gave me this assignment? No angel could make this colony succeed as real Christians. They are hopelessly addicted to sin.

"And what if the Lord waits another twenty years before he sends another colony? Another mistake on my record—and the guilt of knowing that thousands of Algonquins went to hell waiting for another colony to arrive! I can't handle any more guilt!

Scion stood up abruptly and thrust his face into both hands. "And Michael said this colony was to be a global mission base for the Gospel. O, God have mercy! Tens of thousands of people all over the world might not make it to heaven because this colony's failure delayed the birth of that nation. How can I ever face Michael—or anyone else in heaven—or even myself. The shame would be more than I can bear."

Then Scion collapsed onto his knees and sobbed—and sobbed. Angie could not look at him. It was too painful.

After many long moments, Scion became quiet, and Angie looked up. His raised arms and wings formed a glowing arc around his tear-stained, upturned face. Then, he began to groan the way a woman does when she gives birth. His torso bobbed back and forward in rhythmic waves like some Jews do in fervent prayer. This went on for almost an hour.

Angie was a little unnerved. She had never seen an angel pray that way. Then Scion fell forward on the floor Percy's hut, sobbing again. The little angel closed her eyes again to pray for her suffering friend.

After about thirty minutes, Scion stopped crying and whispered with a horse voice, "Father, I can't, but *You* can. I'm not, but *You* are. The battle is yours, my King. My eyes are on You, Father, and on the Lamb." A deep silence covered them both for many more minutes as the Spirit of God ministered to Scion's tormented mind.

When Scion and Angie finally opened their eyes, they both saw a beautiful light around Scion—like a very intense rainbow-colored sunrise. *"Aaaah",* Scion sighed. He knew the Lord had somehow answered his prayers.

"Holy Hallelujah," Angie whispered as she shielded her eyes with one wing. "When you pray, you get under the spout where the glory comes out! We should do this more often!"

Scion grinned. "We will, Angie. The colony still needs us. Despite their many sins, I believe the Lord is going to give them another chance."

CHAPTER 59

*May 10, 1610**

As the newly built *Patience* and *Deliverance* arrived from Bermuda with one hundred and forty-five well-fed settlers, they found only sixty people alive at Jamestown.* Four hundred and forty had died since last August when the seven other ships arrived.* It only took a few days for the newly arrived Governor Thomas Gates to decide that the colony was not survivable.* He ordered everyone to abandon the colony and sail back to England on the two small ships they had built in Bermuda.*

ON THE INCOMING TIDE OF THE NEXT DAY, THE HEAVILY LADEN *PATIENCE* and *Deliverance* bobbed and weaved in the James River as they headed south with two hundred and five souls—many of them angry and some very sick.

"Coming up on Mulberry Island, Governor Gates. Shall I trim the sails for the bay?"

Gates shook his head. "No, not yet, Strackey . . . wait. One of the women just died. They are about to bury her at sea. Just hold your course and tell the *Patience* to hold up too. There is a lot of commotion down in the hold right now. I think her children are not far behind her with sickness. It's a bloody mess. God help us make it home to England without many more casualties . . . or *hurricanes*.

"And ask Admiral Somers if he can guide us back to Bermuda. I'd like to pick up the three men he left there to claim the islands for the king.* We will pick up fresh rations there too.* Also, tell him John Rolfe wants to visit his wife and daughter's graves."

Rolfe heard that last remark, "Thank you, Governor. I am much obliged to you for all you did for me after I lost my family on Bermuda."

"Don't think anything of it, Rolfe."

"Governor, isn't it strange that if our ship had arrived here last August, we might all be dead now. In God's providence, that hurricane saved us from death in Jamestown."

Gates smiled and nodded. "Well said, Rolfe. You are a man of keen insight. I'm sure God has spared you for a special purpose."

"Thank you, sir. I and hoping that the tobacco seeds I cultivated in Bermuda might produce a leaf far better than what England has now."

"Well, if you can get them to grow in England . . ." But Gates could not finish his remark. He had heard a sentry's cry— and it sounded serious.

"Ahoy, below! Ship approaching from around Mulberry Island!"*

"All hands on deck!" Captain Newport bellowed nervously and then muttered to himself, "Oh God, what if it is a Spanish ship. What will we do? We can't fight with so many civilians on board."

"It's one of ours!" Newport shouted. "I see the Red Ensign. It's British!"

Every neck on deck strained to see the mysterious ship. Then, as the ship got closer, a loud voice came across the water: "This is Her Majesty's ship carrying Thomas West, Lord De La Warr, Governor of Virginia.* Turn around and lead us to Jamestown."*

And so they did.* Many cried, both men and women. Their hopes for safety in England were dashed in an instant. Others were jubilant. They called it the "Day of Providence."* But Scion and Angie cringed when they discovered why the Virginia Company had sent Lord De La Warr. The new governor was ordered to wage a military campaign against the Powhatan natives.* A month after Lord De La Warr arrived, he sent Deputy Governor Gates against the Kecoughtan villages.* The soldiers lured the natives into the open using a music-and-dance act by their drummer— and then slaughtered them all.*

Scion was angry—and said so to Angie. "De La Warr sees this as just a military problem.* No negotiations and no apologies for British food raids on Powhatan villages for two years. Many Powhatans starved to death as a result. And no apologies for the British diseases the Powhatans also died of. What else could the Powhatans do but fight back? God will *never* bless this kind of behavior. And I had so much hope for a fresh start in the colony."

Angie quickly flew to Scion's shoulder to comfort him. But neither could talk. All they could do was hang their heads in sadness.

NO RELIEF CAME TO JAMESTOWN—JUST THE OPPOSITE. IN FACT, Jamestown was soon to become more like a bizarre prison than a colony of free English settlers.*

On May 19, 1611,* Sir Thomas Dale arrived in Jamestown to serve as Deputy Governor and "Marshall of Virginia."* Under this stern naval commander, Jamestown waged war *within itself* for years.

"Dale's Code" were military-style laws designed to force the traumatized settlers to submit to his authority. Dale punished people *with death* if they blasphemed God, spoke against the king or biblical truths, raped a Powhatan woman, stole church property, made a false oath, or even traded with the native without permission.* A tsunami of fear, anger, and despair flooded the colony under Dale's dictatorial rule. Outside the fort, the war with Powhatan continued year after year, with no end in sight.*

ONE NIGHT IN 1613, NATIVES CAME AND KIDNAPPED FOUR SETTLERS and stole tools and guns.* No one knew how to rescue them. But then, Captain Samuel Argall* had an idea: capture the chief's favorite daughter and trade her for the English prisoners.*

Pocahontas was captured in 1613

So they captured Pocahontas, but Powhatan refused the proposed trade.* He knew they dared not hurt her. And he was right—but her father never could have guessed what God had planned for his abducted "Playful One."

In the months following her capture by the British, Pocahontas became a *Christian* and was baptized as Rebecca in 1614*—because in Genesis 25:23, the Lord said of another Rebecca, "Two nations are in thy womb."*

Pocahontas is baptized as Rebecca

Soon afterward, an English widower came courting. He was madly in love with the Algonquin princess.* In his letter to Sir Thomas Dale, Rolfe gushed about his passionate feelings for her.* He wrote that Pocahontas was the woman "to whom my heart and best feelings...have been for a long time entangled in such an intricate labyrinth that I wore myself out trying to untangle them."*

Ever the romantic, Angie could not take her eyes off the couple. "Oh, to be human and love like that," she moaned to Scion. "Wouldn't you like to have an angel wife someday, Scion?"

John Rolfe courting Pocahontas

Scion looked at her with mock astonishment, "Surprise, surprise! I am really not the mushy type—but I do have a holy hunch that God has big plans for these two lovebirds! Let's see what happens!"

CHAPTER 60

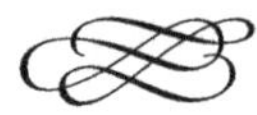

*February 1614**

"They like it!" the short, stocky man shouted as he opened his mail from the supply ship that had just arrived from England. In an instant, he was running toward the governor's home in the center of Jamestown. Curious heads in the glass factory near the docks turned from their work to watch the odd scene.

One older worker of Polish stock spoke up, "Now what is that fool Rolfe up to? He's the laughingstock of the colony—always playing in his garden and growing things you cannot eat! That man needs a real job. And God, that man loves to smoke—day and night. His house reeks of tobacco."

Another man from the highlands of Scotland put down his tools and piped up, "Ya got that right, mate. I think 'es still teched in the head from losing 'is wife and wee daughter in Bermuda. It's been two years, and he still grieves. Poor bloke. All he talks about is gettin' rich and gettin' a new wife. Who'd ever 'ave him? He's nothing but to pity."

An older, bald-headed friend next to him agreed, "Aye, I know my wife would never 'ave 'im. She cannae stand the smell of tobacco, and

I'm agreed. Even King James 'isself 'as written against the weed—'A custom lothsome to the eye, hatefull to the nose.'* Apparently, John Rolfe does not have a royal nose." They both laughed as the man scrunched his nose in mock disgust.

Oblivious to the chatter behind him at the glassworks, John Rolfe sped toward the governor's home with the letter held above his head like a battle flag of a returning victorious army. This was the breakthrough he had dreamed of. Everyone knew the colony was still failing financially. The settlers tried making silk, glass, lumber, soap and collecting sassafras, pitch and tar—but nothing made a profit.* "Now they will listen to me! Now I'll *be* somebody! If only my dear wife could see me now," the happy farmer muttered to himself as he ran.

Seeing Governor Dale on the porch drinking tea, Rolfe burst through the gate, grinning like he had discovered gold in Jamestown. "Governor, remember that tobacco I grew last summer and sent to London for inspection by the merchants? I just got an order for five hogsheads of my next crop! They like it! They said it was almost as good as the Spanish leaf all London is talking about."*

Looking up from his book, the most feared man in the colony seemed even more formidable when interrupted by such outbursts. "Mr. Rolfe, may I remind you that tobacco is not on the list of things our sponsors have ordered us to develop here. Have you forgotten who paid your way here to make them a profit? This is not a social outing; this is a disciplined, orderly, and hard-working colony sent here to make our sponsors rich, and eventually, make us financially strong. Need I remind you again that his Highness, King James I, has written a pamphlet vigorously denouncing tobacco use in any form?* Surely, you do not want to offend the King who gave us our charter to come here! Please, be along now and make yourself useful in one of our industries. That will be all."

Rolfe's cheeks burned. "But Governor, my tobacco will make us all rich and the London Company will finally be happy with us. England is wild over tobacco,* and Spain and France are making a fortune selling it to us.* My new leaf is as good as theirs. This is brown gold, Governor, don't you see?"

Like a bear surprised in its den, Dale suddenly stood up and shouted, "Mr. Rolfe, if you do not leave now, I will call the guard to forcibly remove you and place you in stocks. Now leave my premises and do not return. Go smoke your filthy weed if you must and get sick like your friends back home."

Knowing the governor's reputation for pitiless punishments, Rolfe quickly retreated, bowing several times as he left the property. The men at the glass factory saw him in a hurry, and they had another laugh at the odd, stubborn farmer. "That Rolfe—he must 'ave 'it his 'ead on the rocks when the ship crashed into Bermuda. He's daft, poor bloke."

But Dale was wrong. And so were the glassmen. Within nine months, two large shipments of Virginia tobacco had left the docks along the James River* from three plantations that had agreed to grow Rolfe's new tobacco seeds.* Governor Dale was shocked at the news—but pleased. He even threw a large party for Rolfe to celebrate this new source of income for the colony. Rumor had it that the cynical men from the glass factory also tilted a few drinks in Rolfe's honor. It was a new day for Jamestown.

Word quickly spread across the demonic world along the Atlantic coast: The colony was making money—*lots* of money.

Okeus was furious. He grabbed Snookus around his short slippery neck and growled, "Why was I not informed more about this Rolfe maggot? First, they trick that traitor, Pocahontas, into following the old fool's son—and now this!" Suddenly, Okeus stood up to his full fourteen feet and pulled the trembling, limp body of his octopus assistant right in front of his snarling lips and six-inch teeth.

"Now they have money! Now, more English swamp scum will come. Now—Scion might yet keep his puny, festering, Lamb-loving lair.

Well—what do you have to say about this, you ugly, good-for-nothing blubber-brain?" Okeus roared as he flung Snookus two hundred feet into the air. Then the crazed reptilian ogre looked around for Morph. "This time, I will surely kill you. Morph. You must have known about this."

But when Morph was nowhere to be found, Okeus exploded again in rage—only worse. The monster lunged forward, bellowing *"Yaaaaah!"* and with his powerful, six-fingered claws, he grabbed two demon guards with the speed of a striking cobra. He bit their heads off, then threw his head back and roared so loud it would have stopped a charging Tyrannosaurus Rex in its tracks. Then, he tore the two headless demons into pieces and fed them to the other guards just before the dismembered spirits turned to a red vapor. That seemed to take the edge off his anger—to the relief of every demon in his camp.

But one spirit in the Blue Mountains of Jamaica was rejoicing at the colony's newfound wealth! Voudoc swung through the treetops with his long, greenish-beige monkey arms, screeching, "Okeus is going to fail! The colony is going to stay! Lucifer will be furious. And I can't wait!"

CHAPTER 61

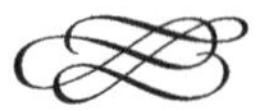

*April 5, 1614**

The sun never seemed so bright. The birds never sang so sweetly. The air never smelled so fresh. At least, that's what the British onlookers thought as they witnessed the first marriage of an Englishman to a native woman in the New World.*

And not just any native woman. This was Pocahontas—the Powhatan princess who had kept the colony alive for years with food from her tribe.* She was already a legend in England. On this day, eighteen-year-old Rebecca* married the man who had made the colony rich: John Rolfe.* If ever the colony could breathe a breath of hope, today was that day.

John Rolfe marries Pocahontas

Jamestown was positively giddy. Peace had come at last—the "Peace of Pocahontas,"* as they called it. Her father had decided to lay down his weapons against the English, and the English did likewise.* The two cultures shared a marriage. Now they would share the land. Five years of fierce war were over. Within two years, Mr. and Mrs. John Rolfe would be presented to the Court of King James in London—an event that sealed the "Peace of Pocahontas" on both sides of the Atlantic. For eight years after this historic marriage, Jamestown enjoyed a springtime of prosperity and growth that brought hundreds of new settlers.

But with all these new settlers, there arose an increasing, unspoken tension with the Powhatans. More and more native land was "borrowed" by newly arrived tobacco farmers without any recompense to local tribes. Native hunting grounds disappeared into one-hundred-acre plantations all along the James River.* Subtle but real racism against natives was rampant. But Powhatan's people did not retaliate . . . *yet.*

June 3, 1616

Sir Thomas Dale,* stepped off the *Treasurer* to the applause of the large crowd in Plymouth, England, on England's southeast shore.* Dale, Mr. and Mrs. John Rolfe, and their infant son, Thomas, had just sailed to England from Jamestown. Governor Dale had endured six weeks of cramped, foul-smelling quarters on that ship because he needed more investments from English donors for his colony. He knew that what was about to happen would ensure that.

"Hooray! Welcome home!" the crowd shouted.

The band struck up "God Save the King"—England's national anthem —as Dale took the podium.

"Ladies and gentlemen, all of us thank you for this wonderful greeting after a long and dangerous voyage from Great Britain's first colony in Virginia to our beloved English shores. Not only do I bring stories of wealth, riches, and new lands conquered for our King, but I bring home a princess—the first native princess in Virginia to embrace Jesus as Lord and to call an Englishman her husband. Ladies and gentlemen, I present to you, Lady Rebecca Rolfe and her one-year-old son Thomas."*

A beautiful, twenty-year-old woman with tawny skin, waist-length, coal-black hair, and a brilliant smile stepped forward carrying a baby. She wore a simple, light blue dress with long sleeves. But her bearing was royal.* The crowd was stunned. They went wild with cheers and shouts of "Long live Lady Rebecca! Long live the Princess!" News of her arrival spread like wildfire. This unique and charming woman was about to conquer London society in a way few women ever had.*

Dale also brought a dozen Powhatans with him,* including Mongo and his assistant shaman, Tomocomo.* Powhatan had sent them to watch over Pocahontas. But both shamans had also come to spy out the land for Opie. Even in the shouts of the crowd, Mongo could hear the voice of his demon, Snookus, inside him.

"Listen to that! They love her already, just as Opie predicted. She is a dangerous bridge to the English. Her fame here could bring many more English to our ancestral lands. Some of our people might even be deceived into following her new god. She has to be stopped!"

"Okay, okay, Snookus, I remember!" Mongo protested. "Now, leave me alone so I can count the English. Opie wants to know how many of them there are in case we have to fight them again. Please go watch Pocahontas. That idiot Morph cannot be trusted to guard her."

Retrieving her baby from her Algonquian helper, Pocahontas got into the carriage with her husband for the long, bouncy ride to London, almost two hundred miles to the northeast. "John, I want to see him as soon as I can. Is that all right?"

"Certainly, my dear. You must see Smith while we are in London. He will always be a friend of our family. There would not be a colony without him. I was so glad to hear last year that he is still alive. I know it broke your heart when they told you he was dead. Please give him my regards. As you know, my meetings with the London Company will keep me busy for some days. They want a full accounting of our progress to get the colony on a firm financial footing. In the meantime, I will make inquiries as to Smith's whereabouts. I hear that he has been traveling out of the country a lot lately . Don't worry, my love. He will turn up eventually. "

As the carriage bumped along, Rebecca could not stop thinking about Captain Smith. *Will he remember me? Will he still like me? He was my first love. If only I had been older when I met him—if only he had stayed in Virginia.*

Thomas let out a burp, and Rebecca laughed at her half-asleep baby, still nuzzling her breast. Then she silently prayed, *O, Father, thank you for allowing me to be a wife, a mother, and most of all, your daughter. My heart is full, and my life is yours—forever. I am content to live or die for you. I ask just one more thing, Lord—let my Captain come to know you as I do.* Then she closed her eyes with a sweet smile and the warm presence of God's Spirit filled the carriage, prompting her to whisper, "Thank you, Father. I know you will do this for me."

CHAPTER 62

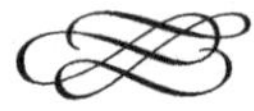

The sumptuous room in the palace was packed with royalty and wealthy businessmen enjoying a night of *King Lear* by the Bard of Avon, the late William Shakespeare who had died the year before.*

But unseen to humans, hundreds of battle-tested angels under Scion's command had formed a wall of flashing swords to repel all of the thousand English demons who had come that to disrupt the historic meeting of King James I, Queen Anne, and the Powhatan Princess, Lady Rebecca Rolfe.

Okeus had put Snookus in charge of the English demons—and the thrill of command made his head woozy with pleasure. So, he decided to disobey Mongo and let Morph guard Pocahontas so he could continue to command the demon assaults on the palace.

Snookus sternly ordered Morph to distract Pocahontas as often as he could. "Don't screw this up, you dolt. I don't want her talking to anyone important. Fluster her. Embarrass her. Frighten her. I don't care how you do it but keep that traitor from talking to the King or Queen. *Got it?*"

But Morph just pretended to comply whenever Snookus looked his way. Morph was much more interested in watching Angie. With her tiny sword raised high, the rainbow-haired scout zipped around Lady Rebecca's head like a warrior hummingbird, protecting the princess from a small group of fear and confusion demons who were dive-bombing into her head in simultaneous attacks. Meanwhile, Scion's imposing presence next to the King and Queen also ensured that no demon could suggest any ill thoughts in them toward the Rolfes.

Meanwhile, Snookus barked a continuous stream of orders to this demon and then that one as they rapidly probed the wall of swords for a weak spot. The floppy-headed octopus absolutely loved commanding one thousand demons against so many angels! Occasionally he would glance at the play below, but he found it painfully boring— until he heard the word *"blood."* Like a cat stalking a mouse, his huge, light-green eyes were suddenly glued to the actor playing King Lear as the king described his daughter, Goneril:*

> But yet thou art my flesh, my blood, my daughter; or rather a disease that's in my flesh, which I must needs call mine: thou art a boil, a plague-sore, an embossed carbuncle, in my corrupted blood.*

"Daughter", "disease", "boil", "corrupted blood"—those echoed in his head. *Great Lucifer,* Snookus exclaimed to himself. *It's a sign from hell. Yes, Pocahontas is a disease to her people—and to Okeus. So, perhaps we should fight sickness—with sickness.*

Finally, the big doors to the hall opened to release the audience after the show.

Escorted by two towering British soldiers, the king and queen ambled toward the opened doors while waving their hands and handkerchiefs to the ingratiating smiles of hundreds seated around them.

Scion walked behind them, calling in other angels to back him up in case of an attack on the royal couple. Once outside the hall, the king and queen stood like two sphinxes as the long line of fawning admirers shuffled by to kiss their hands.

"Will you look at that, Angie?" Scion chuckled. "Those people kissing the king's ring are better actors and actresses than what we just saw on stage."

Angie laughed, but her eyes never left the radiant face of Pocahontas as she walked with regal dignity toward the British Crown couple.

Just then, Snookus shot up through the floor and tripped Pocahontas so severely that she fell forward right at the feet of the king. Before anyone had a chance to react, the agile Powhatan leaped to her feet in a blur of motion, with clenched fists and flashing brown eyes, ready to do battle with her unseen attacker. Seeing none, she calmly turned her gaze to the ruler of England, Scotland, and Wales who stood before her—astonished at her physical prowess.

"My lord . . . I . . . fell. I know not why. Forgive me."

"O, my child, it must have been a rough spot on our floor. Do not be alarmed. We are all amazed at how well you recovered. I can tell you, no other noble here tonight could have righted himself with the skill you just showed."

"It is nothing, my lord. All our women are strong and know how to fight. We are a small nation, so all of our people must be ready to defend our lands when needed."

"Ah, yes, it is indeed a pleasure to meet the famous Mrs. Rolfe," Queen Anne interjected to change the subject. "We have heard of your father, the great Chief Powhatan from Captain Smith. I understand that you saved the captain's life. Is that true?"

Pocahontas felt her cheeks burn. "Well, yes, but it was actually the God of heaven, the Great Spirit, who told me to save him."

"But you were only eleven at the time, I understand," the queen inquired with a motherly smile.

"The Great Spirit has always spoken to me, my queen. He showed me that Captain Smith had a good heart, but it was wounded. The Spirit gave me compassion for him. That's why I helped him and the colony. Now I know that it was God's Holy Spirit speaking to me."

The queen was awestruck and unable to respond for a moment. King James looked at his wife with concern as she struggled to compose herself.

"But you were just a child," the queen finally managed to say, "a native child. How could you…?"

Sensing his wife's dilemma, King James chimed in, "My dear Mrs. Rolfe, we had no idea that your people were like that— that is—like *us*, I mean. Forgive us for not understanding. All we have heard about your people are short business reports. No one has told us of the kindness and depth of feeling you have just spoken of. We are at a loss to know what to say."

The queen took a quick step toward the bowed head of the beautiful princess and embraced her warmly like a mother. For a moment, not a sound was heard in the bustling hallway. The massive angelic host just beneath the palace ceiling bowed their heads in worship, bathing the scene in a heavenly glory, unseen but felt by all. In that moment of terror, the demonic thugs realized they had lost that battle—and perhaps more—as two royal mothers unashamedly wept together for joy.

Slowly, Queen Anne pulled back and placed her hands on Pocahontas's shoulders. She could not stop gazing at her. Finally, as the king gently nudged her that it was time to go, the queen said, "Lady Rebecca, if your people are half as noble as you are, our kingdom would be honored to call you our own." She quickly smiled at her husband and added, "And if you lived here, I would treat you like a daughter."

Rebecca bowed her head and wept again. Then she knelt and kissed their hands. "On behalf of my people and my father, the great chief

Powhatan, we are honored to be part of your kingdom and to serve your God, who is also my God. I pledge our hearts and our spears to you. I commit my life and my children to you. I accept your love and pledge to you my faithful service as your subject and sister in the Lord."

Angie could not contain herself any longer. She wiped away hot tears and let out a war-whoop of victory that startled even the angelic host. Then she shot like a meteor to the pinnacle of St. Paul's Church and sang the "Song of Moses and Miriam" from Exodus 15:*

> I will sing unto the LORD, for He hath triumphed gloriously: the horse and his rider hath He thrown into the sea. The LORD is my Strength and Song, and He is become my Salvation: He is my God, and I will prepare Him a habitation; my father's God, and I will exalt Him.*

As the king and queen settled into their beautiful royal carriage for the short ride home, King James looked at his wife in amazement. "Aye, it cannae be true, but it is."

"What do you mean, James?" the queen asked.

"That feelin'. I haven't felt it in a long time. My blood's still a-boiling with it."

"What in heaven's name are you talking about?"

"That feelin'. It's the same one I had as a wee lad in the Kirk of Scotland when I first met him."

"Him?"

"Jesus, of course," the weary king smiled at his befuddled wife. "When that little native kissed my hand, it went through me like a hot knife through highland cattle butter. Me knees almost gave out. Ya shoulda seen the look on me face, but you were too fastened on her to notice."

"There is no doubt of that. I could not take my eyes off her face. It seemed to glow. I know that sounds silly, but what else can I say? Her face was full of heaven itself. I don't know if I have ever seen such a visage."

"Well said, my lady. Heaven came down when she came near. That's all I know," he concluded with a long, dazed look at his queen.

"James, we must not miss this opportunity while she is here. If God can make Christians like her out of savage natives, then all England, Scotland, and Wales stands to gain."

"Surely, you are right, my queen. Nothing would give me more pleasure than to see the prayers of John Knox answered by seeing the Gospel go forth to Scotland* and to all the world through people like her. Let's hope we can sign a formal treaty with her father soon before Spain sends more spies there to ruin our first colony in the New World."

"You are so wise, my king. Yes, we must act quickly. This princess must be protected at all costs, too. She is the God-given key to our empire there and to the Kingdom of God there. I have never met her equal at court or at church."

"Amen to that, me lassie," the Scottish-born king laughed as he hugged her tightly in his arms. "Let's get home because it is time for the royal bed." He winked as she pretended to smile demurely.

"Bed indeed!" Snookus scowled. He was sitting across from the king, almost beside himself with rage. "Look who's getting in bed with the British: that little *traitor,* Pocahontas—that wretch of a woman, that cesspool of sentimentality, that spiritual brat with fish crap for brains, that putrid bag of water we should have killed a long time ago. She *has* to die— and die soon!"

Sitting next to him, Morph jerked with fright. Angie had told him how important Pocahontas was to the colony. He spoke spoke up quickly.

"Can't we just make her sick enough to stay in England? Or maybe make her son sick so she will stay here? She might be more dangerous to us dead than alive—especially if we assassinate her."

"Shut up, you fool! What do you know? You have the brain of a squashed frog. This is my decision. I say she dies!"

"Okay, okay." Morph pretended to agree. He hoped he could warn Scion about this plot in time. "But, Snookus, how will you do this and not raise suspicion?"

"You weren't listening, Morph. Shakespeare told us earlier."

CHAPTER 63

March 12, 1617

Five days later, the ship that would eventually take Pocahontas and her family back to Jamestown began the slow, two-day passage snaking down the Thames River from London to the English Channel.* The ship had to leave London days before the Rolfes to move downstream incrementally with the tides. "Falling down with the tide" to the channel was done in two stages each day.* Once the ship reached Gravesend, the Rolfes would travel by coach to board the vessel for the forty-five-day voyage in the belly of a dank, dark ship. The Rolfe's delay in London was fortuitous. The search for Captain Smith had been fruitless after months of searching for him. Pocahontas was heartbroken again. Now, word suddenly came that the dashing soldier had been located. He was to meet Rebecca in a London church the following day.

~

FINALLY, THE MOMENT HAD COME. REBECCA ARRIVED EARLY THE NEXT day, nearly breathless with anticipation. She waited for him in the church narthex above a long flight of stairs from the street. Snookus and Morph had arrived with her, taking their positions in the darkest corner of the narthex ceiling. Angie and Scion were also there to guard Mrs. Rolfe against any attacks by Snookus. Morph wanted to signal Scion about the plot to kill the princess, but Snookus had the little cat demon wrapped up tightly in his tentacles. "Stop squirming, furball!" Snookus gurgled. "This is one assignment you are not going to screw up."

At noon, Mrs. Rolfe stood in the church narthex, stunningly arrayed in her finest English clothes. Smith had sent word that they should meet at a small chapel in London near a large park so they would not be disturbed. Above the entrance to the chapel was the Latin inscription ab alto ("from above"). It was a fitting motto for what was about to happen.

Soon, Rebecca heard the sound of heavy boots clomping up the worn stone steps. The sturdy frame of a handsome man in a topcoat, hat in hand, filled the doorway of the church. His head and shoulders were silhouetted in the brilliant sun billowing behind him. The princess felt dizzy with emotions. Instantly, Lady Rebecca melted into a twelve-year-old, love-sick Pocahontas. She could not speak. A tsunami of grief and relief washed over her senses. Since 1609, she had believed he was dead—killed by an accidental gunshot wound.* The news had devastated her. "I never got to say goodbye!" she had wailed.

Pocahontas meets Captain John Smith in London

But now, here he was—alive! She ran and threw her arms around him, clinging to his neck with all her strength, weeping and laughing at the same time. "Captain Smith, you are alive!" she cried. She continued to hug him as if her life depended on it. Smith finally pried her muscular arms off his neck.

"Now, Matoaka, it can't be that wonderful to see an old soldier like me," he joked with obvious pleasure. "Few in London fancy me much anymore, especially after I exposed the lies of the London Company in my book. Now, look at you, a king's daughter!"*

They both laughed. Pocahontas had almost forgotten the sound of his hearty laugh. It was like Powhatan music to her ears. Then she grabbed both of his hands in hers, pulled him close, and looked directly into his sky-blue eyes.

"Captain Smith, your leaders told me you had died of a gunshot wound. Why did they lie to me about that? And why didn't you send word to me all these years that you were alive? Do you realize how much I have suffered because of that lie?" she asked with brown fire in her eyes.

Smith lowered his eyes, pulled his hands away and stood there for a long moment. *Should I tell her the whole truth?* Finally, with pursed lips, he answered, "My little princess, it had to be that way. I did it to protect you and your people."

"What? Your false death protected my people and me? How can that be? You sound like a fool—but I know you are not. You're a . . . good man, but please—tell me what you mean," she pleaded as her voice cracked with emotion.

Smith reached out to cradle her gloved hand in his. With the calloused palm of his other hand, he touched her cheek. Then, looking deeply into her misty brown eyes, he spoke gently, "My dear Pocahontas, in Jamestown, we had become close friends—you, your grandfather, Paquiquino, and I. But I was responsible for feeding hundreds of starving colonists—and my cruel soldier ways took control over me so many times. As you know, I began killing your people when I raided their villages for food. I knew it was wrong—but we were starving.

"One night, I decided I could no longer kill your people to get food. You and your grandfather meant too much to me. I knew I was hurting you both by the raids I led. I knew I had to leave somehow. So, I burned my leg on purpose and pretended it was an accident. I told the others I needed to return to England for proper medical care. I told them to tell you I was dead, so you would not wait for me to return. They were furious. They cursed me for deserting them—but they agreed to the lie. Pocahontas, I am sorry we lied to you, but I had to—to protect you and Paquiquino and your people from me. I was so ashamed of what I had done to your people."

Pocahontas was stunned. Again, she could not speak. But her fiery brown eyes spoke volumes. Her heart was burning for this man standing before her.

"Please forgive me, Little One. In my own way, I did it to protect you," the old soldier whispered with a wince.

"Oh, John . . ." she cried as she buried her face in his thick topcoat. Smith struggled to hold back his own emotions as he held her like a father. For many moments, all he heard was her repeated murmurs, "I knew you loved me. I knew it."

Finally, with great effort, she pulled herself away from his chest and wiped her face dry with a delicate, linen handkerchief the queen had given her. Smith beamed at her. "Yes—I did love you. You are easy to love, Pocahontas. But Rolfe makes a better husband for you than I would have."

Holding her now at arm's length, the old soldier crowed loudly, "And look at you, Lady Rebecca! It is brilliant to see you again. You have become a beauty beyond compare. Why, if I had been fifteen years younger and could have stayed in the colony . . ." He winked slyly to tease her— but his voice was choked with intense emotion.

She blushed and looked down. As she looked up, her face glowed like a bride on her wedding day—her eyes brimmed over with heavy tears, and her hands trembled. *If only . . .* but the thought was too painful to say. Then she moved closer, carefully took off her white gloves and gently took his face into her soft hands. "You were my first love, John Smith. I shall never forget you. *Never.*" And with that, she stepped back from him, her face still glistening with deep emotion as she reached for both of his hands.

"You look so beautiful, Matoaka," he whispered, trying to look calm. But now, his hands shook.

"Do I? I hope so," she responded shyly. "I hope you still like me dressed as a white woman," she laughed, as she turned sideways quickly with a magical swish of her long raven hair.

With fatherly tenderness, he grabbed her outstretched hand and twirled her around in a full circle. "Like you? I will always be grateful for that little Powhatan girl who saved our colony. Why, I wrote in my book that you, Pocahontas, were the instrument for preserving this colony from death, famine,* and utter confusion. I meant every word of that, Little One."

Pocahontas smiled again. "Oh, and did you also mean what you wrote that I was 'a child of eleven years old, which not only for feature, countenance, and proportion much exceeds any of the rest of Powhatan people, but for wit, and spirit, no one surpasses her in this country'?* See, I have learned to read your language, John Smith," she giggled proudly.

"My dear Mrs. Rolfe, I did not tell the half of it. You were and are a truly amazing woman," Smith gallantly added with a tip of his hat. "You really did save the colony."

Blushing again, Pocahontas teared up. "I did it for my father and for you." Smith just looked at her and sighed. He knew this game had to stop.

This talk of love—and now with a married woman—made him feel very uncomfortable. Forcing himself, Smith let go of her hands. "Playful One . . . you really are full of spirit today, aren't you? But all this talk of love . . . well, I am honored, but really, I cannot dwell on such sentiments, especially now that you are Mrs. John Rolfe."

Pocahontas turned slightly away from him. "You are right, Captain Smith, but I had to tell you. I had come that day to the fort to tell you of my love for you. I wanted you to know that girls can marry at thirteen in our tribe . . . if you had wanted me. But you were gone."

She wheeled around to face him again. Her face was full of peace now. "I know now that the Lord had another good John for me to marry. But no one can ever take your place in my heart. If I cannot be your wife, I will call you 'father.'"

Smith raised his eyebrows in concern. "No, dear princess, please do not call me that. I am not your father, just a friend," he responded defensively. "I wasn't cut out to be a good father to anyone."

Pocahontas's face darkened. "What? You invaded my father's country and made him and all of his tribe afraid of you, and now you are afraid to let me call you 'Father'?"* She pointed her finger at him. "I tell you this—I shall call you 'Father,' and you shall call me 'child,' and so I will be yours forever and ever,"* she declared with a fierce but loving look.

Sensing he had met his match, Smith retreated. "As you wish, my child. Father, it shall be, and I am a blessed man to have a daughter such as you."

"O, praise the Lord!" Pocahontas exclaimed as she threw her slender arms around him and pressed her burning cheek next to his muscular chest—close enough to hear his heart beating rapidly. "It feels so good to call you Father." He slowly relaxed and embraced her tenderly for a long moment.

Then, Pocahontas pulled back and looked at him with a mildly urgent look. "So, Father, here is my first question to you as your daughter: Are you a real Christian? Do you love Jesus? Will I see you in heaven? I want you there too!"

Those words struck him like a battering ram to his gut. He froze. Grimacing to suppress the pain he was feeling, the old soldier looked deep into those dancing, mahogany eyes while his mind shouted *You saved the colony, little princess. Would you now save me? I doubt that can be. Not me.*

CHAPTER 64

For a long time, Captain Smith just looked at the dirty, grey marble floor of the church narthex. The old soldier did not want to answer the question Lady Rebecca had just asked. He considered lying to her but quickly dismissed it. *She must know the truth,* he decided—but he didn't want to hurt her. Finally, he forced himself to speak.

"Wow, Pocahontas, you always did get straight to the point," he meekly muttered. "Many years ago, I would have told you what my favorite author, Niccolò Machiavelli,* wrote: 'I desire to go to hell and not to heaven. In the former place, I shall enjoy the company of popes, kings, and princes, while in the latter are only beggars, monks, and apostles.'"*

Smith paused for a moment, and a faraway look came into his eyes. "But knowing Reverend Hunt in Virginia has changed all that. He showed me that a man could really love God with his whole heart and love others unselfishly. I'd never met a person like that. But now I think I see it in you, Lady Rebecca."

"Then tell me you love Jesus! If you love who I am and who Hunt was, it is because we both know Jesus. Reverend Hunt led my grandfather,

Paquiquino, to Jesus. Later, Papa Paq led me to the Lord—and the English told me more about Jesus. Let me lead you to Jesus, my beloved friend—please?"

Smith's sky-blue eyes suddenly brimmed with tears, "Pocahontas, I am not worthy to follow Jesus. I am haunted by what I did as a soldier. I killed so many people in so many places and...and especially in Virginia. Oh dear child, if I am your father, you must forgive me for what I have done to your people. I am guilty. My hands are stained with the blood of your tribe." Smith slowly lowered his greying head down into his calloused hands with muffled cries. Pocahontas tenderly grabbed both of his arms and bowed her head to rest gently against his head.

For a long moment, the foyer of that church was uncommonly hushed—as if it suddenly was transported into another realm. No sound was heard except for the sobs of two very different people bonded by a shared and deep grief—but also by a love for one another that was even deeper.

Pocahontas tilted his face up and looked into his eyes with great solemnity. "Captain John Smith, as an Algonquian princess of the mighty Powhatan, I forgive you for what you all have done to our people. I bless you. You have given us far more than what we lost. You gave us the Gospel. Your colony intended much evil toward us. But God intended your coming to bring my people home to heaven as his very own children."

"Oh, thank you, dear princess. With all my heart, thank you for your forgiveness. You have shown me the same love Hunt showed me. So, yes—I do accept your Jesus as my Jesus. I am tired of being an angry, lonely man. I want to be forgiven and loved. That's all I really want. That's all I ever wanted." Smith's body shook with deep sobs as Pocahontas held him in her strong arms. Then, as she released him, the tired old soldier knelt on the floor—thanking God for Jesus.

"Hallelujah! Hallelujah!" Pocahontas war-whooped so loud it frightened a drunken sailor passing by the church. Snookus cried out in pain. Morph just smiled.

"Hallelujah! Hallelujah!" Scion and Angie shouted, drowning out the hollering of Snookus, who was pinned in the corner by the power of worship.

A dozen angels suddenly swooshed in to sing over the praying soldier. Sensing the angels and God's presence growing stronger, Pocahontas began to dance.

She twirled around her beloved soldier in her Powhatan Victory Dance—the same one she had danced for her father after he had spared John Smith from death and given him to her. But now she danced for Jesus—the Victorious Warrior who had spared her beloved John from eternal death and given him to her as a Christian brother forever. With a swish of her long, ornate dress, she floated like a butterfly across the smooth, marble floor, her hands high above her head, clapping to an ancient Algonquian beat. Closing her eyes, Pocahontas leaped like a deer and pirouetted in the air—only this time, higher and longer than any human should be able. Scion was lifting her up and dancing with her! With gentlemanly grace, he passed her hand to each of the worshipping angels above. They took turns spinning her around as her body circled the ceiling. Pocahontas felt like she was in a dream or in a trance. It all seemed so natural. Then, the most intoxicating incense aroma filled the room just as Captain Smith tried to look up to see where Pocahontas had gone. But only his eyelids could move. His body felt like it weighed a thousand pounds. No one saw her aerial worship except Jesus and the angels . . . and one startled, drunken sailor passing by the open church door—but he quickly fainted.

In the next moment, the Powhatan princess glided to the floor next to Smith. She knelt and prayed, "Jesus, my beloved John had his head on a rock when I first danced over him. Now I have danced over him with his faith resting on you, the Rock of our salvation. His people came to conquer our people, but you have conquered us all with your love." She gently placed her hand on Smith's bowed head. "I bless this man. I bless John Smith as my brother forever . . . in Jesus' name, amen!"

Without looking up, Smith put his hand over hers on his head and tearfully agreed, "Thank you, Jesus. Thank you for sending me to Jamestown to meet Hunt, and this wonderful woman and now you!"

It was done. Smith was saved. Their assignment finished, the angels overhead departed the chapel, laughing and trading high-fives to celebrate another sinner becoming a saint.

As the angels left, Snookus expressed his shock to the secretly bemused Morph, "I thought this would be an innocent diversion for that little traitor. Nothing to worry about—but now this!" Snookus moaned. "She's dancing with angels! If Okeus finds out about this, he will rip my lips off. We must kill her before she gets back to Virginia! Do you hear that, Morph?"

"What can we do?" Morph shot back. "It's beyond us now. Once heaven blesses someone like that, it is permanent. Okeus will just have to deal with it."

"Shut up, you idiot!" Snookus shouted with rage in his eyes. "I will instruct Mongo to get a cloth infected with Gaol Fever.* English demons tell me it is a very valuable pox. The streets are full of beggars sick with it. Her native body will have no way to defend itself against such a powerful white man's disease. Mongo will put that cloth under the pillow of Pocahontas tonight. It should not be difficult. Come with me now. We have to make Mongo act quickly."

Morph was terrified. *How can I warn Scion?* he thought. "But shouldn't I stay here to make sure she does no further damage to us?"

"No! It's too late to worry about that. She will be dead in three days. Come with me! Tonight, we make history. Soon, the peace will end at Jamestown—and Jamestown will die!"

"But Snookus—" Morph pleaded.

"Silence, you imbecile! You are coming with me!" Snookus growled as he grabbed Morph's furry tail with a powerful tentacle and dragged him away.

Morph looked back to see Pocahontas and Smith. His mind swirled dizzily. *How will I ever tell Scion now? Pocahontas is in grave danger. I know Angie is counting on me to protect the princess. But I can't now. I am such a failure—again! How can I face Angie?*

A FEW DAYS LATER, CHAMBERMAIDS AT THE PALACE WHERE THE ROLFES were staying found a filthy rag under the pillow of Pocahontas. Mongo and Tomocomo had carefully laid it there the night before. Snookus made Morph watch it all. When the chambermaids reported this disgusting discovery to their steward, they were told not to tell anyone. "You will lose your jobs if it becomes known that a dirty cloth was found in a royal bedroom," the steward warned.

As Pocahontas was being taken to the ship waiting in Gravesend later the next day, she was already deathly ill. Morph flew ahead to the waiting vessel and quickly buried himself in the bilge compartment, near the keel where the slop of rotten food and human waste ended up. Somehow, that filth seemed cleaner than he felt.

Three days later, on March 17, 1617,* a violently ill Pocahontas breathed her last as she lay in the captain's cabin, surrounded by her husband, their infant son, Sir Thomas Dale,* Scion, and Angie. She had a sickness no Powhatan had ever experienced. She passed into glory with a sweet expression of peace on her tawny face. Her last words were, "It is enough. The child lives."* Everyone wept, especially her husband, John Rolfe, as he stood over the lifeless body of his beautiful wife, clutching their only child close to his heaving chest.

But Scion and Angie's grief was cut short when they saw what no one else could. As the spirit of Pocahontas slipped out of her lifeless body, she leaped like a deer into a dazzling swirl of angels dancing above her. As they all rose higher into the brilliant, rainbow-studded, blue sky of heaven, Pocahontas was clothed with a brilliant white robe, trimmed with golden Powhatan shell beads around all the edges. Throwing back her mane of long, black hair, the shining princess soared toward heaven dancing the Victory Dance of Pocahontas—right into the Throne Room of her heavenly Father. Angie wept as never before—crying tears of sorrow and joy. Scion knelt reverently with his head bowed and his eight-foot sword held high above his golden head. She was home. Princess Pocahontas was now the glorified princess of King Jesus.

As the groans of the mourners grew louder, Mongo and Tomocomo stood outside the cabin door, trying to look as despondent as possible —while trading occasional, secret smiles between them. They knew Okeus would be pleased.

CHAPTER 65

June 6, 1617

John Rolfe grieved the entire four thousand miles on his return to Jamestown. It was like a long funeral. He hardly ate. Even the crew—who were ordinarily boisterous—were subdued. Relatives had agreed to care for his infant son in England while John attended to his busy Virginia plantation and tobacco business.* After what seemed like an eternity, he arrived in Jamestown. The dock was full of cheering Englishmen and whooping Powhatans, eager to see the triumphant Rolfes who had just been guests of the King of England.

Instead, when John stepped off the ship without Pocahontas or their son, he burst into tears as he looked at her father, who was eagerly waiting to see his daughter and grandchild again. Instantly, the old chief collapsed at the dock. Women screamed. Men groaned. A heavy sadness and lingering fear hung over Jamestown. Everyone sensed that the "Peace of Pocahontas" was over. They all wondered what would happen next.

Later that day, after regaining his senses, Powhatan did not have to wonder. He knew that war would not be far behind. He heard that

Opie was already making plans to massacre the colony one day. Finally, the day came when the old chief decided it was time to fulfill the last wish of Pocahontas before allowing Opie to rule in his place.

"Great Chief Powhatan, we are ready to go. The canoe is packed," Chanco announced outside the chief's longhouse.

Chanco

Chanco was the chief's personal assistant—and a secret Christian whom Paquiquino had led to the Lord. The scurrying feet of Powhatan's many wives could be heard as they finished dressing their ailing husband whose left side had recently gone partially numb.

Hobbling outside and leaning on a long, beautifully carved walking stick, Powhatan emerged to join his aide on a trip across the Pamunkey River, a trip he had made many times.

Once the chief was in the canoe, Chanco pushed off from shore as Powhatan's gaggle of wives waved and wept. They had a premonition that this was going to be a bad day.

Opie stood hidden in the trees, grinning. "Maybe he will not come back," he whispered.

Okeus bared his fangs in delight. "He's going into the woods where he will be alone. Now we will finish off that old coot and be done with him. Opie is my man now."

The canoe sailed on the calm waters. Chanco asked, "Where are we going, my chief? To Jamestown? That is a long journey of fifteen miles. Are you strong enough for that?"

"Just take me to Kiskiack. It's only four miles. From there I am going to the Moss Valley," Powhatan grunted with pain.

"I know the werowance there, Ottahotin. I will help you walk there after I tie up the canoe."

"No, you must stay with the canoe," the chief shot back forcefully. "I must be alone there."

Chanco huffed in frustration. He was worried about his chief, but he respected his decision. "As you say. But please call me right away if you fall or need help. The entire tribe is depending on me to care for you today."

After a forty-five-minute trip, the canoe reached the other side of the river. The air was still, and the pine trees stood like tall, silent sentinels along the bank. But jeers, curses, and shouts of victory filled the spiritual realm as hundreds of mocking demons pushed and shoved to watch the final attack on the chief they once served.

"Look, my little ones," Snookus snorted. "He comes here to die. I hope he enjoyed his last meal of corn, beans, and deer at the longhouse. His next one in hell won't be as tasty."

Roars of laughter erupted all around the slimy, blubbery assistant to Okeus. Snookus pointed at four demons with one of his tentacles. "Come, Confusion, come, Torment, come, Terror, come, Destroyer. You have work to do and prizes to win from Master Okeus when this is done. You can ravage any human as you wish if you do well here today."

Three of the demons looked like huge versions of the multi-legged flying insects found in tropical rainforests. But Destroyer was different. Its small eyes, flat head and short legs belied the ferocity with which he killed his assigned prey. Destroyer looked every inch like a massive honey badger—but with wings. Few demons ever dared to mess with him.

High above, Scion gave the signal to Morph and Angie. They flew ahead to ambush the ambushers.

The canoe reached the shore. Powhatan almost fell on the rocks at the river's edge when he got out of the canoe. "Please let me go with you to help you," Chanco urged.

"No, my dear Chanco. I must do this alone. I am meeting with someone you cannot meet now. But I hope you will, one day soon."

"He must be alone . . . very alone to meet us," the four demons cackled as they flew ahead to take their positions.

CHAPTER 66

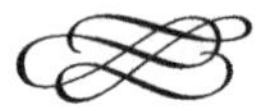

Holding his long, carved walking stick, Powhatan limped into the sweetly scented pine woods. The forest floor was decorated with red columbine and Black-Eyed Susans peeking through the wet pine needles. Powhatan's spirit was lifted just to be in the woods *alone*. Chiefs were hardly ever alone.

Heading toward the tallest oak tree, he finally recognized the path Pocahontas told him about that branched off from the oak. As he rounded the tree, terror flooded his face. Violent images of gruesome deaths fill his mind.

"What is that?" he groaned as he staggered forward, looking for hidden enemies about to attack. Then, suddenly, he felt a searing pain in his chest, and his legs felt like lead.

Watching from a nearby bush, Scion was a little worried, but a quick glance told him that Angie was ready to help soon.

Then a knowing look came upon Powhatan's face. "Get away from me, you filthy spirits! I know you. I sent you against my enemies many times. Begone, I tell you! I will not be tricked by your deceits."

"Sorry, old chief, but Okeus has sent us. You have no power to match his," the feisty demons spat back.

Summoning all of his strength and the pain resistance skills he learned as a warrior, Powhatan struggled forward. He was determined to reach Moss Valley. But just as the struggling chief saw the entrance to the clearing, his mind went blank.

Where am I? Where am I going? Powhatan's thoughts turned to mush, and nothing seemed to make sense. He had an overwhelming urge to just sit down and not move. The world spun around him faster and faster and . . . thump. He fell down, motionless, just before clutching his chest and losing consciousness. Confusion snickered wickedly as the spirit pulled his talon out of Powhatan's torso and nodded to Destroyer. The assassin demon yanked out his curved sword with a loud twang. "Now I will earn great honor with Okeus," he gloated. Terror, Torment, and Confusion all growled in agreement. Destroyer raised his sword for the final blow.

Just then, a voice in the forest screamed, "It's terrible, horrible, unthinkable! What will we do? Okeus is doomed. We are doomed!" It was Morph howling at the top of his lungs.

Confusion was so confused he couldn't move. But Terror was terrified — and jumped off of Powhatan. Then, not knowing what to do, Terror rushed back to see what was happening to his master, Okeus. But once beyond sight of his companions, he ran right into the sharp point of Scion's outstretched sword. His body exploded into a noxious gas, and he was gone forever.

But Destroyer never took his eyes off of Powhatan. He cared little for what happened to Okeus or to anyone else, for that matter. Torment also ignored Morph. He was enjoying his work too much.

Then, despite Morph's continued shrieking, Destroyer raised his fearsome sword again. But before he could bring it down, a sound pierced the forest, drowning out even Morph's cries. This new sound was so high and so loud, it hurt the ears of every man, spirit and beast for miles around. Wine goblets in the governor's home in Jamestown fifteen miles northwest shattered.

The assassin demon froze. Then, with maniacal rage, Destroyer whipped his head around in a complete circle to identify the source of the punishing sound. In that nano-moment, with the speed and agility of a hummingbird, Angie dive-bombed the three demons seven times while belting out that tormenting high C note. On her final aerial attack, the mental walls of Confusion's mind came crashing down. He flew away as quickly as he could, flying with little control, right through trees and rocks before finally crashing into Scion's left wing that snapped out to stop the fleeing spirit. Before his head cleared, it left his body. "Another witness eliminated," Scion muttered fiercely as he put his sword back into the scabbard.

Meanwhile, Torment had recovered from Angie's ferocious audio attacks. He plunged his claw into Powhatan's stomach to crank up his pain. But before the half-conscious chief felt anything, Torment heard the whistling sound of heavy metal as it severed his arm before arcing downward to relieve him of everything between his hips. "Three's a charm," Scion whispered.

Seeing Scion bisect Torment only energized Destroyer. He was not to be denied—not even by a twelve-foot angel and his very sharp sword. Destroyer stood up to his full eight-foot height and roared so loud it could have frightened an angry grizzly bear guarding her cubs. He cursed Scion and the other demons who had fled. This cursing went on for several long moments as he tried to make Scion angry enough to attack him. But Scion just stood there and smiled. Finally, Destroyer got suspicious and looked down at where Powhatan had been moments before. Destroyer shrieked. Powhatan had somehow crawled to within six feet of Moss Valley.

Enraged, Destroyer leapt into the air, raising his sword high above his lizard-like head. With a loud grunt, he pulled the arc-bladed weapon down with both claws to demolish the frail Algonquian leader below him. At the same instant his sword moved earthward, a blinding speck of light flashed before his eyes . . . and stayed there. Destroyer winced and twisted his furry body ever so slightly. The killer's sword continued its violent path, but the blade veered off course just far enough to miss its mark. Destroyer was not sure what was more confusing—that he missed his target or that he was looking at a demon with a blinding light under one wing. Then Angie began to worship. Morph's wing-light burst into full power before the murderer's eyes. Destroyer closed his eyes just long enough for Powhatan to crawl forward and push his hand into the velvety, moss-covered clearing. Before the dazed assassin recovered, an eight-foot blade forged in heaven split him in two from top to bottom, and he evaporated into a thin, foul-smelling red mist.

It was over. Scion, Angie, and Morph all let out a shout of joy. Then, Scion looked at Morph, who was hovering just a few feet away from the two angels. "Well, Morph, we did it—and we could not have done it without your help. Angie was right about you. Thank you for what you just did to help me eliminate those goons."

The little green cat just stared at Scion and then at Angie. Big tears welled up in his eyes. "I . . . I don't know what to say. I always got beat and humiliated for not being bad enough. Now I just did something good for the first time, and you are thanking me. I don't know how to respond to gratitude, but"—his tears dripped down on the biggest smile he'd ever had—"I'd like to get used to that!"

They all laughed. Angie flew over to grab his paw in her tiny hand. "I'm so proud of you, Morph!" Angie gushed as the most unlikely heavenly team ever seen celebrated together.

But then, Powhattan awoke. He groaned and tried to get up, but couldn't. Before he could try again, two giant angels of the Honor Battalion pulled him into the mossy clearing made holy by martyr's blood. Scion smiled. He knew Powhatan was perfectly safe now. Even if they were discovered by a demon patrol now, no demon would dare to enter that angelic safe zone.

My pain is gone. My mind is clear, Powhatan suddenly realized.

As Powhatan lay there, he heard music and singing, more beautiful than he had ever imagined. "They are singing in my language, but they sing of a king I do not know," he mumbled. "The song is of a great warrior who has conquered all my enemies for me. It's also about a land far away, where there is no hunger, no thirst, no wars, no tears, where all people live together in peace in their own longhouse with plenty of corn, squash, and meat."

A ring of angels with flaming swords stood at attention as the aging chief pondered what was happening. "I am to get up and bow," he whispered to himself. "The Spirit I came to meet must be here."

Powhatan slowly got to his knees, looked up to the sky, and cried out: "I am Wahunsenacawh, Chief of Tsenacommacah. My daughter, Matoaka, told me to come here if she did not come back from England. She said I was to call upon you and you would help me . . ."

Powhatan paused for a moment to catch his breath. "The pain of losing my daughter is great, and the peace we had with the English may not last now that she is dead. I am old and sick. I cannot . . ." His voice trailed off into sobs that went on for several minutes. Then, finally, there was total silence. No bird, no animal, no crawling thing moved. A heaviness came over him that he could not explain.

"Father . . ."

The old man froze at the sound of his name. Then he looked up to see his daughter standing next to a man who was the biggest warrior he had ever seen. Pocahontas glowed, but the magnificent warrior was so brilliant, it took his breath away for a moment.

"Yes, Wahunsenacawh, Pocahontas is here with me. She is here because I chose you and loved you and your people before there was a Great Bay or before there was a moon to shine over it."

"Who are you, Great Warrior? I should like to follow in your path and learn your ways."

"I am Jesus, the one who gave his life to save all people from all punishment for things they have done wrong. I died to pay for all the wrong things you have done. I rose from the grave to prove I am God. I offer you what your daughter has—forgiveness for all wrongs and life eternal with me. Will you follow me on my path? I am here to bring you home, Great Chief. Take my hand. Come home to live with Pocahontas and with me forever."

Hot tears flowed down Powhatan's cheeks. He could hardly believe what he was hearing. He knew his father Paquiquino had found peace when he decided to follow Jesus' path. He had seen the change in Pocahontas when she was baptized as a Christian. He thought about the cruelties of Okeus and the terrible things he made his tribes do—even sacrificing people to him. Anger rose inside him. *I hate you, Okeus. You made us kill each other. You made us angry and selfish. You stole our peace. I will not follow you anymore,* he silently vowed.

Looking up to the glowing figure before him, Powhatan slowly extended his hand toward Jesus. As their fingers touched, the old chief fell over . . . into glory—as Jesus pulled his spirit up into the arms of his favorite daughter.

CHAPTER 67

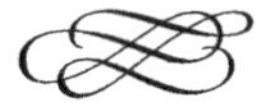

*August 20, 1619**

The barnacle-encrusted hull of an old English profiteering ship called the *White Lion** pulled up to the crude dock at Point Comfort* just south of Jamestown. Flying under Dutch colors,* the *Lion* had recently attacked a Portuguese slave ship, the *São João Bautista,** headed for Mexico from Angola with about sixty Africans.* The Africans were destined for the Mexican slave market.* The *White Lion* had brought about twenty-two* of those slaves to Point Comfort to sell to Virginia farmers.*

The first African slaves arrive at the Jamestown Colony

Everything about the White Lion was creepy. The crew looked and smelled like zombies from Haiti. Their clothes were rags, their beards scraggly, and their eyes dark and empty, like no one was at home inside. Along the ship's railing, the hulking British captain, John Colyn Jope,* stood glaring at the colonists on the shore. He was a dangerous man the Spanish called *El Diablito*. His bloodshot eyes, thin lips curled in anger, and scarred cheeks made him look as menacing as he really was. He captured and sold humans beings to the highest bidder. A hundred demons also traveled on this slave ship. Feasting on the fears of slaves and the sins of slave owners was a tasty banquet for them.

Morph suddenly appeared above the dock. He had heard about this shipment of black people from Snookus—the first black people ever sold in Virginia.* He dove into the ship to see what was going on just as El Diablito addressed his cargo. He saw Angie glide into the water beneath the ship just as he arrived below decks. He smiled. *No one saw her. They rarely do,* he chuckled to himself.

Above, on the main deck, a disfigured British sailor shouted down the hatch to the blacks below, "Wake up, you pigs! Welcome to the Tobacco Coast. Your new masters will want to see your shiny eyes to make sure you have no fever. And you better be on your best behavior. Remember, if you fail to be bought by one of these English idiots, you will pay for it with your flesh. Is that clear? And one more thing—anyone who complains about us to the folks here may not live to tell about it again."

"Yo, you red-and-white one, where is your *jefe?*" the bold island demon demanded as he saw a British officer's personal evil spirit approaching. "We must deal with your master."

"Jefe? Don't give me that Spanish trash talk, mate. We speak English here. This is our land, and these are our slaves. So what does your fat, Caribbean butt-face want?"

"We're here to transfer cargo, yo creep. You know da drill. We got ta torment and play with these bitches for years, and now dey is yours to play with, mon. I need yo scratch on this here note from our jefe, the Great Voudoc, Lord of the Caribbean."

"Voudoc, pludoc, mana mana moodoc. Who cares, jabberguts? Hand over the note, and we'll get the witch doctor's man to sign it. He calls most of the shots here for Okeus, the real boss in these parts."

The Virginia demon snatched the brown, stained note with a snarl and handed it to a goofy-looking cat demon. "Take this to Snookus . . . and be quick about it, butthole!"

As the one-winged demon fluttered and flopped away to the mocking howls of English and island demons, a loud monkey screech in the belly of the ship could not be heard. Voudoc had just run into Morph —a rendezvous neither expected.

Voudoc whispered excitedly, "Are you Morph?"

"Yes, I am. How did you know?"

"Easy, fur ball! Not many cat demons with blue eyes and a bad wing 'round here, I'd say. Besides, you are dat famous cat. Who 'asn't 'eard of 'Da Clown of da Great Bay'? All my demons know 'bout you."

Morph looked mortified. He tried to leave, but Voudoc pulled him closer.

"I am Voudoc, Principality of da Islands. I stowed away on dis vessel so I could see dis day myself. I am here to torment your master. I hate him. He is Lucifer's pet and a fat bully who is full of himself. Today, I've brought da lizard-face Okeus a present he will soon regret."

"Really, Master Voudoc? That sounds too good to be true," Morph chortled. "What kind of present?"

"See these twenty-two blacks?* Dey are from my islands. When I heard dat da colony want slaves, I arrange to get dem on da White Lion. What a relief ta get rid of dem! Des twenty-two are crazy followers of da Lamb—da most dangerous kind. I've never seen humans worship and pray like dis group do. Dey scare the batcrap out of even my biggest demons. Dey are perfect for this!"

Morph scrunched up his dark green face and asked, “Perfect for what? I don’t get it, Master Voudoc.”

“Morph, 'ave you heard of da Trojan Horse? Oh—of course, you haven’t. You’re only a demon. Dis Trojan Horse is something you send ta your enemy ta defeat him—but he think it be just a beautiful gift. If des slaves ever get tagether ta pray, dey will draw da power of our enemy into da colony. Okeus will have to work much harder ta destroy dis colony when dat happen. Dey will be a royal thorn in his big, green butt!”

Morph looked at Voudoc with awe. “Incredible, Master Voudoc. You are more clever than Okeus!”

“Finally, someone who appreciates my true qualities," the monkey spirit laughed. "Look, Morph, later I may need ten or twelve demons ta play another dirty trick on yer master. Can ya help me?”

The cat demon’s blue eyes got wider. “Why, yes, Master Voudoc. I have just the right friends to help you. We all detest Okeus. Just tell us when.”

“Oh, glory ta Lord Lucifer! Thank you. Dis will be so sweet," Voudoc exclaimed with a wide, toothy grin.

Just then, they heard an angry shout topside from the yellow octopus in charge. A large group of slaves was worshipping.

“Hey, what’s that?” Snookus shouted to his demon guards. “Why are those island slugs raising their hands like that? They’re not *praying,* are they?”

As the guards raced to investigate, Morph erupted from the ship’s hull, screeching,

“Hold on, you warthogs! Don’t disturb that bunch. These vermin are from the kingdom of Ndongo in West Africa. They are powerful demon worshipers. I heard them chanting a special spell of blessing for Lord Okeus and this new land. They are under the control of a powerful island spirit who is channeling his power through them to help us succeed against the English. You will ruin the spell if you interrupt now."

Slamming together in a sudden halt, the column of wingless demon guards looked back at Snookus. Snookus hesitated for a moment, then barked, "Okay, forget the chanting African slimebags. Get them ashore as soon as they are done. Mongo will be pleased to use their chants against the English very soon."

LATER THAT DAY, THE WHITE LION WAS QUIET. IT WAS A HOT AUGUST afternoon—perfect for a nap. While white men scurried around on the shore, the newly arrived slaves fell asleep on deck, still in their chains. After an hour, a big African woman named Mongomo awoke. Slowly, the others began to stir and rub their chain-scarred wrists, still throbbing with pain.

Mongomo saw them first—the low-lying buildings with a British flag fluttering in the soft twilight breeze. So, dis be home to us now, she thought. *What a sad-looking place. Da English look so tired. Dey move so slow. What be wrong here? Maybe dey be easy on us and not work us so hard —like on the island. I's hope so. My body, she is sore, and my heart is sad, but we got da Lawd Gaud wit us.*

After a short time of quiet prayer, the ten men and twelve women were dragged from the filthy hold of the ship to the bright sunshine of Jamestown's fort. Dozens of women-hungry men* stared at the scantily clothed females being herded to a nearby warehouse. Spirits of lust smelled the younger men's sinful desires and quickly converged on them, while older, tired farmers eyed the ten muscular males.

"I'll take that big one, the one with the shaved head," a scrawny colonist shouted. "I've got a farm full of tobacco just waiting for a hard worker to make me rich."

The farmers all laughed. They all felt the same way. Another planter remarked, "Why, if I had twenty-five men like that one and a few ladies to clean barns and do housework, I could make more money than my father ever thought to make in a lifetime."

Diving deep into the thick mud of the oyster beds near the shore, Morph found his favorite female angel. "Angie, you will never guess what is happening! Voudoc—the boss in the islands—sent praying, Christian slaves here to torment Okeus."

"Holy Cherubmatzi! Wait till I tell Scion. This will cheer him up. Thanks for the tip, Morph. You know, you'd make a good scout," she said with a warm smile. "Got to go and tell the Boss. See you soon!"

Morph left right after her, in the opposite direction. But his thoughts followed her. *One day, maybe she and I can scout together.* Little did he know that Angie was thinking the same thing.

CHAPTER 68

*May 1620**

As the *Jonathan** sailed into the Point Comfort port on a sunny spring day, three hundred men in their Sunday church clothes jostled each other to get a look at the latest shipment from London.

Just then, a young sailor hanging on the yardarm of the approaching ship waved wildly and shouted to the men onshore, "Women! We have women! Ninety of them!"* The roar of approval that rose from those men could be heard for a mile or more.

"Get out of my way, Johnson! I was here first. I've been in this hell-hole a lot longer than you. I am so ready to get a woman in my house, I think I will explode. No man can hold out this long without going a little crazy. A man needs a woman. That's biblical, right?" Ben Collins laughed. Ben had been in Jamestown as a tobacco farmer longer than most, and he complained almost daily about the lack of women in the colony.

"I'm way past crazy, Ben," a big, bearded, balding man shouted. "I'm rip-roaring ready to kill if I don't get what I want off this ship. Been here six years without a female—except an occasional native girlfriend. They love mirrors, they do!" The two men slapped each other's backs and smiled knowingly at each other.

A ship with ninety unmarried women was about to dock. The "Tobacco Brides" would be sold to the men for one hundred and twenty pounds of 'good leaf' tobacco to pay for their passage over.* Standing along that ship's rail were ninety women of various ages in full skirts, Sunday-best blouses, and shined shoes. Many would become beloved wives. Others would just be hired hands—indentured servants working to pay back their new master for the price of the trip to Virginia.

As the boat pulled up to the dock, Matilda and Betty stood next to the railing and scanned the noisy mob, hoping to find the face of a kind man. "My hair's a mess," she moaned.

"Don't be silly, Matilda," Betty chimed in. "We all look a sight. Smell me. My clothes reek of seasickness vomit. But no matter now, we're here. Well, the Company did say it would be an adventure.* I had to get out of London. No money and no fun. Now, I can get both here."

"Betty, honey, I hope you get all that. But adventure is not the word I would choose to describe what I see now," Matilda cynically responded as she looked at the cursing, shoving crowd.

"Let's face it, Betty—we were suckers. Remember what the poster said, 'Come to Virginia, marry a gentleman farmer, and begin a new life in the New World. He is waiting for you.'*

"But that's not what I heard the captain tell his first mate this morning as we sailed up the river," Matilda spat out with fire in her eyes, "He said that we were coming as servants—indentured servants—to be bought with tobacco.* Yeah, we can be brides all right . . . after working for seven years first.* They lied to us!"

Betty put her arm around Matilda's shoulder and whispered, "It's going to be okay, sweetie. My mum used to read the Bible to me. I remember a story she told me about Jacob, who had to work for seven years to buy his wife, Rachel. The same thing can happen to us."

With a loud thud, the gangplank slammed down onto the dock. Instantly, the men went wild. Shots were fired. Soldiers shouted. All the women blanched with fright.

Betty held her trembling friend close and stroked her hair as a mother would for a distraught daughter. "Matilda, why don't you meet some of my friends I met on the ship? We pray together each night."

"I'd love to meet your friends. There's something about you that I find very comforting. You have so much peace. I need that."

By 10:00 p.m., the ninety women had settled in a big warehouse with sleeping mats on the dirt floor. An old black lady was cleaning the enclosed kitchen at one the end of the building. As the ladies laid quietly in the cool darkness, a sad song wafted out of the kitchen, a familiar song* sung by a woman who has known pain.

Give ear to a Maid, that lately was betray'd

And sent into Virginny, O

In brief I shall declare, what I have suffered there,

When I was weary, weary, weary, weary, O...

Five years I served I, under Master Guy

In the land of Virginny, O,

Which made me know sorrow, grief, and woe,

When that I was weary, weary, weary, weary, O...

I HAVE PLAYED MY PART BOTH AT PLOW AND CART,

In the land of Virginny, O,

Billets from the Wood upon my back they load,

When that I am weary, weary, weary, weary, O…

THEN LET MAIDS BEWARE, ALL BY MY ILL-FARE,

In the land of Virginny, O;

Be sure to stay at home, for if you here do come,

You will all be weary, weary, weary, weary, O….. *

* * *

Early the following day, before dawn, men starting lining up.

"Betty, I'm scared," Matilda confessed as she looked at the drooling crowd of men outside.

"I am too," Betty agreed. "Only God can protect us in this situation. Remember the verse we read at dinner last night? 'I will be with you always.'"

Matilda took a deep breath and whispered, "Jesus, protect me. I have no one else." And then the small, trembling woman stepped into the auction room.

CHAPTER 69

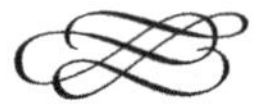

November 28, 1621

"Scion, I . . . I've got n-news," Angie stuttered as she whisked into Scion's view. He was sitting on top of the gate to Jamestown's fort, looking more worn out than the weathered stockade walls behind him. A growing sense of dread about the colony had descended over Scion.

For months he had watched hundreds of terrified African slaves arrive to work tobacco fields for twelve hours a day on the prosperous James River plantations.* In the Jamestown pub, Scion listened to rich farmers joke about how they stole more Powhatan land.* Others bragged about how they beat their slaves into submission for a variety of purposes. One obese man boasted, "My servant woman isn't worth spit

The cruel slavery of Virginia's plantations

in the field, but in bed—oh lordy! Ah reckon ah paid one hundred an fifty pounds of tobac ta buy dat black beauty. Worth evra cent!"

Ben Collins was there. With a sly grin, he whispered how he got his female servant pregnant so she would have to extend her servitude on the farm to pay him back for lost time during the pregnancy.* And yes, he admitted, she was whipped by the colonial rulers for fornication—but he got off with just a warning.* Ben's remarks at the pub sent the half-drunk farmers into spasms of obscene cackles—and loud calls for more Irish whiskey. Then on Sunday, the entire bunch would go to church—a church that never called them to repentance for any of their sins. The parson's salary was, after all, paid in tobacco by the farmers.*

"What is the news, Angie? Another boatload of blacks is coming to be physically, sexually, and verbally abused by our colony? A dozen more women died in the fields last week from exhaustion and malnutrition? Or Bill Hatfield shot another of his slaves when they didn't give him the respect he feels he deserves? Or maybe you came to tell me that Chief Opie is so mad at the lying, thieving English that he wants to massacre the entire colony? That's not news," the big angel moaned. Scion knew God was not pleased with the colony—and that was putting it mildly.

"I just met with General Michael," Angie reported. "He wanted to tell you himself, but he thought it might be easier if I told you first before you met with him."

Scion's face grew pale. Then, with a groan, he held out his huge hand to let Angie alight on it. "Tell me, Little One. It must be terrible news."

Avoiding his outstretched hand, Angie flew to Scion's broad shoulder and sat close to his left ear. She couldn't bear to see his face when she told him.

"Michael said . . . uh . . ." Taking a big breath, Angie whispered, "God has decided to shut the colony down."

Scion's big eyes winced in pain. After a long silence, he whispered in a voice breaking with emotion, "Tell me the details."

Angie looked heavenward for strength, and with big tears rolling down her golden cheeks, she continued, "Michael said that since the northern colony of Pilgrims landed in 1620 at Plymouth, they have distinguished themselves as godly, peaceful people. Father has been especially impressed with how they have loved the natives there. It brought tears to his eyes to see them celebrate meals together. He has decided to build his new missionary nation on that Plymouth settlement— and abandon our Jamestown Colony. God said that he cannot allow the rebellious sins of Jamestown to corrupt the foundations of the holy nation he is going to plant on this continent. Michael said the Lord plans to allow the colony to self-destruct in its own sins. As we well know, Okeus will be more than happy to help them. Michael says we are to finish a few things here and then stand aside and abandon the colony. He's given you seven months to wrap things up."

A long, painful silence ensued. Both angels were in shock.

"If only our colony could have been like Plymouth," Scion moaned. "If only they could have come mainly for God—instead of for gold. If only we could have brought more strong believers here like Hunt. If only the colony had not sinned so much and so often. *If only . . .*" Scion's voice trailed away in gasping sobs.

Angie took a deep breath and forced herself to speak. "He may tell you to step aside . . . while he—" Her voice broke, choking with tears. "Oh, Scion!" She wailed and wrapped her arms as far as they would go around the big angel's neck.

For several long moments, the two of them wept together unashamedly. Angie's tiny tears splashed into the rivulet of tears on Scion's neck.

"So, I have to stand aside like the Lord told Moses to do with Israel?" Scion muttered as if in a daze. "I was afraid this might happen. It's his way, especially with his people. He gives them chance after chance to repent. When they still refuse to repent, he allows them to sin and destroy their lives—just like in the Book of Judges. No wonder the Bible calls this God's 'strange work.' It is so unlike him. He is more loving than anyone could imagine, but he has his limits—especially with his own people who know better."

"That's all true, Master Scion. But perhaps God will give our people another chance—like he gave to the Jews."

"Yes, Angie, he might—but I doubt it. This colony refuses to repent of its sins. It is doomed. It's over . . . all over. I feel like such a failure. I failed heaven long ago—and now I've failed to protect this colony."

Angie had no words to comfort him—or herself.

DEEP IN THE GREAT SWAMP, MOLA CAME UNDER COVER OF DARKNESS to visit Okeus. During the Great Rebellion, he had wanted to follow Lucifer to earth, but Lucifer asked him to remain in heaven. "Watch Scion. Get close to him. Scion is the only angel I fear on Earth. He alone can kill me and the 23. Michael, of course, could kill *any* of us. But he never leaves heaven. The big goon has to protect the precious Throne Room at all times," Lucifer cackled. So, Mola stayed—and became Scion's "best friend."

"What are you doing here?" the enormous reptile huffed indignantly. "I didn't send for you."

"Lucifer is not happy, Okeus. He told you to get Scion away from the colony, but he is still here. Why haven't you told him?" Mola asked.

"I cannot. I will find another way," Okeus mumbled.

"But you must tell Scion!" Mola shouted. "His master has abandoned the colony, but Scion may still try to save it. He may succeed. I know him. Scion can be very clever—and persistent. I know how to really hurt him—and Lucifer agreed to my plan. You have to do it!"

The cocky, six-foot Mola flew right in front of Okeus's formidable face. "Look, *Kai,* I know you two were inseparable thirteen thousand years ago, but this is no time for sentimentality. Planting sin in the colony is not foolproof. All it takes is one firebrand like that loathsome John Knox in Scotland, and the whole colony could repent for its sins and go crazy for you-know-who."

Okeus winced. He knew Mola was right. "All right, Mola, all right! I see your point, but why do I have to be there? Have Snookus tell him."

"Come on, you know that won't work. If Scion doesn't see your face, he will never believe that you are Kai. Once he knows that, he will resign from being Angel of Virginia. We both know that barefoot fool won't cross swords with you. He loves you too much. He would rather slink back to heaven, disgraced, rather than fight you. I know him. He's a naive, dumbass who would rather take a hit than hurt a friend. I will discretely let everyone know that he compromised his assignment because you were here. That will seal his fate. From then on, he will be powerless to hurt us. No one will trust him ever again. Then I can finally leave my fake life in heaven and join you and Lucifer here like I always wanted. I'll get a big promotion from Lucifer, and then I'll be your cruel master down here." Both angels laughed at Mola's weak attempt at humor.

"All right, Mola. You win. I'll do it."

"Good! I knew you would see it our way. Lucifer will be so pleased. I will pass the word to him now. Do your job well. I look forward to joining you down here soon! I leave you with the Dragon's blessing: 'May rage keep you strong and may all your curses come to pass!' Farewell."

As Mola flapped rapidly into the moonless night like a hungry bat, Kai sat down on his hind legs and spiked tail. As his heavy rump thumped onto the squishy swamp floor, his head slumped forward with a jerk. For a long moment, the giant dinosaur demon just stared at the bug-infested ground. His puffy, frog-like lips were tightly pursed, and a deep sadness filled his red eyes. Finally, he raised his head and stared toward Jamestown. With a deep sigh, Kai softly groaned, *"Scion."*

CHAPTER 70

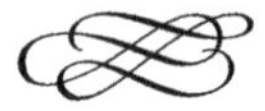

December 7, 1621

Flying into the thick cloud bank just above the Great Swamp, Okeus headed for Jamestown. He knew Scion would challenge him as he approached the settlement.

It didn't take long. Scion and Angie were at their usual post five hundred feet above the fort. From there, they could monitor the status of the Powhatans, the colonists, and nearby demons.

Angie's sensors suddenly detected a strong demonic energy signal.

"Master Scion, you are not going to believe this. Okeus himself is coming our way, low and slow, like he wants to be noticed. What should we do?"

"It's nothing to fret about, Angie. He knows we're finished. He probably just wants to mock us some more. Dark Angels love to mock angels. It's their way of dealing with their own shame and guilt. Let him come. He's no threat now. He's already won. The colony is a sinful mess. Soon, he will destroy it one way or another."

Humming a raunchy British sailor's song to himself to distract his thoughts, the bloated shape of Okeus slowly glided up to where Scion and Angie were waiting. "Ahoy there, mates! A nice day to destroy a colony, no?"

"Cut it out, Okeus. What do you want? I'll give you three minutes, and then you need to go," Scion warned.

"Three minutes? Is that how long you waited before you returned to heaven when you knew the Great Rebellion had started? I heard it took days before you showed your cowardly face again." Okeus turned to Angie. "Did he tell you that, little bug? Your great leader here is a coward. While his friends were fighting and dying to protect heaven, scared little Scion stayed far away."

Angie's fiery purple eyes blazed as her hand gripped her tiny sword. "You ungrateful, lying, selfish, treacherous traitor—and murderer! I know more than you do—probably more than your slave demons know about you. Do they know the truth about you? Do they think you are a demon? Well, guess what? We will blow your cover and tell them you are one of the Dark Angels who has made their lives miserable for eons. You are pathetic. I may be small, but you are microscopic in value to anyone but yourself. I'll bet Lucifer can't wait to betray you and have another one of the 23 lop off your ugly, smelly, lizard head!"

Okeus began to draw his ten-foot sword, but he looked at Scion and thought better of it. "Listen to me, you little freckle-faced mosquito, if I ever catch you alone, you are dead meat. Do you hear me? No one talks to Okeus that way and gets away with it. Better keep your precious sensors in tip-top condition so I don't sneak up on you some night. I have killed more angels than you can count over the last few thousand years. Killing you would be like a tiny dessert after a big meal of real angels."

"Okay, you two. Back off. Angie, go check on the new female arrivals. Protect them in any way you can from the lusty men who bought them," Scion said with a sigh.

"Good luck with that, you gnat!" Okeus bellowed after her as she sped away.

"Well, Scion, at last, we are alone. I have something to tell you that will change everything."

"Okay, fat boy. What's this all about?"

"Insults? I'm so hurt. I may need emotional help if this keeps up. We Dark Angels have feelings too, you know. In fact, all angels have feelings. And once upon a time, I had feelings for another angel. I loved him like no other. He was my hero—smart, funny, brave, unselfish to a fault, and handsome as any angel in heaven. We loved each other so intensely that it made the other angels a little jealous. I didn't care. We had each other. That's all that mattered."

Scion's stomach suddenly felt queasy. "What has that got to do with anything?" Scion snapped back. "You want me to feel sorry for you? You had all that, and you threw it away so that you could slaughter children, burn nursing mothers to death, and decapitate thousands of innocent believers with pagan armies. What a great trade. Why didn't I think of that?"

"Yes, Scion, why didn't you? I know who you are. You are angel 24, aren't you?"

Scion froze. His legs and wings suddenly felt wobbly.

"Why didn't you stick with your closest friends and leave heaven with them?"

Scion remained silent. His head was spinning.

Moving closer to the thunderstruck Scion, Okeus glared into his startled blue eyes and asked, "Why didn't *you* leave with Kai? Why did you give up your closest friend, Scion?"

At this, Scion gasped. "How . . . how did you know? Who are you?"

With a quick head snap, the hulking dinosaur was rapidly enveloped in a foul, green mist. Okeus had disappeared. Out of the bubbling green fog, a twelve-foot Dark Angel stepped into view. His distorted, humanoid face somehow looked both cocky and scared at the same time. Kai had uncloaked.

"Kai, is it really you?" Scion said in a stunned, weak voice. "I thought you were with Lucifer as his second-in-command in hell. Kai . . . I . . . miss you . . . I wish . . . you could . . ."

But then it was over. Scion's emotions exploded inside. The pressure was too much. His vision suddenly went black as his golden, unconscious body hurtled end-over-end toward the dense green forest below. A startled Kai watched him fall—with a numbing mixture of relief and dread. As Scion's spirit body sliced into the soft Virginia earth, Kai quickly re-cloaked into Okeus and raced back to the swamp. He was afraid that one of his demons might see his real identity.

Once there, he roared viciously, "Clear the area! Everyone leave! I must be alone!" No demon needed any prodding when they heard that tone of voice. As Okeus plopped down on his massive tail, he closed his crimson eyes. His breath was shallow and fast—but not as rapid as the thumping of his heart. His thinking blurred. He muttered things he was unaware of. But, in a moment of clarity, he realized his angel hand inside his disguise was fingering a small, jagged-edged object hung around his angelic neck. Then, it hit him like a thunderbolt: it was a piece of jewelry—a gift from Scion long ago. *"Raghhhhhh!* Curse you, Scion!" he bellowed as his legs buckled. For the second time in his life, Kai felt one of the rarest feelings a Dark Angel can feel —*remorse.*

O, Scion. That look on your face! I hated to do it. Now I will have nightmares of you— again. I hope this is the last I ever see you. You'll never know how hard it was to leave you so long ago. But if you continue to oppose Lucifer here, he will order me to kill you. I don't know if I can. Please, Scion—go away! Please...

CHAPTER 71

Later that night, Scion secretly slipped out of Virginia and sped into space—but not toward heaven. His cup of shame, fear, and guilt was brimming over. He had to get away to make sense of what had just happened—and figure out how he was going to respond. After several hours of looking for the right place, he spotted it—Ganymede. He quickly landed and walked to the entrance of a large cavern.

"So, this is where it all began," Scion whispered as he looked into the darkness where he and Kai had pleaded with Lucifer to repent. *If only he had agreed to come back,* Scion sighed.

As he stepped into the cave, the total silence seemed to coil around Scion's grieving heart like a cosmic boa constrictor. Scion knew had to talk out his feelings. His gut was boiling with a furnace of emotions.

"You gave up, Lucifer! You—*the shining one*—gave up on God! You gave up on heaven! You gave up on *me* . . . and took the most precious thing in my life—Kai! And now look at me! *Aaaaagh!* How I hate you!" he howled as he crumpled to his knees.

"And I hate myself! I waited and waited for a way to clear my name. When I finally got the opportunity to prove myself, I blew it. The colony is lost. Thousands of people may go to hell because I failed again. Who in heaven is going to believe that I did my best to save Jamestown when they find out my former best friend was guarding it? I'm doomed.

"And Kai . . . I thought if I found you, I could convince you to come back with me. I thought maybe we could somehow get you restored. If you would only repent. You are banished forever, but anything is possible with God. Look how he forgave humans of all their sins. Kai, it's worth a try!"

Scion grabbed the small medal on the gold chain around his neck—the one Kai had given him long ago.

"Kai, it looks like we will never be together again. I wish I had never met you in Jamestown. All these years, I had hope that we would meet again, and you would repent. But now, I have no hope. You're gone forever. And part of me will die forever.

"How am I going to tell Michael and the rest of the Host when I get back? I'll have to resign from the academy. Everyone will shun me. I don' know if I can do it."

Then, a strange feeling came over Scion. "But what if I didn't go back? What if I . . . O God, can I really say it? What if I *joined Kai*? I would lose heaven—but gain Kai. I know he would welcome me back. I know we could have some beautiful times together—like the old days."

A wave of relief swept over him. It actually seemed like he could choose Kai and not heaven—but that thought terrified him. "O God, I wish I had never been created. This is too hard to bear. I don't want to choose!" he cried out in agony.

And so it went. As giant moon made one full orbit around Jupiter over seven earth-days, Angel 24 wailed and moaned like a motherless child into the infinite deafness of the galaxy. No angel in heaven has ever known such despair.

CHAPTER 72

December 15, 1621

A few days after Scion arrived on Ganymede, a Beta angel picked up an audio signal only spirits can hear while cruising past Jupiter on a routine patrol. It was Scion, *still sobbing*. Within minutes, General Michael dispatched a rescue team. "Bring him home," Michael ordered with tears in his eyes. They had been searching the cosmos for him since Angie reported his disappearance a week ago. Angel Academy broke into spontaneous applause during classes when they heard that he had been found.

After a day of rest, Scion was summoned to Heaven's War Room, where General Michael had his office. Scion entered the massive room whose walls were covered with pictures of angels who had died in eons of battles with Lucifer's forces. Scion just stood—shaken and ashamed. Then, with a quickness that belied his gigantic size, the fiercest warrior in heaven rushed forward to hug his wounded angel. They both wept. Finally, Michael released Scion and motioned for him to take a seat. Scion wiped away his tears and spoke.

"General Michael, I want to thank you again for bringing me back. I knew you would find me, but I had no idea that you would be so gracious. If I had known that Okeus was Kai, I never would've accepted the assignment. But you knew that, didn't you?"

"I did, laddie. In point of fact, I suggested to the Lord that he send ya specifically to deal with Kai. The Lord and I 'ave had many long talks about yer situation. I know ya have suffered fer thousands of years because yer reputation was in question when ya didn't fight in the Rebellion."

"General, I could not return and fight against my best friends. I know I let the Lord down then. Now, I have failed the Lord again."

"Now, now, son. Yer lookin' at it all wrong. We dinnae send ya fer the Lord's sake. We sent ya fer yer own sake!"

Those words struck Scion mute as his mind tried to wrap itself around them.

"Scion, the Lord and I knew ya cannae fight those ya love the most. He understood why ya didn't come back when the battle was on."

"He . . . he d-doesn't b-b-blame me?" Scion blurted out. "But I was never allowed to leave the academy. I thought I was being disciplined."

"O, Scion, I wish I hadda known ya felt dat way. No, I put ya in Angel Academy to protect ya from the other angels who dinnae trust yer loyalty. I knew they would hurt ya more. I knew Kai would show 'is hand one day and then I would send ya to stop him. That t'was the best way to show everyone who ya really are—one of our best angels . . . and just a wee bit crumbled around the edges," Michael chuckled with a kind smile.

"Now, it nay turned oot like I thought. At first, I really thought that ya could save the colony. You and Angie are quite a good team. But Kai was far more clever than I knew. 'Tis easy to see why Lucifer prefers him so much. And the humans in Jamestown were far too easy to tempt. It twasn't yer fault, Scion.

"The Lord and I agree that you need some time off. Angel 442 can wrap things up there. In a short while, the colony will be in great distress. Their sins will destroy them. The Lord and I are very grieved that we couldna save the colony. Sadly, the colonists love their sins more than they love the Lord.

"Maybe in twenty or twenty-five years, we will try again to plant a colony there. In the meantime, the northern Virginia colony at Plymouth is doing well. They 'ave made friends with the natives and their main focus is pleasing the Lord. This is a group the Lord kin use to found that nation.

"So, Scion, I want ya to stay here and serve in the Great Library. 'Tis a good place to rest after all ya 'ave been through. I've instructed the head librarian, Nacham, to give ya a desk in the stacks below the first floor. He says he remembers ya from the academy. He tells me ya changed his life when he was a stinker there. I think he will take good care of ya," Michael grinned with a big wink.

"At any rate, ya will have no proper duties, and so ya can explore the histories of people and nations as ya wish. Perhaps ya will find encouragement and strength to go forward with yer life as you read about the struggles and victories of other people and angels who 'ave gone before ya. God bless ya, my son. Thank ya for doing what ya did ta save the colony."

Weeping now, with his head hung low, Scion could only whisper, "I don't know what to say, General Michael. I am grateful . . . but aside from Mola, I'm not sure any other angels will ever trust me."

"Be patient, lad. In time, in time."

"Well, if you ever need someone to stand guard over the moons of Jupiter, I would certainly volunteer," Scion concluded wryly.

Michael looked at him with tenderness. "Righto . . . Well, ya best be going. I will check on ya from time to time. Till then, be at peace. The

Lord knows yer heart, and he knows ya did yer best. In time, I think other angels will see it that way, too."

"Master Okeus, we just received word from Mola that Scion has been demoted to a librarian. They found him blubbering on a moon of Jupiter and brought him back."

"Thank you, Snookus. At least we will not have to worry about him again."

Okeus turned away, looked up into the dark sky with its twinkling stars, and muttered, "Rest well, my friend—but do not come back here—or I may have to kill you."

CHAPTER 73

January 6, 1622

The swoosh of his shuffling bare feet and his heavy sighs were the only sounds Scion made as he roamed the vast stacks in the basement of the Great Library. There were trillions of records—every detail of every human life recorded by special scribe angels assigned to each person who has ever lived. There were also detailed histories of every nation on Earth. As he scanned the records on Japan, Scion was shocked. "Incredible—I never knew all that. My classes at the Academy should have spent more time here," he muttered as he put the book about Christians in Japan* back on the shelf. But then he saw a different kind of book. It was from Earth.

"Hmm . . . the King James Bible of 1611.* Yes—the very king who authorized the charter of the Jamestown Colony." Flipping the book open, his eyes fell on Ezekiel 22:30:*

> And I sought for a man among them, that should make up the hedge, and stand in the gap before me for the land, that I should not destroy it: but I found none.

Scion had never seen that verse before, but it reminded him of verses he had once taught at the Academy. He quickly turned to 2 Chronicles 7:13–14:*

> If I shut vp heauen that there bee no raine, or if I command the locusts to deuoure the land, or if I send pestilence among my people: If my people which are called by my Name, shall humble themselues and pray, and seeke my face, and turne from their wicked wayes: then will I heare from heauen, and will forgiue their sinne, and will heale their land.

"Now this is amazing. The Lord says he *will heal the land* if his people repent. But Ezekiel 22 says if God could find just *one man* to stand before the Lord on behalf of the land, God would not destroy it.*

Great God in heaven!" Scion exclaimed, all too loudly. "Why have I never seen that before in the Bible? I thought that for God to heal a city or nation—or a colony—most people in that region would have to repent. But Ezekiel says even *one person* can prevent God from destroying a land. *Extraordinary!* Perhaps one person was all God wanted at that unique time. But if one person is enough sometimes, it certainly must be true that God can use *only a few people* to repent for a nation—not the majority, as I thought before."

Just then, a scene flashed before Scion's mind. He remembered a young Jewish boy running up to the statue of Moses near Angel Academy. There was an inscription on that statue that read: "And the LORD repented of the evil which he thought to do unto his people" (Exodus 32:14).

"That's it!" Scion exclaimed. "The Israelites made a golden calf to worship while Moses was on the mountain getting the Ten Commandments from God. God was outraged. He had just rescued the Israelites from Egypt, and as soon as Moses left the camp, they turned back to idols."*

He wondered if those were just isolated verses. Scion flipped the pages so fast they were close to ripping. There it was, Exodus 32:9–10:

> And the Lord said unto Moses, I haue seene this people, and behold, it is a stiffenecked people. Now therefore let me alone, that my wrath may waxe hot against them, and that I may consume them: and I will make of thee a great nation.

"God told Moses to stand aside so he could destroy the rebellious people of Israel," "Scion murmured. "But Moses stood in the gap before God on behalf of Israel, and God did not destroy Israel as he had planned to do.

"Why have I never connected that story in Exodus to Ezekiel 22:30? I guess I need to read the Bible more when I get back to heaven," Scion smirked.

He sat down on the floor and flipped through the pages at lightning speed. "I wonder if I can still read five thousand words a minute," he chuckled to himself. He was on a quest. He could feel his mind and heart coming alive again. Then he found another verse:

> And said, O my God, I am ashamed, and blush to lift vp my face to thee, my God: for our iniquities are increased ouer our head, and our trespasse is growen up unto the heauens.(Ezra 9:6)

"There's Ezra, the Jewish priest standing in the gap for his people. He was repenting for the sins of his entire nation.* Incredible!"

Scion slowly lowered the Bible to his lap and leaned his furled wings against the towering stacks of books. His mind was racing. His heart was beating rapidly.

"If this is true, my life may not be over. If this is true, I may yet save the colony!" But then a thought came like a dark cloud.

“Those are all Old Testament verses. Maybe it’s not true in the New Testament. Or maybe it’s true only for Jews.”

Then, with a jolt of surprise, he blurted out, “But wait a minute—Jesus claimed that he was the Lamb of God who came to take away the sins of the world. So that means Jesus stood in the gap for all mankind—like Moses did for the Jews.*”

Scion gasped. “And now, Christians are God’s ambassadors on Earth.* They are God’s ‘royal priesthood’* who can stand in the gap before God and repent for the sins of others . . . even for our colony!

“Holy Hallelujah! We *can* do it—like Moses did it! Christians in Jamestown can still save the colony! God can still birth that nation from our colony to reach the world for Jesus—and I don’t have to fail again.”

Then, Scion's eyes opened even wider. "Long ago, I failed to return to heaven and fight against my friends—but this time, I’m going back!

“This time, I *will* fight Kai if I have to . . . and with the help of others, we will defeat him—for the Lamb who stood in the gap on the cross for all humanity!”

Slamming the Bible closed, Scion jumped up and danced with his hands in the air. “Hallelujah! Hallelujah! Wait till Angie hears. Wait till Morph hears—he will squawk like an Irish banshee!”

“Like *what*? Who is Morph?” a grinning Nacham asked as he watched Scion twirling in the stacks. “I heard a commotion. I thought some of my old friends had come down here to party.”

Looking sheepish, Scion combed his long blond hair with his fingers and straightened out his wing feathers.

“Are you celebrating because of the new Virginia colony at Plymouth?” Nacham asked. “I heard things are going really well in Plymouth.* Those Pilgrims, as they call them, are something else.

Father God is so pleased with them. He calls them a City on a Hill in a dark continent."

"Dark continent," Scion repeated. "Well, Nacham, there are going be two bright hill cities soon. I'm headed back to Jamestown with some great news."

"But I heard that Father had to abandon that group," Nacham casually remarked.

"Not for long. Have you read the Bible recently? Our Christians there can still save that colony."

"You can do that?" Nacham asked with surprise.

"I can't, and you can't, and the entire Host of Heaven can't—but Christians can! Followers of Jesus are the only creatures in the universe who are authorized to stand in the gap before God so that God will heal and bless the land."

"Incredible. I had no idea," Nacham said.

Tossing the King James Bible to him, Scion laughed, "Look it up. Ezekiel 22:30 and 2 Chronicles 7:13–14."

Scion smiled and unfurled his massive wings. "I must be going. Thank you for your hospitality, Nacham."

"It's been a pleasure to have you here. I have six more years here, and then I get my first Earth assignment. I can't wait."

"You will do well," Scion said. "Remember that day at the academy when you asked me to forgive you for scaring the Jewish family? That's when I knew you would be an excellent angel. Repentance in a man or in an angel is a sign of God's heart in them."

Nacham's face turned red with emotion. "Thank you for saying that, Master Scion. But, before you go—who Morph is and why would he squawk like an Irish banshee?"

Scion grinned and lifted his hand in a short salute. "That, my friend, is a very long answer for another time."

*March 19, 1622**

"This is a good day to kill." Okeus laughed into the minds of Mongo and Opie as they meditated at an altar of broken bear bones and tangled deer antlers in the Great Swamp. They had both come a long way to get final instructions from Okeus himself. This assignment was that important. Deep within his trance, Opie's muscular body convulsed violently as the presence of Okeus surged within him. Opie was now ready.

"The trap is finally set," Okeus gloated. "After four years of deceptions,* we have lulled the English to sleep with feigned friendship and many nights of sharing meals around their home fires." *

"Ha! What a fitting time to kill—Friday, just like the Friday when my father killed the Spanish priests,"* Mongo's voice gurgled in the trance.

"You surprise me with your memory, Mongo. I may have bigger plans for a man like you when we get rid of this British infestation."

"Thank you, Lord Okeus," Mongo fawned. "You are so kind."

"*Me?* Kind?" the scaly dinosaur roared. "*Never* insult me like that!" Okeus growled. "I just want to use you and abuse you. That's all you will ever get from me. That's all any of us will get on Earth. Do you understand?"

Mongo cowered in silence. Then Opie spoke up, "What about our father, Paq, Lord Okeus? He has betrayed us. Will he die too?"

"No, not Father!" Mongo moaned.

Looking at Mongo's upturned face, Okeus slowly bared his frightening orange fangs in a devilish grin. "You will kill him, Mongo. He has brought great dishonor on your family. It is only fitting that one of his sons should bring his treasonous body down to the grave." His eyes danced with hatred.

Mongo shook with fear. "This is not our way—to kill one's father. A niece who has betrayed us, yes, but surely not my father."

Opie spoke, "I'll do it. I can kill anyone who loves our enemy more than his own people."

"No, your brother shall do it!" Okeus snapped. "You are the chief. You must keep your hands clean of such matters in the eyes of your people."

Mongo bowed his head in shamed agreement. He knew his life was at stake. "I will obey, Lord Okeus."

"Yes, you will—or I will kill you *both . . . slowly*," Okeus snorted angrily.

"But what if the whites find out about the attack before we get to all the homes?" Opie asked anxiously.

Human sacrifices to Okeus*

"That won't happen if your brother does his job well," Okeus barked. "Opie, you have an English captive now, do you not? Make sure that the white maggot is skinned alive and offered to me the night before the attack. Then, with a sacrifice as worthy as that, I can give you all the power you will need to destroy every white invader of my domain—including their children."

Opie grinned. "It seems like we are ready. I just hope Scion does not return now and frustrate our plans."

"If he does show up, I have a wonderful distraction planned for him," Okeus boasted with a wicked belly laugh.

CHAPTER 74

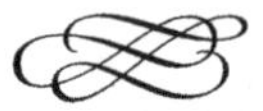

March 19, 1622

"Scion, *you are back*!" Angie squealed with girlish delight as Scion suddenly dropped down into the clearing at Moss Valley with a thud.

Morph buzzed around the clearing, spinning over and over as he flew and shouted, "Yes! Yes! He's back! Yes! Yes!"

Angie looked at Scion and laughed. "Well, I guess that's as close to joy as you get from a demon." The two angels both stared at the whirling, winged cat and laughed hard.

"O, Master Scion. I thought we had lost you for good. I heard what Okeus did to you. One of the guard demons told Morph."

Scion grimaced. "It was one of the worst experiences I've ever had. I used to have nightmares for hundreds of years about something like that happening . . . and then it did. But you know what? I can go on!" Scion shouted and then laughed the biggest laugh he'd ever had on Earth.

Hearing this, Angie and Morph exploded with joy. Happy tears streaming down her face, Angie tried to give Scion a hug around his beefy neck. *Fail!* Morph just fell to the ground, flapping his stubby, black wings erratically with a silly, toothy grin.

After a few moments, they both calmed down. "Master Scion, tell us, tell us! What is your plan?" Angie cried.

"Well, it's a long shot, but God gave the Israelites a lifeline when they got in trouble with him. They rarely used it, but it's there in the Bible."

"Really?" Angie grinned as she wiped her tear-streaked face dry. "Tell me, tell me!" she exclaimed.

"I discovered in the Great Library that God will change his mind about punishing the sins of a group if some of God's people will repent for those sins. Ezekiel 22:30 and 2 Chronicles 7:13–14 describe it clearly."

"Wow, I can't believe I forgot those verses," Angie smiled.

"Exactly! God's great escape plan—the best one the Jews had until Messiah came."

"That's all they had to do?" Angie asked incredulously. "No big sacrifices of bulls, goats, or lambs? No weeks of fasting? No national sackcloth and ashes days like at Nineveh?"

"No, just true repentance by his people in word and deed. Remember, God loved those Jews as his own children. He wanted to make it as easy as possible to bring them back to himself. So, when God judged them in wrath, all they had to do was humble themselves and repent to save their land from God's judgment on the sins of the nation."*

"Well," Angie shouted excitedly, "let's do that! Let's get this Anglican colony to obey those verses!"

Morph piped up. "But how are you going to find enough English colonists here who will repent like that? This is a rough group. That's why Okeus is so sure he can destroy it."

"Wait a minute, Scion!" Angie screamed as she flew right in front of his face.

"Those verses didn't say English people had to repent; it said *'my people.'*"

"You're right, Angie!" Scion blurted out. "You are so right! *Any* believer in this colony can repent for the sins of the colony. We just have to find them and get them together to do it."

Angie asked, "But how? The believers are spread out all over the colony, and many are guarded by demons. If Okeus finds out about this, he will kill them first."

Scion's face darkened. He had to collect and protect those believers somehow. But how? He stared at Morph and Angie for a moment. Then, suddenly, a very non-traditional idea flashed into his mind. "Angie, I think I have it . . . but it will take you and Morph to make it work."

"Both of us?" Morph gulped.

Morph and Angie shot excited smiles at each other. "Did I hear you right, Master Scion? Do you really want Morph and I to help you save the colony? Are you sure this is 'by the book'? I don't want to get you in trouble," Angie said with a wink.

"Okay, okay, Angie. You are right again. I am not the angel I used to be. Believe it or not, I've actually learned some things from watching you both. In fact, I can't imagine any other spirits who can make this plan work better than you guys!"

Angie's and Morph's jaws dropped. Angie thought, *Who is this angel, and what did they do with Scion?*

"I can hardly believe I am saying this—but it's true," Scion belly-laughed as he scooped up the two small spirits, one in each of his massive hands, and brought them close to his face. "You both have taught me a lot. I used to be terrified of making mistakes. I thought following rules rigidly was the only way I could survive down here. But real life is different from school, isn't it?"

Looking affectionately at the mangy little furball in his left hand, Scion whispered, "Morph, you were put on the wrong team for a long time. But we all now know that Jesus touched you in a special way so that you would help us save this colony."

Morph looked at Angie, and Angie looked at Morph, silent and stunned. Then, Angie's hand moved toward Morph's arm. Morph saw it. Fear filled his face, but inside, a warm feeling began to flow—a feeling he had not experienced since he had watched Paquiquino become a follower of Jesus.

Seeing what was happening, Scion cupped his hands together, and the two spirits slid into each other awkwardly with a bump, making Angie grab Morph's paw to steady herself. Scion smiled as her five bright pink fingers entwined within the dark, furry paw of the trembling demon.

For a moment, no one moved or spoke. They all knew this was a moment that God had ordained in some mysterious way. Then, after a few seconds, Scion shouted with new authority in his voice, "Well, folks, it's time to get to work. We have a colony to save!"

Angie and Morph realized they were still holding hands and quickly shook loose of each other, looking embarrassed—but not upset. Then, shaking their woozy heads a bit, they both leaped into the air to await Scion's orders.

"Okay, first, we're going to need a bunch of the believers to help us." Scion was now on the ground with one knee, drawing in the dirt between the deep moss. "Okay, here's the James River and the Pamunkey River. There are about twenty different plantations along both rivers with believers we need for a big prayer meeting. Bring some African slaves and some of those indentured English women.

We also could use some Powhatan believers, especially Paquiquino. And some British believers, of course. We need to gather them here at Moss Valley at 10:00 p.m. tomorrow night.

"The believers are closely guarded by demons. So, Morph, this is where you come in."

"Me?" Morph winced. "Just *me*? What about Angie?"

"Well, Morph," Scion began in his best professorial voice, "normally, I would have Angie work with you—you being a demon and all that. And, normally, I would require a detailed outline of how you plan to get those believers out from under the snotty snouts of those guard demons, but now...," Scion had to stop and chuckle. "Now, just go do it! After all, who knows how to trick a demon better than a demon?" Scion laughed.

With eyes bulging with surprise and glee, Morph bared his fangs in delight, saluted like a pirate with his deformed wing, and shot off with a brazen *"Meooow!"*

Scion and Angie doubled over with laughter. "We just sent a demon to do an angel's work, Angie!" Scion blurted.

Angie looked up at Scion and spoke very deliberately, "*No,* Master Scion. *We* didn't. *You* did!"

Scion pursed his lips for a moment. "I guess I did! I really did! I probably just broke about a dozen rules from Angel Academy. And I liked it!" Scion exclaimed. "Hallelujah! I'm free! Free to be me—*finally*! "

Then, looking suddenly serious, the big angel admitted, "If I let them, my old fears could still get the best of me. I know we are sticking our necks out now—especially after God has decided to abandon this settlement. But much is at stake. I really can't expect Michael to understand what we are about to do—especially using Morph. Hopefully, if we can help save the colony, he will be grateful. In any case, *Alea iacta est*—'the die is cast,' as Julius Caesar once said."

"Oh, you know that quote too!" Angie joked.

"Yes—I taught it to you in class, smarty-pants," Scion smirked. Then with a serious look, he said, "I have to go now and meet with Okeus one more time to make this work."

CHAPTER 75

March 21, 1622

As he flew west, Scion checked the two pointer stars of Ursa Major —*Dubhe* and *Merak*—and lined them up to find the North Star to calculate the time.* The imaginary line from the North Star that showed the time was about forty-five degrees to the right of vertical. Scion mumbled to himself, "Amazing what you can learn in the Great Library. These humans are pretty clever to have figured out centuries ago how to tell time this way. It's almost 9:00 p.m. I've got to distract Okeus for three hours. Lord, help me!"

As he approached his destination, he looked for the big, oval lake that sat like an evil eye in the middle of the vast swamp. "There it is," Scion muttered with grim determination.

When the Powhatan god spied him, he demanded with a snarl, "What are you doing here, you pig?" Twelve of his most intimidating guards snapped to attention and drew their swords.

"I'm here to talk—to make you a deal. I may have failed this colony, but I'm not ready to give up on saving you." At those words, the guards looked at each other nervously.

"Silence! My demons are listening. Come this way. We'll talk."

Okeus shuffled his sixteen-foot reptilian body to the other side of the clearing near the lake, so they could talk privately. Scion followed.

Okeus plopped down on his tail and stared at Scion with pure contempt. "Okay, what is it *now*? I thought we were done. Did you come to ask for mercy? *Forget it.* My job is to stop all followers of the Lamb from coming here. By tomorrow, they will all be dead, and your old, foolish lord will have to build his little missionary nation somewhere else. It just breaks my heart."

"I know all about your plans, Kai."

Okeus's eyes squinted nervously. "You *do*? How?"

"I'm afraid you don't have a need to know. And as we both know, there are real dangers from leaking classified information," Scion smiled slyly. "No, Kai, I did not come to plead for the colony. I know you have won, and I have failed. I come to plead *for you*. I've spent over thirteen thousand years mourning for you. Before I leave Virginia for the last time, I want to give you one more chance. Come back with me. I really believe God *would* forgive you. *Just ask* for his forgiveness and repent for your rebellion. He is very gracious. He always wants mercy to triumph over judgment."

"Oh, *shut up*, Scion! That's a bunch of religious fish snot, and you know it! I'm no idiot. I read the book where his son says that the devil and his angels go to hell. That would be *me*. You're wasting your time. All of us cooked our goose when we let Satan trick us into fighting Michael and his army. *What a joke*! Michael was only going to banish Lucifer. But Lucifer told us that all of his friends were going to be kicked out of heaven too. So naturally, *we fought*.

"No, Scion. I got sucked into one lie; I'm *not* going to be deceived by another. You're wasting your time. Just go back to heaven and enjoy the silence of the library. I'm sure your buddy Mola can cut a deal with Michael so you will be safe from the other angels."

"Mola—how do you know about him? What has he got to do with anything? I'm talking about you and me right now."

"I have my sources—just like you do. I also know that sniveling little Voudoc has been trying to get back at me. He sent those blasted black lamb-lovers here to torment me. He is also recruiting some of my own demons to oppose me. As soon as I finish with your colony, I'm going to pay a certain foolish, butt-faced monkey a visit he will *not* forget!"

"Kai, how can I prove to you that I am serious about helping you?"

"You can't! Go back to the library where you belong. I never want to see you again!" the exasperated dinosaur roared menacingly.

Scion frowned. He knew he had to act now. He moved closer to Kai and exclaimed, "I know how I can prove it! I'll be right back. I am going to get you a list of every demon who has tried to rebel against you. Stay right where you are, friend!" Scion shouted as he leaped into the bright, moonlit sky.

The guards heard the angel call Okeus "friend." Okeus turned and saw the confusion on their faces. *Batcrap! I'd better do something to calm those dolts down. I cannot afford any rumors about a friendship with Scion,* Okeus quickly concluded with a loud belch.

Looking over at his very unnerved guards, Okeus twirled his claw next to his skull and shouted, "Don't worry, maggots! He's gone mad. Losing the colony has damaged his feeble mind. Can you believe—he says he is leaving to get a list of my demons who have betrayed me? This will be rich! Now I know he has flipped! Wait till Lucifer hears this one!"

Sixty minutes later, Scion touched down again in front of Okeus. But, unbeknownst to the hulking, seaweed-green lizard, thousands of curious demons now filled the forest around his swamp throne. They had secretly abandoned their guard posts near Jamestown when Morph told a few of them what Scion was about to do. The news spread quickly. Every demon who heard about it was determined to see what was going to happen. Nothing like this had ever happened in the Great Bay. Incredibly, the horde of curious demons had all snuck into the forest nearby, unobserved by Okeus or his guards. The guards were still very distracted after Scion's last visit.

With five thousand pairs of yellow demon eyes fixed on him, Scion handed Okeus a small piece of paper. "Here is your list of traitors. Hopin, Scopin, Mopin, Flopin, Dunt, Fard, Snoozle, Og, Butz, Guano, Splatz, Doltt . . . and Morph."

Okeus farted loudly with excitement and spat green mucus on the ground several times, "*Morph*—I knew it! I knew it! Now I will pull him limb from limb. And the other twelve idiots on the list—my favorite clowns—they are all worthless, broken scumbags."

Okeus waved the little list triumphantly over his thickly scaled head and loudly announced to his guards, "Look, look, you scumbags! Your master even commands angels to rat out my traitors! So tomorrow, we will give my Judas demons a proper death salute at the tip of our blades!"

A crescendo of roars filled the night air—but not one demon budged an inch. "This is the stuff of *legends*," one guard whispered. "I can't wait to tell Warrts when I relieve him at the Rolfe plantation tomorrow."

Turning back to his smiling angel visitor, Okeus softly whispered, "Okay, Scion, what is that going to cost me? Come over here where no one else can listen to your foolish chatter." They moved closer to the edge of the dark lake.

Just as Scion began to speak, Okeus turned his head away. The love shining out of Scion's sky-blue eyes was too painful for him to observe. "Kai, all I want is for you to give up everything you don't want," Scion whispered. Kai recoiled in confusion.

"You hate Lucifer, and you don't want to burn forever. Give them both up! Abandon Lucifer, repent to God, and avoid the fire. That's what it will cost you!"

Okeus cringed, but only slightly, lest his watching guards think something was wrong. He whispered, "You are ridiculous! Look at my realm! My loyal subjects. What more could I want? I also have benefits here you cannot imagine." Turning to Scion now, Okeus added with a wicked smile, "Have you ever been inside a person like I have? I can feel what they feel in their skin! It's incredible! I'm hooked on it. You really should try it!" he taunted.

Glancing at his intrigued guards, Okeus stomped over to Scion, grabbed him by his muscular left arm, and yanked him up close to his bared, six-inch teeth. As the powerful reptile god gazed at the calm angel dangling before him, a shudder went through his body. He saw Scion looking at him like he used to look at Kai. With great effort, Okeus forced his mind to focus elsewhere. Then, so every demon guard could hear him, he ferociously blared, "Just go away, you demented failure—before I do something you will really regret!"

Suddenly, thousands of demons sucked in their sulfurous breath as Scion smiled, reached out, and gently put his hand on the powerful, reptilian claw that held him. No one had ever touched Okeus and lived. Scion knew he had to be discrete. "*Please,* Kai," Scion whispered, "come back. You mean so much to me. Let's be friends again like we once were."

Okeus was unnerved. He couldn't look at Scion a second more. The dinosaur's big red eyes suddenly disappeared under his thick, reptilian, nictitating eye membranes. It was a stalemate. They both knew it.

CHAPTER 76

Scion nervously glanced at the three stars again. *Dear Jesus! We need more time.*

Suddenly, Snookus spurted over to Okeus. The gangling octopus whispered something that made Okeus instantly release his grip on Scion. Then, with a single swoosh of his forty-five-foot, semi-transparent green wings, the startled lizard leaped into the air. He hovered at one hundred feet and quickly scanned the perimeter.

He bared his six-inch fangs as he spotted them—thousands of sentries hiding in the trees around the camp. "What the hell are you all doing here?" he demanded. "I did not summon you!" He dove to a tall pine tree, grabbed it with a massive claw and shook it like a ragdoll. Ten terrified demons fell to the mud. "Why are you not guarding Jamestown?" Then, glaring at another group hiding in the bushes, he barked, "And what caused you to stop guarding the river plantations? Don't you remember what we are doing tomorrow?"

Then, Okeus spun around and looked back at Scion with fire in his bulging crimson eyes. Bursts of yellow fumes chugged from his mouth as his anger rose like lava surging upward within Krakatoa. Every demon sensed it. They cringed in horror.

"You did this!" he screamed as he pointed his right claw at Scion. "You did all this to distract my guards and lure them here. You did all this to trick me! That's why this ridiculous affair took so long. Lies! All lies! I knew it! Everything you said to me was just a lie!" After alighting back on the ground, Okeus savagely pulled up a small maple tree and threw it at Scion. Then, in a blind rage, Okeus grabbed a demon who had fallen out of the pine tree moments earlier.

"See this, Scion? This worm is you! This is what I am going to do to you, you backstabbing loser!" And with that, Okeus bit off the demon's head and tore its body apart limb by limb. In an instant, hordes of evil spirits exploded out of the forest and raced back to their assignments, screeching in terror. Only a few throne room guards stayed in the camp—and their knees shook uncontrollably.

Scion calmly walked toward the bloodthirsty dinosaur. "Yes, you are right. I needed to distract your sentries for a bit . . . but what I said about you is all true. Deep inside, you know it's true."

Pulling out his fearsome, curved sword with a twang of hardened steel, Okeus rushed toward Scion, his eyes glazed with crazed anger.

"Okeus, please . . . stop. I don't want to fight. I will leave now."

"*Too late!* You can't make a fool of me in front of my demons and just fly away!"

With a kick of one huge lizard leg, Okeus jumped into the air above Scion and came down, blade-first, to impale him. But angels move much faster than a Dark Angel in a bulky disguise. So, Scion deftly outmaneuvered the leaping lizard every time—and with a smile. He knew he was gaining precious time.

After several unsuccessful attempts to skewer Scion with jumps and thrusts, Okeus knew he had to discard his cumbersome disguise. He quickly calculated the cost. *My guards might tell all my demons that I have been deceiving them once they see I am a Dark Angel. No problem. I'll just kill them before they do.*

With a quick shake of his head, the fearsome dinosaur dissolved again into a dark green mist. Kai now stood—a twelve-foot Dark Angel with orange wrinkled skin, dark gray hair, red eyes under a black, hooded robe covering most of his face. His guards shrunk back and almost fainted. They huddled together for safety.

"Well, that's better, Kai. I'll bet your guards are wondering what your next trick is," Scion teased.

Looking at Scion like a bull ready to charge, Kai bellowed back, "My next trick is to demonstrate how to subtract 1 from 24! And to think we were once friends. I thought you might be different. You're just like the rest of them—a liar and a fraud! Tonight, pretty boy, you die! *Arghhhhh!*"

Kai leaped into the air and brought his sword down on Scion with the speed of a panther and the strength of one hundred grizzly bears. But Scion shot in the air and, without thinking, flashed his sword just in time to deflect Kai's crushing blow, causing sparks to erupt from the blades like fireworks in the night sky.

"So, you still know how to use a sword, Scion. I am surprised the academy didn't dull your skills," Kai laughed scornfully as he maneuvered to a better position for his next attack.

"Actually, I taught swordsmanship at the academy," Scion shot back with renewed fierceness in his voice. "Please, Kai. Stop this! I don't want to fight you. I will leave now."

"No, Scion. This is the end of our relationship . . . and the end of you!"

With that, he charged. Scion had no choice but to fight. And fight they did—back and forth for a ferocious hour. Thrust, parry, lunge, whirl away. Over and over. Kai was all offense. Scion was all defense.

"Are you ready to give up, Kai? I can play this game for a long time," Scion laughed, leaning against a tall oak tree. "You cannot kill me. And I will not kill you—because I choose not to. So why don't we—"

As Scion spoke, Kai slipped a hidden dagger out of his right sleeve. When Scion momentarily took his eyes off of him, Kai thrust the blade toward Scion. It found its mark and sliced deeply into Scion's right wrist, causing him to drop his sword. In an instant, Kai's sucker-kicked the defenseless angel against the old oak tree. Scion slid down the trunk into a heap, stunned and wounded.

Just as quickly, Kai's left hand seized a large, twin-forked spear nearby and pinned Scion's head to the trunk between the spear's horizontal forks. With his right hand, Kai raised his sword above his head and aimed it so the blade would slide down the shaft of the spear and neatly sever Scion's head from his neck.

For a moment, Kai seemed to hesitate. Scion didn't resist. He just looked at Kai with squinting, pleading eyes. He sensed that his time had come. As the enraged Dark Angel was about to strike, he bent over so that he could better see the terror in Scion's eyes.

But then something happened that neither angel expected.

In the nanosecond before Kai's muscular forearm began to pull the massive sword in a downward arc, Scion kicked Kai's head with his right foot in a last desperate defense move. Then, as Kai's neck snapped back, a small object on a gold chain flicked into view. Kai saw it.

Instantly, Kai howled like a man about to be burned alive, *"Noooooooo! Noooo! Then* Kai's sword and spear dropped from his limp hands as he crumpled to the ground, clutching the gold chain as if it were choking him to death.

Scion sat stunned for a moment and then yanked the forked spear off his neck, hardly believing what he was seeing. Kai was lying on his side, shaking, grunting and cursing furiously, eyes shut tight. Finally, after what seemed like an eternity to Scion, the Dark Angel stopped moving, sat up on one elbow and just stared at Scion. His face was contorted with fury—and a desperate pleading at the same time. At first, Scion head felt dizzy with a storm of confused emotions. Then, like a brilliant ray of sun piercing the storm, Scion's face broke forth into a smile with so much love that it pierced Kai like a red-hot poker.

"Aaggggh! Get out of here, Scion!" Kai screamed.

For several moments, Scion was intensely conflicted. His heart told him to stay with Kai—but his mind prevailed. The demon guards were already swooping in to rescue their master, even though they now knew he was a Dark Angel.

So, with a loud clap, Scion's golden wings snapped open, and he shot into the cold, damp night air to rendezvous with Angie and Morph at Moss Valley. As he leveled off at ten thousand feet, Scion looked back at the Great Swamp, sighed once more and smiled. Then he flipped over on his back and pulled into a steep dive toward Jamestown, shouting into the rushing wind with a giant grin, "I am alive! My colony is going to live! *Tonight,* they will stand in the gap! Our plan is working!"

But Kai's mind was not.

He had not moved since Scion left— not even to change into his dinosaur disguise. His guards just stood around him, dumbfounded and frightened. Kai just sat on the bug-infested swamp floor staring at the angel-wing medallion he clutched in his trembling hands.

CHAPTER 77

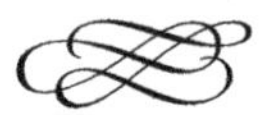

That Night

Cholie, a Caribbean slave, called the secret prayer meeting to order at 11 pm. Seventeen other women—six Powhatan squaws, five Englishwomen, and six other Caribbean slaves—sat in the circle, cross-legged on woven mats in Moss Valley while four men—Paquiquino, Chanco, Jehu, and John Rolfe—stood quietly behind Cholie. Everyone felt the sacredness and solemnity of the moment. Scion, Angie, and Morph hovered above, back to back, each scanning a third of the night sky for any approaching demons.

"Ya know why we is here," the graceful slave began. "Many of us, we is from Africa and England and be bought and hurt by da men on what dey call plantation. But God, he done send us ta make a *habitation,* not a plantation—a habitation for God's family through prayer, just like ole Joseph be sent for evil reasons ta Egypt in dat book God call Genesis. What da man mean for evil, God mean for good, as da good book say.

"Many sisters' ave done died, workin' hard in da fields or from da bad sickness. But da Spirit, he keep us alive ta call on the Lawd so dat he save dis colony. I dream last night, sister Jennifer' eard da Lawd say dat da power of darkness, dey be plannin' big evil on da colony."

Another Caribbean woman spoke up, "I pray last week. Da Spirit show me big hatchet try ta fall on da cross. Den, big arrows hit da hatchet. Hatchet slow down and da cross be cut but not broken."

A heavy stillness fell upon the gathered women. They all felt the Holy Spirit drawing them into prayer. Humming or groaning sounds could be heard as each believer worshipped the Lord. Then, an older Powhatan woman sang a spontaneous song to Jesus in her Algonquian tongue. The Caribbean ladies joined the music with their own words in their native languages. Others just hummed the tune, lost in a state of deep worship. Suddenly, Scion looked at Angie with wide eyes. The harmony of the voices had somehow shifted into a sound that went beyond normal human music. At the same moment, the atmosphere became electric with the presence of Almighty God as he slowly drew near the twenty-two worshippers.

"Lawd, we do worship thee! We do love thee! Come down an save us, O Lawd. We trust in you, Lawd, ta help us in dis valley of da shadow of death," Cholie intoned in her velvety island voice.

As she prayed, Scion could feel new strength flowing into his body. He also began to glow brighter as the Lord's presence drew closer.

"Fader God, forgive us!" Cholie cried out as she fell to her knees with her hands outstretched to heaven. "Dis colony done sinned against you. Fergive us, yer children, fer our sins and da sins of all da people who did come here before us."

Then, old Paquiquino slowly stood up. He had a regal bearing that everyone noticed. "My brothers and sisters, I speak a message from my brother who now in heaven, Pastor Hunt. Just before he die, he give me message from God's carvings that he call Bible." Pulling a wrinkled sheet of yellowed paper from a small deerskin pouch around his neck, the aging warrior handed it to Jehu to read.

After clearing his dry throat, the big Spaniard read 2 Chronicles 7:14,

> If my people which are called by my Name, shall humble themselues and pray, and seeke my face, and turne from their wicked wayes: then will I heare from heauen, and will forgiue their sinne, and will heale their land.

Scion blinked tears from his eyes as he realized something. *Hunt already knew what I discovered in the library!*

Paquiquino looked at each one in the group and then declared, "God give this land to my people. My people sin. Your people sin. Tonight, we must follow the carving Hunt give me. Tonight, we must do what carving say, so God can make our land good again."

Cholie and her English friend, Elizabeth, stood and prayed, "Lawd, we sorry. Please fergive us fer—"

"The love of money," Elizabeth admitted with a blush. "For loving money more than we love you. For trusting in money more than we trust in you."

A beautiful Jamaican got to her feet. Under her thin, ragged clothes, her back was streaked with scars from whippings. She cried out, "Fergive dis colony, Lawd, fer hurtin' people ta make da money!"

A gaunt, white woman with deep-set eyes prayed, "For trickin' us ta come from England as servants and then workin' us ta death."

"For looking to the stars for help and not to you, Jesus," a wizened Algonquian woman added.

"Forgive dis colony fer using us fer sex," a beautiful Cuban girl cried out, her high-pitched voice cracking with emotion.

"For addicting us and our families in England to tobacco," a sickly Englishwoman added despite her frequent coughs. John Rolfe nodded silently, with tears in his eyes.

"And for stealing native lands so that we grow more tobacco," the middle-aged, red-headed Englishwoman confessed.

"For we Spanish coming here to deceive the tribes so we could steal their lands!" Jehu blurted out in pain.

"For hating and killing the priests who came to tell us about Jesus," Paquiquino barely whispered.

"Amen! O Lawd have mercy on us, have mercy on dis colony!" the whole group prayed together. Rivulets of tears ran down all of their faces. "Give us another chance, Lawd. Do not abandon us."

Then, they all stood up. The four men joined the women in a circle with arms around each other in a slow rocking motion. Soon, the entire circle was swaying rhythmically back and forth as deep moans and weeping continued. Scion and Angie also wept but Morph couldn't. He just felt numb.

Almost imperceptibly, like a ship at sea slowly drifting into a thick fog bank, the twenty-two intercessors became engulfed in the heavy presence of God. Bodies fell to the dirt floor, face down, utterly overcome by the glory of the Lord. Some wept and whimpered as God healed their broken hearts. Others laughed hilariously, filled with his joy. Cholie was on the ground, grunting and groaning as if she was giving birth.

In invisible realms, she was.

Without a thought, Scion suddenly glorified into a white-hot light, his wings slowly extending to their entire majestic twenty-four feet, covering everyone below. Then, just as quickly, Morph darted under Scion's left outstretched wing, his blue eyes tightly shut. It was a light so intense that it could kill any demon.

Angie whispered with a giggle, "Wow—I can't even open my eyes, Scion. If I did, that light would burn out my purple pupils!"

Scion just smiled. "Oh, Angie, I could do this forever. When the Lord's presence gets this close, the pleasure of his presence is almost more than I can bear," Scion exclaimed under his breath.

"So, you say. I'm in pain!" Morph hissed from under Scion's wing. *"Ahhhhhhgh!* It torments me on the outside. But," he sheepishly admitted, "in a crazy way, I feel really good inside," Morph concluded with a loud snicker.

Angie had to tease him, "Your poor little demon spirit does not like the glory of the Lord? That just breaks my angelic heart. Maybe you'd better scat, cat!"

"Are you an idiot? My wing spot is glowing so bright now I'd be seen and shredded by demons before you could count to ten. Besides—and you're going to be shocked—'cause I am—I actually get *more* strength from this happy feeling inside than I ever got from the sins of people. It's *fantastic!* Someday, I will have to tell my friends about this!"

But then Scion heard something. A roar, like a massive tornado, was descending from high above. Seven dozen large warrior angels suddenly appeared and circled Moss Valley.

The Lord is here, Scion and Angie realized at the same time. They bowed their heads low as the Lord of Glory arrived with great majesty among the twenty-two intercessors still transfixed in deep worship on the forest floor. Instantly, every human felt the presence of Jesus. They could move or even open their eyelids. The weight of his glory was so profound even breathing was difficult.

Then, Jesus raised his nail-scarred hands toward heaven and began to pray as crashes of throaty thunder echoed across the cloudless night sky.

"Abba, you promised that if your people repent, you would forgive their sins—present and past. You promised that you would heal the land of your judgments against it. I call upon you now to honor my shed blood for your children here and fulfill your word to them. These twenty-two have stood in the gap on behalf of this sinful colony. Hear their prayers and set this land free from your righteous judgment. Thank you, Father, for giving me whatever I ask."

Instantly, the twenty-two sensed that God had heard their prayers. Feeling the strange weight come off her body, Cholie quickly stood to her feet and shouted, *"It be done!* We' ave released da victory of Calvary on dis place. God, he done hear us! Da Lamb of God' as conquered for us!"

"Wahoo!" With a victory whoop, the rest stood, locked arms, and formed two concentric rings. Then, without a word, both circles instinctively danced in opposite directions. It was a Jewish *Horah* dance of victory, even though the jubilant intercessors did not know the term. The Spirit led them, just as he led Miriam in her victory dance at the Red Sea.

Just above their heads, the eighty-four angels joined in the dance. They created three vertical layers of dance circles, each higher group fewer in numbers than the one below.

"Looks like a wedding cake of dancers," Angie giggled. "I want to dance! Come on, Scion!"

"No, really, Angelique, I'm much too old for that, you know, uh . . ."

Just then, Jesus looked at Scion and *winked!*

Scion saw it, smiled and then gently took Angie's tiny hand. "I believe this is our dance, Angel Angie," the tall, bright angel announced with a boyish smile. Angie curtsied with a demure grin and a low bow—while her other hand shielded her eyes from Scion's slowly diminishing glow. Morph just hung on to Scion's fluffy wingpit—eyes closed but grinning wildly like a cat in an endless field of catnip.

Then, as Jesus watched like a proud father, Angie and Scion glided together in a slow arc above Moss Valley with the grace of a butterfly and the majesty of an eagle. The "angel-cake dancers" cheered and spun faster.

But no one enjoyed the spectacle more than the Lord. As he arose to return to heaven, Jesus clapped his hands and laughed so loudly that it shook the gates of hell itself.

His colony had just been reborn!

CHAPTER 78

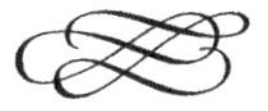

March 22, 1622*

Cruel was the wind that blew in the blood-red dawn that Friday.

All through the night, several thousand half-naked* Powhatan warriors slithered into positions along a fifty-mile swath of the James River—home to thirty-one English tobacco plantations.* Plantations such as the Powell's,* Ewen's,* the Treasurer,* Barrows Hill,* Bennett's,* Bassie's Choice,* Mulberry Island,* Smith's Hundred,* Hog's Island,* Westover,* Berkley Hundred,* and especially John Rolfe's Plantation.* The colony had become rich growing Rolfe's tobacco—on stolen Powhatan lands.

As the sun rose into the cloudless winter sky, waves of warriors began to seep into settlement homes along the river. They arrived to share breakfast with families, as they had done many times. Cabin doors swung open with hearty greetings. The night before, about a hundred Powhatans had brought gifts of deer, turkey, fish, and fresh or dried fruits to the plantation families.* "We be back tomorrow when sun up. We eat with you," the warriors promised.

"The fox is in the henhouse," Okeus muttered as he swooped along the river, watching his followers distribute the food. "We have fattened them for the kill, haven't we, Snookus?"

"O Master, Lord Lucifer will be so proud of you. He has often said that slaughtering 'friends' reminds him of how he won his freedom from heaven."

But Richard and Isabelle Pace* and their 13-year-old son, Billy, would not receive breakfast visitors that Friday morning. At 2:00 a.m. that morning, a Powhatan warrior who had become like a son to the Paces* rushed into their home. He was breathless and terrified. Chanco* had run from Moss Valley several miles away and then paddled a stolen canoe across the wide James to warn his adopted family.

"Father Pace, my brother tell me that Chief Opechancanough* send braves to kill all whites tomorrow when sun come up! You must run! You must warn others!"

"Chanco,* my son, are you sure? Your people have been so friendly to us for years."

"Yes, Father, I sure. My brother have war-paint on. His eyes full of hate. He tell me to kill all of you!"

When Isabelle heard that, she fainted and fell into the arms of her husband. "I'll get your Matchlock, Papa!" Billy shouted as he ran for the heavy 10-gauge rifle on the wall.

"Never mind the gun, son. It's heavy. You need to run fast and get the boat ready so we can row to Jamestown tonight and warn the governor. As soon as Ma comes to, we'll meet you at the dock. I'll bring the gun and supplies."

Looking at the young, weeping native, Richard whispered, "Come here, son!" Chanco flew into the arms of the powerfully built tobacco farmer as they both burst into tears. They knew many Powhatans and

English would not survive this assault. It was the end of the "Peace of Pocahontas."* War had come . . . again.

TWO UNARMED BRAVES EMERGED FROM THE DARK FOREST TO KNOCK ON the door of the MacDonald family. The thick wooden entrance swung open. "Here, laddies, come in. We really appreciate the victuals ya brought last night! But nay clothes in this weather? My goodness' sake. Yer both better men than me," he laughed. "Ma will have bread ready soon. Sit down by the fire and get warm," Donald MacDonald smiled. "Ya must be a wee bit frozen. Use the iron pokers thar ta stir it up a bit, will ya?" With a sly look, both Powhatans picked up a heavy, iron poker.

"George, put down your Bible and get two of Ma's wool blankets for our visitors, and then go out to the barn and get that venison they brought last night."

Turning to the two crouching figures by the fire, he proudly announced, "In just a few minutes, my wife will warm the cockles of yer heart with some of her best stew."

But the two warriors did not respond. That be odd, the farmer thought, but he shrugged his shoulders and turned to see if George was back. George loved to dawdle and feed the goats when he went to the barn.

After a while, George returned with the leg of deer. As he approached the house, he noticed that there was no smoke from the chimney and the door was wide open. Once inside, he stood, perplexed. The main room was freezing cold. He could see his breath.

"Ma? Pa?" No answer. Then, out of the corner of his eye, he noticed a slight vapor rising from the floor behind the large kitchen table. Trembling now, he walked around the table to see his parents. Their Powhatan friends had bludgeoned his parents to death with their own fire pokers. The mist was emanating from their warm blood running across the cold, wooden planks of the uneven floor. Instinctively, he ran to the back door of the cabin. Blood-stained moccasin tracks were smashed into the snow . . . headed toward Jamestown. His wail of grief pierced the whining wind in the tall pines. But no one heard it.

EARLIER, AT MIDNIGHT ON THAT FRIGID FRIDAY, JEHU AND JOHN ROLFE pulled their scratchy, British woolen blankets close to their necks as the biting wind whipped through Moss Valley. The Powhatan women had just returned to their villages.

Thirty minutes later, Chanco rose to leave. "I must warn my white friends," he said. As he left, the five English women looked at each other and got up.

Jehu and Rolfe motioned for them to sit down and stay warm. "It's too dangerous out there now for you to be roaming around. You will be killed if the braves see you."

"We know it's risky, but we have to warn the other servants," one said. "They don't know Jesus yet." And so, after prayers for protection, the five left just as war cries began to filter through the snowy forest.

"Our braves are coming this way," Paquiquino whispered. "We must all leave now!"

"But they will see our tracks in the snow," Cholie cried softly.

Jehu spoke up, "Not if you go to the Pamunkey and walk in the water's edge. It's not far. The water will hide your tracks. Turn right when you reach the river and follow it to our fort at Point Comfort.* Tell them Mr. John Rolfe sent you. You will be safe there."

"Good thinking, Jehu," Rolfe nodded gravely.

Then, Paquiquino spoke, "Jehu and John Rolfe—you follow women south. I go north and make tracks and noises, so braves think we all go north." Jehu and Rolfe looked at each other for a long moment. "No, Paq," Rolfe finally said, "We will stay with you. Together, we can make more tracks and more noise. That will protect the ladies better."

"Hmmm. Rolfe, you have white face, but you think like Powhatan," Paquiquino grinned. "Yes—stay with me. Come!"

As the women headed toward the Pamunkey River just to the east of Moss Valley, the three men began walking north along the river's edge. They moved swiftly, but not too fast. They wanted to be heard. So each man took turns yelling and talking like both men and women. The old chief was especially good at screaming like a terrified woman!

"It's working," Jehu puffed into the frigid air. "I can hear war-whoops coming closer!" Just as the Spaniard said that, one foot flew out from under him as his shoe slipped on a mossy rock. Before he could hit the freezing water, the wiry arm of Paquiquino caught him.

"Paq, you sure saved me that time! I almost got a cold bath. In this weather, that would have done me in, for sure," Jehu laughed. Paquiquino smiled.

"My brother, I wish I do more for you. I owe you much." But the river's noise and their own numbed senses kept them from seeing what was just ahead. Two husky braves with stolen kitchen knives were hiding in the bushes—and their blades were bloody. They had just helped murder seventy-eight farmers* at Martin's Hundred,* about seven miles southwest. Without warning, the braves burst out of the bushes like flushed quail. They both ran to kill the two white men who had apparently captured the father of their chief.

One attacker shouted, *"Rolfe!"* Mongo had told them there was a handsome prize for whoever killed him. As the warrior raced by Paquiquino to claim that reward, Paquiquino put his leg back and tripped. The native hit his head on a rock—just enough to knock him out. Then, after motioning to Rolfe to keep on running, Paquiquino jumped on the other attacker who was about to slit Jehu's throat.

As the old chief pulled his fellow tribesman off of Jehu, the young warrior looked confused. He was too young to recognize the chief's father. "Why you stop me, old man? All whites must die! Our chief send us to kill all English devils!" the warrior shouted with great rage.

Stepping between Jehu and the brave, Paquiquino put his hand on the war-painted shoulder of the confused Algonquin. "No, my friend. *Not* this man. He is my brother. Many moons ago, I killed white men who came here—but this man is different. I cannot allow you to kill him now. His God is now my God. We are spirit brothers."

For a moment, the warrior just stared in disbelief. No Powhatan had ever said anything like that to him. Then, he suddenly raised his knife and cried out, "I obey Okeus, not white man's god! I must kill!" With a lightning-quick lunge, he rushed around Paquiquino and slashed the arm of Jehu.

Paquiquino retaliated by knocking the brave into the snowy bushes with his shoulder. Then, the spry old warrior jumped onto the assailant's chest while grasping the arm that held the knife. "*Run,* my brother, run! Run—and live for Jesus!" the old chief yelled to Jehu.

And run, he did—faster than he ever had since he escaped as a boy in those same woods decades ago. With tears streaming down his half-frozen cheeks, he stumbled through the snowy peninsula for several miles toward Martin's Hundred for help—but he would find none.

As Jehu melted into the thick forest, the young warrior began to get the advantage over the much older man. But just as he thought he could turn his blade against Paquiquino, the wily chief hit him in the throat with his folded knuckles—a move a Spanish conquistador had once taught him.

The warrior choked, his windpipe compressed. He dropped the knife, clutching his throat with both hands and coughing violently. As he did, Paquiquino picked up the knife. "I will go now. Do not follow. Go back to your family," Paquiquino warned sternly. As he turned to leave, the warrior leaped up and grabbed him around the neck from behind, his other hand reaching for the knife. They struggled and fell to the ground. In the furious fray that followed, the younger warrior was wounded in his side— but his strength and endurance were winning out over the exhausted old man beneath him.

Soon, Paquiquino realized he could not defeat the younger man and that Jehu was safe now. So, he relaxed his grip on his opponent—and smiled. For a second time, the warrior paused. No foe had ever done that. As Paquiquino peacefully lay beneath him, the confused native noticed that the old man's face seemed brighter. The brave also felt something come over him that made him shiver—a powerful spirit—a spirit of great peace. He panicked. He knew he could not kill the strange old warrior now: a good spirit was protecting him. The perplexed brave was about to get up and run when he heard the shouts of his fellow attackers drawing closer. Their war cries awakened his hate. Now, he could kill.

With a blood-curdling yell, the warrior lifted his knife and drove it deep into the chest of the old man. Just as the brave yanked the blade out to strike again, Paquiquino whispered, "I forgive you, my son. Go in peace."

The brave's eyes grew wide. *What have I done? This is no ordinary man. I have killed a man of peace. Ahone must be with him. I have killed a son of Ahone! I am cursed.* Then the terrified warrior ran screaming like a man on fire into the silent forest.

Behind him, Paquiquino lay calmly in the blood-stained pearly snow. His heart was about to stop, but at that moment, he felt a joy surging inside him that no Powhatan or English words could express.

Suddenly, he saw them—a squad of angels from the Honor Battalion wafting down from heaven in worship. He lifted one hand to join them for a few moments until his breath stopped . . . and then he saw Jesus— walking down the trail toward him, arms open wide.

"Paquiquino, my son. I have longed for this day."

CHAPTER 79

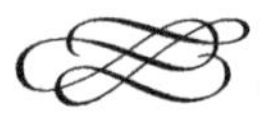

All that morning, hell reigned in Virginia. Of the twelve hundred settlers, more than three hundred and fifty were killed* while preparing and serving breakfast to native friends—now assassins. Most were killed by the same hoes and axes the English loaned the natives to help them on the farm.* Men, women, and children of all ages were bludgeoned to death so as not to leave any behind who might try to seek revenge. It was the same scene in dozens of plantations that morning. Chief Opechancanough's plan was working.* He and his warrior chiefs began to celebrate as reports came that the destruction they had planned for years was now happening.

"Great Chief, we have killed many whites. We even killed John Rolfe! None survived at Henricus* and Wolstenholme Towne* at Martin's Hundred plantation.* We burned churches, houses, tobacco barns and took many weapons.* We captured many women and children to share with other braves."*

"What of Jamestown? Does it burn now?" Looking down, the wounded warrior replied, "No, my Chief. Someone warned them.*

When we came there, they began to shoot at us right away. They killed ten of my warriors. We left the fort. It is too strong now."

Opechancanough spat on the ground and growled, "It is enough. We will starve the rest to death* . . . as my father did before. They almost left then. This time, they will—for good."

FLOATING HIGH ABOVE JAMESTOWN, THE BLOATED DINOSAUR GLOATED serenely as he enjoyed the fierce Powhatan war whoops and the cries of dying settlers. "Ha! The colony is done for sure, Snookus. Their lord has abandoned them, and now they will starve. Soon, this greedy nest of foolish Lamb-lovers will be gone!"

But in a small, warm cabin at Point Comfort, a tip of land south of Jamestown,* Cholie and her troupe of intercessors had found shelter that morning. They were praying feverishly for God to save the colony —and the Lord was quick to answer. The Holy Spirit sent angels to alert godly Pilgrims in the northern Virginia colony in Plymouth. Pray now for your sister colony in Jamestown. They are in great danger, the angels whispered. The same angelic message came to another small settlement of Pilgrims on the peninsula* forty-two miles to the east of Jamestown. Angels also made a call on Old Heathfield Anglican Church in Sussex, England,* to rouse the saints there to pray for Jamestown. Robert Hunt had been their pastor before sailing for Jamestown.*

Soon, like a mighty cannon barrage, fervent prayers from multiple locations were being lobbed into a large, golden bowl in heaven.

"Father, is it enough? Can we intervene now?" Jesus eagerly asked the Lord.

"Not yet, Son. I am eager to help them, but I am waiting for a few more prayers from the saints to fill the prayer bowl. I must have *their partnership in prayer*! Remember—we are training them to rule with us in heaven one day. The Spirit is giving them the will and the power to pray. When they do, their prayers will prevail. Then, you can activate your plans!"

And so, the saints continued to pray. But thirty minutes later, it happened. The prayer bowl in heaven overflowed.

Instantly, Okeus sensed something. He grew nervous. He clawed at a strange itch beneath the thick scales on his long, green abdomen. Snookus also felt a stab of pain in his floppy torso. Evil was lifting. The battle was shifting.

"Damn it! Someone is praying!" the angry dinosaur grunted. Then, he looked at Jamestown with shock. Hundreds of families were crowded behind the high walls* while many others were still fleeing toward the walled town.* Oddly enough, no warriors intercepted them.

"They're getting away!" Okeus bellowed. "What the—? Where are my warriors? What the hell is Mongo doing? Damn him! I will rip that little turd apart for this." Finally, after several minutes of furious snorting, growling, farting, and cursing, Okeus grabbed Snookus by his throat and demanded, "Is my Portal ready or not?"

"Yes, Master, but please do not open that portal—it is only for the greatest emergencies against *angelic* attacks. Lucifer will be very angry if we use it without his permission against mere humans. Remember that Dark Angel in France who broke that rule? Lucifer stomped him death. It was awful"

"Of course, I remember. But that idiot was a *nobody* to Lucifer. I am one of his favorites!"

"You certainly are, Master—but, as we know, Lord Lucifer has also killed many friends."

"Just tell the Horde commander to be ready for my signal. My plan will work and Lucifer will agree when he sees the results."

Just then, the Powhatan god saw Scion in the woods two miles north of Jamestown. The twelve-foot angel was swinging his eight-foot sword back and forth in brilliant, deadly arcs, vaporizing dozens of demons who were clinging to warriors chasing fleeing colonists. Angie was there, too. She whirled around the Powhatan warriors, uncloaked, to distract them. It worked. The demonically deprived braves fell to the ground in confusion.

"Look at that fool!" Okeus barked. "And his little brat-girl right in the thick of it too. I will kill them *both* of them today!"

Then, for an instant, an unwelcome thought ricocheted inside the Dark Angel's mind. *Scion—why did you have to come here! You and your . . . rotten friendship. You are probably going to get me killed someday. But today, I rule—and today, you will die!*

A gargantuan fart sealed his decision as he shouted, "Open the Portal! Let the hounds of hell come forth! Let terror reign! Let death rule!

"Let *Okeus* be glorified today!"

CHAPTER 80

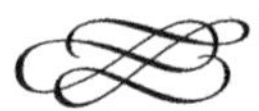

A few demon scouts landed on the ground not far from Jamestown. They quickly shapeshifted into native warriors and headed for the fort. But the main body of the Horde did not move an inch. Neither did Okeus, Snookus, Scion, or Angie. For about five seconds, they each tried to wrap their numbed minds around what they were seeing: God did not dispatch warriors to rescue men and angels that day. Instead, he sent *worshippers!*

In that moment of shock, the twenty-four angels swooshed down under the dark cloud of the Horde like a tiny circle of golden lights, swirling counter-clockwise faster and faster. They were invisible to people, but every spirit was mesmerized by them.

Then it began. The angel voices of Heaven's Royal Throne Room Chorale hummed a melody no human had ever imagined or heard. The rumble of deep, resonant male voices thundered multilayered harmonies that made Scion and Angie shiver with pleasure. As the angelic music drew closer, the air was electrified with waves of peace and joy felt by humans and non-humans alike. The hair on Scion's arms stood straight up. Angie sprang into the air and spun like a top, humming her own counterpoint melody to the chorale's masterpiece.

Settlers all over the James River peninsula dropped to their knees in worship but wondering why. But Okeus and Snookus could only cry out in pain as the music of heaven engulfed them. Incredibly, the temperature on the Jamestown peninsula rose 45 degrees within minutes. Snow began to melt—as did the intense terror in the fort. Without a bloom in sight, the tantalizing smell of wildflowers filled the forest. English guards looked over the walls of Jamestown and saw a few fully-armed "Powhatan warriors" now standing like statues at the treeline—their eyes bulging with fear.

Then, without warning, Okeus and Snookus fell out of the sky and plopped into the large, over-filled latrine near Jamestown, screaming like little girls. Then, the twenty-four Throne Room Angels began to sing the worship song that Jesus loved the most. All heaven clapped for joy, and all hell groaned with dread.

At first, it was soft, like a lullaby, almost hypnotic to hear. Millions of demons in the motionless Horde had never heard such a song. The effect was powerful. The hatred in their eyes softened. Their scaly or furry shoulders relaxed. Some lowered their swords, now hanging in drooping claws and paws.

Then, with an imperceptible crescendo, the angelic voices grew louder and even more beautiful. As the song filled the invisible realm of the forests, Angie began to sing . . . and then Scion. In that instant, the choir stopped singing and just hummed again in harmony to accompany the two angels kneeling on the ground beneath them.

It happened slowly, but the angels saw it and smiled. They had seen it before.

Scion began to worship. With new strength surging back into his golden, twelve-foot frame, he pushed himself to his feet with one hand, holding Angie with his other.

Looking up at the swirl of knowing smiles above him, he suddenly understood why the Lord had not sent warriors. He planted his feet slightly apart and gently placed his worshipping friend on his left shoulder. Looking up to heaven, he slowly raised both arms into the air. Instantly, his twenty-four-foot wings snapped open so fast it sounded like a thunderclap. Then, throwing back his head and gleaming platinum hair, the Angel of Virginia bellowed out the praises of God with a force that made many proud demons wet themselves.

Then, Scion's body pulsed with ever-brighter waves of light—brighter, then brighter and brighter. Okeus and Snookus saw the growing intensity of light as they peeked out from the crap pit. Okeus cursed and farted as he realized what was about to happen. Instantly, he rolled his heavy body facedown while tackling Snookus and pushing both of their faces deeper into the human muck. Without any command to do so, the entire Horde quickly backed back up higher into the sky. Scion and Angie just stood there, their eyes closed, lost in worship.

Then, twelve trumpets pierced the air with seven glorious victory blasts. Every animal in the forest laid down. Birds flew to the ground. Even bugs sought shelter in fallen, rotting logs. And then—faster than a hummingbird's wing—a white-hot sunburst of light exploded from Scion into a blinding glory cloud that covered the entire Great Bay sky! Instantly, millions of flying demons in the Horde were annihilated before they could even twitch. Then massive cloud rushed out in every direction at great speed, disintegrating every airborne demon in its path.

Scion, Angie, and the twenty-four worship leaders quickly soared to twenty thousand feet to watch the wave of glory splash against the hazy western mountain ridge and up and down the entire eastern seaboard. It was a total victory! No flying demon survived the cloud as it cleansed the entire east coast of Virginia from Plymouth, Massachusetts, to just above the Spanish Florida border.

But Dark Angels knew they were immune. From a high cloud fifty miles south of Jamestown, Voudoc had been watching this great battle. As he saw the explosion of light over the peninsula, he cackled like a happy monkey, "That damned angel did it again. Good for him!

I guess my work is done here for now. Time to go home" As he turned to look back at the approaching glory cloud once more, he ran right into the muscular arms of two massive Watcher Angels who grabbed the little white-faced monkey by both wings. "Let me go! Let me go! The cloud is coming. It will kill me! Oh, no—it is here!" Voudoc yelled. "Let me go, you big baboons!"

But the two Watchers just hung onto Voudoc and smiled at each other with a wink. As the glory cloud sped past them, one Watcher looked at the frightened monkey spirit and smirked, "So, you didn't die, little monkey man. *Wow*—that must mean you are not really a demon. We are *so* shocked you would lie to us. But you know what? I have a holy hunch you are none other than Voudoc, Principality of the Islands—and a former partner of Okeus, perhaps?" the big angel snickered and rolled his eyes. "Angie said we might run into you. That cloud couldn't hurt you—and you *know* it. You are a Dark Angel." Tightening his vise-like grip on the small prisoner, the fierce angel roughly yanked the intruder close to his golden face. "You lied to us, little monkey. We no like traitors from heaven or liars, comprende? Don't try that act again on us, monkey brains. The next time we may not be so nice. Huh! And you call *us* baboons? Some nerve, creep.

"But you are free to go, Mr. Whoever-you-really-are rebel. You can't return to heaven—but I have been ordered to tell you that heaven thanks you for assisting Scion. Now, scoot along furry butt-face before I get into a bad mood." Then, the intimidating guard smartly drop-kicked Voudoc south with a parting look that most demons never want to see on an angel up close.

A visibly shaken Voudoc did not need to be told twice. The Dark Angel raced back to Jamaica's Blue Mountains to comfort his frightened demons who were cowering in their caverns because of Scion—*again*.

CHAPTER 81

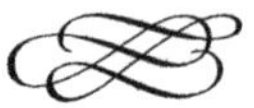

A few demon scouts landed on the ground not far from Jamestown. They quickly shapeshifted into native warriors and headed for the fort. But the main body of the Horde did not move an inch. Neither did Okeus, Snookus, Scion, or Angie. For about five seconds, they each tried to wrap their numbed minds around what they were seeing: God did not dispatch warriors to rescue men and angels that day. Instead, he sent *worshippers!*

In that moment of shock, the twenty-four angels swooshed down under the dark cloud of the Horde like a tiny circle of golden lights, swirling counter-clockwise faster and faster. They were invisible to people, but every spirit was mesmerized by them.

Then it began. The beautiful voices of Heaven's Royal Throne Room Chorale hummed a melody no human had ever imagined or heard. Deep male, resonant voices hummed multilayered harmonies that made Scion and Angie shiver with pleasure. The beauty and majesty of their acapella vocals held every ear spellbound. These were the Lord's personal worship team. Their music released the power and glory of Almighty God as no other heavenly choir could.

As the humming drew closer, the air turned electric with waves of peace and joy felt by humans and non-humans alike. The hair on Scion's arms stood straight up. Angie could not control herself. She sprang into the air and spun like a top, humming her own counterpoint melody to the chorale's masterpiece.

Okeus and Snookus cried out in great pain as the music of heaven grew louder. Incredibly, the temperature on the Jamestown peninsula rose 45 degrees within minutes. Snow began to melt—as did the intense terror in the fort. Without a bloom in sight, the tantalizing smell of wildflowers filled the forest. English guards looked over the walls of Jamestown and saw a few fully armed "Powhatan warriors" now standing like statues at the treeline—their faces full of fear.

Okeus and Snookus screamed like little girls as they fell out of the sky and plopped into the large, over-filled latrine near Jamestown.

In that timeless moment, the two-dozen angels stopped humming and began to sing the songs of God's Throne Room. All heaven clapped for joy and all hell groaned in pain.

At first, it was soft, like a lullaby, almost hypnotic to hear. Millions of demons in the motionless Horde had never heard such a song. The hatred in their eyes softened. Their scaly and furry shoulders relaxed. Some lowered their swords, now hanging in drooping claws and paws.

Then, with an imperceptible crescendo, the voices grew louder and even more beautiful. As the song filled the invisible realm of the forests, Angie began to sing . . . and then Scion. In that instant, the choir stopped singing and just hummed again in harmony to accompany the two angels kneeling on the ground beneath them.

It happened slowly, but the angels saw it and smiled. They had seen it before.

Scion began to worship. With new strength surging back into his golden, twelve-foot frame, he pushed himself to his feet with one hand, holding Angie with his other.

Looking up at the swirl of knowing smiles above him, he suddenly understood why the Lord had not sent warriors. He planted his feet slightly apart and gently placed his worshipping friend on his left shoulder. Looking up to heaven, he slowly raised his arms into the air. Instantly, his twenty-four-foot wings snapped open so fast it sounded like a thunderclap. Then, throwing back his head and gleaming platinum hair, the Angel of Virginia bellowed out the praises of God with a force that made many proud demons within miles wet themselves.

Scion's body pulsed with ever-brighter waves of light—brighter, then brighter and brighter. Okeus and Snookus saw the growing light as they peeked out from the crap pit. Okeus cursed and farted as he realized what was about to happen. Instantly, he rolled his heavy body over facedown while tackling Snookus and pushing both of their faces deeper into the human muck. Without any command to do so, the entire Horde instinctively backed back up into the sky. Scion and Angie just stood there, eyes closed, lost in worship.

Then, the chorale hummed louder as twelve angels strummed their lutes and twelve trumpeters pierced the air with seven glorious victory blasts. Every animal in the forest laid down. Birds flew to the ground. Even bugs sought shelter in fallen, rotting logs. Every forest creature knew something *big* was about to happen.

And then—faster than a hummingbird's wing—a white-hot sunburst of light exploded from Scion into a blinding glory cloud that covered the entire Great Bay! The cloud of glory instantly annihilated millions of flying demons in the Horde before they could even twitch. Then massive cloud rushed out in every direction at great speed, disintegrating every airborne demon in its path.

Scion, Angie, and the twenty-four worship leaders quickly soared to twenty thousand feet to watch the wave of glory splash against the hazy western mountain ridge and up and down the entire eastern seaboard. It was a total victory! No flying demon survived the cloud as it cleansed the entire east coast of Virginia from Plymouth, Massachusetts, to just above the Spanish Florida border.

But Dark Angels knew they were immune. From a high cloud fifty miles south of Jamestown, Voudoc had been watching this great battle ever since he heard that Okeus had opened the Virginia War Portal. As he saw the explosion of light over the peninsula, he cackled like a happy monkey, "That damned angel did it again. Good for him! I guess my work is done here for now. Time to go home" As he turned to look back at the approaching glory cloud once more, he ran right into the muscular arms of two huge Watcher Angels who grabbed the little white-faced monkey by both wings. "Let me go! Let me go! The cloud is coming. It will kill me! Oh, no—it is here!" Voudoc yelled. "Let me go, you big baboons!"

But the two Watchers just hung onto Voudoc and smiled at each other with a wink. As the glory cloud sped past them, one Watcher looked at the frightened monkey spirit and smirked, "So, you didn't die, little monkey man. *Wow*—that must mean you are *not really* a demon. We are so shocked you would lie to us. You know what? I have a holy hunch you are none other than Voudoc, Principality of the Islands—and a *former* partner of Okeus, perhaps?" the big angel snickered and rolled his eyes. "Angie said we might run into you. That cloud couldn't hurt you—and you *know* it. You are a Dark Angel." Tightening his vise-like grip on the small prisoner, the fierce angel roughly yanked the intruder close to his golden face. "You lied to us, little monkey. We no like traitors from heaven or liars, comprende? Don't try that act again on us, monkey brains. The next time we may not be so nice. Huh! And you call *us* baboons? Some nerve, creep.

"But you are free to go, Mr. Whoever-you-really-are rebel. You can't return to heaven—but I have been ordered to tell you that heaven thanks you for assisting Scion. Now, scoot along furry butt-face, before I get into a bad mood." Then, the intimidating guard smartly drop-kicked Voudoc south with a parting look that most demons never want to see on an angel up close.

A visibly shaken Voudoc did not need to be told twice. The Dark Angel raced back to Jamaica's Blue Mountains to comfort his frightened demons who were cowering in their caverns because of Scion—*again.*

CHAPTER 82

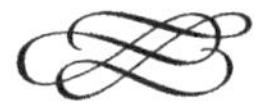

As the golden glory cloud dissipated at Virginia's southern border with Spanish Florida, the Royal Throne Room Chorale returned to heaven to report to General Michael. Within moments of hearing their report, the Captain of the Host of Heaven decided to do something he had never done: he was going to visit Earth—and specifically to meet with Scion and Angie. When the two heard about Michael's official visit, to say that they were a bit nervous would be a significant understatement.

"Gosh, Angie—I wonder if Michael is coming to scold us?" Scion fretted. "We lost three hundred and fifty settlers today*—almost of third of the colony."*

"We did the best we could, Master," she kept repeating to comfort Scion—and herself.

Finally, an hour later, he arrived above the Great Bay. Before landing to greet his two angels, Michael surveyed the heart-breaking scene from the air as he glided on thirty-six feet of wings. Smoldering dots of blackened earth stretched almost fifty miles along the James River. The smoke of a hundred burnt buildings drifted across blood-stained snow on both sides of the river. Michael had to bite his lip when he heard the soft sobbing of many women and children hiding from attack in the snowy woods. Many more families were crammed into the narrow streets of the Jamestown fort, huddled together to stay warm. But he was grateful to also see that dozens of other plantations farther inland had been untouched by the carnage. His heart filled with gratitude. *Praise be to Jesus! The Jamestown Colony has indeed survived.*

Finally, the massive eighteen-foot archangel landed near the anxious duo. They had been watching him reconnoiter the region with growing fears that he had come to rebuke them. But as soon as they saw Michael's broad smile and his hand extended toward Scion, the two breathed an immediate sigh of relief.

"Yer to be commended, ya are, Scion. You and Angel 442 have done something few of us on the War Council thought ta be possible. And ya did it despite the wicked schemes of Kai—yer former best friend. No one kin doubt yer loyalty to the Kingdom now. The colony will survive and thrive . . . and so kin you!"

"General Michael, you are too kind. Yes, I did stop Kai from destroying the colony . . . but I failed the Lord in another way. Once we lost our best intercessor, Reverend Hunt, sin grew like weeds among the settlers. I didn't know how to stop that. As you know, the Lord wanted a holy colony to found his new missionary nation. But my colony is not that holy, I am sorry to say."

"It's happened before ta God's people, son—like in the Lord's parable of the tares and the wheat," Michael solemnly responded. "But God's power kin always reverse the damage. He will prevail here, in time, as the people continue to repent and seek him."

"That's my hope, General. This colony has suffered so much. Fourteen thousand have come here since 1607*, but only twelve hundred were still alive before yesterday's attack!* Now that number is down to eight hundred and thirty-three.* The survivors in Jamestown are so traumatized that they are afraid to leave the fort. Many may yet starve because of low food supplies."

"Ya, it' as been terrible. I hate war, laddie—and 'tis na over. Now that they've been attacked, the colonists will feel justified in taking even more Powhatan land. If only this colony coulda be like the Plymouth colony up north.* They excel in lovin' the host people of the land,"* Michael sighed sadly.

"But I bring some very gud news from the Lord to ya: God has granted this colony and the nation it kin birth a four-hundred-year reprieve. If that new nation kin turn from the sins planted here and live fer God within four hundred years, he has promised ta do great wonders on the Earth through it."

"Glory to God! That is wonderful news, General!" Scion exclaimed.

But then Scion became serious. "It's all because of those dear people who stood in the gap for the colony, *isn't it?* If they had not repented, God would not have saved us, right?"

Looking at Scion now with a gentle smile, Michael replied, "Yer so right, me laddie. Unless people repent for their sins and for the sins of their people, the Lord kin do only a little for them. Remember that statue near Angel Academy?"

"I certainly do. It's a statue of Moses. He saved his people from God's judgment. He stood in the gap for Israel by pleading for forgiveness and mercy."*

"That right, Scion. God's always looking for a Moses so he can restore what sin has destroyed.

Putting his massive hand on Scion's shoulder, Michael gazed deeply into the angel's blue eyes and said, "Scion, you and yer intercessors were that Moses to this colony! Ya got them ta stand in the gap. I'm so proud of ya, my son. I tooka chance on ya, and ya dinnae let me doon!" Michael concluded with a fatherly kiss on Scion's upturned forehead. As he did, Scion began to weep. Thousands of years of believing that he was a failure began to melt away. Scion put an arm around Michael's waist and clung tightly to him for a long moment. Angie smiled and cried tears of joy.

Finally, Scion stepped back and said, "General, we both know that even Moses needed Aaron and Hur to hold his staff up all day to win a war. If you think I am a Moses, you must also honor the two who held my arms up in this great war against Kai. I could not have saved the colony without them."

Angie giggled and winked at her boss. She knew what was coming.

"Two? Ya must be mistakin', laddie. I only gave ya *one* assistant, this here 442, whom ya now call Angie."

Scion gulped and just stared at Michael for a long moment.

"Well . . . well, uh . . . uh . . ."

"Fer the Lord's sake, man, spit it oot."

CHAPTER 83

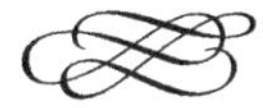

The moment of truth had arrived—Scion had to tell him.

After taking a deep breath and rubbing his twitching face several times, Scion finally looked up at the perplexed face of the giant angel and said, "Well, this is my first Earth assignment, and as you know, I am a stickler for doing things by the book."

Angie giggled again and put both hands over her wide grin.

"Well, you see, there is this, uh . . . other creature—a sort of half-breed, if you will. Without him, the intercessors could not have gathered to repent for the colony."

"A half-breed?" Michael chuckled as he scrunched up his face in confusion.

"Well, uh . . . actually, uh . . . a spirit, touched by heaven."

"Oh, that sounds good. Ya mean a *fervent* Christian? But ya said t'was a half-breed. I guess I'm confused, Scion. Just who is this other assistant?" Michael moved his face closer to Scion's so he could hear his response clearly. He was now thoroughly intrigued by what Scion had to say.

Just then, Angie zipped in between their faces and looked right into one of Michael's dazzling blue-green eyes. She smiled ever so sweetly and proudly announced, "Why, General Michael, you will be happy to know that your protégé, Scion, has broken new ground in protecting God's precious humans. Through his brilliant powers of observation and adaptability in combat, Scion has recruited a covert assistant from the ranks of demons—but one who has been uniquely equipped by Jesus himself for Kingdom work." Angie backed away with a low bow to the General and a huge wink toward her astonished partner.

You could have knocked Michael over with a feather—even from a hummingbird. For a Scottish archangel who loves to talk a lot, "to blither," he was speechless. His mouth was open, but no sounds came out. For a long moment, no one spoke. Scion could only stare straight ahead at Michael's midsection with the glittering gold belt buckle that read "CHH"—Captain of the Host of Heaven.

Michael finally blinked several times and looked at Scion, and then at Angie, and blinked again. "Well, I dinnae expect that. So, could one of you tell me a little more about this . . . uh . . . special demon?"

Angie could tell Scion was still mortified, so she spoke first. "General Michael, this is the New World, and we are building a new nation that will change the entire world. Our Lord said once that new wine demands new wineskins. Collaborating with this demon is one of our' new wineskins,'" Angie concluded with a queenly wave of her hand. Michael was clearly taken aback.

"Well, Angel 442, I kin see yer point, but I'm a wee bit confused—I thought all demons were our enemy.' Ave I missed something in the last fifteen thousand years? Just why do ya believe this creature could possibly be a help ta the likes of we angels?"

Scion spoke now. "General, with all due respect—and gratitude—this demon worked with us for months to deceive the forces of Kai and thwart the plans of Kai . . . even at great personal risk to himself. He distinguished himself in gathering vital intelligence on enemy plans and movements we would not have otherwise had. And, if my research is correct, the Lord himself used demons at least twice in the Old Testament to do his will. I don't know the name of the demon God sent to torment King Saul for his rebellion or the demon God used to trick the prophets of evil Ahab, but I do know our demon's name. His name is Morph."

Trying to hide his shock, Michael could only say, *"Really?* Extraordinary!" The eighteen-foot archangel was fearless in battle—but this story about Morph challenged his theology on a massive scale. Relaxing his tense shoulders a bit more, Michael went on, "Alright. I'll give ya that. God uses demons at times fer His purposes. Tell me more about this new type of demon, this . . . Morph, as ya call 'im."

Seeing the big angel's genuine interest now, Angie jumped in again. "When Jesus went to hell to announce his victory over Lucifer, Morph got struck with the light blasting from Jesus. He still carries a spot of that light under his left wing. Because the light of Jesus marked him, he is incapable of being evil enough to accomplish his assignments. His attempts to tempt or torment people usually fail miserably. The other demons hate him and mock him all the time because of that. That's why I call him a half-breed. Part of him tries to be a demon, but the other part of him seems to be controlled by *heaven."*

"Extraordinary," was all Michael could say, his sense of disorientation growing with each new revelation about Morph.

Michael finally got control of himself. With tears welling up in his eyes, he spoke softly and carefully, "My dear friends, if what ya tell me is true, this could be one of the greatest discoveries in the history of heaven."

Scion and Angie gasped and hung onto his every word.

"I dinnae ever expect da Lord ta do anything like this," Michael finally managed to whisper. He tried to clear his throat a couple of times, and then, with a voice full of emotion, he said, "I knew the Lord' as planted clues to da Gospel in idol-worshipping tribes all over da world fer' undreds of years. And, yes, God used a couple of demons in the Old Testament for his purposes. But a demon marked by Jesus ta further da Gospel. Nah—never! Every angel in heaven will be totally shocked."

Now Scion's brain was going into high gear. "But why not? Jesus wrote in the Bible that hell is made for the devil and his angels.* But the Bible never says demons are angels—or vice versa. To be sure, most demons are very evil and will certainly be condemned to hell. But if demons are not all automatically doomed to hell like Jesus said Dark Angels are, there is a chance that some demons may have a purpose in the Kingdom—just like those pagan prophets God used to predict the coming of missionaries to their tribes."*

All Michael could mutter was, *"Extraordinary* . . . just extraordinary! I want to meet him. *Now!"*

CHAPTER 84

As Angie sped off to fetch Morph, Michael and Scion waited in silence. The tension was palpable.

In a few minutes, the two appeared. Morph's siamese-blue cat eyes bulged with fear as he approached the most enormous angel he had ever seen—with the most fearsome sword he had ever seen.

"Welcome, little Morph," Michael graciously announced.

Instinctively kneeling before Michael—as he had seen the subjects of Powhatan do—Morph suddenly felt a massive but gentle hand pull him upright. His furry face lit up with joy.

"Ya should not bow to any angel, Morph," Michael whispered. And as Scion and Angie gasped with surprise, Michael got down on one knee before Morph and said, "If yer who they say ya're, then I am at yer service, Morph. Any enemy of my enemy is my friend. And, judging by what Scion says ya did to save the colony, ya may be one of the biggest enemies Lucifer has right now."

Standing up now, Michael went on. "Come up here, Morph, and tell me how ya helped my friends here defeat the plans of Kai. I need to know how ya operate if we are gonna be working together in the future."

Morph didn't speak or budge, so Angie grabbed his paw with a big smile and slowly pulled him up to eye-level with Michael, who was sixteen feet above Morph's head. Morph froze in panic when Angie touched his paw, but then, he reluctantly complied. After placing him near Michael's golden face, Angie moved back.

| Morph

Speaking as softly as he could so Morph would relax, Michael asked, "For starters, just how did ya help Scion gather the believers ta repent?

Morph turned to Angie and pleaded, "Angie—I am so nervous. I c-can't. . . unless you hold my paw."

Angie nodded, struggling to hold back her tears, and said, "Yes—of course, yes!" as she moved closer to Morph.

Michael had to blink again—this time really hard. Here was an ugly, furry cat demon with its paw in the tiny hand of a beautiful angel—

and they were both smiling at each other. *No one in heaven is going to believe this,* the General groaned silently.

Morph finally forced himself to turn away from Angie's deeply comforting gaze. Morph now felt stronger, but he squeezed her hand so tight it made her wince in pain as he struggled to talk.

"Angel Michael, here . . . here's how . . . uh . . . we . . . we did it. After Scion told me who he wanted at the prayer meeting, I knew we needed help. We had to get twenty-two people from several locations to one spot in the woods at 10:00 p.m. So, I contacted some friends of mine." He looked at Angie again for reassurance. Her smile was still there—but with a slight flinch due to the pain in her tightly squeezed hand.

"Oh, an who might they be, laddie? Other half-breeds like yerself?"

"Not exactly. You see, a lot of demons get damaged on the job. Sometimes, we get cut up while fighting angels. But more often, our masters lop off one of our arms, wings, or legs because we didn't do exactly what they wanted. When that happens, we get treated as freaks. No one wants us around them.

"Go on, Morph. Tell me more," Michael said.

"Well, my twelve closest friends are defective demons, like me. But they are also famous as the official throne room entertainers for Okeus. They all agreed to help me—even though they knew it could be a death sentence if they were caught. So, that night, I got my twelve friends to distract the demon guards at several plantations, native villages, and at Jamestown—all places where the twenty-two lived. Those guys danced or sang or just acted stupid—but the guards ate it up. That gave us enough time to get everyone to a place called Moss Valley several miles away."

Michael scrunched up his face and rubbed his chin for a moment, and then remarked, "But 'twas dark, and the area is thick with forests. Didya' ave other demons lead 'em through da woods? I cannae imagine any woman following a demon into dark woods," Michael commented with a frown.

Turning to Angie again, Morph looked into her flashing purple eyes for several seconds before going on. "No, I had help from an angel whose beauty would charm a wounded bear." Angie blushed.

Morph saw it, swallowed hard, and continued. "Fortunately, all the believers lived near Jamestown and on the same side of the river as Jamestown. So, once the guards started to watch one of my friends perform, Angie flew to each believer in their huts and whispered, "Go outside. The Lord is calling. Go where no one can see you."

Once the Christian was outside in a safe place, Angie quickly uncloaked and sang to the Lord. Just like me, each believer knew they could trust a beautiful, worshipping angel. One by one, they were led to our rendezvous point on the hill just above Jamestown by the light from Angie's body. Once there, she pointed them to another light above Moss Valley."

"Light? What light?" Michael asked.

"That . . . would be *me,*" Morph admitted sheepishly, lifting his left wing as he nervously squeezed Angie's hand too hard again.

Michael looked at Morph and Angie, still grinning at one another. Then he looked at Scion and just shook his head. "Scion, do ya' ave room fer another confused angel in yer classes? I may 'ave ta start over."

At last, Morph gave Angie's hand one more painful squeeze and let it go as he moved closer to General Michael.

"General, my friends risked their lives that night. I am very proud of them. But now, Okeus knows who they are, and he will be hunting them down. He will not spare them. They will all die horrible deaths if he finds them—and he will, unless we help them."

Scion now spoke. "Yes, General. I told Morph that if anyone could help his friends stay safe, *you* could. I'm sure the Lord would allow your angels to guard Morph's friends somewhere if you asked," Scion suggested confidently.

Michael shook his head in wonder. "May God be praised! First, I am hearing a demon show concern for' is men like any leader should—and then an angel is asking fer angelic protection of demons! What's next—a birthday party fer Lucifer?" he grimaced as he walked away to think, rubbing his jaw with his massive right hand. After a few moments, he came back to the group.

"Morph, those twelve demons do need ta be protected, but . . . we cannae giv 'em protection as Scion suggests. The Lord would nay allow it. I dunnae know what we kin do.' Tis a veritable conundrum ta me," the General responded with a heavy face.

"It's a what?" Morph asked Angie. Angie just shook her head and quickly lowered it.

Suddenly, to everyone's amazement, Morph somehow forgot all his fears. He flew closer to Michael's face and shouted, "General, my friends *will die* unless you protect them! Scion said you would work it out somehow. Please, don't let us down, General. They risked their lives for your colony! They trusted me. I trusted Scion. I can't tell them we betrayed their trust! I cannot, and I *will not!*" Morph spat out with hot anger.

"General Michael, you are Captain of the Host of Heaven and Defender of the Throne of God with millions of angels at your command! General Michael, you *must* do something!" Morph demanded.

Deep shock registered on the face of the three angels. Instantly, Morph knew he had crossed a line—a dangerous line. He realized he had just spoken like he always wanted to—but had never dared. And now he had just rebuked the General of the Armies of Heaven. He quickly shrank back from the three angels, ready to flee for his life.

CHAPTER 85

Scion and Angie looked at Michael, hoping he would not leave in disgust at Morph's outburst. Amazingly, Michael returned their gaze with a look of surprise, compassion, and sadness. The great General of heaven did not know what to do. Scion knew he had to do something quickly to salvage this situation.

Reaching out boldly, Scion touched Michael's left arm and stuttered out, "Uh, Ge-Ge-General . . . uh . . . I have another idea to share with you. It's . . . another 'new wineskin' tactic I thought of," he stammered, glancing desperately toward Angie.

"Hmm. All right, laddie. Let's hear it. It cannae be worse than what yer friend just proposed. And ya kin be sure that I'm going ta lookup that remark Jesus made about wineskins when I get back. Somehow, I dinnae think 'tis the kinda thing our good Lord meant."

"It may be, General, after you hear it. Remember those cities of refuge* the Lord gave Israel in the Old Testament? They were places of safety for those who killed someone accidentally. The avenger of the deceased could not touch them as long as they stayed in one of those cities.* I once read about such a place, even now in a land called Hawaii. The natives call it *Pu'uhonua o Honaunau.*"*

"Yes, I've 'eard of it. Go on. Be brief, please. I've had a little too much of yer 'new wine' already, methinks."

"Well, to be honest, I suspected you might say no to Morph's request. And I certainly understand the importance of rules, as you do, General. So, I also told Morph that if you could not get angelic protection for his twelve, I would seek permission to have them relocated to a place where they would be safe for a long time. So, while you had me stationed in the Great Library not long ago, I found a possible location for the twelve . . . if the General agrees."

"The General is listening," Michael impatiently grunted.

"Right," Scion responded as he looked nervously again at Morph and Angie.

"In a word, I propose to offer Morph's twelve what we could call the Demon Assistant Protection Program. DAPP, if you will. If you agree, General, the twelve will be taken to *Nozaki Island*.* It is inhabited by hundreds of zealous, persecuted Japanese Christians*—not far from Nagasaki, in southern Japan.* I read all about this island when I was recuperating in the Great Library.

"The prayers of the saints on Nozaki are so strong that many angels are already assigned to protect it. Only the stupidest demons and Dark Angels would dare to go there. The twelve in the DAPP can live in one section of the island, far from the Christians. If the twelve do try to mess with the local believers, they will soon discover what a bad idea that is. Those persecution-hardened brethren on Nozaki are like spiritual warfare samurai!"

Michael blanched, "Extraordinary! No, it's beyond that. It's just plain weird! It's the weirdest thing I 'ave heard of in one hundred thousand years!

"Scion, I sent ya here ta heal yer heart and clear yer reputation. Now ya want me ta do somethin' that would change me own heart and me own reputation. Look, I know that God reserves the right ta do things differently all the time, but this—this is ridiculous! DAPP? Really? We hardly ever do such things for humans—and ya want me ta do all that fer the likes of demons? I've spent me life fighting demons. I'd be laughed outta the War Room if I did that. I'm just dumbfounded that ya could expect such a foolhardy thing of me."

Scion and Angie's faces fell. Morph looked terrified. Michael just glared at them, snapped his wings open, and shot into the stratosphere.

He was gone. Their only chance of saving the twelve—and he was gone.

The three moved closer to each other and tried to hug each other. Morph hugged tiny Angie with one furry arm and drew her close to his furry neck, just under his chin. At the same time, Scion held Morph and Angie close to his chest, now heaving with emotion.

Then the tears began. Scion's tears dripped on Morph's face, mixing with Morph's own tears until they dripped on Angie's swollen eyes below Morph's face. The colony's needs had made them a team. Now, deep pain melted their hearts together in a way none of them could have imagined.

Soon, as she often did when life seemed out of control, Angie began to sing a haunting melody about the power of love. At first, the song made Scion and Morph even sadder as they thought about the imminent deaths of Morph's friends. But, by the second verse, Scion felt something move in him. He was afraid to admit it, but it felt like hope. He began to glow a little, and so did the spot under Morph's wing. They both looked up to see Angie's face already shining with joy. Morph released Angie and she spun into the air, exuberantly dancing. It was the same victory dance Pocahontas had danced over

Captain Smith in the village and in the London church. Scion and Morph were awestruck as they watched her leap and twirl before the Lord. The Presence of the Holy Spirit fell on them, thick and heavy.

This tender reverie was suddenly interrupted by the loud flapping of enormous wings. Michael was back—and he was singing—and not just any song! It was the same song the Holy Spirit had just given to Angie! What could this mean? they wondered. Their hearts felt like they would burst if Michael did not quickly explain why he came back —singing their song.

Upon alighting, he looked at each of them with the fire of heaven burning in his beautiful blue-green eyes, "Fergive me, friends. I had ta leave. My mind t'was about ta explode. Yer new wine and new wineskins were more than I could take any more," he admitted with a grimace. "First, ye partner with a demon. Then the demon is a half-breed, secret agent from heaven. Then, his defective demon buddies 'elp save the colony, and now ya want me ta approve a protection program fer those weird little critters on an island full of God's people who will protect them by their prayers! Did I get that right?" Michael asked with a profoundly serious look on his face.

Scion and Angie only nodded. They were too overwhelmed to say anything.

Michael now got down on one knee again and so he could look in the eyes of all three trembling spirits before him. The three sucked in their breath. In the General's huge, stern face, they sensed his unchallenged authority as the Captain of the Host of Heaven and Defender of the Throne of God. Unconsciously, they all reached out to touch each other for support.

"Okay, like I said, 'tis weird. 'Tis VERY weird, but . . . I *LIKE IT!*" Michael shouted with a smile as big and bright as heaven itself. "I *really* like it. I may be drunk on yer new wine—but I like yer plan ta protect the little, crippled critters."

"What changed your mind, General Michael? You seemed so set against our plan when you left," Scion asked.

"Well, true. I was in a flap. I had ta think. Except fer the Great Rebellion, I 'ave never been faced with such a dilemma. I had ta get a bigger view of things, so I flew ta the moon. As I sat there watching this blue orb float in space, it occurred ta me that Earth is full of broken and sinful people—always 'as been. And Earth is full of evil demons too—but, unlike humans, they never 'ad a choice ta choose anything but evil. So, it seemed right as rain that if Jesus could suffer and die ta be the Savior of wicked, lost sinners—me thinks we kin 'elp a few misguided demons fer riskin' der wee lives to 'elp us save the colony!"

Scion and Angie burst into tears and uncontrolled laughter at the same time! Morph just hovered in total shock, eyes as wide as Angie's smile.

Then, Angie leapt into the air to dance the dance of Pocahontas—again. Twirling into a blur with the speed of a hummingbird and leaping with the grace of a doe in flight, Angie sliced through the air with breathtaking figure-eight arcs of liquid movement—all the while singing the song the Spirit had given to her and Michael.

After several minutes of spell-binding, aerial artistry, Michael leaned over to Scion and whispered, "Does she always do stuff like that? I may 'ave ta get some more Betas assigned to me when I get back. It just makes me feel . . . well . . . like dancing *meself,*" he chuckled. Then, he stood up and called them to attention.

"Friends—and I include you, Morph—I say, *let's do it*! Let's protect those who risked der lives ta protect our colony," Michael gushed as he threw his arms up to celebrate. In an instant, the other three rushed to hug him—or at least tried to. Scion playfully grabbed Michael's right arm. Angie nuzzled Michael's left ear. Morph got a grip on one finger and pressed it to his jowl. It was a group hug that would have made any other angel or demon who saw it cringe.

But *someone* did see that hug from afar—and that Someone did not cringe. In fact, Jesus threw his head back and laughed a cosmic belly laugh so big that it rippled across the entire universe to the joy of angels everywhere.

EPILOGUE

For the next twenty years, conflict between the colony and the Powhatans continued in bloody and treacherous spurts.* It all ended when old Chief Opechancanough and his brother Mongo were finally killed in 1646* after their last desperate attack on the English in 1644.* Meanwhile, the seeds of sin in the Jamestown colony were germinating into a dark and painful harvest—a harvest that would come to maturity in four hundred years.

But for the unseen saviors of Jamestown, everything was better. Scion resigned from Angel Academy and was promoted by General Michael to Archangel of Virginia—the last of the six Continental Archangels!

Angie became the Recon Angel of Virginia, Special Assistant to Archangel Scion. A week after the Powhatan attack of 1622, all heaven celebrated Angie and Scion with a magnificent royal parade down the streets of gold, led by Pocahontas, Chief Powhatan, Paquiquino, and John Rolfe. The all-female Beta Choir led the music the way Angie liked it—a blend of jazz, bluegrass, and Caribbean worship songs. The joy of heaven was so contagious that many distinguished guests spontaneously joined the celebration by dancing in the streets all that morning—Abraham and Sarah, Moses and

Miriam, King David and his wife, Michal, the Apostles Paul and Peter —even General Michael himself. Mola did not attend. He didn't "feel well" that day.

The two heroes of Jamestown now enjoy the gratitude and respect of most angels. A few older male angels were still not ready to accept the Virginia "new wineskins." Beta females were now in high demand in every sector of God's Kingdom. General Michael now has two Betas assigned to his personal security detail. Some say he selected them based on how well they could dance in worship—but many male angels quickly called that fake news.

But none of the heavenly celebrations compared with the joy Scion and Angie felt when they joined the other five Continental Archangels in one more Seraphim Starburst over Virginia later that year. Scion thought about smuggling Morph and Angie under his left wing for this exclusive maneuver, usually reserved only for archangels. But Jesus knew what he was thinking and told him, "Scion, those two never have to sneak into any of our events on Earth—and if any angel tries to keep them out—just send them to me."

So ride with Scion they did. Angie irritated the other five archangels to no end with her ear-piercing singing. Morph got dizzy from one hundred continuous vertical rolls skyward. He puked after they landed—but he loved it!

The twelve crippled "hero demons" love their new home in southern Japan. It's full of the peace they had each longed for ever since they were spawned. No Dark Angel darkens their world. On the other hand, there is not much to do on that tiny island. But the twelve concluded that a dull life was far better than the sharp sword of Okeus at their throat. So, they fritter away their time making the ocean crabs fight pitched battles with each other on land and in the sea. They especially love using the Heikegani crab,*

since its shell looks like the face of an angry Samurai*—or demon! Each of the twelve has at least two crabs as pets. They have also

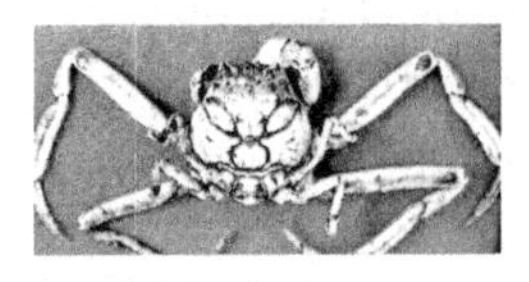

Heikegani Crab

named hundreds of crabs after the crippled friends they left behind in Jamestown. The twelve do have "crabby" days—but on the whole, they are content just to be safe.

Jehu Robinson sailed back to England in 1623.

But before he left Jamestown, he met five-year-old Thomas Rolfe, who came to Virginia with an uncle to claim his deceased father's estate. Jehu told Thomas how heroically his father died saving a tobacco farmer's family during the 1622 massacre. Thomas eventually married the youngest daughter of the family his father had protected.

After Jehu arrived in London, he gave a secret report about the colony to the man who had sent him there as a spy—the Spanish Ambassador, Pedro de Zuñiga.* Zuñiga thanked him profusely for smuggling out a map of Jamestown Fort in 1608* and then asked him if Spain could gain control of Virginia now.

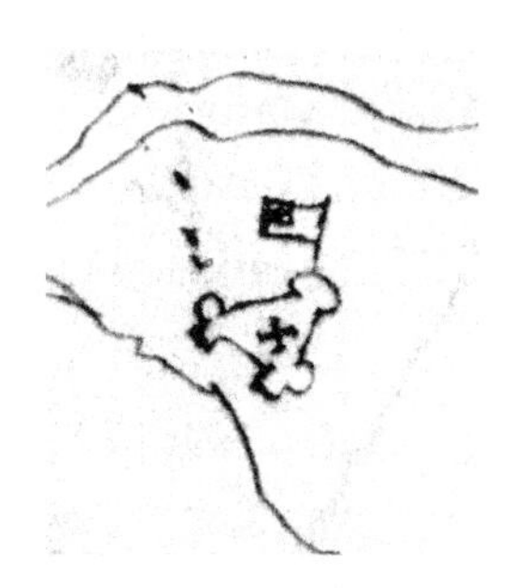

The 1608 Zuñiga map of Jamestown Fort*

Jehu strongly advised him to ignore that region because the natives and that British colony would be far too aggressive to be easily conquered. It worked! Spain never again tried to settle in Virginia.*

Later, Jehu would meet John Smith in London each Friday night at the Boar's Head Inn to imbibe several warm beers and share stories about Virginia, usually with lighthearted laughter—but sometimes with tears. They always ended each evening by drinking a hearty toast to Pocahontas and Paquiquino. Both Jehu and Smith lived out their last days as fast friends. Jehu even paid for John Smith's funeral. The adult children of Reverend Hunt sang at Smith's memorial service, and Mrs. Hunt read a 1608 letter from her husband describing how he had grown to love the grouchy, mercenary soldier who always did his best to help others in need.

Back in Jamestown, Chanco continued to live with the Pace family* as a beloved, adopted son, especially after their own son, Billy, was killed in a subsequent Powhatan attack. Chanco's tribe thought the whites had captured and enslaved Chanco, so they never blamed him for warning the colony about the 1622 attack. His role as the "Paul Revere" of the 1622 Massacre was kept a secret by the settlers in order to protect Chanco from retaliation by Opechancanough. Chanco's brother knew, but he loved Chanco too much to tell anyone. When Chanco died years later, the story of how he saved the colony was finally revealed. Almost the entire population of Jamestown attended his funeral. Many of the survivors and their children wept openly.

In the months after the 1622 attack, Okeus was enraged that he could not find Morph or his twelve clown demons who helped Morph. But the worst was yet to come to the proud Principality of the Bay. Lucifer told Okeus that he had to replace the one million Horde demons Scion had vaporized after Okeus activated the portal without permission. Okeus was too angry and humiliated to respond. He just grunted and farted, as usual, as he was escorted to the Abyss. To replace the lost demons, Lucifer made Okeus serve Vermixen in the spawning rooms by cleaning the sticky, black ooze out of the mouths, noses, and rear ends of newly spawned demons. To punish him even more, Lucifer made Okeus take off his dinosaur disguise. The Abyss demons found endless entertainment in mocking this once mighty Dark Angel, now working knee-deep in spawn slime month after month.

Finally, Okeus was released to return to Virginia—minus a few toes on one claw after his final and harrowing meeting with Lucifer. However, the Dark Lord did allow the disgraced Principality to put his dinosaur disguise back on before leaving.

But before he ascended to the Earth's surface, Okeus dropped down on both knees and begged, "Lord Lucifer, I appeal to you. Forbid your demons here to tell my demons that I am a Dark Angel. My demons would be furious. I am sure that they would rebel and desert me. I beg you, Master. Protect me!"

Lucifer laughed hideously, grabbed Okeus by the throat, and threw him upward to the mouth of the portal. "Get out of here, you disgusting lizard! Yes, I will protect you—for now. But next time, I will not be merciful. You can count on that."

A few minutes later, the bloated form of the Algonquin god popped into view out of the swamp War Portal—much to the surprise of the sleepy demons there. After a brief and awkward welcome by his guards, Okeus thanked Snookus profusely for running things while Okeus was "on assignment" elsewhere.

Snookus smugly nodded this appreciation—but he never laughed at any of Okeus's jokes after that.

Shortly after Okeus returned, Morph paid him a surprise visit. He brought a tightly wrapped bag—a gift from Scion—and a personal message from the new Archangel of Virginia.

Okeus snatched the bag from Morph's small claw with a swipe of his huge paw and threw it on the ground as he growled with pent-up rage, "What's the message, you little pus-bag!"

Okeus was stunned when he saw that Morph was not at all intimidated. In fact, a big, toothy cat smile covered his dark green feline face as he spoke to Okeus, "Scion told me to tell you that if you will not kill or harm me in any way, Scion promises not to tell your demons that you really are a Dark Angel." Okeus's red eyes ballooned with rage. He grunted, cursed, and farted royally as he stomped around, spitting and mumbling to himself for quite some time. Finally, he agreed to Scion's terms and ordered Morph to leave. But suddenly, just as Morph turned to depart, the defeated dinosaur leapt up and swatted Morph with the flat part of his sword so hard that Morph was knocked halfway across the Great Swamp. But after recovering from that parting "love-tap", Morph laughed and twirled in the sky all the way back to Jamestown.

But shortly after Morph left, no one was laughing in the Great Swamp. Instead, every demon within ten miles of Okeus was traumatized when they heard their master howl in immense pain. Okeus had just opened Scion's gift bag and saw something he had long forgotten: two shoes. His shoes—the ones Scion had borrowed just before the Great Rebellion. A note tied to one shoelace said: "My dearest Kai, when you left heaven—and me—I vowed to never wear shoes again. It's just my way of remembering you. I want you to know that."

Red-hot tears gushed into his squinting eyes as the giant reptile crumbled to his knees with a heavy thud, clutching the tiny shoes in both paws close to his heavily armored and heaving chest.

ANGIE AND MORPH ARE STILL GOOD FRIENDS. THEY AGREED TO continue to share vital back-channel information with each other to protect the colony from future problems. Scion and Angie still love to take restful breaks on the glistening beaches of Bermuda. Now and then, Okeus hears rumors about the two angels lounging under a swaying palm tree with a furry demon —but Okeus ignores it. As the years go on, Morph and other demons continue to look for The One who is prophesied to set them all free from slavery to the Dark Angels. Some of them sense that day may not be far off.

BACK IN THE GREAT BAY REGION, OKEUS STILL LOVES TO GLIDE ACROSS the rivers and waters of the Great Bay to survey the land he rules—but now he flies only at night— and without Snookus.

One warm Sunday night, from far above the bay, Okeus smiled as he saw dozens of campfires of his Powhatan followers sprinkled among the dark trees. But his huge head drooped as he heard the singing of hundreds of children in the Jamestown Church. With a deep sigh, he admitted to himself again that he had failed Lucifer. Those worshipping children reminded him that he had no hope of destroying the colony before it became a great nation—and worse, a great Christian missionary nation.

But one ember of hope still glowed in him: that one day he could somehow do something right to escape the crushing shame of almost killing the best friend he ever had.

O, well. It's time to go home, he mused. My guards will wonder where I am—and who knows what mischief that snooty Snookus is up to.

So, the tired, old spirit slowly banked left toward the evil-eye lake. As he did, he shifted his moist eyes to the river of brilliant, twinkling stars splashed across the moonless Virginia sky. A faint moan escaped his lips: "Scion, Scion . . ."

ANOTHER BOOK BY BOB FOX

Healing America's Soul

Our national sins are painfully obvious and numerous. The love of money is our greatest sin. It is the sin that drove America's founders to abuse Native Americans, African Americans and even each other for generations. Jesus says we have to choose serve money or God. We still often chose both.

Those major sins patterns in America all began in the Jamestown Colony of 1607.

Drug abuse, racism, Christian disunity, pornography plus violence and sexual sins against women—all these sin patterns began in the Jamestown Colony.

Because God loves America passionately, He has to discipline us. America's only hope to avoid God's painful discipline is for the American Church to do what God says in II Chronicles 7:13-14:

When I shut up heaven and there is no rain, or command the locusts to devour the land, or send pestilence among My people, if My people who are called by My name will humble themselves, and pray and seek My face, and turn from their wicked ways, then I will hear from heaven, and will forgive their sin and heal their land.

It's not too late. Repentance in word and deed for our sins and the sin patterns of our forefathers can allow God to "heal our land" once more. .

This book give you the historical facts and the biblical theology to do just that.

REVIEWS

If you think **Angel 24** is worth reading, please take a moment to give it a good review online or elsewhere. Your review has great power to help someone else benefit from Angel 24's message about the power of repentance to restore God's blessings on America.

If you send me a copy of your review, I will send you **a special digital gift** I think you will like. Send it to: bob@angel24book.com

Thank you for being a reader of either book!

HEALING

LESSONS FROM JAMESTOWN
PROMISES FROM GOD

BOB FOX

ABOUT THE AUTHOR

HIS ENTIRE LIFE HAS PREPARED HIM TO WRITE THIS BOOK

Bob Fox is an emerging author of spiritual warfare fiction. Angel 24 is the author's second book on the 1607 Jamestown Colony. In 2001, he wrote a biblical and historical analysis of the colony which is called *Healing America's Soul.* That history book is the basis for *Angel 24.*

Authoring a book on Britain's Virginia Colony in Jamestown seems so appropriate for Bob's background.

He has dual citizenship in America and in Great Britain. His American father was a WWII soldier who met his Scottish mother in London in 1946. Bob was later born in Scotland. Soon afterwards, like all the British Jamestown colonists, Bob emigrated and sailed to America on a ship.

Since 1986, Bob and his wife, Beth, have lived within an hour of Jamestown, Virginia. They have been married for over 50 years and raised four godly children who are now parents to their thirteen wonderful grandchildren.

From childhood, Bob always wanted to be a missionary. But right after college in 1969, he became a Vietnam-era Marine Corps recon pilot, flying tactical jets. Since 1978, he has served mainly as a pastor of churches across America, as well as a database manager, reserve

Navy Chaplain, painting contractor and international shipper of humanitarian goods.

Along the way, Bob earned a BA in History from George Mason University and a Masters of Divinity in Theology from Fuller Theological Seminary.

But, if you really want to know this author, Bob would tell you that ever since he was a young boy, his greatest treasure and his greatest pleasure was being an adopted child of God (Romans 8:15-16, Ephesians 1:4-5). His greatest burden is to help others become a child of the Father through faith in Jesus.

The Author can be contacted at:

For a **free digital gift** from the author, email to: bob@angel24book.com

More info at https://angel24book.com

Facebook: https://www.facebook.com/angel24book

Facebook Messenger: https://m.me/angel24book.

Made in the USA
Middletown, DE
09 December 2021